SAVAGE SCARS

THE ULTRAMARINES AND the Scythes of the Emperor were each spearheading one of the other two main assault groups, with the smaller squads of the other Chapters each attacking a secondary objective. Despite this, or perhaps because of it, Sarik was determined that his Chapter would claim its share of the glory, and he would lead his brethren to victory. General Gauge's main force would only be able to land once a bloody wound had been torn in the heart of the aliens' defence network.

Satisfied that the assault groups were all on target, Sarik scanned the surrounding area for his own objective. A kilometre distant, in the midst of a cluster of tall rock columns, Sarik located the massive tau sensor pylon.

'White Scars!' Sarik shouted above the high-pitched whip-crack of tau projectiles splitting the air overhead. 'Move out.' With savage joy welling within him, he added, 'Let's complete our mission before the Ultramarines complete theirs!'

By the same author

ROGUE STAR
SWORD OF DAMOCLES

· SPACE MARINE BATTLES ·

RYNN'S WORLD
Steve Parker

HELSREACH
Aaron Dembski-Bowden

HUNT FOR VOLDORIUS
Andy Hoare

PURGING OF KADILLUS
Gav Thorpe

FALL OF DAMNOS
Nick Kyme

A WARHAMMER 40,000 NOVEL

SAVAGE SCARS

Andy Hoare

BLACK LIBRARY

For my mates Gadge, Craig and Jay.

A BLACK LIBRARY PUBLICATION

First published in Great Britain in 2011 by
The Black Library,
Games Workshop Ltd.,
Willow Road, Nottingham,
NG7 2WS, UK.

10 9 8 7 6 5 4 3 2 1

Cover illustration by Clint Langley.

A CIP record for this book is available from the British Library.

US ISBN: 978 1 84416 565 0

Distributed in the US by Simon & Schuster
1230 Avenue of the Americas, New York, NY 10020, US.

Printed and bound in the US.

IT IS THE 41st millennium. For more than a hundred centuries the Emperor has sat immobile on the Golden Throne of Earth. He is the master of mankind by the will of the gods, and master of a million worlds by the might of his inexhaustible armies. He is a rotting carcass writhing invisibly with power from the Dark Age of Technology. He is the Carrion Lord of the Imperium for whom a thousand souls are sacrificed every day, so that he may never truly die.

YET EVEN IN his deathless state, the Emperor continues his eternal vigilance. Mighty battlefleets cross the daemon-infested miasma of the warp, the only route between distant stars, their way lit by the Astronomican, the psychic manifestation of the Emperor's will. Vast armies give battle in His name on uncounted worlds. Greatest amongst his soldiers are the Adeptus Astartes, the Space Marines, bio-engineered super-warriors. Their comrades in arms are legion: the Imperial Guard and countless Planetary Defence Forces, the ever-vigilant Inquisition and the tech-priests of the Adeptus Mechanicus to name only a few. But for all their multitudes, they are barely enough to hold off the ever-present threat from aliens, heretics, mutants - and worse.

TO BE A man in such times is to be one amongst untold billions. It is to live in the cruellest and most bloody regime imaginable. These are the tales of those times. Forget the power of technology and science, for so much has been forgotten, never to be re-learned. Forget the promise of progress and understanding, for in the grim dark future there is only war. There is no peace amongst the stars, only an eternity of carnage and slaughter, and the laughter of thirsting gods.

'In the year of Our Emperor 742.M41, the most glorious forces of the Imperium launched a crusade of conquest into the Lithesh Sector, to regain control of those worlds so long estranged from the Rule of Terra by warp storm activity and the raids of the pernicious eldar. But woe, for it was discovered that far worse a fate had befallen those benighted worlds. A previously unknown xenos species called the tau had infiltrated and undermined the proper governance of a string of worlds along the edge of the celestial anomaly known as the Damocles Gulf. Foremost amongst those to have discovered this duplicity was the rogue trader Lucian Gerrit, patriarch of the Clan Arcadius.

The Imperium could not, would not, stand by as more worlds fell from the fold. The firebrand preacher Cardinal Esau Gurney of Brimlock preached a full crusade against the tau, holding that the Gulf must be breached, the tau home world located and the entire species exterminated.

The call to arms rang out across the sector and beyond, and was answered. The Space Marines of the Iron Hands, White Scars, Ultramarines and Scythes of the Emperor heeded that call, as did a dozen planetary governors who raised new regiments for the Imperial Guard to prosecute the Damocles Gulf Crusade. The rogue trader Lucian answered the call too, his Warrant of Trade earning him a place on the crusade's command council.

But so too did the figure of Inquisitor Grand, and the council soon split into two factions – those centred around Grand and Gurney, who desired only the complete destruction of the xenos tau, and those allied to the rogue trader, who sought in various degrees honour, glory or profit, but not dishonourable slaughter.

The first battles were fought on the nearside of the Damocles Gulf, and saw the world of Sy'l'kell conquered with relative ease and a tau fleet bested at Hydass. But already the council was being torn asunder by internecine rivalries and Gerrit's daughter Brielle appeared to assault the inquisitor, for reasons unknown, and flee. She was assumed dead thereafter, much to her father's despair, though he still had his son Korvane to stand by him.

Having purged the world of Viss'el, the crusade pierced the Damocles Gulf, and fell upon the world of Pra'yen with the righteous fury of the faithful. But disaster almost befell the Emperor's warriors there, for it proved that the tau were a far greater threat than any had imagined. The tau were not some minor race residing on but a single world, but were possessed of an entire stellar realm.

As the crusade pressed in to capture the capital world of the Dal'yth system, Dal'yth Prime, more tau forces closed in. The fate of the Damocles Gulf Crusade would come to rest in the hands of three individuals – the White Scars Veteran Sergeant Sarik, the rogue trader Lucian Gerrit, and his daughter Brielle, who had fallen by her own hubris into the hands of the tau water caste envoy called Aura.

Mustering its forces, the crusade prepared for 'Operation Pluto' – the Dal'yth Prime landings. All would depend on those landings, and the actions of but three very different individuals.'

Extract from preface of *The Truth of the Damocles Gulf Crusade* (unpublished, author unknown)

CHAPTER ONE

DEEP WITHIN THE dense stellar cluster that was the crucible and the cradle of the alien species known as the tau, the frigate *Nomad* was a dark shadow against the roiling blue nebulae permeating the entire region. The cluster seethed with anomalous energies not witnessed anywhere else in the galaxy, a phenomenon that the most learned of Navigator-seers and astro-cognoscenti had entirely failed to explicate. The stars here were young and the very fabric of space somehow charged with raw potential, and the same appeared to be true of the species that had evolved here. The tau had developed from primitive nomads to a heretically advanced, space-faring empire within a handful of millennia. The tau's very existence was now a threat to the Imperium's rule in the area, and the Damocles Gulf Crusade had been set in motion to restore order and adherence to the rule of the God-Emperor of Mankind.

But Veteran Sergeant Sarik cared little for inexplicable

nebulae or esoteric stellar phenomena. He didn't even care a great deal about the tau or any other alien species, so long as they adhered to the one, defining principle by which he himself led his life. That principle was honour, and to Sarik, everything else was secondary.

Sarik was standing on the bridge of the *Nomad*, the lambent nebulae washing his weather-beaten, honour-scarred face and causing his folded eyes to glow with ice-blue luminescence. His polished white armour glinted in the light of alien suns. Sarik was the master of his vessel, a one-and-a-half-kilometre-long Nova-class frigate bearing the white and red livery of the White Scars Chapter of the Space Marines, but truth be told, he held little love for the role. He yearned to fight on solid ground, to engage his foe not in ship-to-ship combat at a thousand kilometres but in the brutal, face-to-face savagery of close-quarters melee.

Turning his back on the lancet-paned forward viewing portal, Sarik strode the length of the bridge, reading in every step the deep throb of the plasma drives as they propelled the *Nomad* through the void at full speed. The air was heavy with the smoky scent of the purifying unguents used to bless the vessel, its machine systems and the crew that tended her. The scent reminded Sarik of the cold, windswept plains of home, the world of Chogoris, for the Techmarines of the White Scars worked into the incense the resin of the rockrose gathered from the uplands of the north. Dozens of sounds filled the bridge, from the chattering of the cogitation banks and logic engines to the muted conversation of the bridge-serfs as they coordinated dozens of secondary operations, none of which were of immediate concern to the master of a vessel crewed by several thousand souls.

One of the bridge-serfs was a man called Loccum, a veteran with the rank of *conversi*, an appointment that honoured him with the right to address his Adeptus Astartes masters directly. Unlike many Adeptus Astartes, however, Sarik eschewed the aloofness so often displayed by the superhuman Space Marines, and while he might not converse with his crew or others as peers, he nonetheless valued their skills and their opinions.

Loccum glanced up as Sarik approached, and reported, 'Pathfinder squadron is approaching segment delta-nine, brother-sergeant.' The man was permanently connected to the frigate's machine-systems by a complex web of mind impulse link cables, and every fragment of visible skin was a matrix of Chogoran tribal tattoos. 'In-loading remote telemetry now.'

'Shunt it through, please, Loccum,' Sarik replied, frowning as he focussed on the icons tracking their way across the glowing blue screen of his command lectern. Machine chatter blurted out of the bridge phonocasters, a harsh sound that grated on Sarik's nerves whenever he heard it. He was reminded again how much he yearned for the howl of wind in his ears and the feel of a clean breeze on his face. The machine noise cut out as suddenly as it had appeared, a series of figures and icons resolving on the lectern's screen.

'Damn,' Sarik cursed, as he took in the full import of the lines of data scrolling across the lectern. A semicircular form appeared at the edge of the screen, representing the enemy-held planet towards which the pathfinders were probing. In between the squadron and that planet three new returns blinked ominously. The Imperial Navy pathfinder squadron ranging ahead of the *Nomad* were the elite of the crusade's scout forces, the master of each vessel a man Sarik knew personally.

He would not see them blunder into an alien trap, not while he could influence matters.

'Confirmed,' said Loccum. 'Three capital-scale defence platforms.'

'Initiate tight-beam communion,' ordered Sarik. 'We have to warn them.'

Loccum hesitated, causing Sarik to look up in response to his silence. 'Well?'

'Brother-sergeant,' the bridge-serf replied. 'Orders from fleet.'

'I am aware of fleet's orders, conversi,' Sarik said, using the serf's rank title to remind him of his status. 'If we must risk detection, so be it.'

Loccum bowed deeply in response to Sarik's order, and turned to a nearby vox terminal. The data script that was being fed back to the *Nomad* before being relayed to the bulk of the fleet continued to scroll across the lectern. The three icons that represented the alien defence platforms indicated that they were deployed in a relatively tight cluster, approximately 100,000 kilometres from the world they protected. Sarik's lip curled as he recalled the last time the fleet had faced one of those platforms. Then, it had been just one platform, but so heavily armed it had inflicted a fearsome toll on the Damocles Gulf Crusade fleet. Men had died by the thousand, screaming silently into the void as their vessels had burned around them, a death that Sarik considered an unsuitable one for such brave servants of the Imperium.

That station had finally been destroyed when Sarik himself had led a boarding action, consisting of a composite force of Space Marines drawn from the White Scars, Ultramarines and Scythes of the Emperor Chapters. The Space Marines had destroyed that platform's power plant, sending it burning like a meteor through the atmosphere of the world the alien tau knew as Pra'yen.

Sarik glanced up at the conversi, who noted his attention and replied, 'Seventy per cent, brother-sergeant.'

Grunting, Sarik resumed his study of the lectern's screen. He was looking for any sign of tau vessels, praying that the pathfinders would not be drawn into an ambush. The scout vessels were built for speed and stealth, and would stand little chance if they were engaged. The fleet had already faced a sizeable tau force as it had pushed into the system, and communications intercepts indicated that more were incoming.

A group of augur returns resolved out of the background noise, some distance ahead of the scouts.

'Tight-beam communion established,' announced the conversi. 'On main terminal now.'

'Nova-zero-leader,' said Sarik, using the pathfinder squadron leader's call sign. 'This is *Nomad*. I read multiple contacts inbound on your trajectory. Report status.'

'Received, *Nomad*,' replied the comms officer aboard the lead pathfinder, his voice clipped and metallic over the heavily shielded vox-link. 'Conducting passive augur reading of the platforms. Will relay to you when complete, over.'

The icons on the lectern blinked as the tau vessels rapidly closed on the pathfinder squadron. 'Enemy vessels have you in their sights, Nova leader,' Sarik growled. 'You don't have time for a full reading.'

There was a pause, before the pathfinder replied, 'We know that, *Nomad*, over.'

Sarik scowled and his grip on the edge of the lectern tightened as his frustration mounted. Inside, he honoured the pathfinders for their dedication to their duty, but he saw no reason for them to throw their lives away. 'They'll be on you before you can complete the reading, you know that.'

'We have our orders, *Nomad*. Fleet has to know of those platforms,' the comms officer insisted. 'Whatever it costs.'

Sarik forced himself to calm before responding. 'Nova leader, I honour your courage.' He did not say such a thing lightly, and many Adeptus Astartes would never have considered saying it at all. 'But if you do not take immediate evasive action, fleet will never hear your report. You'll be dead.'

'We can't simply–' the officer replied, but Sarik cut him off. 'Listen to me, Nova leader, and we'll get fleet their reading and share a victory horn together later. This is what I want you to do…'

AS THE NOMAD had ploughed onwards towards the pathfinder squadron's position, Sarik had monitored the vox-channels. The elite crews of the scout vessels had accepted his plan, and were enacting it with supreme skill and courage. Even as the tau vessels closed, all but one of the scouts had veered off on a new heading, on Sarik's order, drawing the aliens away.

Only one pathfinder vessel now remained on station.

'Nova leader,' Sarik said, aware of how isolated the scout crew must be feeling. 'Status, please?'

'Preliminary readings compiling now, *Nomad*,' replied the comms officer of Nova leader. 'Initial cogitation suggests all three defence platforms are of a different configuration to those we have previously faced, over.'

Sarik's mind raced as he considered what devious new combination of offensive and defensive alien technology might await the fleet as it closed on the platforms.

The tau had proved able to adapt rapidly, their forces displaying a wide range of unpredictable technologies. 'Different?' he said. 'How?'

'Unclear at this stage, *Nomad*–' the scout replied. Before he could complete his transmission, the channel burst with a sudden scream of feedback. Sarik knew from previous fights with the alien tau what such vox interference often foreshadowed. Yet another of their abominable weapons systems.

'Conversi Yosef,' Sarik addressed the tech-serf manning a station nearby. 'Source?'

'Enemy contact, brother-sergeant,' the crewman replied. 'Augur spirits sing of a homopolar energy surge analogous to mass driver weaponry previously encountered.'

Sarik had no idea what that meant, his gorge rising at the prospect of losing even a single fellow warrior of the Emperor to these aliens. Yosef's words spoke of the technological heresy of the tau, but they were as impenetrable and repellent as a sorcerer's hex to Sarik. 'Meaning?'

'The xenos are opening fire, sir.'

'At?'

'At the scouts, sir.'

A moment later, a bright blue pulse illuminated the scene beyond the bridge's armoured viewing port. Bitter experience had taught Sarik just how lethal the aliens' weapons could be, and he braced himself against the sturdy lectern, even though he doubted the shot was aimed at the *Nomad*.

He was correct. Although the distance was far too great to see any detail of the attackers, the glowing readout on the lectern told him all he needed to know. The blurred return that was the group of enemy vessels was resolving into five separate icons as the scouts' augurs got a better fix on them. One of those icons, the vessel that had just fired, blinked as a line of cogitation data scrolled rapidly beside it. The machine script described just how alien the vessels were, their manoeuvring characteristics, displacement and weapons systems so different from the Imperium's warships and Sarik's anger rose at the thought of techno-heresy of the tau.

The vox-channel came to life as the comms officers of each of the scout vessels reported in. Sarik breathed a sigh of relief that none had sustained any major damage. Nova-zero-three had been the target of the attack, and had suffered a temporary failure in flight control as the shot had passed dangerously close. The scout vessel's tech-adept was even now tending to the outraged machine-spirits and nursing his systems back to life.

'They're going for it,' Sarik growled, as the icons representing the enemy ships changed course to power after the bulk of the pathfinder squadron. Nova leader still appeared mightily vulnerable, but at least the enemy were being drawn away. 'Helm,' said Sarik. 'Take us in.'

Helmsman Kuro, a bridge-serf who had served aboard the *Nomad* for three decades and whose voidsmanship was nigh legendary, hauled on his mighty brass control yokes, setting the vessel to come around to the new heading.

'Intercept at seven zero delta by five nine sigma,' Sarik snapped, before addressing Conversi Loccum. 'Do we have resolution yet?'

'In-loading now, brother-sergeant,' the serf replied, his face underlit by his readout and his eyes flicking impossibly fast as he rapidly scanned the reams of cogitation script passing across its glowing surface. 'Enemy vessels appear to be pickets, sir. Light displacement only.'

'Thank the primarch,' Sarik breathed. While the alien vessels might prove superior to the pathfinders, they would hardly be a match for the *Nomad*. That left the three defence platforms to face. Sarik determined to worry about those later. Right now, his attention was focussed on closing the trap without the loss of any Imperial lives.

Even as Sarik watched the icons swarming across the lectern screen, another bright blue pulse illuminated the bridge. Silence followed, during which Sarik fixed his gaze on the icons representing the pathfinder vessels. Far from machine phosphorescence, each was a crew of dozens of brave men and women.

Then one of those icons turned red. Involuntarily, Sarik held his breath.

'Pathfinder Nova-zero-two hit, brother-sergeant,' Conversi Yosef reported grimly.

'Damage?' Sarik replied, fearing the worst having seen all too closely the potential of the alien weapons.

'Port drive disabled,' the serf said. 'Reading grievous reactor failure.'

I'm sorry, Sarik said inwardly, no doubt in his mind as to what would happen next.

A second bright flash illuminated space, and a small sun flared into existence thousands of kilometres away, before collapsing in upon itself within the span of a second. The icon representing Nova-zero-two blinked once, then vanished. Sarik mouthed a silent Chogoran prayer to ease the passage of the dead into the halls of their ancestors, before resuming his duty.

'Helm, open her up,' Sarik ordered. Flicking a switch on his lectern to activate the internal vox-net, he said, 'Fire control?'

'Brother Qaja here,' the reply came back. 'Go ahead, brother-sergeant.'

'Qaja,' Sarik addressed the Space Marine who supervised the gun-serfs, a warrior Sarik had served alongside for decades and counted amongst his closest of brothers. 'I want your crews to concentrate fire on any enemy vessel that so much as *thinks* about breaking off from the decoy group to engage Nova-zero-zero. Understood?'

As Brother Qaja signalled his understanding, Sarik turned to Conversi Nord, the bridge-serf manning the shields station. 'Nord, we're about to draw a lot of fire, from the enemy scouts for certain, but possibly from the defence platforms too if they have the range. Be ready.' The conversi nodded his understanding, and Sarik turned his attention back to the screen on his lectern.

The tau pickets were closing on the bulk of the pathfinder squadron. The *Nomad's* projected course would bring her into weapons range within minutes. The tau vessels opened fire on the scouts again. The scouts had scant point defence capability, but what few weapons they did have opened fire as one, stitching the void with streams of bright fire.

Screaming silently in, the tau pickets swept directly through the pathfinder's formation, reminding Sarik of a pack of silversharks attacking a shoal of moonwyrms. The brave pathfinders ploughed on, relying on their speed to push through the enemy. The tau vessels were fast, as Sarik knew they would be, but they were also supremely manoeuvrable, each vessel selecting a victim and latching onto it whatever evasive actions the pathfinder attempted. Just hold on, Sarik thought, counting down the seconds until his own weapons would be in range to intervene.

'Nova-zero-three's in trouble, brother-sergeant,' a crewman said. Sarik glanced upwards through the armoured portal, but besides the staccato flashes of distant weapons discharges, the opposing vessels were still far too distant to be seen with the naked eye. The readout on the lectern, however, told the full story.

The scout vessel with the call sign of Nova-zero-three was being closely pursued by a tau picket, the human pilot jinking sharply from side to side in an attempt to avoid the constant hail of high-velocity projectiles streaming through space towards him. The scout pilot was good, Sarik could tell, but so too was his pursuer. The scout's life must surely be measured in seconds.

'Intercept?' Sarik said, denial welling up inside him.

'Closing to long range now, brother-sergeant,' Conversi Kuro replied.

Sarik activated the vox-net link to Brother Qaja. 'Fire control,' Sarik said, 'Zero-three needs our help – I got him into this situation, and by the primarch I will get him out. Fire when ready.'

'Aye, brother-sergeant,' the other Space Marine replied. A line of targeting script scrolled across the readout beside the icon representing the enemy picket. 'Fire control cogitation plotted. Opening fire.'

A moment later, the *Nomad's* weapons batteries spoke, the report shuddering through the frigate's hull as titanic energies were unleashed. Each shell was as large as a tank, and had been hauled into the breech of its cannon by gangs of sweating Chapter-serfs, who even now would be racing to load the next. A barrage of shells was propelled from the forward guns at supersonic velocity, tearing across the intervening gulf of space in a matter of seconds.

So close were the pursuer and the pursued that

Brother Qaja had been forced to take aim at a point in space aft of the enemy picket, hoping to catch the alien in the shell's blast and avoid damaging the scout. More callous gunnery masters might not have taken such precautions, but Qaja knew his commander well and was in any case of a like mind. The first salvo of shells blossomed into raging orange fire, but Sarik saw instantly that the shot had fallen short.

'Nova-zero-three,' Sarik hailed the pathfinder. 'Cease evasion, full power to main drives and hold on.'

The scout did not reply, and Sarik had not expected him to, for all of his efforts would be focussed on simply staying alive. Nonetheless, Sarik's instruction was heeded. The scout vessel ceased its jinking and powered straight ahead, its forward velocity increasing now its path was true. Within seconds, the gap between the two vessels had increased.

A piercing shrill filled the small bridge.

'Enemy has cogitated terminal lock,' Conversi Yosef announced.

'Qaja,' said Sarik, his heart pounding with the ferocity of battle. 'Do it, do it now!'

The frigate shook as its forward weapons batteries roared a second time, unleashing another salvo of gargantuan ordnance into space. Even as the shrill warning tone continued, Sarik finally saw that the two vessels were entering visual range. The pathfinder streaked past to the *Nomad's* starboard, and a second later the shells exploded violently to the fore.

A sheet of raging fire exploded across space, the infernal orange chasing away the serene blue of the nebulae. The glow lent Sarik the aspect of a fearsome beast from Chogoran legend, his polished white and red armour gleaming and his fierce eyes burning with reflected flames. His face twisted savagely in the furnace illumination and he pounded the lectern with a clenched fist with dark exuberance. The glass of the lectern readout cracked under the impact, but Sarik didn't notice.

The icon representing the tau picket was engulfed in a rapidly expanding circle that described the blast radius of the second salvo. The icon blinked out of existence. It had been caught in the blast, and even had it survived, it would not be in any state to continue the pursuit.

'*Nomad*,' the vox-channel burst to life, 'this is Nova-zero-three. Our thanks, we are indebted to you.'

'Never mind that,' Sarik growled, his hunter's instinct reasserting itself over his battle-lust as he scanned the readout. 'What's your status?'

'Alive,' the comms officer aboard Nova-zero-three replied wryly, causing Sarik to snort in amusement. 'But flight control is compromised and the machine-spirits are grievously angered.'

'Then get clear, zero-three,' Sarik ordered, 'before the Emperor gets bored of keeping you around.'

'Acknowledged,' Nova-three replied. 'Will form up on your trajectory.'

'Negative, zero-three,' Sarik replied. 'We'll catch you up. Out.'

'Sir?' inquired the helmsman, sensing a change in plans. 'Your orders?'

'Zero-nine by delta, offset three point five, helm,' Sarik ordered. A series of unfixed readings scrolled across the lectern readout, indicating the appearance of a potential new contact.

'Screen the defence platforms?' Conversi Kuro said over his shoulder as he hauled on the steering levers.

'Aye,' Sarik replied. 'Time?'

'Five minutes,' the helmsman replied.

'Nova leader?' Sarik said, opening a vox-channel to the squadron leader. 'What is your status?'

'Augur readings compiled, *Nomad*,' Nova leader replied. 'Communing with fleet now, but I think we have company.'

'I see it, Nova leader,' said Sarik, as a new augur return flashed on the lectern's screen. The *Nomad's* cogitator banks set about analysing the return, comparing it to vessels the crusade had faced in its previous battles against the alien tau.

'Medium displacement, brother-sergeant,' Conversi Loccum reported, his mind impulse link feeding him the raw information before it even appeared on the lectern screen. 'Cruiser analogue, similar to those faced previously.'

'Not something we want to face alone, then,' Sarik growled, the warlike side of his spirit battling with the veteran warrior-leader side. 'Nonetheless,' he continued, 'fleet needs those readings. Helm, bring us prow on with the enemy. Fire control?'

'Already there, brother-sergeant,' Qaja replied over the internal vox. 'Full yield lance?'

Sarik grinned savagely, his honour scars twisting into a swirling pattern as he gripped the lectern with both hands. 'Aye, Qaja. And make it count.'

Addressing the bridge-serf at the shields station, Sarik said, 'Nord, forward banks to maximum. This might hurt...'

The veteran sergeant had barely completed his remark when a blue pulse filled the forward vision port. Sarik braced himself, and a moment later, the tau's hyper-velocity projectile struck the hastily raised forward screen.

The entire view from the portal exploded with seething white energies as the enemy's attack was dissipated against the *Nomad's* forward shield. Sarik squinted against the fierce illumination, but his pride refused to let him shield his sight entirely. The frigate shook violently as the projectors struggled to shunt sufficient power to counter the attack, warning klaxons sounding as the bridge lights flickered.

'Report!' Sarik shouted above the banshee wailing of the sirens.

'Shields holding,' Nord yelled back. 'But only just!'

Sarik's grip on the lectern redoubled as he imagined his hands strangling the life from the captain of the alien vessel. If only he could engage his foe face-to-face. Snarling, Sarik looked to the lectern screen, confirming that the pathfinders' squadron leader was finally coming about on a heading that would take the vessel back towards the fleet. His gaze followed the icon's projected course towards the far edge of the screen, where he saw…

'All stations!' Sarik bellowed. 'I want every last ounce of power on the shields.'

The frigate's main systems powered down one by one as the crew enacted Sarik's order, the siren dying away to silence as all available power was diverted to the shield generators. Soon, only the shrill whine of the labouring projectors was audible. Only the harsh light cast by the lectern screen lit the bridge, the surface laced with racing numerals. A new icon resolved in the mid-range band, to the *Nomad's* aft.

'Energy spike!' Loccum reported, his voice seeming shockingly loud in the sudden near silence. 'Brace!'

Sarik didn't need to be told. Another cold blue pulse filled the portal, a white pinprick of light in the black void marking its source. An instant later, the hyper-velocity projectile slammed into the *Nomad's* forward shield, and this time, the screen could not contain the terrific energy of its impact.

With a staggering release of blinding energies, the frigate's forward shield collapsed. The solid mass of the tau projectile was transformed into raw energy as it passed through the screen, and struck the *Nomad's* blocky, armoured prow.

The gut-wrenching impact passed through the vessel in seconds, the deck beneath Sarik's armoured boots buckling with a tortured metallic scream. Secondary explosions ripped along the vessel's spine, scores of Chapter-serfs dying in an instant as ravaging flames scoured entire compartments or the cold vacuum of space plucked them away. The helm station erupted in a shower of molten brass, blasting Conversi Kuro backwards even as he was consumed in flames. The lectern screen died, plunging the entire bridge into near darkness, the only illumination that of guttering flames.

Bracing himself on the lectern, Sarik drew himself to his full height, looking around him as he did so to confirm his crew's predicament. His bridge, his personal domain over which he was undisputed master, was burning around him. Why had the conflagration-suppressors not engaged?

Sarik looked down at his dead command lectern, and realised that the impact of the tau weapon had ripped the soul from his vessel, its core logic engines and cogitation transmission conduits crippled, or at the very least silenced for a spell, at the worst possible moment.

The flames picked up as they rushed along the length of the bridge, consuming terminals as they progressed. Conversi Nord dashed across the deck towards the sprawled form of the helmsman, Kuro, rolling his body over as he knelt down beside it. It was immediately obvious that the veteran bridge-serf was burned beyond aid, the flesh of his face sloughing away in smoking chunks.

Conversi Loccum's station was as yet untouched, but Sarik saw that it was directly in the path of the onrushing flames. Hard-wired into his mind impulse unit, there was nothing Loccum could do to avoid imminent and horrific death.

Having lost one valued servant, Sarik vowed in that instant not to allow the other to suffer a similar fate. He knew what he had to do.

'Bridge crew!' Sarik yelled over the raging flames and the shattering of glass terminal screens. Conversi Loccum had closed his eyes, his tattooed face almost serene in the face of death. 'Vacuum protocols, purging now!'

Sarik turned and hauled down on a large brass lever. The manually operated purge valve mounted in the vaulted ceiling irised open and the hatch to the rear of the bridge locked shut with a resounding clang. A new siren started up, its rapid rise and fall specifically keyed to the purge protocol. Those bridge-serfs not already at their station made quickly for their seats, following long-rehearsed purge drills. Sarik had no need to strap himself into a seat, his superhuman grip on the lectern sufficient to hold him against the coming storm of depressurisation.

Seconds later, that storm erupted.

With explosive force, the air in the bridge compartment was sucked through the valve almost directly above Sarik's lectern. He redoubled his grip, screwing his eyes tight shut and forcing the air out of his lungs to avoid internal injury. Loose objects were sucked upwards towards the valve, the grate across its surface stopping them jamming its mechanism. A bone-hewed Chogoran charm scythed through the air and cut a deep gash across Sarik's scalp, before shattering on the bulkhead overhead. Parchment strips affixed to terminals fluttered wildly in the rush of air, and then fell still. Suddenly, all was silent. Sarik opened his eyes to see that the flames, starved of oxygen, had extinguished.

Sarik pulled back on the lever, manually initiating the re-pressurisation cycle. The purge valve irised shut and the hiss of oxygen inlets filled Sarik's ears. He took a deep breath, unaccustomedly pleased to taste the stale shipboard air. The taste of burned metal would hang in the air for hours, he knew, and a fine mist was already forming as the newly pumped-in oxygen condensed in the chill space. Within thirty seconds the bridge was returned to one standard atmospheric measure, the emergency averted and Loccum and the other bridge-serfs saved.

'Sound off!' Sarik called out. As a Space Marine, his genetically enhanced biology was proof against the worst effects of the depressurisation, but Sarik was less certain how his bridge crew might have fared.

Coughs and splutters sounded from the darkness, before the first of the crew replied. 'Loccum!' the man called out. 'Vox-net awakening, but Kuro is down.' Sarik was filled with relief that Loccum had been saved from a horrible death, and immeasurably proud at how quickly the conversi resumed his duties.

'Nord,' the bridge-serf at the shield station called out. 'Residual only, projectors down.'

'Understood,' Sarik replied, looking down at the blank, cracked screen of the lectern. 'If you're out there...'

'Incoming vox communion, brother-sergeant,' said Conversi Loccum, his terminal awakening even as he spoke. A moment later the bridge was filled with churning static as the ship-to-ship vox-channel burst to life.

'*Nomad*,' a voice came over the static-laced vox-channel. 'Pathfinders are clear. Get your drives on-line and follow them out. We'll deal with this.'

Sarik grinned savagely as he recognised the voice of his friend and ally, the rogue trader Lucian Gerrit, master of the heavy cruiser *Oceanid*.

'You're sure you don't need help, Lucian?' Sarik replied. 'It wouldn't be the first time, after all!'

The rogue trader's only reply was a devastating broadside, which struck the closing tau vessel amidships and broke it in two. The enemy ship's drive section sheered away from its central spine, inertia and residual thrust carrying it forwards to pass the *Nomad* at perilously close range.

Two competing reactions welled up inside Sarik as he watched the spectacular destruction of the tau vessel. Part of him knew vindication, revenge for the deaths the tau had inflicted on his crew and the damage they had done to the *Nomad*. The other part, which Sarik rejected the instant he became aware of it, knew something akin to jealousy, for it had not been him, but another, who had dealt the killing blow. Sarik knew the emotion was ignoble, born of his fierce warrior heritage and nothing to do with the noble traditions of his Chapter or the Adeptus Astartes as a whole. He would confess his weakness to his ancestors later, he vowed.

As the flaming debris passed across the view from the bridge portal, Sarik saw the *Oceanid* move forwards, assuming a vector that would take it into battle with the three alien defence platforms.

'Lucian,' said Sarik, his momentary weakness replaced by concern for his friend. 'You can't take those platforms on alone...'

'Don't worry, Sarik,' the reply came back, and Sarik knew that the *Oceanid* was merely the tip of the spear. 'We'll save some fun for you.'

Sarik moved around his lectern and strode along the length of the bridge, coming to stand before the armoured glass of the forward port with his hands gripping the stanchions. As he watched, the entire fleet came into view, gargantuan battleships and cruisers gliding past in stately procession. In echelon behind the *Oceanid* came the other two vessels of the rogue trader's flotilla, the cruisers *Fairlight* and *Rosetta*. As the three ships began to open fire at extreme long range against the distant defence platforms, the majestic form of the *Blade of Woe*, the crusade's flagship, came into view. Even Sarik, who had seen the sight many times before and far preferred to prosecute his wars on land, could not help but be impressed by the battle cruiser's vast form. Its sharp prow was sculpted into the form of sweeping eagle's wings, and every square metre of its ancient armour was carved with litanies and the features of revered Imperial saints. Its portholes were delicate lancet windows, the armoured glass a riot of colours depicting scenes of glorious battle. One by one, the warships sailed past the *Nomad*, passing her by on every side and accompanied by their nimble escort squadrons and swarms of smaller vessels.

And then, the strike cruiser *Fist of Light* came into view. Though smaller than the *Blade of Woe*, the Space Marine vessel, which belonged to the Iron Hands contingent of the crusade forces, radiated menace as if the cold outer steel skin shielded a raging furnace at its heart. Where the Imperial Navy warships were stately, with sharp prows and covered in Gothic detailing, the Space Marine vessels were blunt-prowed and unadorned. Their flanks were not encrusted with devotional statues, but sheathed in the thickest ceramite armour known to man. The *Fist of Light* was the largest Space Marine warship in the crusade fleet, the remainder frigates and destroyers. Her armoured flanks were painted black, white and steel grey, the predominant colours of the Iron Hands heraldry, and they were pitted with countless thousands of small craters, each a battle scar earned over many centuries of service to the Imperium of Mankind.

The fleet crossed the point at which its longest-ranged weapons could open fire upon the alien defence stations. Initially, these weapons were those mounted in dorsal turrets, or torpedoes fired from cavernous tubes mounted in the armoured prows. The *Blade of Woe's* weapons batteries spoke first, for they had the longest range, great salvoes of city-levelling ordnance blasting across the void to smash into the tau stations. Yet, the display was inconsequential compared to what would follow when the ships' masters ordered their warships to turn and present a broadside to the alien platforms. The Imperial Navy's battle doctrine dictated that its vessels' firepower was concentrated in mighty batteries on either flank. A single salvo could drive off, cripple or even destroy almost any enemy vessel, as the tau had already discovered to their detriment.

The *Nomad's* systems began to reawaken, the lectern screen flickering to life, though it remained shot through with churning, grainy static. Though too far distant to be seen with the naked eye, even that of a Space Marine, the screen indicated the presence of a number of the crusade fleet's supporting vessels. Tenders stood by should a warship need repair or towing clear of the battle. Tankers and mass haulers carried vast quantities of fuel and other commodities. Transports carried the crusade's ground troops, each of them home to an entire regiment of Imperial Guard. Most of the ground troops belonged to one of the Brimlock regiments, raised from the planet on which the crusade against the expanding alien empire of the tau had first been preached. Right on the edge of the readout was an icon representing the huge conveyance *Toil of Digamma*, a vessel of the Adeptus Mechanicus that transported the Legio Thanataris Titan Legion, known as the 'Deathbringers'. The towering god-machines carried in its cavernous bays would be crucial in the forthcoming planetary assault.

As mighty as the crusade fleet was, Sarik was painfully aware that it lacked sufficient carrier capacity. Scant few interceptors were available to defend the larger warships against enemy fighter-bombers. These would be able to inflict a terrible blow were they to get amongst the lumbering transports that followed behind the main fleet.

Conversi Loccum spoke up. 'Signal from fleet, brother-sergeant. The platforms burn. It is done.'

Looking around him at his smoke-wreathed bridge, sparks still spitting from wrecked consoles, Sarik shook his head. 'It is far from done.'

'Addendum to signal,' the crewman said.

'Go on,' Sarik replied, a sense of foreboding rising inside him.

'All crusade council members are to gather aboard the *Blade of Woe*, brother-sergeant. Immediately.'

'Reason?' Sarik said.

'None given, brother-sergeant, but the signal has the highest priority level.'

'Better request *Blade* sends a cutter then,' Sarik sighed. 'We're going nowhere fast in this state.'

'Aye, sir,' the conversi replied, opening a channel to the *Blade of Woe* to arrange for a naval runabout to collect Veteran Sergeant Sarik, and ferry him to the hastily gathered council of the Damocles Gulf Crusade.

SARIK WAS THE last to arrive at the majestic *Blade of Woe*, and he noted straight away that the atmosphere aboard the flagship was unusually strained. Ordinarily, following a victory such as that the crusade had just won, the mood would be celebratory, but right now it was tense. The feeling had only increased as Sarik had made his way from the main docking bay to the council chamber. Now that he stood at the ornate chamber doors, he had a feeling he was about to find out why.

The portal ground heavily aside, and the voice of the council's convenor announced, 'Veteran Sergeant Sarik, of the Adeptus Astartes White Scars.' The convenor's iron shod staff of office slammed into the deck at his feet, indicating formally that Sarik was recognised and welcomed.

The sergeant stepped through the portal, into the council chamber.

Though a large space, the chamber was lit in such a way that little more than its huge, circular table was visible, illuminated by several dozen floating servo-skulls, the crown of each surmounted with a flickering candle, runnels of solidified wax covering their surfaces. The wan candlelight overlapped where the servo-skulls converged, illuminating the table below, while others picked out the councillors seated around it. Sarik saw immediately that four of the seats were unoccupied. One seat was his, and the remaining three had belonged to councillors lost in the crusade's previous engagements.

Apart from the table, the only other thing visible was a large pict-slate mounted on one wall. The slate's surface showed the image of the three enemy defence stations breaking up or burning to death under the fleet's withering bombardment. The scene had been slowed down and was being played in loop, as if the suffering of each was being repeated over and over again, so as to reiterate the Imperium's glory. In truth, the stations had proved not nearly so well armed and armoured as previous ones the crusade had encountered, a fact for which its leaders should be grateful.

As Sarik crossed to his seat, one of the councillors stood, a dozen candle-bearing servo-skulls converging on him from above. The position of chairman of the council rotated with each sitting, and for this convocation, Logistician-General Stempf of the Adeptus Terra fulfilled the role.

'The brother-sergeant has arrived,' Stempf announced, the tau defence stations reliving their death throes behind him. 'And so we can begin.'

As Sarik seated himself, he cast a glance to the man to his left. Lucian Gerrit, the rogue trader, met his eye and shrugged. Gerrit was in many ways the archetypal rogue trader, a privateer and something of a scoundrel, though Sarik found him far less vainglorious than most men of his class. Like Sarik, Lucian lived his life according to a strictly defined sense of honour, which, also like Sarik, was at times at odds with the machinations of the galaxy and of the fates. Lucian was a large man, his head shaved except for the extravagant topknot sprouting from his crown, a style not unlike that worn by Sarik and his Chogoran brothers. He wore a dress coat resembling that of the high-ranking officers of the Imperial Navy, but festooned with more gold braid than even the most decorated of admirals would dare display. Sarik had learned to see past the affectation, knowing it was part of the role that the rogue trader played and that, if anything, it was a ruse designed to hide the man's true self and confound the weak and the stupid.

Sarik looked back at Stempf, a man he had grown to strongly dislike over the previous months. The Logistician-General cultivated what he hoped was an ascetic air. Yet Sarik, gifted with the superhuman senses of the Adeptus Astartes, could not help but detect the cloying reek of illicit narcotics that permeated his adept's robes.

In common with the bulk of the crusade's Space Marine contingent, Sarik preferred to remain aloof from men like Stempf and from the incessant politicking that bedevilled its command council. The leaders had become increasingly factionalised, splitting into two opposed power blocs. No doubt the situation would get worse before it was resolved.

'Gentlemen,' Stempf continued, warming to his role as chairman of the crusade council. 'We have this hour received an astropathic communiqué of such import that I have convened this session of the council.' The other councillors exchanged glances. Stempf had not shared the details of the communication with any others, even with the leaders of the bloc to which he was aligned, the firebrand Cardinal Esau Gurney and the dark person of Inquisitor Grand.

The Logistician-General nodded to the council's convenor, who struck his staff of office against the decking again, the metallic thud resounding around the chamber. From the still open portal, a hunched, robed figure emerged, and made his way to stand beside Stempf.

'Master Karzello,' Stempf said as he stepped to one side, allowing the man to stand before the council.

Master Karzello was the crusade's senior astropath, the head of the choir whose psychic mind-voice allowed them to communicate across the interstellar voids with the distant Imperium of Man. Such distances made communications by conventional means impossible, but the most powerful of astropaths could receive and send messages across many hundreds of light-years of space. The seething aetheric energies and unknowable stellar phenomena that afflicted the region made even this means of communication unreliable at best, and next to impossible at worst. Nonetheless, Master Karzello was one of the most skilled astropaths in the entire segmentum, so his appearance before the council was greatly portentous.

A dozen candle-bearing servo-skulls swung away from the Logistician-General, to cluster around the master astropath, throwing his wizened features into flickering relief. The man was ancient, kept alive long past his natural span of years by repeated applications of the rejuvenat treatment available only to the most senior and valued of the Imperium's servants. The treatment was slowly poisoning the master astropath, even if it was keeping him alive. He was so thin that his skin looked like a paper-thin layer of crumbling parchment, barely covering his bones. He had no eyes, for as an astropath his sensory organs had been blasted away by the process that had created him. His body was only kept upright by an arrangement of clanking brass callipers and leather braces that bore his frame and animated his limbs. Furthermore, his robes, though crafted of the finest deep-green void-silk, were encrusted with filth, filling the council chamber with the acrid reek of bodily fluids.

When Master Karzello spoke his physical voice was no more than a whisper. His words were heard not by the ear but by the mind, for despite his bodily frailty, the astropath was gifted with one of the most powerful minds in the region.

'Honoured counsellors,' Karzello began, his psychic voice resounding with such vitality that it drowned out his real one. 'I bear a message. A message from the Inquisition.'

All eyes turned towards the black-robed and hooded Inquisitor Grand. Sarik's gorge rose as he considered what machinations the agent might have conspired in order to gain total power over the Damocles Gulf Crusade. At Pra'yen, Grand had used his rank to overrule the fleet's command structure, but in so doing had made himself more enemies than allies. Was this communiqué a means of cementing his power and taking total control of the crusade?

'Under what cipher?' the cold voice of Inquisitor Grand interjected. Sarik exchanged a second glance with the rogue trader by his side, for here was a mystery unfolding before them both.

The ancient astropath turned his skull-like face towards Grand, and replied, 'That of Lord Kryptman.'

All in the council chamber knew the name of Lord Inquisitor Kryptman, the scourge of xenos the length of the Eastern Fringe. The rogue trader at Sarik's side nodded subtly across the table, and Sarik followed the gesture, seeing that Grand and his arch-ally Gurney were engaged in hushed conversation.

'Please, Master Karzello,' Stempf pressed. 'Continue.'

The astropath's head turned back towards the table centre, the motion accompanied by the whining of dozens of tiny motors. 'Lord Inquisitor Kryptman states that his most trusted emissary shall soon be joining the crusade.'

Grand looked up sharply at this, though his face was unreadable beneath the black hood of his voluminous robes. It seemed to Sarik that the candle-bearing servo-skulls were giving the inquisitor a wide berth. He could hardly blame them.

'This emissary carries the seal, and her words are to be obeyed as those of Lord Kryptman himself. That is all.'

As Stempf stood and the master astropath shuffled out of the chamber, every counsellor began to speak as one. Taking advantage of the din, Sarik leaned towards his neighbour and asked, 'What do you make of this?'

'Ordinarily, I'd say the involvement of another inquisitor would seal Grand and Gurney's control of the crusade for good...'

'But?' Sarik pressed, frustrated with the need to involve himself in the crusade's politics, but knowing he might have to.

'But I'm not so sure. We both know Grand could just wave his Inquisitorial rosette at the council, dismiss us all and take personal control of the whole crusade.'

'Yet, he has not done so,' Sarik replied. The dealings of the Inquisition were even more obscure than the council's, and Sarik had even less desire to become embroiled in them.

'Indeed,' Lucian said thoughtfully, his expression shifting before he changed the subject. 'How go the preparations for the drop?'

'General Gauge has decided to take advantage of the

aliens' delay in reinforcing their world,' replied Sarik, relieved to talk of something other than politics. 'We move within hours.' Sarik grinned. 'I for one look forward to the feel of solid ground beneath my feet, and a weapon held in my own hands once more.'

'THE ENEMY FLEET is moving in, my lady.'

Brielle Gerrit, daughter of the rogue trader Lucian, stood high up on a tiered gallery, looking down on the busy, brightly-lit tau command centre. The chamber could not have been more different than the equivalent on an Imperial vessel. The lighting was bright and the air clean, the stark white, curved structures pristine and devoid of the tracery and script applied to every surface of most Imperial vessels. Alien tau attended to their stations with calm efficiency, and not one of them was hard-wired into his terminal. Instead, the operators' hands worked effortlessly across banks of glowing readouts, utilising machine-intelligent interfaces considered heretical across the Imperium.

Like her father, Brielle wore the distinctive garb of her class, a flowing dress coat of the finest deep blue fabric lined with elaborate gold piping. Brielle wore her hair in a mass of flowing plaits, the natural black tipped with purple and violet streaks lending her an outlandish appearance entirely at odds with her surroundings. Her eyes were dark and brooding, and lined with painted swirls that further emphasised her exotic features.

Brielle's grip on the railing tightened and her knuckles turned white, but she made no response to the man who stood beside her. Naal, Brielle's companion, wore the dark grey, hooded robes of an Imperial scribe, but that was far from what he truly was. His face bore a tattoo of an Imperial aquila, bearing witness to a former life he had long ago abandoned in favour of service to the tau empire.

Brielle continued to stare fixedly at a vast holographic display below, her mind swimming with doubt as she desperately sought a way out of her predicament.

'My lady?' Naal repeated.

'Thank you, Naal,' Brielle said finally, not taking her eyes off the vast display that filled the centre of the command deck.

'The tau wish to remind us that we have a task to perform. The envoy will be with us shortly. He expects your full report on the crusade fleet's strength.'

I'll give him his report, Brielle seethed inwardly. I'll find a way out of this mess yet...

'Brielle,' Naal pressed, his tone low and conspiratorial. 'Brielle, you joined the tau willingly, and they offer you much in return. But there is a price, as well you knew.'

Brielle rounded on the man who was at once her co-conspirator, her lover and her jailor. 'They offer much,' she hissed. 'But how much of it is of any worth, tell me that?'

Naal glanced furtively about the command centre, before leaning in to speak. The whole space was brightly-lit and spacious, and there was nowhere for the pair to hide from suspicious eyes. 'The tau have made you their envoy to the entire Eastern Fringe, Brielle. Who amongst your line holds such power, aside from your father?'

Brielle resented the mention of her father, who she had no doubt believed her dead before the Damocles Gulf Crusade had even commenced its assault into tau space. 'I'm a rogue trader, Naal,' she said. 'Such power is hardly a novelty to me.'

'I understand that, my lady,' Naal said. 'But you joined the tau at least in part to recover what status you lost when your stepbrother was named your father's successor. Remaining in the clan was a dead end, or so you yourself believed when you agreed to join the tau and forge your own destiny.'

That much was true. Brielle had indeed seen something of value in the tau's collectivist philosophy, something which she could be a part of after her family had rejected her. But she had recently come to realise that she had acted foolishly, and in haste. In truth, she had allowed herself to be seduced by the aliens' words and ideals, seeing something in their notions of the 'Greater Good' that she could be a part of. Later, as the scales had slowly lifted from her eyes, she had seen that she had merely sought to escape the cruel twist of fate that placed her forever in the shadow of her stepbrother and robbed her of her rightful inheritance as bearer of the Warrant of Trade of the Arcadius Clan of rogue traders. Then she had sought to turn the situation to her advantage, her rogue trader's instincts asserting themselves once more. But it was now clear to Brielle that there was no profit to be made in working with or for the tau, no matter the plaudits they heaped upon her. She desired only to escape them, and already, a plan was forming in her mind...

'My lady?' Naal interrupted her brooding. 'Por'O Dal'yth Ulor Kanti approaches.'

BRIELLE LOOKED UP as the tau diplomat, who preferred to be addressed as 'Aura', approached. His long silver robes and fluted collar shimmered in the light of the command centre, dancing with the multihued reflections cast by the huge holograph below.

'Mistress Arcadius,' Aura said as he inclined his head towards Brielle. As with all tau, his face was flat and blue-grey in colour. Compared to a human's it was relatively plain, with black, almond-shaped eyes, a wide, flat mouth, no nose and an odd, slit-like organ in the centre of the forehead. 'The time is upon us. You will soon be attired as am I, in the robes of an emissary of the water caste, and you will go before the humans and demand their surrender. But first, as we have discussed, you must appraise us of their full military potential, that our brothers and sisters upon Dal'yth might put a stop to human aggression and force them to negotiate, as reasonable beings.'

Reasonable beings? Brielle suppressed a snort of derision as memories of Inquisitor Grand and Cardinal Gurney came unbidden to her mind. What they had done to the tau prisoner they had taken in the opening phase of the crusade was hardly the act of reasonable beings…

'Mistress Arcadius?' Aura repeated.

Gathering her thoughts, Brielle bowed to the tau envoy. 'Indeed, Aura,' she said. 'I will be happy to provide a full appreciation of the enemy's capabilities.' Aura turned, his silver robes shimmering as they swept behind him. Steeling herself for what she was about to do, Brielle followed in his wake.

CHAPTER TWO

VETERAN SERGEANT SARIK grunted as the drop-pod lurched violently and its retro thrusters flared to life. Not much larger than a tank, the drop-pod was essentially an armoured passenger compartment attached to a hugely powerful retro thruster, and although it would be recovered later, after the coming battle, it provided an essentially one-way journey directly into the heart of battle. Such operations had led to the Adeptus Astartes being labelled the 'angels of death', warriors of vengeance who descended on their foes atop pillars of fire. The White Scars were masters of the lightning strike, drop-pod deployment just one of their many forms of attack.

The tactical cogitation readout in the centre of the pod's cramped passenger compartment told Sarik that it was seconds away from slamming into the surface of the world the alien tau called Dal'yth, the world the Damocles Gulf Crusade had come to conquer in the name of the Imperium.

'Steel your hearts, brothers,' Sarik called out to his four companions. The other five brethren of his ten-man squad were in another drop-pod, his squads deployed as five-man units for the initial drop. 'Your ancestors' eyes are upon you!'

The thrusters reached full power, and no more words were possible. Withstanding forces that would incapacitate any unaugmented human being, Sarik readied himself for the glorious moment when the drop-pod would touch down and release him into the crucible of battle. All that remained now was to mouth a final prayer to the primarch of the Chapter, honoured be his name...

And then the impact came. Even with its descent arrested by the drop-pod's potent thrusters, the shock was stupendous. Every bone in Sarik's body was jolted, despite the huge bars that restrained him and kept him from being turned to pulp. The thrusters died and a klaxon wailed. With a pneumatic hiss the restraint bars lifted upwards. The bulkhead in front of each Space Marine dropped away to form an assault ramp, which slammed to the earth with a resounding crash. Harsh light filled the pod, followed a moment later by the unfamiliar air of the new planet.

'Out!' Sarik bellowed, surging forwards and grabbing his boltgun from the nearby quick release cradle. In an instant each Space Marine was bounding down his ramp and setting foot on the ground of the alien world of Dal'yth.

The ground was dry and sandy, coloured the dull ochre of a semi-arid land. The sky above was a serene shade of jade, and Sarik could see thin, column-like mesas rising into the skies all around the drop zone. The temperature was warm and the air appeared clean, though Sarik's armour systems would need a few more minutes to declare the atmosphere entirely free of toxic elements. Sarik's preparation told him that while other regions of the surface were host to cultivated farmland, this particular area had been left in its natural state, untouched by the aliens' hands or their heretical technologies, and not a single plant was visible.

Sarik rejoiced in the feel of solid ground beneath his feet and the knowledge that his enemies were nearby. Soon, the deaths of so many of the *Nomad's* crew would be avenged.

'The ring of horns!' Sarik called out, using the unique battle-cant of the White Scars Chapter to order his warriors into a defensive perimeter around the drop-pod. The act of issuing orders to his fellow White Scars was a simple, long-missed pleasure; one denied Sarik at the bridge of his frigate. Hyper-velocity projectiles spat across the jade sky, fired from a distant defence turret towards more Space Marine drop-pods streaking through the air upon churning black contrails. The passage of the rounds through the sky was marked by silvery lines of disturbed air rather than the smoking black contrails of the Imperium's ordnance.

Sarik grinned savagely, knowing that even the aliens' heretically advanced anti-drop defences could not hit so small and fast-moving a target as a drop-pod, for the vehicles plummeted at impossibly fast speeds, slowing only at the last possible instant. Nonetheless, Sarik noted several shots coming perilously close to the drop-pods, evidence, if any were needed, of just how fearsomely effective the aliens' weapons truly were.

Sarik activated the tactical display within his helmet, reams of battlefield and command script suddenly appearing across his field of vision. Status runes indicated that the six White Scars drop-pods were all safely down, and the thirty warriors were all deployed as per their mission orders. A line of text scrolling across the lower portion of his vision told him that the other Space Marine contingents were also under way, each with the objective of destroying one of the sensor pylons that formed an extensive network across the entire surface of Dal'yth.

The White Scars were one of the smaller contingents amongst the two hundred or so Space Marines accompanying the crusade, the Iron Hands, Ultramarines and the Scythes of the Emperor far more numerous. The Ultramarines and the Scythes of the Emperor were each spearheading one of the other two main assault groups, with the smaller squads of the other Chapters each attacking a secondary objective. Despite this, or perhaps because of it, Sarik was determined that his Chapter would claim its share of the glory, and he would lead his brethren to victory. General Gauge's main force would only be able to land once a bloody wound had been torn in the heart of the aliens' defence network.

Satisfied that the assault groups were all on target, Sarik scanned the surrounding area for his own objective. A kilometre distant, in the midst of a cluster of tall rock columns, Sarik located the massive tau sensor pylon.

'White Scars!' Sarik shouted above the high-pitched whip-crack of tau projectiles splitting the air overhead. 'Move out.' With savage joy welling within him, he added, 'Let's complete our mission before the Ultramarines complete theirs!'

'WHITE SCARS DEPLOYED,' the chief of staff reported. 'Ultramarines groups in nine minutes, Scythes of the Emperor group in twelve minutes. All other sub-groups within twenty minutes.'

'Good,' replied General Gauge, turning from the huge pict screen that dominated the main wall of his command chamber aboard the *Blade of Woe*. The entire space was crowded with command terminals, glowing readouts and blaring phono-casters describing every detail of the landing operations. Tacticae advisors and Imperial Guard staff officers manned dozens of stations, and vox-servitors and Munitorum logisters shuffled from one to the next, collating and dispensing raw data in ream after ream of parchment. Located in the heart of the *Blade of Woe*, the command chamber was Gauge's personal domain and it could have been a high command bunker at the front line of any of the Imperium's sector-spanning wars.

Gauge faced Lucian and the others of the crusade council who had assembled to witness the assault on Dal'yth Prime. 'Gentlemen,' the scarred, craggy-faced veteran soldier addressed his fellow councillors. 'Phase one of Operation Pluto is under way.'

The general nodded to the chief of staff, and then turned back towards the huge pict screen. The image resolved into a real time capture of the surface of Dal'yth Prime, transmitted by an orbital spy-drone controlled by one of Gauge's command staff. The dry atmosphere of the world below contained few clouds, so Lucian and the councillors were afforded a clear view of the main continent's eastern seaboard.

'As you can see,' General Gauge indicated the centre of the image, 'this region is ideal for our purposes. The land is relatively flat, and the sea to the east and the mountains to the north will mask our landing operations from those two directions.'

The staff officer worked the controls of his command terminal. The image on the pict screen blurred, and then came back into focus having magnified the central region.

'Sector zero shall be the site of the main landings,' Gauge said. Lucian caught a glint in the old veteran's eye, something that told him the general would be quite happy leading the planetfall operation from the very front. He smiled wryly as the general continued. 'The main landings can only commence once the tau's sensor network has been disabled,' Gauge gestured towards a number of blinking, red runes that represented the primary objectives being assaulted by the White Scars, Ultramarines and the Scythes of the Emperor, 'here, here and here.' Lucian saw that around a dozen secondary objectives were also marked, but the general was only interested in the primary ones, for now at least.

Each of the three primary runes represented a vital node in the planetwide sensor network. Taking out those nodes would blind the tau to the exact details of the main landings. The landings themselves could never be hidden, but at least the tau could be put at a major disadvantage if they could not clearly see what was happening at the landing zone. The defenders would be forced to commit their forces piecemeal, probing for the Imperium's armies.

'What of their air assets, general?' Lucian asked, his mind calculating every possible risk to the successful landing of the main crusade ground forces.

'That is the great unknown, Lucian,' Gauge answered, with unusual honesty for one of his station. 'All ground forces will be equipped with as many anti-air weapons as they can carry, and what sub-orbital fighter capacity we do have will be fully committed. But frankly, we really have no idea what the tau might throw against us.'

'Then why not wait, general,' said Cardinal Gurney, standing resplendent in the finery of his office. 'Or bombard the entire world into submission.'

'Cardinal,' Gauge bowed his head ever so slightly as he spoke. 'I am merely enacting the will of the council in this matter. I was given the task of conquering Dal'yth Prime, and that is what I intend to do.' Then he looked the cardinal straight in the eye. 'I have done this before.'

'General,' Lucian cut in, forestalling any further interruptions or objections from Gurney and his faction. 'When will the main landings begin?'

'That, friend Lucian, is in the hands of the Adeptus Astartes.'

THE DRY GROUND at Sarik's feet erupted into plumes of dust as the turret atop the sensor pylon brought its weapons to bear on him and opened fire. He continued running for another ten paces, before throwing himself to the right into the cover of a large boulder.

The other warriors of his squad, who had reformed into a single ten-man unit having disembarked from the two drop-pods, had caught up with him. Brother Qaja, the Space Marine who commanded the *Nomad's* fire control station when the squad was serving as the frigate's command cadre, was the first to join him. He seemed unencumbered by the huge plasma cannon he carried in both hands, and by the massive, humming power source on his back.

Sarik reached up and released the catches around his neck, then lifted his helmet clear and shook his long, black topknot loose. He took a deep breath, allowing his genetically enhanced senses to taste the air, testing it for contaminants and other indications of the nature of the immediate environment.

Qaja too had removed his helmet, and appeared to be laughing.

'Something amuses you, brother?' Sarik said, grinning with the joy of battle despite himself.

Brother Qaja shook his head, his long, plaited moustaches waving freely. 'My apologies, brother-sergeant,' Qaja said. 'I am merely grateful to be on solid ground once more, with my enemy before me and my battle-kin at my side.'

'Aye,' Sarik grinned. 'I feel it too, brother.' Sarik risked a glance around the boulder, hoping to get a fix on the turret that pinned him and his squad down. No sooner had he leaned around the outcrop than he was forced to pull his head back sharply. A torrent of rounds erupted against the rock, sending up plumes of vaporised stone and shards of razor-sharp shrapnel.

Nonetheless, Sarik had learned all he needed. The pylon was a mere fifty metres distant, its white tower rearing high above the arid landscape. Its form reminded Sarik of the funnel of a great sea-going vessel, and it was covered in domes and blisters that bristled with sensor veins. Sarik had seen a ring of smaller structures around the base of the pylon, and halfway up its flanks the turret from which the hail of blue energy bolts was being unleashed.

Furthermore, in the brief instant he had been exposed, Sarik had caught sight of at least one squad of enemy warriors about the base of the pylon, weapons trained on the boulder the Space Marines sheltered behind.

'Brother Qaja,' said Sarik. 'I want that turret silenced. Squad,' he called out, 'Cover him!'

With that, Brother Qaja hoisted the heavy bulk of his plasma cannon, his face split with a feral grin at the prospect of the coming destruction. Sarik nodded once, and the Space Marine stepped out from the cover of the rock and brought his heavy weapon to bear on the turret.

Even as Qaja raised his plasma cannon, Sarik and the remainder of the squad emerged from either side of the boulder, each taking aim at one of the enemy warriors. At the very same moment, they opened fire.

The boltguns spat explosive death towards the aliens, who should have been cut down in a bloody swathe. But instead of striking the tau warriors and exploding inside their bodies, the rounds detonated in mid air without striking a single one.

'Energy shield!' Sarik bellowed, frustrated once more by the perfidiousness of the aliens' technology. The tau warriors brought their own long-barrelled rifles to bear on Brother Qaja. Before the Space Marine could fire, a dozen blue energy bolts lanced towards him as the alien soldiers opened fire through what was clearly a one-way energy shield that allowed the tau to fire from behind its protection.

Brother Qaja was caught in the storm, the blue bolts slamming into his power armour and vaporising large chunks of ceramite and the flesh beneath.

Sarik bellowed a wordless curse at the sight of his closest battle-brother gunned down before him. The two warriors had shared such glories and such tragedies that a wound to one was a wound to the other. Rage and pain welled up inside Sarik and reason threatened to flee his mind entirely, so strong was the urge to avenge his fallen brother.

But Sarik's curse turned into a howl of joy as he saw

that his battle-brother was far from dead. Dragging himself up onto one knee, his face a mask of grim determination, Qaja levelled his cannon at the turret.

As the turret's multi-barrelled weapons tracked him, Qaja opened fire. His target was high up on the side of the massive sensor pylon, and was not protected by the energy shield that had saved the alien warriors on the ground. The plasma cannon spat a roiling ball of raw energy, which lanced upwards and slammed into the turret. The side of the pylon erupted in an explosion of blinding violet light as the turret disintegrated, showering the tau below with liquid gobbets of the fabric of the pylon, turned molten by the plasma blast.

Sarik saw his opening. 'White Scars!' he bellowed, filled with battle-rage. 'On them!'

Limbering his boltgun and drawing his chainsword, Sarik surged out from cover, his battle-brothers close behind. As he passed Brother Qaja, he saw that the warrior was grievously wounded, but willing and able to fight on. The plasma cannon whined as it drew power for a second shot.

The world became a blurred rush of sights and sounds as Sarik powered across the open ground in front of the pylon. His armoured boots pounded the dry ground and his blood thundered in his ears. His heart sang with the sensations of battle and he roared a savage cry to lead his warriors onwards. As the range closed and the White Scars approached the nearest of the smaller structures circling the pylon, the enemy warriors opened fire again. The weight of fire had lessened, for a handful at least had been incapacitated or killed by the molten debris showered on them from above by the destruction of the turret. Small yet deadly bolts of blue energy split the air scant centimetres from Sarik's body or stitched the ground at his feet. Miraculously, Sarik crossed the open ground without being struck and slammed into the nearest structure, a projector for the invisible energy shield.

Sarik took cover behind the structure as a second bolt of plasma blasted through the air and struck the flank of the main pylon. Sarik could not see its effect, but he heard it a moment later. One of the tau was screaming in what could only have been pain, and another was coolly issuing orders in their alien tongue, the voice made oddly artificial by the helmet the leader wore. Trusting Qaja to do his duty, Sarik went about a hurried examination of the structure he had reached.

The projector was around three metres tall, and made of the same hard, white material as the main sensor pylon. Sarik pressed his hand against it, seeking to judge something of its properties. Even through the armour of his gloves, he felt the hum of machinery within, and judged that he had been correct in his guess as to its function.

Sarik's squad was closing on his position. He had but seconds.

'Keep going!' Sarik bellowed, activating the blade of his chainsword so that the diamond-hard, monomolecular-edged teeth came screaming to deadly life. Gripping the chainsword's hilt in both hands, he plunged it tip first into the side of the projector.

The structure had been built to survive small-arms fire, the white surface withstanding the strike until Sarik redoubled his efforts and the screaming blade began to pierce the armour. Another second and the chainsword was plunged halfway into the structure, and then Sarik felt its tip come into contact with the systems hidden inside.

A muffled explosion sounded from inside the projector, but Sarik gritted his teeth and forced the chainsword even deeper. His battle-brothers reached his side, and he pushed harder, bringing his full strength, augmented still further by the dense fibre bundles of his power armour, to bear.

A second explosion sounded from with the projector, and a crack appeared across its face. The air became suddenly charged, as it does the instant before a lightning bolt strikes the ground. Sensing danger, Sarik pulled his chainsword from the ragged wound it had inflicted, and pushed himself backwards.

The air pulsed with searing white light, and the projector exploded, showering the White Scars with fragments of shrapnel, their power armour deflecting the worst of it. The detonation of the first projector was followed a moment later by the next two along, and then by the next, until within seconds every projector around the main sensor pylon had exploded in sequence.

Sarik let out a joyous war cry as his battle-brothers charged across the ground that had previously been denied them by the invisible energy shield. Mad laughter came unbidden to his throat as he pulled himself upright, the sound of chainswords rending alien flesh and bone filling the air.

THE MAIN PICT screen dominating General Gauge's command centre lit up with flashing runes as the tacticae logic engines plotted the progress of each of the Space Marine attack forces. 'All assaults now under way,' Gauge's chief of staff reported. 'First assault report their target was surrounded by some form of one-way energy shield; all commands advised.'

'Main viewer,' General Gauge said. As the assaults on the sensor nodes had developed, the command centre had become increasingly busy as Gauge's staff officers made final preparations for the main landings, which would follow as soon as the tau's sensor grid was disabled. As the image on the screen shifted, almost every head in the crowded centre turned towards it, the tension building as the stakes got higher with every passing minute.

Near silence descended, the only sound coming from the ever-chattering vox-net channels. The image on the screen now showed the scene of the White Scars' assault on their objective, and Lucian knew that his friend Sarik would be down there, at the very speartip of the Damocles Gulf Crusade.

As the spy-drone relaying the picts passed almost directly over the scene of the White Scars' assault, the shape of the main pylon came into view. A ring of burning structures was visible around it, and to the west a group of white-armoured figures moved relentlessly forwards towards their objective. A string of bloody corpses marked their defeat of the alien warriors that had defended the objective.

And then, Lucian saw movement at the top of the pylon, a number of circular shapes, each roughly a metre in diameter, detaching themselves from the structure to circle steadily about its flanks.

'General Gauge?' Lucian said.

Gauge had not yet seen what Lucian had, but Cardinal Gurney had. 'I am quite sure, rogue trader, that the mighty Astartes require no aid from us,' the cardinal sneered.

Though no professional soldier, Lucian was not a stranger to the battlefield, and as he watched it became clear to him that the White Scars had yet to detect whatever was deploying on the far side of the pylon.

'Wendall?' Lucian said, deliberately using General Gauge's first name. Gauge nodded smartly in response.

'Give me that,' Lucian said to the nearest staff officer as he grabbed the vox-set from the man's head. 'Patch me through,' Lucian said as he placed the set on his own head and adjusted the pickup. 'Now.'

'I really think–' Cardinal Gurney interjected, before General Gauge shifted sideways to block his view.

'Vox-communion established, my lord,' the staff officer reported.

'Sarik?' Lucian said, his eyes fixed on the screen as he spoke.

'Gerrit?' the response came back a moment later. 'Make it quick. I'm a little busy.'

'Understood,' Lucian replied, not wasting time with formalities. 'You have company. Two four, high, from your location.'

'Thank you, Lucian,' Sarik's voice came back. 'You just can't help it, can you…' The channel went dead as the Space Marine closed the link.

'You really should stop doing that,' came the amused-sounding voice of Admiral Jellaqua, who had crossed to stand beside General Gauge. The admiral was a large man bedecked in reams of naval finery and his jowly face was split by a friendly grin as he spoke. 'You'll only annoy him.'

'I know,' said Lucian. 'But someone has to…'

'The scythe-wing strikes at dawn!' Sarik yelled, his battle-cant warning providing the White Scars with more information than any formally composed order could have done in the scant seconds it took to issue.

Two-dozen boltguns were raised towards the direction indicated, while the heavy weapons troopers braced themselves to open fire with heavy bolter and missile launcher.

Scanning the jade sky for contact, Sarik caught sight of movement near the pylon's summit. Within seconds, a fast-moving swarm of disc-shaped objects was swooping down, angling towards the White Scars.

'Gun drones!' Sarik called out, recognising the machines instantly, for he had faced them in the opening ground battle of the crusade. 'Aim for the undersides!'

As the drones descended towards the Space Marines, the twin-weapons mounted beneath their dish-shaped bodies opened fire. More of the blue energy bolts spat towards the White Scars, but before the tau machines could find their range, the Space Marines were following Sarik's order. Bolt-rounds filled the air, the force's heavy bolter adding the weight of its firepower a moment later. In seconds, the alien machines were blown apart as bolt shells penetrated the weaker armour of their undersides, detonated within, and scattered burning wreckage across a wide area.

The last of the debris pattered to the dry ground at his feet and Sarik activated his armour's strategium uplink. Runes blinked across his vision, and a stream of text told him what he needed to know. The battle-brothers of the Scythes of the Emperor were reporting their objective ready to take, the threat of another Space Marine force completing their objective first bringing a feral growl to Sarik's throat.

'Brother Kharisk, bring the melta charges,' Sarik called out. 'I want this place wrecked, now!'

* * *

GAUGE'S CHIEF OF staff looked up sharply from his command terminal, one hand to the vox-set at his ear. 'Enemy flyers!' he shouted over the noise of General Gauge's command centre. 'Inbound on all objectives!'

'Status?' General Gauge replied.

'Sergeant Sarik reports ready to place charges, estimate detonation within five minutes,' the officer replied. Lucian breathed a silent sigh of relief that his warning had got through in time, and the White Scars had been ready when the gun drones had attacked. By all accounts, the other pylons had been similarly defended, and the other Space Marine contingents had not fared so well. The Ultramarines had suffered one casualty, and the Scythes of the Emperor two, though none of the injuries was life threatening. To a Space Marine, few injuries were.

'Ultramarines ready to detonate charges,' the officer reported. 'Scythes still facing resistance from enemy infantry.'

'Gentlemen,' General Gauge addressed the gathered members of the crusade council as he turned from his chief of staff to face them. 'We arrive at the point of decision, the point at which all may be decided, the entire crusade. Given the previous... disagreements within the council, I would take this opportunity to show resolve, and to demonstrate that we are united in our purpose.'

'I propose the final order to begin the landings be put to a formal vote of the crusade council. Right here, right now.'

Lucian kept his expression outwardly calm, but inside his mind raced. The general had surprised even his closest allies on the council, as the expression on Admiral Jellaqua's jowly face confirmed. Perhaps he had done so as a precaution against the other faction, centred on Cardinal Gurney, catching wind. Inquisitor Grand was known to be a powerful psyker, and even if he did not resort to tearing the thoughts directly from the minds of his rivals, there were few secrets that could be kept from one who bore the Inquisitorial Rosette.

At the beginning of the crusade, before the mighty fleet had crossed the Damocles Gulf and plunged blindly into the region claimed by the tau empire, the council had consisted of twelve members. Three of that number, however, had been slain at the height of the crusade's last space battle, the ships on which they had chosen to travel lost, scattered to atoms in the void. Replacing those three councillors was a task the body had yet to undertake, but it would need to be done, and soon, if the council was not to become dominated by the likes of Cardinal Gurney. Two more members were absent, for they represented the Space Marine contingent of the crusade: Captain Rumann of the Iron Hands Chapter was aboard his vessel, the *Fist of Light,* directing his ground troops, while Veteran Sergeant Sarik of the White Scars was leading his own warriors from the front, as ever he did.

That left General Gauge, Admiral Jellaqua, and Lucian himself on one side of the council, and Cardinal Gurney, Inquisitor Grand and Logistician-General Stempf on the other. Ordinarily, Lucian would have been able to count on Sarik's agreement, not because the Space Marine had allied himself to a particular view, but because the two were simply of a similar mind most of the time. Captain Rumann was less predictable, keeping his own, inscrutable counsel in most matters.

'What motion do you propose, general?' said Inquisitor Grand, his voice low and threatening. 'And what is the alternative, should it be rejected?'

So that was Gauge's ploy. The tough old veteran, born on the Deathworld of Catachan and elevated through the ranks on the power of his will and the strength of his arm, was attempting to force the council's hand once and for all. In previous sessions, it had seriously been suggested that the crusade turn back, to return later with a fleet so vast it could reduce the entire tau empire to ruins. Thankfully, saner counsel had prevailed. While Lucian sought to profit from the enterprise, his allies sought honour, and neither outcome would be possible should the tau be completely obliterated.

'I propose the motion that we vote on authorising the landings or we withdraw the fleet,' Gauge said.

Silence settled upon the assembled council members, but each was painfully aware that the enemy's flyers were closing on the Space Marines on the surface below, every second bringing them closer to their targets.

'I second the motion,' Lucian stated. 'Let each cast his vote, while we can still make it count.'

'Very well,' rasped Inquisitor Grand, barely containing his displeasure. Why, if he was so displeased, did he not simply brandish his Inquisitorial rosette? The astropathic transmission relayed in the council chamber came back to Lucian's mind, before the inquisitor gave his answer. 'I vote in favour of the motion.'

Now things were really getting interesting, Lucian thought, his glance meeting that of Admiral Jellaqua for a fleeting moment.

'As do I,' said Cardinal Gurney, who stood beside the inquisitor. 'And I,' added the Logistician-General.

Within moments, Lucian, Gauge and Jellaqua had all indicated their agreement with the motion, and the vote was sealed. For the first time in the long months of the crusade, the entire council had, to all intents and purposes, presented a unanimous front. Even if the two Space Marines had disagreed with the motion, which was inconceivable, it would have been carried by a majority. But Lucian could not help but wonder what the vote had achieved, unless Gauge sought to demonstrate power over the rival faction.

Lucian's thoughts were interrupted as Gauge's chief of staff spoke up. 'Enemy flyers closing on White Scars objective. Contact in one minute.'

SERGEANT SARIK HAULED himself onto the platform at the top of the towering sensor pylon, directly below the structure's antennae mast. The platform was circular and ten metres across. It clung to the side of the pylon precariously, the dozens of spear-like antennae above swaying slightly as a stiff breeze rushed through them.

'Brother Kharisk,' said Sarik as a second White Scar climbed up onto the platform behind him, one more battle-brother following close behind. 'Get to work. High command reports we have enemy flyers inbound.'

Nodding, the Space Marine crossed the platform to stand directly beneath the antennae mast. Assessing the structure with an efficiency that Sarik had come to value highly throughout his tenure as the warrior's squad leader, Brother Kharisk unclipped three bulky, tubular melta charges from his belt, and set about placing them where they would do the most damage.

With Kharisk deploying the charges, Sarik turned to the next Space Marine to climb up onto the platform, Brother Qsal. The warrior carried a stubby missile launcher, which he handed to Sarik as he hauled himself up. Sarik took the weapon in one hand, and with the other aided his battle-brother onto the platform. Despite the additional strength afforded the brother by his power armour, Brother Qsal was carrying a double load of ammunition for his launcher, consisting of additional krak missiles to combat enemy aircraft.

'You know your duty,' Sarik said as he handed the missile launcher back to Brother Qsal. The warrior shouldered his weapon, and crossed to the platform's edge to begin his vigil.

With both of his warriors in place, Sarik took the opportunity to examine his surroundings. The surface of Dal'yth Prime spread out below Sarik, his vantage point several hundred metres up affording him a stunning view all the way to the distant horizon. The land was dry and sandy, and dotted with tall, flat-topped mesas of dark red rock. Over the curve of the western horizon, beyond the area that had been designated as the crusade's landing zone, were clustered a number of small cities. Assaulting those areas, General Gauge had claimed, would draw the tau to defend them, allowing the crusade to dictate the terms of battle. Sarik prayed the general was correct, for he had faced enough aliens to know that their reactions could rarely be predicted in such human terms. To the north, the dry land rose to form the foothills of a distant mountain range, which, it was hoped by the general, would protect the crusade forces from attack from that quarter as they carried out the landing operation. Again, Sarik determined not to put all of his trust into such a presumption, although the basic notion was sound.

Fifty or so kilometres from the pylon, the arid landscape gave way to the sea, which was a deep, blue-green band across the entire eastern horizon. The only vapour clouds in the jade sky were far out over that sea, and as a son of the wild steppes of Chogoris, part of Sarik's mind pondered what natural process kept them from sweeping in over the land and watering the parched earth. If it were true that the tau preferred their worlds dry, perhaps they used some form of planetwide atmospheric engineering, just as there were polluted industrial worlds in the Imperium where rain was made to fall at the end of each work shift to wash away pollutants.

Towards the south lay nothing but desert, dotted with the flat-topped, dark red mesas. The crusade's high command had discerned no threat from that quarter, ascertaining that the desert was empty and no enemy was likely to threaten the landings from that direction. The thought that the tau might prefer their worlds arid came back to Sarik's mind...

Brother Kharisk stood back, the melta charges all set at the base of the antennae mast.

'Brother Qsal,' said Sarik, his eyes fixed on the clear skies to the south. 'Do you detect anything out of the ordinary?'

'No contact, brother-sergeant,' Qsal replied, panning his weapon slowly across the skies.

'South, high,' Sarik said, a sense of foreboding welling inside of him. 'Maintain overwatch.'

Brother Qsal turned in the direction Sarik had indicated, and resumed his watch, though the skies looked empty. Perhaps the war spirit residing in the missile launcher's machine core would detect what the eye could not.

'Brother-sergeant?' Brother Kharisk said from behind him. 'Charges set.'

Command runes blinked across Sarik's vision, telling him that the other Space Marine contingents were also reporting that they were ready to begin the final phase of their assaults.

'Understood, prepare to...' Sarik answered, before he was suddenly struck by the notion that something was very wrong. He turned a full revolution, his eyes scanning the panorama intently. 'What was that...?'

'Brother-serg–' Qsal began, and then Sarik's world exploded around him.

A storm of blue energy bolts ripped into the platform, tearing great chunks from the white material. The air was filled with the ultrasonic whine of the bolts ripping through the air, and for a second, Sarik could hear nothing else. Sarik threw himself to the deck as a second blast of energy bolts ripped into the platform around him.

Something large screamed overhead and was gone before Sarik could identify it. He rose and looked about for the aircraft, but there was nothing to be seen, the jade skies as empty as they been but a moment ago.

The sharp scent of burned resins filling his nostrils, Sarik turned to his brothers, ready to order Qsal to locate the enemy flyer and engage it. He saw that the attack had chewed great wounds from the platform but left the sensor antennae masts completely intact and functional, a testament to the skill and the intent of who or whatever had fired on the Space Marines. Then Sarik saw that Brother Qsal was dead, torn into ragged chunks as dozens of the energy bolts had cut him apart. Brother Kharisk was simply gone, thrown from the high platform by the sheer weight of fire.

Sarik's next thought was for the mission. He would leave his mourning until later, as any good leader should. With Brother Kharisk gone, the melta charges could not be detonated remotely, for the warrior had carried their control device. Sarik would have to set the charges' timers manually, and get clear before they detonated. But such thoughts were instantly driven from his mind as a high-pitched whine caught his attention.

Following the sound, Sarik looked southwards, and caught sight of a rippling in the skies above the desert. Focussing on the sound, the source of which was travelling rapidly from south to east, Sarik saw it again, this time far closer, and knew what he must do.

Not taking his eyes from the subtle rippling in the air, Sarik went down on one knee, and without looking located and picked up the missile launcher Brother Qsal had carried. A moment later, the tube was at his shoulder, and he was squinting through the sights as the whine increased in pitch and volume, growing closer to the pylon as the seconds passed.

With a flick of his thumb, Sarik lifted the cover over the firing stud. Even as he did so, the air before him rippled, revealing for a brief moment the sleek, predatory form of a tau aircraft beginning a strafing run on his position.

Even as Sarik pressed down on the firing stud, the tau aircraft opened fire. The air was suddenly filled with a hundred blue energy bolts, stitching the platform at Sarik's feet or ripping through the air scant inches from his body. The moment his missile fired, Sarik threw himself to his right, diving into the cover of the base of the antennae mast as the platform disintegrated under the relentless tide of fire.

With a deafening whine, the enemy aircraft passed by overhead, its form fading again as it disengaged its weapons systems, shunting power back to whatever xenos-tech cloaking system had previously hidden it from the eye.

The tau flyer might be invisible to the eye, but it was not hidden from the senses of the machine-spirit guiding the krak missile that even now streaked through the air in the aircraft's wake.

The missile banked left, following hard on the heels of the invisible flyer. Then it banked suddenly right and dived straight down towards the ground, matching the invisible alien pilot's desperate efforts to evade death.

And then the missile exploded in mid-air, and whatever alien technology was hiding the flyer from view failed. Sarik voiced a feral war cry as the now visible aircraft shuddered and began to disintegrate. At the last, the main fuselage was torn apart as its drive section detonated, a thousand pieces of flaming wreckage plummeting to the ground several hundred metres below.

Sarik howled an ancient Chogoran victory chant, giving thanks to his ancestors that the human-forged weapon had bested the perfidious alien war machine.

'Command to Sarik,' the Space Marine's earpiece suddenly barked, interrupting his impromptu celebration. 'We read multiple additional flyers closing on your position, over.'

Glancing towards the melta charges at the base of the antennae mast, Sarik replied 'Understood, command. Detonation in three minutes.'

'Be advised,' Sarik added as he scanned the jade skies. 'Enemy aircraft are utilising some form of optical shielding. They're invisible to the naked eye.'

'Understood,' the voice replied. 'Disseminating to all commands.'

'THE ORDER IS given,' announced General Gauge, the pict screen relaying the top-down scene of a vast mushroom cloud climbing into the air, marking Sergeant Sarik's destruction of his objective. Addressing his chief of staff, Gauge said, 'Commence landing phase.'

Scores of Imperial Guard staff officers and Departmento Tacticae advisors set about their preordained tasks, each relaying orders into vox-horns and putting into motion the planetary assault on Dal'yth Prime. This was the moment the crusade had been building towards for so long, from the earliest sessions of the crusade council when all of this was little more than a dream. Countless cogitation terminals lit up with rapidly scrolling lines of text, status reports flooding back and forth, describing the drama unfolding in orbit above the tau planet.

Lucian felt relief that his friend Sarik had completed his mission, though two of his warriors had fallen during the assault on the sensor pylon. Of the other Space Marine contingents undertaking their own missions against other pylons, a handful of injuries and two more deaths had been reported, all of which spoke volumes of their courage and dedication, and of the tau's readiness to defend their world. With the primary sensor pylons destroyed, however, the landings could commence, safe in the knowledge that the tau would be blinded to the true extent of the Imperium's invasion.

Lucian was reminded of the deeds of a number of his ancestors, those bold men and women who had earned the Arcadius Warrant of Trade and forged the clan's fortunes, carving its name into the annals of Imperial history for all time. The name of one of his forbearers rang especially loud, that of old Abad Gerrit, the hero of the Scallarn Pacification. As a child, Lucian had been enthralled by the huge holochrome rendition of old

Abad, depicting the scene of the rogue trader leading an army of ten thousand followers against the orks that had enslaved the entire Scallarn Cluster.

At that moment, Lucian realised that above all else, he desired to be a part of such battles, to earn such glories for the Arcadius clan as had his predecessors. As much as he tried to dismiss the notion, his mind raced as he considered the possibilities. To join the crusade on the ground, to take part in its battles, would have both the immediate effect of elevating his position on the council, and of further securing the clan's long-term fortunes. Maybe someday someone would sculpt a holochrome of him, side by side with Sergeant Sarik as they conquered tau space...

As the landing operation began in earnest, Lucian marvelled at the sheer spectacle of the event. Dozens of screens showed fleet assets moving into position as lumbering troop transports prepared to disgorge hundreds upon hundreds of drop-vessels. These ranged in size from ships ferrying a single squad or platoon to the surface, to those carrying entire companies of armoured vehicles. The greatest and most impressive were those of the Adeptus Mechanicus, by which the mighty god-machines of the Titanicus would be deployed to the surface. For each man that would land on the surface, another hundred at least supported the action, each forming a vital link in the chain. In truth, the Damocles Gulf Crusade was a relatively minor undertaking in the grand scheme of the Imperium's wars, yet here and now, at the heart of the command centre, it had all the grandeur of any of the great battles of the last ten thousand years.

General Gauge stood at his command postern, surrounded by his cadre of staff officers, listening to a constant stream of reports and status updates. The central pict screen now showed the view over the landing zone as seen by a sub-orbital spy-drone a dozen kilometres overhead. Reams of data scrolled across a dozen smaller screens, each contributing to the general's picture of the grand invasion.

A winged death's head icon appeared in the centre of the main screen, indicating the successful landing of the first wave. That force was made up of a composite company of Space Marines drawn from several different Chapters. A second such company landed, via two-dozen drop-pods, five kilometres to the west of the first. It immediately deployed as a blocking force to intercept any tau ground forces that attempted to counter-attack along the road network that led to the western cities.

The operation unfolded over the following hours, General Gauge scarcely needing to issue any further orders, for the landings had been planned in meticulous detail. Regiment after regiment made the drop. While the elite Space Marines landed in small, five-man drop-pods, the Imperial Guard deployed in far larger drop-ships, each capable of ferrying an entire infantry company and its equipment, a troop of Leman Russ tanks, or an armoured infantry platoon mounted in Chimera carriers. The landings were not unopposed, however, for while the tau pulled back what ground units were near the landing zone, they committed large numbers of flyers to contest the landings, which General Gauge's force was hard-pressed to counter.

The tau air force launched sortie after sortie against the landing forces. The initial attacks were directed against the two composite companies of Space Marines, but that allowed the first wave of the larger transports to land largely without incident. The Space Marines withstood dozens of attacks by enemy flyers so fast that they stood little chance of engaging them. Nonetheless, the Space Marines did manage to shoot down a handful of aircraft using their missile launchers, each successful engagement being met with a hearty cheer from the staff of the command centre.

With the tau flyers concentrating on the Space Marines, the Imperial Guard were able to land several mobile air defence companies of Hydra flak tanks. Though one transport was engaged as it plummeted through the atmosphere and shot down with the loss of a dozen tanks and several hundred lives, the remainder were able to deploy successfully. Within three hours the landing zone was covered by an air defence umbrella that made it impossible for the tau to harass subsequent waves. With the immediate airspace secured, infantry companies from the Rakarshan Rifles and the Brimlock Dragoons pressed outwards to secure the ground in all directions. The bulk of their number headed west to establish dominance over the road network leading to the coastal cities.

At the last, satisfied that the landing zone was secure, General Gauge ordered the deployment of the crusade's heaviest units, the vast landers from which the mighty engines of the Legio Thanataris would walk. With the Deathbringers' fastest moving machines, their Warhound Titans, pressing forwards, the ground war could truly begin.

THE VIEW FROM the flat top of the rocky mesa was quite stunning, allowing Sergeant Sarik to take in the awe-inspiring scale of the landing operation. Several kilometres behind Sarik, the sensor pylon still burned, its once pristine white form reduced to a twisted, blackened mass as a column of choking smoke rose high in the atmosphere. The landings were well and truly under way, the white sun of Dal'yth setting in the rapidly darkening jade sky.

Having destroyed the sensor pylon and ordered the tending of his dead and injured battle-brothers, Sarik had linked his force up with the other Space Marine contingents to assist in the securing of the landing zone. The tau units in the area had swiftly disengaged, however, and mounted an impressively coordinated withdrawal before the Space Marines could engage them effectively. Sarik was forced to admit that the tau warriors were worthy opponents, and that they fought with honour. The aliens' fast-moving tactics reminded Sarik of those employed by the nomads of his home world of Chogoris, whose use of swift mounts allowed them to launch lightning raids before withdrawing in the face of enemy counter-attack. Already, Sarik had disseminated this point to the other Space Marine units of the crusade, and advised them how such tactics might be met, and countered.

The flat desert below the tall mesa was now swarming with troops and armoured vehicles. The first Imperial soldiers Sarik's White Scars had linked up with were the veteran light infantrymen of the Rakarshan Rifles. They moved quickly to press into the surrounding desert, and had begun aggressive patrolling in order to repel any enemy that sought to observe or interfere with the operation. The Rakarshans were followed by the crusade's more heavily armed and equipped units, whose tanks, mobile artillery and armoured carriers were even now filling the air with the roar of their engines, the grinding of tracks and the smoke of their exhausts. As more and more heavy landers touched down, the first streams of men and vehicles swelled to become rivers, until thousands of Imperial Guardsmen and hundreds of tanks were pressing outwards.

All the while, the tau flyers continued to contest the landings, and though few had penetrated the air defence umbrella the Hydra flak tanks had established, those that had been able to slew scores of men with each strafing run. Fortunately for the operation, only a handful of the flyers were equipped with the stealth field Sarik had faced on the pylon. The Departmento Tacticae advisors surmised that these were an elite wing of the tau air force. The Imperium would be ready for them next time.

Sarik's chain of thought was interrupted as he became aware of a deep, rumbling drone sounding from above. The heaviest lander yet was descending upon a column of fire and smoke. The vessel came ponderously in to land, and another three followed in its wake. The roar of the vessel's landing jets was deafening, even from several kilometres away. In basic form the lander resembled the drop-pod Sarik and the other White Scars had made planetfall in, yet its scale was truly vast. The vessel was three or four times taller than its width, its hull configured in a hexagonal form above the largest retro thruster Sarik had ever seen on a ship capable of atmospheric operation.

As the lander descended, an invisible anti-grav field was projected below it, an arcane and ill-understood system that would ensure the vessel's precious cargo was deployed with all possible care. The anti-grav field pressed down upon the earth as the vessel neared the ground, the invisible forces crushing everything beneath it flat, including a tracked cargo tender which failed to evacuate the landing zone in time. The grav field dampened the area so effectively that the clouds of dust that should have been thrown up by the retro-thrusters were crushed downwards to form a carpet of sand across the land.

As the first lander touched down, Sarik felt the desert beneath his feet tremble as millions of tons of steel and ceramite ground into the bedrock. It felt to Sarik as if he witnessed a primeval contest of the elements: that wrought in the forges of the Adeptus Mechanicus battling against the raw stuff of Dal'yth Prime's continental plates. The contest continued for long minutes, until eventually the tremors faded away, leaving Sarik with the impression that the world beneath his feet would remain scarred by the coming of the Titanicus forever. Soon, a dozen of the landers had touched down, each towering a hundred metres and more into air that shimmered with the residual heat of atmospheric entry.

The anti-grav fields deactivated, contingents of tech-priests and their servitors emerged from dozens of hatches and busied themselves around the heavy landers. Prayers and chants filled the air as the tech-priests supplicated themselves before the vessels, which in themselves were a manifestation of their Machine-God, the Omnissiah. The cloying scent of holy lubricant and incense oil drifted across the desert, mixing unpleasantly with the scent of burning resin blowing in from the ruined sensor pylon.

Finally, the sides of each lander lowered downwards like the petals of a titanic ceramite flower, accompanied by the grinding of metal gears and the thud of the huge ramps striking the earth. Vast clouds of dust were thrown up as the ramps hit the ground, and through them emerged a group of loping Warhound Titans of the Legio Thanataris. Each was a towering war machine bearing weapons of the scale normally only seen on starships. Though far from the heaviest of the Titans the Legio could field, these had the speed to range ahead of the crusade's ground forces, moving swiftly with a characteristic stooped gait, to engage anything the tau might be able to field. As they formed up into a predatory pack on the blackened earth of the landing zone, the Warhounds' heads, each sculpted to resemble a mighty wolf-like face, tracked back and forth across their new hunting ground. It almost appeared as if the Titans sniffed the air as they sought the spoor of their prey.

Sarik mouthed a prayer to the spirits of his ancestors, thanking them for the part he would enact in the coming battles as his heart yearned to begin the fight. Limbering his boltgun, Sarik turned to make his way from the mesa, filled with anticipation for the glory the coming battles would surely bring.

DEEP IN THE bowels of the heavy cruiser *Oceanid*, Lucian and his son Korvane approached the mighty armoured portal of the vessel's armoury. This was no conventional store of arms and munitions, but the inner sanctum of the rogue trader dynasty, the holy of holies that kept safe some of the most prized of Lucian's possessions. Only the ancestral stasis tomb beneath the blasted surface of sacred Terra held more valued treasures, such as the Arcadius Warrant of Trade and the holy banner of the line's founding.

Lucian's mind was made up; he had decided to travel to the surface of Dal'yth Prime. He would lead a battle group of Imperial Guard units against the tau defenders, and in so doing bolster his position on the crusade council whilst continuing the glorious traditions of his line.

'Father,' said Korvane, the inheritor of the clan, as the pair halted before the armoured portal. Though a handsome man, Korvane's features lent him a shrewd aspect many found disquieting. Lucian's son wore the same style of clothes as his father, a dress coat styled after that of the Imperial Navy officer classes, though he had always eschewed the more overt forms of finery and naval affectation. While Brielle had been raised at Lucian's side, literally standing beside him on the bridge of the *Oceanid* as soon as she was able to walk, Korvane had been brought up in the refined surroundings of the Court of Nankirk, learning his trade in the cutthroat circles of the upper echelons of Imperial aristocracy. His experiences had taught him to conceal his passions and his thoughts, to shield them from potential rivals lest he reveal some exploitable weakness. Lucian knew that Korvane would disapprove of his plan.

'I really must–'

'I know, son,' Lucian interrupted, as hidden gears engaged and the portal ground slowly upwards. 'I know. But this is something I have to do.'

'Something you *want* to do,' said Korvane, as the pair stepped through the open portal and into the darkness beyond. As they passed over the threshold, hidden mechanisms detected their presence, confirmed their identity, and activated the lumens. The darkness fled as row upon row of arms and armour were illuminated.

'And what if I do?' Lucian countered, crossing to a row of armoured suits as he spoke. 'You were raised in the court, son, and I'm glad of it, for the skills you amassed there have served us well. Many of our battles of late have been fought with words, and others with lance battery and broadside. But sometimes, our battles must be fought in the traditional manner. Up close, and personal.'

'And General Gauge,' said Korvane. 'He agrees to this?'

'That he does, Korvane,' said Lucian. 'Gauge is a veteran of more battles even than Sergeant Sarik. He understands the value of one of our faction getting involved, of being *seen* to get involved, at the front line. I think he may be a little jealous, actually...'

'But what will it actually achieve?' Korvane replied. 'What good will this do our cause on the council?'

'Much,' said Lucian, selecting a suit of ancient power armour. Its scarred and pitted surface was polished to a sheen that reflected the overhead lights. 'Grand and his lap dog cardinal would have us exterminate the tau out of hand. They even state they have the means to do so, though I have yet to see evidence that any of the crusade's vessels is carrying anything like a virus bomb. If the landings go well, that position will become less tenable, and we can steer events to our own ends.'

'Which are?' Korvane pressed.

'You know as well as I, son,' said Lucian. 'Whatever happens, however the crusade is concluded, we must come out of it in the ascendant. The concessions we could win, the charters we could earn... Emperor, if we play this right, Korvane, we could end up as viceroys of this entire region!'

When Korvane did not respond, Lucian turned from his examination of the suit of power armour to face his son. 'What?' he said.

'Has it not occurred to you, father,' Korvane said darkly, 'that you might not return from this grand adventure?'

Lucian sighed, placing a hand upon his son's shoulder. It certainly had occurred to him.

'Son,' said Lucian. 'Before I depart for the surface, I have something for you. Just in case.'

Korvane turned his back on his father, but Lucian pressed on regardless. He raised his hand, palm upwards, to reveal a simple ring in its centre.

'You must take this,' said Lucian.

Korvane looked at the glinting ring held out before him. 'What is it?'

'It is the most valuable thing on this ship.'

When Korvane appeared not to understand, Lucian continued. 'It's a gene-keyed cipher bearer. The crystal contains the access codes for the Clan Arcadius stasis vaults.'

'On Terra?' Korvane said, the full import of Lucian's words slowly dawning on him. 'The warrant?'

'Indeed, son,' said Lucian. 'Should I fall upon Dal'yth Prime, it's yours, all of it. But not,' he raised his hand to Korvane, 'without this.'

For a long moment, Lucian thought his son would refuse the ring. After a pause, Korvane reached out and with obvious trepidation, gently took it.

'It was to be Brielle's,' said Lucian. 'But when I married your mother you become my son.' He nodded towards the ring in Korvane's hand. 'And that became your birthright.'

Korvane's expression darkened at the mention of his stepsister's name. Korvane's entering the clan had displaced Brielle, who was Lucian's child from his first marriage, from her position as heir, and she had hated him ever since. Korvane still bore painful scars from a nigh catastrophic accident that had befallen his vessel, an accident which he, if not Lucian, believed to have been her last deed before she disappeared at the outset of the Damocles Gulf Crusade. As Lucian regarded his son's face, a new resolve appeared in his eyes, and he placed the ring upon a finger.

'While I'm gone, you will watch my seat on the council,' said Lucian. 'Do you understand?'

Korvane nodded, and Lucian continued. 'There are three empty seats that must be filled. They must be filled with men sympathetic to our cause, not to Grand and Gurney's. This is your battle, which you must fight here, while I fight below. Are we agreed?'

'We are agreed,' Korvane replied solemnly. 'I shall not let you down, father.'

'Good,' said Lucian, relieved that he had done what he must. 'Now, you can help me into this power armour.'

CHAPTER THREE

SARIK'S COMMAND RHINO ground forwards as he led the Space Marine assault column across the inland plain west of the landing zone. Having boarded transports landed from orbit, the crusade's Space Marines had divided themselves into several groups, each approximately the size of a conventional company. Each group had then linked up with a pair of Warhounds. The spearheads would each advance along a separate axis, pushing hard and fast into enemy territory, and engaging and destroying any tau forces they encountered. In the unlikely event that the spearheads encountered resistance they could not simply smash aside, they would bypass it, leaving it for the heavier units behind them to deal with.

Throwing back the hatch of the Rhino armoured carrier, Sarik's ears were assaulted by the deafening tread of the nearby Warhound Titan. The huge bulk of the mighty war machine blocked out much of the dawn sky above. Sarik reminded himself that the Warhounds were but the lightest of Titans, and that their compatriots were at least twice as large again.

Shaking the tail of his long topknot out of his eyes, Sarik scanned the vista ahead. The land was still arid, but the column had left the majority of the towering rock mesas behind them. The column was following the tau road network, which led west directly towards their target, the city of Gel'bryn. The air was fresh, and Sarik's genetically enhanced senses could taste in it the underlying taint of pollutants unleashed into the atmosphere by the huge landing operation.

'Driver!' Sarik bellowed over the noise of the nearby Titan and the rush of wind. 'Loosen formation. That beast won't even notice if he treads on us.'

If the driver gave any response, Sarik did not hear it, but the Rhino soon veered off to the war machine's right. The going here was good due to the wide, smooth roads. Sarik's spearhead was advancing quickly as the roads allowed them to avoid the rougher terrain.

'Sergeant Sarik,' a voice said over the command channel. 'This is Princeps Auclid of the *Animus Ferrox*, do you receive?' Sarik glanced upwards at the Titan his transport had just passed, knowing it was the commander of that mighty iron beast that spoke.

'Go ahead, *Animus Ferrox*,' Sarik replied.

'Sergeant,' the princeps began. 'Augurs are reading a concentration of enemy armour a kilometre ahead. Be advised, we are adopting battle stance. I suggest you give us some room. Out.'

Fully aware of the dangers posed by remaining too close to a Titan engaged in battle, Sarik relayed the order to his squads. Titan weapons were capable of unleashing fearsome energies, which could prove lethal to nearby units. They tended to attract a lot of return fire too, which the Titans might be able to withstand, but that its friends almost certainly would not.

Sarik scanned the arid landscape, his warrior's eye ever alert for signs of trouble. The advance continued, the units of the spearhead adopting a loose formation in order to allow the huge Warhounds space to fight when the time came. The land rose as the spearhead came upon a range of low hills, and soon the Warhounds were cresting a shallow rise, each around a hundred metres ahead of the Rhino-borne Space Marine squads.

'Alert!' Princeps Auclid's voice came over the vox-net. 'Enemy missiles launched, source unknown.'

A dart-like missile streaked directly downwards from the sky and impacted on the invisible void shield projected around the Warhound.

The missile exploded ten metres above the Titan, erupting in a flash of white light, a roiling cloud of black smoke billowing outwards. The Warhound ploughed through the bank of smoke, its head, fashioned after the war machine's namesake, scanning left and right as it crested the rise.

Cursing the alien trickery, Sarik sent the dozen Rhinos of his force forwards with a curt order, whilst allowing the Scout Titans to continue at the front. The missile that had struck Princeps Auclid's war machine would have torn a Rhino wide open.

'Second missile inbound,' said Princeps Auclid. 'Still no source...'

The second missile struck the *Animus Ferrox* in the right flank, from a high angle, yet once again the void shield held firm and the iron beast strode on.

As Sarik's Rhinos reached the crest of the rise, the pair

of Scout Titans were already stalking down the opposite slope. The land ahead was different to the terrain the spearhead had passed through. The arid desert gave way to a belt of scrubland, which ten kilometres ahead became arable land scattered with cultivated fields and stands of regular, planted trees. There was still no sign of the enemy that had fired the missiles.

'All squads,' Sarik voxed to his Space Marines. 'Increase visual scanning. Inform me the instant you see *any* sign of movement.'

The upper hull of each of Sarik's carriers featured a double-door hatch. These swung outwards as Space Marines emerged to scan the surrounding landscape for any sign of the enemy heavy weapons teams firing the missiles.

'Brother-sergeant,' a voice came over the net. It belonged to Sergeant Arcan of the Ultramarines Chapter, his Rhino following directly behind Sarik's own. The sergeant was riding high in the roof hatch and scanning the surroundings through a set of magnoculars. 'I have a contact. Twelve nine, high.'

Sarik followed the squad leader's warning, in time to see a salvo of rockets arcing straight up into the air from behind a stand of trees a kilometre distant. In the span of seconds, the missiles had streaked upwards through the sky, closed the distance, and slammed into the *Animus Ferrox*.

A blinding white light flashed, and the Scout Titan was engulfed in a billowing cloud of black smoke. At least some of the missiles had been stopped by the war machine's void shields, but in the process had overloaded the projector. The invisible shield had collapsed in upon itself.

The Warhound's torso swivelled left and right on its

reverse-joined legs, its huge weapons eager to engage its tormentor. Sarik keyed his command terminal and sent Princeps Auclid the coordinates of the stand of trees the missiles had been launched from.

'My thanks, White Scar,' the princeps transmitted in reply. There was frustration in the man's voice, no different to how Sarik himself would have felt under sniper fire. The Warhound turned to bring both its weapons to bear at once on the coordinates indicated. The ammunition feeds of its Vulcan mega-bolter whirred as thousands of rounds were chambered ready to fire, and the coils of its plasma blastgun pulsated with the staggering energies it was ready to unleash.

Another salvo lanced upwards into the air, the launch point somewhere behind a stand of purple-leaved trees. This time, Princeps Auclid saw it too, and opened fire.

The Warhound's Vulcan mega-bolter was, in effect, a cluster of oversized heavy bolters, each one far larger than even a Space Marine could carry. The sound of the weapon firing was like a bolt of silk being ripped violently in two. Sarik gritted his teeth against the horrendous report, and fought the urge to cover his ears. Up ahead, the stand of trees the missiles had been fired from simply exploded into constituent particles. Trunks were ground to pulp, and the pulp to a fine mist, by the merciless fusillade.

Surely, nothing could live through that.

But something had. As the breeze carried the mist away, a curved and sleek form was revealed. It took Sarik a moment to register just what the form represented. It was a vehicle, but its construction was more akin to the gracefully wrought forms of eldar tanks than those of the Imperium, which were solid, brutal and supremely functional in their design. Then Sarik realised that the vehicle was not driven by a track unit like the majority of Imperial war machines, but by some manner of anti-grav generator. Once more, the similarity to the fiendish works of the eldar came to his mind. For such technology to be so widely employed was a sure sign of the depths of the technological heresy to which the tau had descended, and reason in itself, in the mind of the Imperium, to prosecute a campaign of extermination against their empire. Sarik's heart beat faster at the prospect of combat against such a foe, but the vehicle was already rising on its invisible anti-grav cushion. With a whine of turbo jets, it swung around and was gone.

As the mist of the pulped trees drifted across the road in front of the Warhound, Sarik caught sight of a thin, red beam of light scything through it, which disappeared the instant the mist was caught on the air and dispersed. He followed the beam to where it had originated, and saw another stand of purple-leaved vegetation.

'Princeps Auclid!' Sarik called into the vox-net. 'The fire is indirect, there are observers in the treeline, they're using some form of–'

Sarik's words were cut off as the Warhound opened fire on the nearest treeline. Sarik saw the red beam lance outwards a second time. The alien warrior holding the source of the beam did so with countless thousands of mass-reactive bolts thundering overhead in what must have been a deafening barrage. Despite his loathing of such alien technology, Sarik acknowledged the skill at arms such a feat represented.

And then another salvo of missiles came screaming in from a high angle. The faintest glint of red light reflected from the side of the Warhound's canine head.

A second later half a dozen missiles slammed into that exact point. The Warhound's void shields had been stripped, and even though the ornate cockpit was heavily armoured, it exploded as the missiles struck. The mighty war machine staggered backwards, its machine systems suddenly bereft of control.

'Get clear!' Sarik bellowed, ducking back inside his carrier as the driver gunned its engines. '*Animus Ferrox* is wounded!' Folding down a periscopic sight, Sarik witnessed the last moments of the *Animus Ferrox* as his armoured carrier powered away from the Titan's awesomely destructive death throes.

The Titan shook, as if its war spirit fought to keep its crippled form upright even without the guidance of the princeps, who had been killed the instant the missiles had destroyed the head. Then one of its mighty clawed feet slipped and the towering machine listed precariously to one side. The last thing Sarik saw before his Rhino bore him away was the entire machine toppling to the ground, thick black smoke boiling from the ragged wound where its cockpit-head had been.

Then Sarik's Rhino was shaken violently as the Warhound hammered into the road and an instant later exploded. Secondary explosions ripped out, the Rhino's driver fighting all the while to maintain control of the bucking armoured transport. Orange flames licked at the edge of Sarik's scope, and the pristine white heraldry of his transport was turned to scorched black by the raging fires of the Warhound's destruction.

When the explosions finally ceased, Sarik ordered his driver to halt. The white of the road surface had been scorched black, great banks of smoke lit from within by airborne cinders gusting past. The *Animus Ferrox* was reduced to little more than its armoured carapace shell at the centre of a huge crater strewn with blazing wreckage. Sarik bit back his grief that such a mighty, proud war machine could be struck down by alien weaponry with such seeming ease. It was one injustice amidst a galaxy of wrong, but the tau would pay for it nonetheless, he vowed, in blood.

From out of the smoke reared the form of the Warhound's twin, the *Gladius Pious*. The second Titan paused a moment as it passed its slain companion, before stalking forwards to take its position at the head of the advance, its weapons tracking back and forth across the treelines either side of the road.

Sarik opened a channel to the *Gladius Pious*. 'Princeps, this is Sarik. I honour your fallen kin, and I suggest a change of plan.'

'Go ahead, Sarik,' the princeps replied, his bitterness and grief at the loss of his fellow obvious in his voice. 'But make it quick, I read multiple armour contacts.'

'Understood, Princeps...?'

'Atild, brother-sergeant,' the princeps replied.

'Listen to me, Princeps Atild,' Sarik continued. 'The tau are marking their targets with some sort of laser designator, which the missiles are following. They're being launched blind, and the launchers are redeploying as we press forwards.'

'I understand, Sarik. But what can we–'

'My force will press forwards,' Sarik said, aware that at any second another salvo of missiles could come streaking out of the skies. 'We'll clear the treelines of observers and flush out the launchers. If we force them to fire over open sights, you can engage them before they get a chance to do so. Agreed?'

'Sarik, you'll be exposing yourself to–'

'I know, princeps,' Sarik interrupted, growing

frustrated with the exchange. Titan crews, even those of the comparatively light Warhounds, were accustomed to dominating any battlefield. They were ill-disposed towards relying on infantry, even elite Space Marines, to clear the way for them. Nonetheless, Sarik knew that the princeps had just lost a valued fellow warrior of his order, and so he gave the man some leeway.

There was a pause before the princeps answered, during which Sarik scanned the sky impatiently, fighting back the urge to press the other man for a response.

'Agreed, Astartes,' the princeps finally replied. 'I am in your debt.'

'You can thank me later, princeps,' Sarik replied, finally able to enact his plan. In moments, he was leading the column of armoured carriers forwards to clear the treelines of tau spotters.

EVEN AS THE Space Marine spearheads were pressing westwards in their breakout from the landing zone, the crusade's Imperial Guard units were mustering to launch the second wave of the advance. While the Space Marines represented small but highly elite formations, the diamond-hard tip of the spear, the Imperial Guard would form the inexorable main bulk of the attack, an unstoppable mass that would roll over and flatten anything it encountered.

Lucian stood in front of the assembled ranks of the force that he himself would soon be leading into battle, his heart swelling with pride. No Arcadius had gone to war at the head of such a formation for several centuries, a fact that Lucian hoped would seal his place in the annals of the clan forever.

The Dal'yth Prime landings were still taking place, but the majority of the combat units had been ferried to the surface and local air superiority largely consolidated. The plain was filled with thousands of marching troops and hundreds of growling armoured vehicles, and overhead dozens of impossibly large heavy landers plied to and from the vessels in orbit. Lucian had made planetfall in his personal shuttle and made his way immediately to meet his new command.

The force was drawn from the veteran light infantry companies of the Rakarshan Rifles, an ad-hoc battlegroup of around a thousand men and women who were acknowledged as the finest infiltrators and mountain troops in the entire crusade. In addition to their reputation for highly professional soldiering, the Rakarshans were the subject of folklore amongst the peoples of the Eastern Fringe, their ferocity in combat making them greatly feared by their enemies. The tau had never heard of Rakarsha, but Lucian had promised his troops that together, they would give the aliens cause to dread their coming.

As the last troops took their places, the formation was called to attention by bellowing sergeant-majors. They were an impressive sight indeed. They wore uniforms designed to blend in with the predominant subtropical environment of their home world, and these had been retained, for the pale green and dusty brown patterning was well suited to the arable lands around the tau cities. While the camouflage was eminently practical, the Rakarshans carried plenty of reminders of the culture that had spawned them. Each carried a short, curved blade at his belt, which by tradition was not to be drawn from its jewel-encrusted scabbard except to taste blood. Some said that should a drawn blade not spill the blood of a foeman, it should do so from its bearer. In addition, the Rakarshans each wore an intricately knotted headdress made of rich, purple cloth wrapped about their heads. Mounted above the forehead was a single black feather taken from a mountain vulture, a creature held as nigh sacred by the superstitious peoples of Rakarsha.

A pair of officers stood at the centre of the formation. Major Subad would serve as Lucian's executive officer, enacting his orders and supervising the more mundane aspects of the battlegroup's operations. Sergeant-Major Havil would be the battlegroup's senior non-commissioned officer, in whose hands the discipline and moral well-being of the warriors would rest.

When the troops were finally all in place, formed up in perfect lines by platoons and companies, all fell quiet, apart from the ever-present background noise of the more distant tanks and the landers flying overhead. Lucian stood perfectly still, impatient for the ceremonial handover of command to begin so that he could be about the business of conquest.

The two officers walked smartly forwards. Major Subad was a tall, lean man who to Lucian's eye had something of the ascetic about him. One of his eyes had been replaced by an augmetic lens, which twinkled like a rare gem from his dark, sharp-nosed face. The major wore a headdress similar to those worn by his troops, not one, but three tall feathers mounted at its front. Though the major looked to Lucian more a man of intellect than of action, he bore an impressive, curved power sword at his belt. Lucian judged that by the man's bearing he was fully capable of using the blade to masterful effect.

At the officer's side came Sergeant-Major Havil, a giant of a man with a coarse beard and dark eyes that surely saw all that occurred in the ranks. He too wore the traditional headdress of his home world, surmounted by a single black feather. In his hand the sergeant-major carried a polearm as tall as he was. Its head was a huge, double-bladed power axe. Though the weapon was encrusted in gorgeous gems and was undoubtedly a regimental heirloom, Lucian suspected that it was also wielded in battle, and would reap a fearsome toll amongst the enemy.

Both officers halted in front of Lucian. Sergeant-Major Havil stamped his feet with parade-ground precision, and bellowed an order in the tongue of his home world so loud it made Lucian's ears ring. The rogue trader decided instantly that he liked the sergeant-major. The man reminded him of a cthellian cudbear.

In response to the order, every rifleman in the formation came smartly to attention, stamping down in flawless precision as they shouldered their lasguns. A gentle breeze stirred the feathers of their headdresses, but otherwise, the ranks stood perfectly motionless. It was a sight to stir the heart, making Lucian pleased that his political manoeuvrings had resulted in him taking command of such a splendid force of warriors.

Then, Major Subad bowed at the waist, straightened, and addressed Lucian. 'Battlegroup Arcadius is hereby commissioned, and its command is vested in Lucian Gerrit, bearer of the Warrant of Trade of the Clan Arcadius. Let it be recorded in the regimental rolls, and let the foes of the God-Emperor tremble!'

Lucian bowed in return, then took a step towards the major, holding out his right hand. The two clasped forearms, and the deed was done. Battlegroup Arcadius, Lucian smiled inwardly at the name, was his to command.

'My thanks, Major Subad,' Lucian replied, looking from the hawk-faced officer to the ranks of veteran warriors arrayed behind him. 'Is the battlegroup ready to receive orders?'

'That it is, my lord,' the major replied. 'All companies have been assigned orders of march and merely await your command to advance to glory.'

Lucian chuckled slightly at the officer's turn of phrase, filled as it was with beaming martial pride. The Rakarshans spoke an archaic dialect of Low Gothic and he would have trouble communicating directly with the ranks himself. The major, however, spoke High Gothic fluently, and would translate Lucian's commands as he passed them down the line. Nonetheless, Lucian thought it might be worth learning some of the Rakarshan dialect, as he might be fighting beside these fierce warriors for some time to come.

'Well enough, major,' Lucian said, grinning widely. 'The command is given. Let the advance to glory begin!'

SARIK VAULTED THE trunk of a large tree that had been felled by the Scout Titan's supporting fire, raising his boltgun one-handed and unleashing a rapid-fire burst at the tau warrior who sheltered in the foliage up ahead. Bolts stitched the alien's torso, his blocky, sand-coloured armour penetrated in half a dozen places. An instant later, the mass-reactive shells exploded within the warrior's body, and he fell to the ground a ragged mass of ruined flesh.

Sarik tracked his weapon back and forth across his surroundings, his squad moving up behind him.

'Clear.'

The chest armour of Sarik's victim was ripped wide open, as was the flesh beneath it. A pool of blood swelled outwards, seeping into the dusty ground. The alien's blood was not red, but a deep blue-purple. The xeno-genitors attached to the Departmento Tacticae postulated this was because their circulatory system relied not on iron, as in human biology, but on cobalt. The only thing that mattered to Sarik was that they bled, and that they died with honour.

Stooping, Sarik retrieved the weapon the dead warrior had carried. As with all the tau firearms Sarik had encountered, it was rectangular and hard-edged, lacking the ornamentation many weapons of human manufacture displayed. The grip was too small for his gauntleted hands. It was designed to accommodate the tau's hands, which featured an opposable thumb and three fingers. Mounted atop the weapon was a device Sarik had not seen before, though he guessed straight away what it was. Lifting the weapon, he squinted into the device. As he suspected, it was a sighting mechanism. Tracking the weapon back and forth across the clearing, Sarik depressed a stud at its side and a needle-thin beam of red light lanced out from the front.

Sarik guessed that a second stud at the weapon's side would establish a machine communion with a remote, vehicle-mounted weapons system. The link would be maintained as the missiles homed in on the target indicated by the red beam.

Feeling suddenly tainted by his contact with the alien technology, Sarik threw the weapon to the bloodstained ground beside its former owner.

The alien that lay slaughtered at Sarik's feet was the third his squad had killed, and reports from the other elements of the spearhead indicated that a further dozen had been engaged. The Space Marines ranged ahead of the lone Warhound Scout Titan, clearing each stand of trees of the observers. The weight of missile fire had rapidly dropped off as the tau had discerned the Space Marines' tactics, allowing the advance to proceed again.

As the spearhead progressed, the stands of trees became increasingly regular as it pressed in to cultivated farmland. In the distance, small, white domed-shaped structures were nestled in amongst the vegetation, the first signs of the conurbations that the spy-drones had indicated lay all around the tau city.

Moving to the edge of the plantation, Sarik prepared to call his transport forwards towards the next area of cover an alien spotter might be concealed in. At the edge of his hearing, which was far superior to that of any normal man, Sarik detected a rising drone, like turbines slowly powering up. The sound was emanating from behind a low rise, and could represent only one thing.

'Squad,' Sarik called into the vox-net. 'Enemy armour located. I want the missile launcher forward, and all other brethren on overwatch.'

A battle-brother appeared behind Sarik and knelt down beside him. He shouldered the very same weapon that Sarik had used the previous day against the tau flyer that had slain its previous bearer. The sound increased in volume, and Sarik saw a curved prow edge its way out from behind the rise, followed by the low, almost piscine form of the rest of the tau vehicle. Last to be revealed was the splayed, wing-like structure of the multiple launcher mounted high upon its back, its paired vanes underslung with three missiles each.

The launcher was slowly rotating. An undetected observer must have managed to bring his laser designator to bear on the *Gladius Pious*. Sarik turned to the battle-brother at his side, about to issue the order to engage, when he saw a red reflection glinting from the Space Marine's helmet.

Sarik dived forwards, shunting his fellow Space Marine aside at the very moment a missile fired to life and streaked through the air towards the pair. Both hit the ground hard, rolling apart as the missile burst through the foliage. With a supersonic scream, the missile passed by a mere metre over Sarik's head and struck the bough of a tree on the other side of the clearing. The entire plantation erupted as the missile detonated, shards of wood transformed into potentially lethal shrapnel by the power of the explosion.

Rising, Sarik scanned the clearing, which had been reduced from an orderly plantation to a scene of devastation. None of his warriors was injured, but that would not last if the observer drew a bead on any of them a second time.

Opening a vox-channel to the *Gladius Pious*, Sarik said, 'Princeps Atild. The enemy have changed their tactics. They are targeting us, but the spotter remains concealed. I suggest you engage possible locations while we deal with the launcher, over.'

'Understood, Sarik,' the princeps replied. 'Activate transponders and stand by.'

Relaying the order to the squad leaders under his command, Sarik activated his transponder unit. The device would transmit the location of each Space Marine and Rhino in the spearhead to the Warhound's strategium, so that the Scout Titan's weapons would not be turned upon its allies. Ordinarily, the transponders might be left to continually transmit, but the Departmento Tacticae had warned that the tech-heresies of the tau were so dire they might be able to detect the transmissions. The Space Marines were not prepared to take that risk.

'All units, stand by,' Sarik said over the command net, the blood rising within him.

Then the skies erupted as the Warhound turned its Vulcan mega-bolter on the nearby treelines, sweeping the weapon left and right as thousands of explosive bolts hammered into any and every possible location a tau spotter might be concealed in.

'Squad forward!' Sarik bellowed, praying his voice would be carried over the vox-net, for it was not audible over the deafening torrent of fire. 'Take it down!'

Sarik burst from the cover of the plantation and emerged into the open. A second later the warriors of his squad were at his side, and the black-armoured Scythes of the Emperor were not far away. Before them, the tau grav-tank had engaged the huge thrusters mounted on its flanks and was rising up as its retractable landing treads folded into its underbelly. The thrusters swivelled downwards to give it additional lift, and as the power built they emitted a high-pitched whine so loud it was soon competing with the thunderous report of the Warhound's mega-bolters.

Stowing his boltgun, Sarik drew his chainsword and brandished it high so that his warriors would follow his example. Then he brought the snarling blade downwards, pointing it directly at the tau grav-tank. A missile lanced from the treeline the Space Marines had just left and slammed into the side of the slowly rising grav-tank.

The missile struck a thruster unit on the grav-tank's side, and although the vehicle's thick armour deflected the worst of the blast, the engine was crippled. The vehicle slewed around, its remaining thruster screaming as it fought to maintain lift.

The grav-tank's nose dipped towards the ground, and Sarik sprang forwards, putting all his strength and that granted him by his power armour into sprinting across the open ground before the vehicle could recover and escape. As Sarik closed with his target, the pilot finally regained control and the vehicle began to rise again.

Finally, Sarik was on his foe, his battle-brothers a mere step behind. As the grav-tank rose, the air beneath it rippling with the anti-grav field that kept it aloft, Sarik leaped upwards, and caught hold of one of the secondary control vanes at the grav-tank's prow.

Pulling himself up onto the curved surface, Sarik looked for a handhold. Finding none on the alien machine, he located a crew hatch high on its spine and threw himself towards it even as the grav-tank gained altitude. The barking report of half a dozen boltguns sounded from below as Sarik's warriors opened fire on the anti-grav generators keeping it aloft.

His grip on the curved surface threatening to desert him, Sarik finally got a hold on the small hatch, and dug his armoured fingers in around its collar. Hauling with all his might, Sarik bellowed a wordless war cry, which turned into a joyous outburst of savage victory as the hatch peeled back under his efforts.

The grav-tank dipped violently, whether from the effects of his battle-brothers' fire or the pilot panicking Sarik could not discern. A red battle fury descended upon him. He plunged his arm inside the hatch right up to his shoulder plate, and pulled furiously on the first thing he grabbed hold of.

As Sarik retracted his arm, the grav-tank dipped crazily forwards. He dragged the pilot through the hatch and held him in the air victoriously. Then he brought the tau's body downwards upon the spine of the vehicle. He broke his victim's back across the hard armour, before flinging the ragged form to the ground below. It was only then that Sarik's berserker rage lifted, as the grav-tank slewed wildly out of control towards the structure it had been hidden behind.

In the final seconds before the tau vehicle slammed into the dome-shaped building, Sarik threw himself from its back, propelled clear by a last, powerful thrust of his legs against its hull. Even as he fell backwards towards the ground Sarik saw the grav-tank strike the building, gouging a great wound through the structure. Sarik struck the ground, the breath hammered from his lungs by the force of the impact. Then the vehicle upended itself, its nose ploughing through the building, before the entire structure collapsed upon it with a mighty release of dust, smoke and falling masonry.

'One down,' Sarik snarled, rising once more to his feet. An entire empire to go...

THE LANDSCAPE AHEAD of Lucian was dominated by low rises and dense vegetation, making it a perfect hunting ground for the veteran light infantry of the Rakarshan Rifles. To the south, a vast column of black smoke rose many kilometres into the sky, marking the death of one of the Legio Thanataris Scout Titans. Lucian had monitored the advance of Sarik's spearhead over the command-net, and warned his own companies to be vigilant for the missile grav-tanks and the observers directing their fire. Perhaps because the Rakarshan Rifles used no vehicles, they had not attracted the attentions of these supremely deadly armour killers.

Now, Dal'yth's sun was high overhead, and the battlegroup's advance was proceeding well. The Rakarshans had been transported forwards on Officio Munitorum conveyances, each large enough to carry a whole platoon and its equipment, before pressing forwards on foot. The warriors were well suited to the terrain, and were able to make intelligent use of the folds in the land and the regular stands of cultivated trees, whilst maintaining a rapid and steady advance.

Enemy resistance had been relatively light at first, with the lead platoons pressing through what ambushes they had encountered. The Rakarshans had proved themselves fearsome attackers and many had blooded their ceremonial blades already. The ambushes were growing in frequency, however, as the tau adjusted to the Rakarshans' tactics and redeployed their highly mobile forces to counter them.

'Communiqué from command,' Major Subad said, his hand raised to the vox-set at his ear. 'Spy-drones report a substantial concentration of enemy infantry amassing in the conurbation ahead.'

Lucian raised a gauntleted hand to shield his eyes from the white sun, and squinted in the direction indicated. The land rose and fell in a series of low hills, the eastern slopes of each covered in row upon row of the now familiar, purple-leaved fruit trees. Nestling in a shallow valley around five kilometres ahead, Lucian saw a cluster of white, domed structures, and in amongst them, evidence of enemy infantry moving to and fro.

'Looks like they intend to make a stand,' Lucian said, as much to himself as to his second-in-command. 'If they want a fight…'

'Standing orders require us to bypass them, my lord,' Major Subad interjected, 'and leave the main body to engage them while we press on.'

Lucian looked the officer in the eye, gauging the tone of his statement. 'How far behind is the main body?'

'Command states the advance has become stalled on several fronts, my lord,' said Major Subad.

'So there's a very real chance that if we bypass the enemy position, they will escape before the main body can engage?'

Major Subad's bionic eye glinted in the sun. 'A very real chance indeed, my lord,' he said.

'Then clearly, it is our duty to engage the enemy. Pass the word, major.'

Lucian remained at his vantage point, maintaining his watch on the tau while his forces prepared for the assault. During a brief conference with the company commanders it was decided that the battlegroup's heavy weapons, mainly missile launchers and heavy bolters, would deploy to the enemy's front and pin them down. Meanwhile, one third of the battlegroup would advance north-west, hooking around the enemy's flank to assault them from what should be a lightly defended front. Finally, the remainder of the battlegroup's companies would work their way around to the enemy's rear, block his escape route and guard against enemy reinforcement.

When the three elements were finally ready to begin their advance, Major Subad approached. 'My lord,' the major said. 'Will you be joining us?'

Lucian looked to his second-in-command and raised an eyebrow. 'It would be an honour, major,' said Lucian. 'Where would you have me?'

Subad's face lit up, and he bowed to his commander, before answering. 'The flanking group would very much benefit from your presence, my lord. I myself shall lead the blocking group, while Sergeant-Major Havil directs the heavy weapons. I shall vox you when all units are ready.'

'Well enough,' Lucian answered, keen to press on. Taking his leave of his officers, Lucian strode towards the companies he would be leading into battle, an adjutant vox-operator close behind him. The companies were mustered amongst a large cultivated fruit tree plantation, each platoon having moved forwards to its ready position in near total silence. Lucian felt suddenly very aware that while his troops were lightly equipped and camouflaged, he himself was wearing hulking power armour adorned in the deep red and gold trim of his clan's livery. No matter, he told himself. A good commander should be seen and heard, leading from the front, as much an inspiration to his own troops as an object of fear to the enemy.

The Rakarshans were eager to advance. Each was grim-faced and dark-eyed, every movement fluid and ready for battle. Lucian had seen hardened Imperial Navy armsmen look more nervous before boarding a harmless cargo scow, and he almost felt pity for the tau warriors. Almost.

'All units in position, my lord,' Major Subad's voice came across the vox-net. 'Advance at your command.'

'Stand by, major,' Lucian replied, locating the riflemen of the foremost platoon. He crossed to the unit's position, and nodded to its lieutenant before replying to Subad. 'You may begin, major.'

There was a brief pause, before the sound of a missile launcher being fired from Sergeant-Major Havil's fire support element filled the air. The missile streaked from its launcher upon a billowing black contrail, its firer hidden amongst the fruit trees of another plantation south of Lucian's position, and detonated upon striking one of the dome-shaped buildings. The resulting explosion was the signal to the entire battlegroup that battle was joined.

The air was suddenly filled with the deafening roar of dozens of heavy weapons opening fire at once, thousands of rounds of explosive ammunition hammering into the settlement.

Taking his cue, Lucian drew his power sword from its scabbard and turned to the platoon commander beside him. Though the man was much younger, his eyes were filled with the desire to advance. Lucian nodded, and the man yelled an order in the Rakarshan tongue.

An instant later, the riflemen were charging from cover and so too was Lucian. The sunlight was harsh after the shade of the fruit plantation, and it took Lucian a moment to get his bearings. Ahead of him was a cluster of low, white buildings, towards which the Rakarshans were advancing. The riflemen moved quickly, darting from one piece of cover to the next, each platoon covering another with weapons sweeping the buildings ahead. Despite the disciplined manner of the advance, Lucian knew that the final seconds would be a wild, ferocious charge as ceremonial blades were drawn.

Then came the whip-crack of a hyper-velocity projectile splitting the air nearby. The tau had seen their advance, and were firing on the flanking group.

The leading riflemen opened fire on the cluster of buildings, from where it appeared the shot had been fired. Lucian pressed forwards, making use of what cover he could, knowing that to fall to an alien sniper at this stage would be an ignominious way to start, and end, his military adventures. Lasgun rounds sang through the air, hammering into the white buildings and stitching dirty black scorch marks across their flanks. A second hyper-velocity shot scythed past, and Lucian imagined he saw a thin line etched through the air in its passing. A grunt sounded from somewhere behind, followed by the thud of a body hitting the ground. First blood to the tau, Lucian thought grimly, knowing that his flanking group could not afford to become stalled so soon in its advance.

'You men!' Lucian shouted to a platoon opposite from his position behind the trunk of a tall fruit tree. 'With me!'

The riflemen looked back at Lucian, their faces blank. He might as well be offering to make them a cup of recaf. Raising his power sword high, Lucian decided to lead by example.

Lucian stepped out into the open and swept his power sword towards the tau position. The Rakarshans got the idea immediately, and those nearest to him limbered their weapons and drew their ceremonial blades, springing forwards to join him.

A shot whined past Lucian, way too close for comfort, and sent a shower of grit into the air scant metres behind him.

'Forward Rakarshan!' Lucian bellowed, to be answered a moment later by the ululating war cry of the riflemen.

The charge towards the cluster of buildings was a mad dash, Lucian only absently aware that a relentless rain of blue energy bolts was being unleashed from somewhere up ahead. He heard several screams of pain from the accompanying riflemen, but he knew that to falter now would be fatal.

Closing on the nearest building, Lucian was confronted by a tau warrior emerging from cover to bring a long-barrelled weapon to bear. The warrior wore a blank-faced helmet, its single lens locking on to him as the alien swung his weapon upwards to draw a bead.

As he closed the final metres, Lucian brought his power sword up and back, and then finally his charge hit home.

Lucian's blow struck the alien warrior's weapon, scything it in two in a shower of blue sparks. The tau uttered an unintelligible curse and stepped backwards, even as a second warrior emerged behind him. Lucian let his momentum power him forwards, and shouldered his full weight into his enemy's chest, pinning him with a bone-crunching impact to the wall of the building.

The alien slumped to the ground, his body pulverised. Lucian drew his plasma pistol with his free left hand and swung it upwards towards the second tau.

Before the pistol was fully raised, the other fired his weapon, a shorter, carbine type firearm well suited to the close quarters battle. The carbine's discharge was almost blinding at such a short range, the energy bolt slamming into Lucian's shoulder armour. The impact blew Lucian backwards, his body striking the ground with a gut-wrenching thud. An instant later, he was looking directly up into the barrel of his enemy's weapon.

'*Gue'slo*!' the tau said, the words sounding metallic as they came from his helmet speaker.

'I've had guns pointed at me by far more scary people than you, tau,' Lucian sneered.

On hearing Lucian speak the name of his race, the alien cocked his head slightly. '*S'nae'ta*...'

'*S'nae'ta* indeed...' Lucian replied, playing for time as the Rakarshans pressed forwards.

The word must have been an insult, for the tau shouldered his weapon, his finger closing on the trigger.

Then the tau's head snapped back violently as a las-bolt slammed into it from the side. The alien warrior dropped heavily to the ground at Lucian's side, the blue-grey of its face visible through the smoking crack in the helmet. A hand appeared in front of Lucian's face.

'Rha ji?' the Rakarshan trooper said.

'Great,' Lucian grunted as he took the rifleman's hand and got to his feet. 'Does no one speak the Emperor's holy tongue around here?'

Before the Rakarshan could answer, the air was filled by a storm of las-bolts as the rifleman's platoon charged forwards and passed the building. As they closed on the tau positions, the riflemen drew their ceremonial blades and unleashed an ululating war cry that stirred cold dread in Lucian's heart. He could scarcely imagine what it would do to the tau.

The tau defending the cluster of buildings fired a last, desperate fusillade and half a dozen Rakarshans went down. The high-velocity weapons tore straight through their bodies, but unlike many weapons used by the Imperium, they did not kill outright. Instead, they left the victim to bleed out on the ground, out of the fight but a drain on resources as medics would have to deal with them and stop their cries demoralising their unwounded fellows.

Then the Rakarshans were upon their foe, and their blades were drinking deep of the purple blood of the tau.

'Leave some for fleet intelligence!' Lucian yelled as he rejoined the riflemen. 'Leave some... Emperor's balls, will you just...'

With the Rakarshans unable to understand Lucian's words, he had no choice but to wade in amongst them, locating a rifleman whose blade was raised to deliver the killing blow to a tau warrior at his feet. Lucian stepped in and grasped the man's wrist, staying his blow.

'No!' Lucian said firmly. 'Intelligence. We need to get at least...'

'Band'im?' the Rakarshan said, the savage light of battle fading from his eyes.

Lucian relinquished his grip on the other's wrist, and the rifleman lowered his blade. 'Aye lad, band'im. Band'im right now.'

The Rakarshan nodded his understanding, and then drew his ceremonial blade across his palm, drawing blood, before sheathing the weapon in the jewelled scabbard at his belt. A crowd of riflemen was gathering about the scene as Lucian turned on the tau.

The warrior's helmet had been torn off in the melee, and he had a blackened wound at his shoulder where a las-bolt had struck home. There was no blood; the heat of the blast had cauterised the wound, but would have flash-boiled the surrounding tissue making the entire arm useless and collapsing the adjacent lung. If they even had lungs. 'Looks like the war's over for you, tau,' Lucian said. Then, remembering the mess Inquisitor Grand had made of the first tau the crusade had taken prisoner, he added 'Better get you to Gauge's staff...'

An explosion sounded from somewhere amongst the settlement, followed by a last burst of heavy bolter fire before the sounds of battle finally ended. The sound of whining turbines came from the far side of the cluster of buildings, rising in pitch before fading as the vehicles fled.

'Vokset, sir,' the vox-operator said as he handed Lucian his headset.

'That I understood,' Lucian said. Like most Low Gothic dialects Lucian had encountered, the Rakarshan tongue contained elements common across the

Imperium. It was just a matter of deciphering the underlying terms. 'Gerrit here. Go ahead.'

'The enemy are retreating, my lord,' said Major Subad over the vox-net. 'They put up an honourable fight, but they are now fleeing west by anti-grav carrier.'

'Understood, major,' Lucian replied. 'Congratulate the men on a battle well fought and meet me here. Have Havil deploy a screen to the west in case they counter-attack. Out.'

As the rifle platoon's lieutenant arrived and set about ordering his men to secure the area, Lucian took stock of the tau settlement the Rakarshans had captured. The dozen or so buildings were constructed of the off-white, resin-like compound he had encountered in previous battles, and were low and domed. They were so unlike anything humanity built or dwelt within, all clean lines devoid of ornamentation. Despite their functional appearance, there was something elegant about the design of the buildings, for there was obviously some alien aesthetic at work.

Lucian located the door of the nearest building, comparing its design to that of the defence station that had been captured at the outset of the war and used for a brief time as its base of operations for the planetary assault on the tau-held world of Sy'l'kell. A shallow recess to one side of the door concealed a simple command rune, which Lucian pressed, causing the door to hiss as pneumatic systems engaged and opened the portal.

Lucian stepped inside, his eyes adjusting to the relative gloom. He kept his plasma pistol drawn, just in case any defenders lurked inside. As his eyes adjusted, Lucian saw that the room he had passed into was some sort of workshop, with dozens of tools arrayed in orderly rows across the walls. A moment's study told Lucian that the tools were little more than agricultural implements, but they appeared not to be designed for use by the tau, whose four-fingered hands would surely be unsuitable to wield them. The tools looked more like they were designed for use by some sort of...

A shadow swung across the periphery of Lucian's vision, and his plasma pistol was up and pointing right at it in an instant. Floating two metres off the ground directly in front of Lucian was a small, dome-shaped machine, a single lens blinking red as if it were studying him. Beneath the curved dome hung a cluster of multi-jointed limbs, each terminating in an empty socket that Lucian guessed was designed to use the tools arrayed across the walls.

Lucian kept the plasma pistol levelled at the drone as it bobbed in the air in front of him. 'So you're the hired help,' he said, marvelling that the tau should use such a wondrous machine for the simple task of tending crops and fixing broken fences. The red-lit lens blinked, and the machine emitted an electronic chatter, less harsh, but not unlike the sounds Lucian was accustomed to hearing around the cogitation terminals aboard his starship.

'Intelligence,' he said, lowering his plasma pistol a fraction. 'Of a sort at least. You'd be popular with the tech-priests. They'd take you to bits, not be able to put you back together again, then declare you a heretic...' he added wryly.

As if in reaction to Lucian's comment, the drone backed into the shadows with a sharp movement.

'You understood that, didn't you,' Lucian said, part of him feeling faintly ridiculous, another estimating how much the machine might fetch amongst those who collected such items of 'cold trade' curiosity. 'Of course,' Lucian muttered. 'Your masters have been in contact with isolated colonies for decades.'

'My lord!' Major Subad said as he burst into the room. 'I have it covered, back away slowly...'

Lucian could not help but smile as the Rakarshan commander entered the room in full combat stance, a gold-chased laspistol fixed on the bobbing drone. 'It's just a glorified shovel, Subad,' Lucian said, but the major's expression told him the man was on the verge of blowing the harmless drone to pieces. The drone seemed to see this too, and backed even further into the corner of the room.

'My lord,' Subad said, not taking his eyes from the drone. 'This is heresy. Crusade intelligence warned us of them. You must have read the briefing slates.'

'Those were gun drones, major,' Lucian said. 'This is no war machine.'

The major looked far from convinced. 'But it thinks, my lord, look at it!'

'Aye,' Lucian said. 'That's curious, isn't it?'

Major Subad's eyes widened and he turned his glance to Lucian. '*Curious*, my lord?'

'Well enough,' Lucian sighed. He could hardly expect the man to share a rogue trader's attitude to the unknown. 'Why don't you post a guard at the door and we'll keep it safe in here?'

The major nodded fervently at Lucian's suggestion, and began backing away towards the door. When Lucian had stepped out into the light, Subad sprang out, his laspistol still trained on the shadows inside.

Lucian pressed the command rune and the door hissed shut, locking the infernal thinking-machine inside the building.

'Major,' Lucian said as the officer finally lowered his weapon. 'You and your men are going to have to learn the difference between a gun drone and the sort of machine in there. If the tau use such machines as warriors, they probably use even more as menials.'

'They employ techno-heresy as servants?' Subad said, his expression incredulous.

'I would guess so, major. We know they espouse some extremist collectivism they call the Greater Good, so perhaps...'

'My lord!' Subad hissed. 'Please, we have our orders. That obscene doctrine is not to be mentioned. It is *unclean*.'

'Yes,' Lucian sighed. 'I've heard that Cardinal Gurney fears the troops might desert in droves if they got wind of the notion that all were equals...'

'Indeed, my lord,' Subad said, apparently not noticing what Lucian had hoped was a witheringly caustic tone. 'The Commissariat are alert for signs of taint.'

'Pfft!' Lucian said. 'Myopic fools who can't see past the muzzles of their own bolt pistols. Please, if one of those jumped-up demagogues so much as looks at one of our boys, you'll let me know, won't you?'

Now Major Subad's face was a mask of horror.

'COME ON, MAJOR,' Lucian said, deciding it would be better to steer the conversation away from such dangerous topics as techno-heresy and xenosyndicalism. He slapped a hand on the officer's back as the two walked away from the building towards the main body of the troops. 'Update me, if you would be so kind.'

Subad nodded, visibly composing himself. 'Yes, my lord, forgive me...'

'Nothing to forgive,' Lucian interrupted. 'I've just seen

much more of the galaxy than you. I should have taken that into account.'

Subad straightened up and tugged down the front of his battle dress. 'The assault went as planned, my lord, with one exception, for which I offer my most humble and sincere apologies.'

'Go on, major,' Lucian said raising an eyebrow.

'A number of the enemy escaped using carriers we had not previously detected. If you want patrols platoon flogged I can–'

'Flogged?' Now it was Lucian's turn to be horrified. 'Why would I want them flogged?'

'You want them put to death, my lord?'

'No!' Lucian said, exasperated. 'Neither. Not now, not ever. Is that clear?'

Major Subad managed to look both relieved and confused at the same time, but nodded his understanding before continuing. 'The battlegroup inflicted at least one hundred and twenty kills.'

'Captives?' Lucian asked.

'Captives, my lord?'

'Yes, major. Captives. Band'im.'

'Oh. Band'im, yes. Just the one.'

'The one I took.'

'Yes, my lord.'

'Have the Band'im passed back to Gauge's staff cadre at sector zero,' Lucian said. 'Not to Grand's goons. Understood?'

Major Subad nodded his understanding, though he looked distinctly uneasy at the mention of the inquisitor's name. Lucian pressed on. 'Casualties?'

'Twelve dead, my lord. Twenty or so light wounds, twelve are being mustered for medicae evacuation to sector zero.'

At least the wounded wouldn't be flogged for getting in the way of enemy bullets, Lucian thought, though he kept the idea to himself in case it gave the officer ideas. 'What of the general advance? Any reports?'

'Yes, my lord,' Subad said, producing a data-slate from a pouch at his belt. His face grew dark as he scanned the first few lines of text.

'Initial advances pushed back what few enemy units opposed them,' Subad said, paraphrasing the information presented on the slate's screen. 'But the main advance has been opposed by multiple hit and run attacks and ambushes. It has broken up into separate thrusts, and each is facing increasingly heavy resistance.'

Lucian scanned the settlement, which was crawling with riflemen dashing to and fro doing whatever it is soldiers do straight after a firefight. 'Then we'd better push on then, hadn't we, Major Subad? Remind me,' Lucian added absently. 'What's the tau name for the city we're taking, major?'

Subad consulted his data-slate. 'Gel'bryn, my lord?'

'Gel'bryn,' Lucian said. 'Something tells me the road to Gel'bryn isn't going to be an easy one, major.'

THE GLADIUS PIOUS stalked ponderously away, its huge armoured feet uncaring of the destruction wrought in their passing amongst the plantations and farm buildings. Princeps Atild had informed Sarik that the Warhound had been ordered to reinforce another of the spearheads. The Iron Hands had encountered heavy resistance in sub-sector delta twelve, while the spearhead Sarik led had made far better progress once it had broken through sector beta nine.

Sarik's Rhino ploughed onwards along the road towards the distant city of Gel'bryn, the column heading westwards as it penetrated ever deeper into alien territory.

According to Sarik's command terminal, the city was still some fifty kilometres away. His force was the furthest forwards, a fact that stirred fierce warrior pride in Sarik's heart, even though the White Scars made up only one part of the spearhead he commanded. The column, consisting of three squads from Sarik's own Chapter, two from the Ultramarines and three from the Scythes of the Emperor, plus supporting Predator tanks and Whirlwind missile tanks, had sustained multiple casualties and three deaths as it had pushed onwards. The fallen had been evacuated by Thunderhawk gunship, and the composite Space Marine company was travelling through a sector almost entirely given over to agriculture.

'All squads,' Sarik said into the vox-net. 'Remain vigilant for ambushers. Maintain overwatch on all arcs.' The terrain was closing in again, the crops and plantations offering ample hiding places for the spotters that had directed the tau grav-tanks to fire so effectively on the Warhound.

'Lead,' Sarik transmitted to the Ultramarines Rhino travelling ahead of his own. 'Watch your forward sinister. There's cover there the enemy might use.'

The Rhino's Ultramarines tank commander swung his pintle-mount storm bolter in the direction Sarik had indicated, covering the dense stand of fruit trees as the vehicle rumbled by.

The Ultramarines carrier cleared the trees and the column wound its way past a cluster of what appeared to be abandoned agricultural machines. Sarik studied the machines as his Rhino ground past, studying their pristine white, gracefully rounded forms and considering for a moment whether he should order them destroyed in case the enemy should use them as weapons.

Even as Sarik decided the machines were no threat, the air was split by a hissing roar. Sarik recognised the sound of a fusion reaction boiling the air up ahead, and shouted from his open hatch: 'Ambush! Pattern Nova!'

A sharp explosion split the air and the lead Rhino shuddered to a halt, its left track splaying outwards as its armoured flank was flash-melted to white hot slag. The Rhino veered right as flames belched from its left-side traction unit, shedding the track entirely.

Sarik hauled himself from the top hatch of his Rhino and vaulted over its side, bolt pistol drawn in one hand and chainsword in the other before his armoured boots had even touched the ground. The rear hatch slammed down and his squad emerged, each brother taking position to cover a different arc with his boltgun.

Last out was Brother Qaja, his plasma cannon tracking back and forth as he came to kneel beside Sarik. The battle-brother had been patched up following the injuries he had sustained at the sensor pylon, but Sarik had been told by his force's Apothecary that the warrior would need heavy cybernetic augment-treatments when Operation Pluto was concluded.

'Target, brother-sergeant?' Qaja said as he swept the land ahead with his heavy weapon. 'Do you see them?'

'I see nothing, brother. Get the squads dispersed,' he said, before running forwards towards the lead Rhino, which was now almost entirely engulfed in flames as the melted armour on its flank began to solidify. None of the Ultramarines riding inside had yet disembarked.

As Sarik reached the rear end of the carrier, a secondary explosion burst from its foredeck. It was the pintle-mount's ready ammo cooking off, telling Sarik that the damage was far greater than was visible from the outside.

'Sergeant Arcan!' Sarik bellowed over the roar of the flames. 'Sergeant, do you hear me?' When no answer came, he sheathed his bolt pistol and chainsword and moved right up to the rear hatch.

'Can anyone hear me?' he bellowed. Again, no answer. There was only one thing for it. Flexing his armoured gauntlets, Sarik fed power to their fibre-bundle actuators to bolster his own, already formidable strength. He reached an arm out to either side of the hatch, locking the armoured shells covering his fingers to provide an anchor. After a final deep breath, Sarik hauled on the rear door with every ounce of his strength. The carrier's armour was designed to be proof against the many and deadly threats it would face whilst fighting across the numerous battlefields of the 41st Millennium, and was not so easily beaten. Sarik took a second deep breath and bled more power from the fusion core at his back to his armour's actuators. Warning tones sounded as the armour's war spirit protested its mistreatment, then the hatch buckled at either side and Sarik hauled one more time.

With a roar, Sarik tore the rear hatch from its mounting and flung the metal down. A dense cloud of greasy black smoke billowed out to engulf him and Sarik's genetically enhanced senses filtered and analysed the taste and scents assaulting him. The strongest was burning flesh.

'Apothecary!' Sarik bellowed before diving inside the stricken carrier. In a moment the smoke had begun to clear and Sarik's eyes, well capable of operating in darkness, beheld a tragic sight.

The blast that had struck the Rhino's flank had

burned a concentrated jet of nucleonic fire into the passenger compartment. Sergeant Arcan had been standing in the open rooftop cupola, and his entire lower body had been seared to atoms, its upper half still slumped in the hatch. The three battle-brothers nearest the wound in the side of their vehicle must have been boiled alive inside their armour, which had been melted into a hideously deformed parody of its former shape.

A movement caught Sarik's eye as an Ultramarine stirred. A second fusion blast sounded from somewhere outside, and Sarik heard running footsteps approaching from behind; the Apothecary, he hoped.

'Help is on the way, brother,' Sarik told the Space Marine, whose once deep blue armour had been reduced to scorched black by the titanic energies unleashed inside the vehicle. 'Hold on, and have faith.' Another secondary explosion sounded from the forward area of the troop bay as more ammunition detonated, showering the sergeant with micro-shrapnel. He reached forwards and grabbed the nearest Ultramarine by the shoulder plates, hauling the stunned warrior from the open rear hatch as the Apothecary joined him.

The Space Marine medic added his strength to the effort, and the wounded Ultramarine was dragged clear by their combined efforts. In another minute, the two warriors had pulled another three clear, and more Space Marines had arrived to aid the rescue effort.

'Do what you can, brother,' Sarik told the Apothecary before rushing back to join Brother Qaja.

'Status,' Sarik said.

'Squads are deployed as per Pattern Nova,' Qaja said.

'Enemy?'

'None located, brother-sergeant,' Qaja said, not taking his eyes from the terrain as he spoke.

'None?' Sarik growled. 'These xenos and their trickery...'

A third fusion blast roared through the air, burning a searing orange wound across the flank of one of the Whirlwind missile tanks further down the column. The blast was hard to track, twisting and distorting the air as it was boiled by nucleonic forces. Nevertheless, Sarik got an idea of the origin point.

The only problem was, he could see nothing there. A ripe Chogoran curse escaped his lips as he scowled at the thought of yet more alien technology at work against his Space Marines.

'All squads,' Sarik growled into the vox-net. 'Suppressive fire, delta nine, two hundred metres, wide.'

Every battle-brother deployed on the column's left flank opened fire at the kill zone. The air was filled with hundreds of mass-reactive bolts, the crops in the target area ripped to shreds as the ground was pounded by exploding rounds.

'Cease fire!' Sarik called out, watching intently for signs of movement in the kill zone. 'Just wait...'

Then the sound of some kind of rotary gatling weapon powering up came from further down the column and an instant later a storm of blue energy bolts sprayed towards the Space Marines. Most struck the sides of the sturdy Rhino transports without inflicting any damage, but a battle-brother of the Scythes of the Emperor was thrown violently backwards as a bolt struck his shoulder plate. The warrior was unharmed, but he was forced to discard the wrecked shoulder guard and jettison the arm section as he stood to regain his position in the firing line.

'Tau infantry,' Sarik said. 'But they're using the same stealth devices we've seen in their elite flyers.'

'Orders, brother-sergeant?' Qaja said.

Sarik scowled as he scanned the surrounding terrain. It was dominated by low rises and depressions, a patchwork of crop fields and fruit plantations receding into the distance. The rise and fall of the land reminded him of the Baatarn Lowlands, an area his nomadic tribe had passed through when he was a child. His uncle, the tribe's seersman, had told him a tale of the mist-spirits said to haunt the place...

'Smoke...' Sarik muttered.

'Brother-sergeant?'

'Did you ever hear the tale of how the Tuvahks defeated the Kagayaga at Baatarn?' Sarik said, a sly grin forming on his face.

'Of course, brother-sergeant,' Qaja replied. 'Codicier Qan'karro related it at the last Feast of Skies. I don't see what–'

'All squad leaders,' Sarik said into the vox-net. 'Have one of your men gather smoke grenades from the Rhino launchers and stand by.'

Another burst of blue bolts sprayed through towards the Space Marines, this time from further down the column still.

'They're circling us like blood-sharks on a wounded mooncalf,' Qaja said through gritted teeth.

Within thirty seconds the squad leaders had all reported back over the vox-net that they were armed with smoke grenades taken from the multi-barrelled launchers at the front of each carrier. 'How did the King of the Tuvahks escape the Kagayaga, brother?' Sarik said, a feral light gleaming in his eyes.

'He...' Qaja said, before realisation dawned. 'He smoked them out, brother-sergeant.'

'All squads, deploy smoke grenades. Wide dispersion, fifty metres. Now!'

As one, the battle-brothers of each squad armed with the smoke grenades hurled them forwards. Upon striking the ground, each grenade detonated, creating an instant cloud of white smoke that billowed out from the impact point. Within seconds, a wide area fifty metres in front of the column's left flank was enshrouded in drifting banks of smoke.

'What now, brother-sergeant?' Qaja said.

'Wait and see, brother,' Sarik said. 'All squads, maintain overwatch. Look for movement in the smoke.'

Quiet settled the length of column as the Space Marines on its left flank focussed their attentions on the drifting smoke. Clipped exchanges went back and forth between the squad leaders as they coordinated their arcs, ensuring that every quadrant was covered.

'Contact!' a battle-brother from a Scythes of the Emperor Devastator squad on the extreme end of the line reported. 'Zeta nine, transient.'

'Hold your fire,' Sarik ordered. 'What did you see?'

'Movement, brother-sergeant,' the Space Marine said. 'A parting of the smoke, but nothing solid.'

'Your vigilance does you honour, brother,' Sarik replied. 'Stand by. Qaja, you have the squad.'

Sarik moved swiftly along the column, exchanging brief words with the squad leaders as he passed them. As he reached the Scythes of the Emperor Devastator squad, its sergeant indicated the battle-brother he had spoken to.

'Show me.'

The warrior lowered his heavy bolter, resting its gaping barrel across his knee, and pointed into the drifting smoke bank with his free hand. 'There, brother-sergeant. The smoke parted for a moment, as if something were about to emerge.'

'But nothing did.'

'Contact!' another of the Scythes of the Emperor hissed, bringing his missile launcher to bear on a point to the squad's extreme left. Sarik saw it too.

'They're working their way around us,' Sarik said. 'All squads. Ten round fusillade, fifty metres, delta quad, on my mark.'

As the squad leaders signalled their acknowledgements and ordered their firing lines ready to enact Sarik's direction, the sergeant looked to the next squad along, a Scythes of the Emperor tactical squad. Clapping a hand on the shoulder of the Devastators' sergeant, he said 'Remain on station.' Then turning to the sergeant of the tactical squad, he said, 'Sergeant, I need five men.'

The squad leader selected five of his warriors and with a curt gesture sent them over to Sarik. 'Brothers, remove your helmets. Our foes are hidden to our sight, but not to our other senses. With me!'

As the five Scythes stowed their helmets at their belts, Sarik turned and was off, running towards the roiling bank of smoke. He crossed the fifty metres and plunged into the mists, halting the instant his vision was swallowed up by featureless white. A moment later, he heard the Scythes move in behind him and likewise halt. Even at a range of two metres, the warriors were barely visible. It was only their black armour that made them stand out at all, while Sarik's white armour would make him all but invisible even at that close range.

Sarik took a deep draught of the air, slightly overemphasising the action so that the other Space Marines would hear it and follow his example. To Sarik's enhanced senses, the air tasted overwhelmingly of garlic, though in reality that was the phosphorus employed in the smoke grenades. Sarik sensed his multi-lung implant engage as it protected his kidneys from the toxic effects of the chemical smoke. Taking another deep breath, he mentally filtered out the strong odour of garlic, and detected something else, something sharp, like bleach.

'Ozone?' one of the Scythes of the Emperor whispered at Sarik's side.

'Indeed,' Sarik whispered back. 'Some sort of energy field. Follow me.'

Sarik rose and commenced a stooped run, breathing steadily as he followed the sharp scent. As he moved, the smell grew in intensity, until his suspicions were confirmed. The tau were nearby, and the energy fields they were using to shield their movements were giving off the sharp smell of ozone as they reacted with the atmosphere.

Sarik halted, and was joined a moment later by the five Scythes of the Emperor.

'Follow my lead,' he hissed as low as possible. 'And stay close and quiet.'

Then he was up again, the Scythes close behind. The smell of ozone grew almost overpowering and Sarik could sense he was almost upon his prey. Then the mist parted as if something just larger than a man was walking through it, and Sarik dived forwards headlong.

Sarik's dive was arrested in mid air as he slammed into something invisible. The unseen form must have been substantially armoured, for the impact almost took the breath from Sarik's lungs. He went down, the invisible opponent beneath him, and felt the figure thrashing wildly as it fought to escape.

The dark shadows of the Scythes of the Emperor passed by, and Sarik knew they too were engaging more unseen enemies. None made a sound.

Sarik made a fist and punched down hard towards the smoke-shrouded ground. His fist stopped half a metre from the ground, striking a hard surface. A muffled grunt sounded, confirming that the tau warrior was clad in some form of hard, but not invulnerable armour. Guessing where its head was, he made a grab, and found its neck, clamping his fist around it.

Sarik used his free hand to draw his combat knife. The enemy struggled all the more, and something blunt slammed into Sarik's left shoulder plate. It could only have been a weapon, for a moment later Sarik heard the universal sound of ammunition being chambered. Knowing he had but seconds to prevent the enemy from firing its weapon and at best giving his presence away and at worst blowing his head clean from his shoulders, Sarik plunged the monomolecular-edged blade towards where he judged the enemy's chest must be.

The blade struck solid armour, but Sarik brought it downwards until it found yielding flesh. With a brutal upwards thrust, Sarik plunged the knife deep inside the enemy's innards, feeling the tau shudder and thrash as he did so.

Then hot, purple blood spilled out of the invisible wound, staining Sarik's forearm. He withdrew the blade, and a shower of blue sparks, accompanied by the overpowering stink of ozone, erupted in front of him. He stood, and before his very eyes, his enemy faded into existence.

The warrior was wearing an armoured suit of matt black. The armour covered most, but not all of its body, and Sarik saw that his knife had found the soft joint between thigh and groin armour plate. The warrior's right arm carried a blunt, tube-shaped heavy weapon, and at its back was a device that Sarik judged to be the generator that powered its stealth field.

A series of muffled grunts and impacts told Sarik that the Scythes had encountered, and violently neutralised, more of the enemy stealth troopers. He listened until all had gone quiet again, and a moment later the five Space Marines reappeared.

'There are more of them, brother-sergeant. At least twenty, to the north.'

'Did they hear you?'

'Yes. They are inbound.'

'Good,' Sarik said, assuming a prone position on the ground. The smoke was beginning to clear. 'You might want to take cover, brothers.'

The Scythes of the Emperor took position beside the White Scar, and the six warriors concentrated on the smoky depths where the enemy lay. 'Come on then...' Sarik whispered.

Then he saw it. The smoke parted as at least a dozen figures ghosted towards the Space Marines.

Sarik opened the vox-channel. 'Mark!'

The air erupted and the ground was churned as bolt-rounds hammered in from the Space Marine gun line. Heavy bolters added their throaty roar to the sharp staccato of the boltguns and the smoke banks sizzled as balls of plasma lanced through. Though un-aimed, the fusillade could not help but strike the foe. Sparks flew as rounds struck invisible bodies over and over again. Then the tau attempted desperately to return fire and a stream of blue energy bolts spat out from the invisible heavy weapons. But the tables were turned; the tau could not see their targets, and they were cut down before Sarik's eyes. As each fell, their shattered forms resolved, broken armour and body parts scattered across the ground.

The return fire died away, and within seconds ceased as the surviving tau retreated in the face of the Space Marines' overwhelming fusillade.

'Brother-sergeant,' a voice cut in over the vox-net. 'Estimated fifty contacts, closing in behind us'

LUCIAN AND HIS two subcommanders looked west through their magnoculars into the setting sun. The skies had turned a deep turquoise the like of which Lucian had never seen before, with a faint glimmer of stars appearing overhead. Below the white sun, the distant towers of Gel'bryn glinted in the fading light, tempting the rogue trader with the riches and opportunities to be found there.

The city was small by human standards. In the Imperium it was often convenient to pack the multitudes in as tightly as possible, as near to their workplaces as could be achieved, in order to control the means of production with brutal but vital efficiency. The ultimate expression of this harsh reality was the hive cities of such worlds as Armageddon, Ichar IV and Gehenna Prime, each of which could equal the industrial output of any other planet in the Imperium short of a forge world of the Adeptus Mechanicus. Instead of packing their population into a relatively small number of massive cities, the tau evidently preferred to establish thousands of smaller settlements across an entire planet, and Gel'bryn was the largest of those on Dal'yth Prime. Lucian suspected that each city was relatively self-sufficient too, if the surrounding farmland was anything to go by. The use of advanced technology, forbidden or simply lost in the Imperium, for such simple tasks as farming was beyond anything he had seen in his decades of contact with all manner of xenos species. It suggested a highly ordered society in which individuals were free of the drudgery that was the reality of everyday life in the human Imperium.

But despite their seeming reliance on technology and their aberrant social order, the tau had proved a highly capable foe. While their skills in close combat were no equal to the sheer ferocity of the Rakarshans or the Space Marines, their advanced weaponry made up for that deficiency. The Departmento Tacticae was slowly piecing together a picture of the tau's capabilities, which it was disseminating to the ground force commanders as quickly as the reports could be compiled. The Imperium had learned more about the aliens' battlefield doctrines in the last forty-eight hours than it had in the entire crusade, for in previous ground battles Imperial forces had encountered little more than line infantry. Now reports were flooding in from all fronts of anti-grav armoured vehicles, target designator-equipped artillery spotters and a myriad of equally unanticipated, yet highly deadly foes.

'Be advised,' the voice of the Departmento Tacticae advisor crackled over the vox-net. 'Spearhead Sarik reports contact with enemy heavy infantry equipped with some form of stealth field. Ex-loading tacticae script now.'

Lucian lowered his magnoculars and took the data-slate handed to him by Major Subad. He scanned the reams of information being transmitted from General Gauge's command centre on the *Blade of Woe*, ignoring large portions of it and zeroing in on what was most relevant.

Item; main advance stalling, Imperial Guard units engaged by multiple ambushes resulting in fractured progress. Regimental Provosts to increase activities pending Commissarial intervention.

Item; advance to be consolidated into three main fronts. Battlegroup Arcadius to advance along present axis to probe city outer limits. Space Marine composites to amalgamate as soon as possible to reduce main enemy concentration. Titans to amalgamate ready to face enemy destroyers.

Item; second wave Imperial Guard units to proceed in attached order of march. Armoured and cavalry units to be made ready for push against enemy units consolidating along River 992. Armoured infantry to move up in support of armour. Mechanised units to muster as per attached orders.

'Havil, better get the boys fed and watered,' Lucian told the sergeant-major as he lowered the data-slate. 'Subad, draft a warning order. We're going in. I want us moving by nightfall.'

THE OUTSKIRTS OF Gel'bryn lay ahead, the details lost to the static-laced, monochrome green of Lucian's prey-sense goggles. Battlegroup Arcadius was advancing towards a small conurbation on the eastern shore of the watercourse designated 'River 992', beyond which lay the city and the bulk of the tau defenders. Patrols platoon was a kilometre forward, the very finest of the Rakarshans' scouts leading the rifle companies forwards under cover of darkness.

Though he had wanted to go in with the foremost platoons, Lucian had been told in no uncertain terms that he was nowhere near the equal of the Rakarshans when it came to stealth and field craft. His insistence on wearing his ancestors' suit of power armour tipped the argument. Lucian was currently positioned halfway down the line, where he was less likely to give away the Rakarshans' approach.

Lucian knew that the advance into the outskirts would not go undetected for long, for it had been established that the tau had their own low-light technology. Though he kept the heretical thought to himself, it seemed likely to Lucian that the tau's technology was superior to the Imperial forces' in this, and many other fields. Though the Rakarshans' own night-vision devices were offset by the tau's, they had other advantages and skills to draw on. The Rakarshans moved with such utter silence that one could be marching right next to Lucian and he would not have heard. Their use of cover and concealment was beyond any human unit Lucian had ever witnessed. In fact, they were almost supernaturally good.

With a slight start, Lucian realised that he was alone, no Rakarshans visible in the darkness around him. He continued his advance nonetheless, knowing that there were probably over a dozen of the stealthy riflemen within ten metres of him. The terrain dipped as it ran down towards the distant river, beyond which the Tacticae advisers reported a concentration of the enemy units gathering.

'Sir!' an urgent whisper hissed out of the darkness. Less than three metres in front of Lucian was a Rakarshan section leader, barely visible in the shadows behind a low shrub. Spread out behind him was a whole rifle section, which Lucian had not even known was nearby.

Lucian halted, lowering himself into a kneeling position beside the corporal. 'Report.'

The section leader clearly spoke a small amount of standard Low Gothic, for Lucian could just about understand him when he said 'Enemy, right flanking.'

Lucian adjusted the gain on his goggles and studied the terrain to the right of the group. The land continued to dip as it ran towards River 992, which sparkled in the middle distance. Three hundred metres to the east was an orderly plantation of the ubiquitous purple fruit trees, but to Lucian, they harboured nothing but dark shadows.

'You're sure?'

'Yes, sir. Ghosting in the thick.'

'Well enough,' Lucian said. 'If you're sure.' Lucian looked around for the signalman who had been his shadow for the last day or so. He was not surprised when the man appeared from the darkness nearby.

'Advise Subad we've detected movement in the woods to the east. Tell him I've ordered a sweep, but the advance should continue.'

The signalman passed the message on, shielding the pickup of his vox-set with his hand as he spoke in hushed tones.

'Right lad,' Lucian whispered to the corporal. 'Let's go see what we have.'

The man's eyes narrowed in disapproval and he nodded to indicate Lucian's power armour. 'You go first then,' Lucian conceded.

The section leader saluted silently and in a moment was gone, along with his men. Lucian engaged his prey-sense goggles again, and could just about make out the Rakarshans' thermal signatures as they dashed across the open ground towards the plantation. Lucian cycled through his goggles' range bands, looking for any sign of an enemy in the treeline. He found none, but that did not mean there was no enemy there. If the enemy the Rakarshans had detected were the stealth-fielded heavy infantry the White Scars had encountered, then it was incredible the Rakarshans had detected them at all. According to the tacticae reports disseminated to the various commands, the stealthers were not just shielded from the eye, but from other targeting devices too. Perhaps even from the war spirit that animated Lucian's prey-sense goggles.

Lucian was overcome by the notion that someone was watching him. He told himself it was nonsense and moved out in the Rakarshans' wake, but could not entirely shake the feeling. Wanting to be ready for combat, he drew his plasma pistol, and was just about to activate its power cycle when the signalman put a restraining hand on his forearm. He was right of course; the high-pitched whine of the containment coils drawing power from the plasma flask would ring out like a bugle signalling a cavalry charge. Lucian nodded his thanks to the signalman and re-holstered the pistol, drawing his power sword instead, but not activating it for now. The sword could be powered up in a second, so he could leave doing so until really needed, whereas the pistol could take long seconds to be readied to fire.

Lucian continued as quietly as he could, leaving a generous distance between himself and the leading Rakarshans. He was painfully aware of every little sound his suit made, marvelling that he had never noticed any of them before. The fusion core of his backpack gave off a low hum, while the actuators at the suit's joints hissed and strained with his every movement. Ordinarily, the sounds were practically inaudible, but in the dark night, with a concealed enemy potentially training a crosshair on Lucian's forehead, they were appallingly loud.

'Sir!' the signalman hissed, dropping to a crouch. Lucian followed the man's example, and scanned the treeline through his goggles. Still nothing.

'What?' he whispered, his voice barely more than a breath.

'The riflemen, my lord,' the man said. 'They have detected movement beneath the trees. It must be an ambush.'

Lucian located the riflemen, who were spread out in a line about a hundred metres ahead, each taking cover behind the low lying shrubs that studded the area. Lucian felt suddenly that whatever would happen next was down to him to decide. He was used to such situations in the void, where his actions in a space battle might doom himself and thousands of crewmen, but this was something else. What would Sarik or Gauge do, he thought?

Both would fight through the ambush, he knew. And they would do so from the front.

Turning back to the signalman, Lucian was about to give the order to press on when a thunderous burst of gunfire erupted from the treeline. Five Rakarshans went down, dead or wounded, Lucian could not tell which. 'Damn this,' he spat, and drew his plasma pistol from its holster.

'Charge!' Lucian bellowed, uncaring of the high-pitched whine of his plasma pistol powering up. He stood, the signalman following his example, and strode forwards. A second burst of gunfire sounded, pale blue bolts whipping through the air all too close.

'That's it!' Lucian yelled as he picked up his pace towards the treeline. 'Come out and play!'

Lucian strode past the Rakarshan section leader, the man's face staring up at him with a stunned expression.

'Now's your chance, lad,' Lucian hissed. 'Get moving!'

Understanding dawned on the Rakarshan's face and Lucian grinned like a fool. In an instant, the man was leading his riflemen away, starting a wide loop that would bring them towards the hidden enemy's left flank.

Now Lucian was picking up speed as he neared the dark treeline, and a third volley of gunfire split the air. The projectiles were the same condensed energy packets fired by other tau weapons, but the discharge of the weapon firing sounded distinctly different, somehow cruder and certainly noisier.

The signalman was directly behind him, and thankfully, so too were several other sections. Lucian brandished his power sword and thumbed it to full power, arcs of white lightning leaping up and down its length. The nearby Rakarshans followed his example, limbering their lasguns and drawing their ceremonial blades.

Now the treeline was only twenty metres ahead, and Lucian heard a ripple of lasgun fire from fifty metres to the left. The Rakarshans had engaged. An ululating hoot sounded from within the trees, and was repeated along its whole length. The sound was utterly alien and savagely barbaric, and not like any other Lucian had heard so far on Dal'yth Prime.

Then the trees rustled, and a dark shape leaped to the ground in front of Lucian, followed within seconds by a dozen more. The figures glowed bright green in Lucian's prey-sense goggles, and were tall, muscular and whip-fast in their movements. In the last few moments, Lucian tore his goggles free, knowing they would hinder his three-dimensional awareness in the brutal melee to follow.

The creature in front of Lucian let forth a high-pitched, almost avian-sounding cry, and charged in. It lifted its rifle, which was fitted with wickedly sharp spikes at barrel and butt. Lucian brought his power sword high to parry the blow, and the rifle erupted in sparks as it was cut in two.

The creature kept on going, brandishing the two halves of its ruined weapon like hatchets. If anything, it was now more dangerous. With a twist, Lucian turned his forward momentum into a sideways lunge and brought his power sword down in a wide arc aimed at the creature's middle. It anticipated the move and sprung backwards with an angry hoot.

The war cries of the Rakarshans and the whistling calls of the aliens erupted all about, and a swirling melee engulfed the entire treeline.

Lucian's foe leaped through the air, directly for him, and he raised his power sword again. In a split second, he saw that he could not hope to deflect both of the alien's weapons, so he parried one, reducing it to a useless stump, and turned his shoulder to the other causing it to glance harmlessly from a shoulder plate.

The creature hissed its anger in Lucian's face, its sharp, beak-like mouth open wide as if it meant to bite into Lucian's flesh. The alien came on, barrelling into Lucian and forcing him backwards as its weapon scraped down his chest armour. Lucian saw an opening and brought his power sword up to plunge it into the thing's chest, but again, his foe twisted aside and sprang clear.

For a second, Lucian and the alien circled one another, the shadowy forms of bitterly interlocked combatants swirling around them in the dark and grunts of pain and anger filling the air. Its beady eyes were fixed on his and sharp quills at the back of its head rattled as they stood on end like the hackles of some enraged predator.

Lucian feinted to the left, and the creature dodged his blade with preternatural speed. But that was what he had hoped it would do. With his left hand, Lucian brought the plasma pistol up, levelled it directly at the alien's head and pulled the trigger.

The darkness erupted into violet brightness as the plasma bolt spat from the blunt pistol's barrel and consumed the alien in a roiling ball of searing energy. Lucian's vision swam with nerve-light and he was momentarily blinded. As he blinked furiously to clear his vision, Lucian heard the wet thud of meat striking the ground and knew his foe was dead.

A Rakarshan yelled something from nearby. Though Lucian did not understand the words, he guessed their meaning and ducked blindly. The sharp hiss of air parted by a razor-sharp blade sounded a hand's span above his head, and Lucian knew the rifleman had just saved his life. He straightened again and as his vision finally cleared he saw another three of the alien warriors closing on him.

'Daem'ani!' a Rakarshan yelled, an unfamiliar note of fear in his voice. The shout was taken up by a dozen other riflemen, and in a moment Lucian was surrounded by Rakarshans.

The aliens threw themselves forwards at the exact same moment the Rakarshans charged. The two lines crashed together in a thunderous explosion of steel and blood. A rifleman beside Lucian was struck hard in the face by the spiked stock of an alien's rifle, the blade lodging itself in the man's head. Before the creature could pull the blade free Lucian lashed out with his power sword and severed both of its arms in a single sweep. The creature hooted in pain as it collapsed writhing to the ground, blood spurting from its wounds.

Even before the wounded alien had been trampled flat beneath the Rakarshans' boots, another had stepped into its place. A rifleman leaped forwards, repeating the earlier cry of 'Daem'ani!' at the top of his lungs, his ceremonial blade lashing outwards to gut the creature. The alien saw the blow coming and parried it with its rifle, using it as a duel-bladed stave and slamming its end into the soldier's stomach. The Rakarshan doubled over under the impact and the alien brought the other end of the rifle down across his back, crushing him to the ground beneath the brutal strike.

A high-pitched whine from Lucian's plasma pistol told him it had recharged and was ready to fire another blast. He raised the pistol and this time brought his right forearm across his face as he squeezed the trigger so he was not temporarily blinded by its discharge.

Lucian had no time to aim his shot, but had no need to. The enemy were coming on in such numbers that he could scarcely miss. The plasma bolt burned a hole right through the torso of the first enemy in its way and incinerated the one behind it. The enemy faltered in their assault, and in that moment Lucian saw that scores more of them were pouring from the treeline.

'We're outnumbered!' Lucian bellowed. *By at least three to one, and rising.*

The section leader was nearby, and Lucian grabbed him by the shoulder. The man's eyes were glowing with madness, as if he were consumed by overwhelming and unreasoning fear of what the Rakarshans had named 'daem'ani', and a berserker's rage to destroy the foe. The man appeared not to notice Lucian, so he shook him violently until his eyes came into focus. 'Order your men back, now!'

More hoots and whistles sounded from the woods, and Lucian knew the small force had no chance if it did not fall back straight away.

'Fall back!' Lucian yelled. 'Move and cover, you know the drill!'

But the Rakarshans did not understand. 'Damn you,' Lucian growled, looking about for his signalman, who he knew to speak near flawless Gothic. The man was on the ground, bleeding profusely from a wound across his chest, a dead alien warrior sprawled out next to him.

'How do I tell them to fall back?' Lucian said as he crouched next to the signalman. 'What's the word of command?'

'Fall back, my lord?' the signalman said through gritted teeth. 'There is no word for fall back in our tongue...'

Lucian bit back a curse and sheathed his power sword. Hooking his free arm around the signalman's waist, he raised his plasma pistol at the onrushing aliens and let off another blast. The shot struck an alien square in its roaring, beaked head, decapitating it and setting its still-standing body alight.

The aliens nearest to the conflagration leaped back from the fire, hissing and whistling in obvious fear. Lucian took a step back, dragging the wounded signalman with him. 'Tell them to follow me,' he growled. 'You must have a word for that!'

'Mu'sta,' the signalman grunted as Lucian dragged him back. 'Tell them that...'

'Mu'sta!' Lucian yelled. 'Mu'sta, ya bastards, mu'sta!'

Within seconds, the surviving Rakarshans were gathering about Lucian, two of their number taking the wounded signalman from him and propping the man up between their shoulders. Lucian fired another plasma bolt at the aliens, who were even now recovering from the shock of seeing one of their number decapitated and immolated at the same time.

The Rakarshans followed Lucian's example, firing into the aliens even as more emerged from the treeline. Lucian backed away, though he kept firing as he went, and soon the Rakarshans had the idea. The corporal appeared to have recovered his wits too, for he set about ordering the sections to deploy or cover one another alternately. Soon the Rakarshans were halfway back up the rise and out of immediate danger.

Lucian lowered his prey-sense goggles over his eyes again, in order to judge the numbers of aliens the Rakarshans had fought. Zooming in on the scene, he saw something that filled him with utter revulsion. Three of the aliens were crouched over the body of a fallen rifleman. One was scooping up a great, looping handful of the man's guts and sucking on the end. Another was biting down hard on a forearm, while the third was doing something behind the corpse's head that Lucian was glad not to be able to see clearly.

'You sick, sick bastards...' he muttered, unaware that the section leader had come up beside him.

'Sir?' the man said.

Lucian turned from the horrific scene and lifted his goggles. 'Nothing son, nothing. Come on, we need to get the battlegroup organised, and I need to talk to someone from Tacticae intelligence...'

BRIELLE STOOD IN the centre of the domed viewing blister high on the spine of the tau vessel *Dal'yth Il'Fannor O'kray*. It was like standing on the outer hull of the ship itself, for the blister was made not of solid material, but an invisible force field. Brielle felt a combination of trepidation and thrill as she looked out past the gleaming white hull to space beyond. A swarm of spacecraft traversed to and fro across the void, every possible class and configuration represented, from pinnace to mass transport.

Brielle turned slowly on the spot, taking in the full panorama of the scene until she came to face Naal.

'What?' Brielle said, her dark eyes glinting with mischief.

'You lied to them, Brielle,' Naal said, and gestured to the vista beyond the invisible field. 'And this is the result.'

Brielle turned from him again, her mood growing dark. Of course she had lied, it was the only way she could see to avert disaster and dissuade the tau from using her as an emissary to demand the crusade's surrender. The vessels crossing the void beyond the energy dome were preparing to evacuate huge numbers of tau civilians from Dal'yth Prime, while a warfleet was mustering further out to retake the planet with overwhelming force. If the tau knew what Brielle did, they would chase the humans all the way back to Terra. The crusade had been launched in haste with no idea of the tau's capabilities, was riven with internecine rivalries and massively overextended following the months-long crossing of the Damocles Gulf into tau space.

'The *result* is that the tau have pulled back from Dal'yth,' Brielle said. 'I've saved thousands of lives.'

'For now,' Naal said. 'But that wasn't why you told them the Imperium has twenty more battleships inbound. You wanted to create chaos and confusion. Why, Brielle?'

The observation blister was plunged in shadow as a huge refugee transport passed the *Dal'yth Il'Fannor O'kray*, a shoal of tenders and launches buzzing around. It was just the first of several hundred such transports the tau had rushed to the Dal'yth system with the intention of evacuating as many civilians as possible. Brielle's warning of how humanity treated aliens was no lie, and the tau had taken it to heart.

'Because this has got to end, Naal,' Brielle sighed. She felt a great weight lifted as she finally said what she had been feeling for weeks.

'Then you have to go before the crusade council as Aura requests, and settle this.'

'That isn't what I meant.'

'Then what, Brielle? What do you–?'

'I want out!' she said, stalking away from Naal towards the invisible shield that held the void at bay and kept her alive. 'I exaggerated the crusade's strengths so the tau would pull back. We both know that the crusade council is split. Gurney and Grand, if he's still alive, want total war, my father wants profit and the others want honour. If my father can turn the council around before the tau can muster a big enough force to repel the crusade, this can all be settled. And I can go home.'

Naal's face showed his utter shock at Brielle's revelation. The Imperial eagle tattoo on his forehead, a relic of past military service, seemed to fold its wings as he frowned at Brielle, then cast his glance to the floor.

'Why did you not tell me earlier?'

'You may share my bed, Naal,' Brielle said as she rounded on the man. 'But we both know where your loyalties lie.'

'What are you saying?'

'You're for the tau. You always have been. I don't know what led you to them, and I know you can't go back. But I can.'

'Brielle,' Naal sighed. 'I was just a Guard captain before I joined the tau, before I heeded the Greater Good. I was just a captain and yet I'm marked for death across an entire segmentum. You're the daughter of nobility, Brielle. There's nowhere you can hide. You have no choice.'

'My father can protect me from the likes of Grand.'

'Your father thinks you're dead.'

'Then he'll be happy to see me again then, won't he?'

'Please, Brielle,' Naal said with an edge of sadness to his voice. 'Look around you. There are no inquisitors here. There is no judgement and no repression.'

'So long as you do *exactly* what they say, Naal, come on...'

'That's the point of the Greater Good, Brielle,' Naal pressed. 'They don't have to tell you. You just do it, for the good of all.'

'And if you don't?'

'You do.'

'And if *I* don't?'

'You will, Brielle. In time...'

'You can't really think this is right, Naal, not deep down.' Brielle reached up and tenderly caressed the eagle tattoo on his temple. 'Does this mean nothing to you?'

Naal took Brielle's wrist in his hand. 'Of course it does. I love the Emperor. I just hate the Imperium. The aquila represents the former, not the latter.'

'What made you this way, Naal?' Brielle whispered, her eyes narrowing as she tried to find something, anything, inside his.

'You wouldn't understand, Brielle.'

'Then why not come back with me. Put it right. Together.'

'Brielle, if I did that, he'd–'

Naal's words were cut off as the circular iris-hatch set into the deck hissed and a column of white light shone upwards as the opening widened. Brielle and Naal stepped apart like guilty lovers, both turning to face the tau envoy, Aura, as he rose upwards on a platform through the hatch.

Aura looked around, casting his sad gaze out into space for a moment before turning it upon the two humans and affording them a shallow bow. 'Lady Brielle,' the envoy addressed her in his usual formal, yet strangely maudlin tone. 'As you can see, the transport fleet gathers to deliver our people from destruction.' Did he count Brielle in that 'our people'? 'And the fleet musters even as we speak.'

Brielle inclined her head, acknowledging Aura's statement without saying anything herself.

'When the fleet arrives, there will be much bloodshed, on both sides. Even now, with our enemy attacking us in such great force, we would avert disaster and bring peace.'

Brielle and Naal shared a furtive glance before the envoy continued.

'You will go before the enemy's leaders and demand their surrender…'

'Their *surrender*…?'

'Yes, Lady Brielle,' Aura continued. 'You must inform the humans that if they do not submit and take their place in the tau empire according to the dictates of the Greater Good, they will be destroyed. Utterly.'

'You will be briefed and prepared for your duty, Lady

Brielle. You will go before their leaders adorned as I, as an envoy of the tau empire. This will be your finest hour, Lady Brielle, and it will be remembered across the entire empire.'

'Of course,' Brielle said, though her mind was in turmoil. She had been so sure the tau would have seen sense when she had so grossly overstated the crusade's strength, yet they wanted not just a ceasefire or even a surrender, but to coerce the crusade's forces to join them...

'Of course,' Brielle repeated. 'For the Greater Good...'

CHAPTER FOUR

SERGEANT SARIK'S FORCE was pushing forwards now, driving the tau stealth-troopers back towards a low rise as the light of dawn filled the skies. The Space Marines had taken casualties when the tau had attacked the rear of the column, including both Whirlwind missile tanks being taken out of action as stealthed tau infantry used their equivalent of the Imperium's tank-busting melta weapons from close range. Sarik's warriors had rallied, and over the course of a three-hour firefight learned how to detect the presence of the infiltrating tau.

As Sarik advanced at the head of his tactical squad, he saw another such sign. The air would ripple just before the tau opened fire, as if their weapons were bleeding power from whatever generator powered the stealth field. Sometimes, if an observer was looking in their exact direction, a change of light would cause the enemy to become visible for a fraction of a second, and if they were not moving and the light remained unchanged, they might solidify and become plain to see.

Most importantly, the Space Marines were learning how to predict the enemy's movements and where to look for them. The details had already been voxed to the other Space Marine commands, and the stealthers were being driven back all along the front.

'Contact front!' Sarik called out as he opened fire at the half-visible foe. 'Strike them down!' A line of small explosions stitched the ghostly figure and its stealth generator failed with an eruption of blue sparks. The enemy resolved into a black-armoured warrior, its helmet blank-faced and with blocky, segmented armour plates across its chest, shoulders and thighs. Mounted on one arm was a tubular heavy weapon, which it was raising to point directly at Sarik.

The sergeant shouted a warning to his squad and weaved sideways as he advanced. The tau fired and a hail of blue energy bolts scythed the air where the Space Marines had been advancing a fraction of a second earlier. The alien stepped backwards as it fired, tracking its weapon left and right. The ground at Sarik's feet was churning with dozens of impacts as he powered on, and several shots glanced from his shoulder plates and greaves, biting neat-edged scars across the ceramite.

A grunt of pain sounded from behind Sarik as a Space Marine of the Scythes of the Emperor went down, an energy bolt having clipped his cheek and torn off half his face. The warrior went into a roll as he fell, and having barely lost momentum was up again. His enhanced physiology caused his blood to clot the instant it met air, his features a mass of scabby tissue with the inside of his jaw visible through the ruined cheek.

Sarik's warriors returned fire as they ran, the

combined boltguns of his own squad and the nearby Scythes of the Emperor hammering into the alien stealther. The enemy lowered his heavy weapon and assumed a wide-legged stance. A second later he leaped straight backwards, having activated a short-distance jump generator on his back. This was the first the Space Marines knew of the capability, and although it took them by surprise, the alien did not get far.

At the height of the alien's powered leap, a missile streaked in over the Space Marines heads, fired from one of the Devastator squads at the column's rear. The missile slammed into the alien with unerring accuracy, its war spirit predicting its target's trajectory and altering its course at the last possible second. Both missile and alien exploded three metres up, showering chunks of ruined armour and flesh across a wide area.

As Sarik approached the crest of the rise he saw another ripple in the air, followed by a burst of blue flame. Three more tau stealthers resolved in the air, their jump burners drawing power from their stealth generators. Sarik opened fire and his squad followed his example, filling the air with fin-stabilised, deuterium-cored bolter rounds. But the aliens were fleeing the Space Marines and with their jump packs engaged were soon bounding down the opposite side of the rise and away from the Space Marines.

'All squads,' Sarik said into the vox-net. 'Let the cowards flee. Consolidate on me.'

The squads of Sarik's spearhead were soon in position near him, the sergeants ensuring each was correctly deployed. There were obvious gaps in the line, where squads had taken casualties. Most of the wounded were able to fight on thanks to their genetically enhanced physiques, but the worst, in particular the Ultramarines caught in the stealthers' ambush, had been evacuated for treatment.

'Rhinos,' Sarik voxed the vehicle commanders further back. 'Maintain position and overwatch. All squads, form up on me for probing advance forward.' Sarik had to remind himself not to use the White Scars' battle-cant, which used context- and culture-specific references that could not be deciphered should a transmission be intercepted. But with warriors from more than just his own Chapter under his command, Sarik was forced to use more standard battle-code.

'Brothers,' Sarik addressed the squads. 'We advance around this rise. Devastators,' he indicated the Ultramarine and Scythes of the Emperor heavy weapons squads, 'overwatch just below the crest. White Scars tactical squads,' he nodded to his own squad and the other two of his Chapter, 'right flank. Remaining squads to the left.'

'Brothers,' he went on, conscious that the enemy stealthers were unlikely to have withdrawn far. 'This could be a trap.' Consulting his data-slate, which displayed a grainy, low-resolution aerial reconnaissance image marked up with numerals and symbols, he went on, 'Limit of exploitation is Hill 3003, to the west. Move out in one minute.'

As the Space Marines checked ammunition levels and swapped out depleted magazines for fresh ones, Sarik consulted his data-slate for an update from crusade command. Almost a hundred reports had been disseminated since the last time he had checked, most of which he felt justified in ignoring as they related to matters outside of his immediate concern. He skimmed reports on the enemy's aerospace strength, noting that the crusade had managed to land a small number of its precious fighter-bomber wings. Understandably, these were being kept in strategic reserve to be used only when desperately needed. The Imperial Navy deployment officers and the Departmento Tacticae intelligence advisors considered launching them into anything but totally empty airspace practically suicidal.

Noting the fighter-bombers' call sign, Sarik read on through the list of reports. Space Marine spearheads to amalgamate – Captain Rumann of the Iron Hands had ratified that order and the other Space Marine units were moving towards the rendezvous point even now, meaning Sarik's would be the last unit there. The Titans were amalgamating too, preparing for a push further down the line. The tau were massing beyond River 992, and the Rakarshans had encountered resistance on its east bank.

At the mention of the Rakarshans, Sarik opened the report, knowing that the unit was led by his friend Lucian Gerrit. The report was vague, having been penned in a hurry, but warned that the tau were not the only xenos on Dal'yth Prime. Lucian's battlegroup had encountered a group of tall, agile and highly aggressive alien savages. Tacticae had cross-linked them to troops encountered on Sy'l'kell at the outset of the crusade, and concluded they were the same group. Sarik's gorge rose as he read the grisly account of the aliens consuming the bodies of the fallen. He promised there and then he would not allow such a fate to befall even one of the battle-brothers under his command.

Then a minute had passed and the squads were ready to move out. Sarik stowed the data-slate and unlimbered his boltgun. He took his place at the head of his squad, which would be the second to move through the low defile around the base of the rise.

Checking that the two Devastator squads were in position to cover the Space Marines' advance, Sarik ordered his warriors forwards.

As Sarik rounded the base of the rise, the land ahead opened up into a dense patchwork of fields and plantations. Hill 3003 rose from amongst the crops and trees, and beyond it, glistening silver in the morning light, was River 992.

Beyond the distant river, made hazy and indistinct by the small amount of vapour still lingering in the morning air, was the city of Gel'bryn. The city's towers shone bright in the full light of the sun, and each was revealed to be gracefully curved in form, almost as if it had been grown rather than constructed. The tallest of the towers must have been five hundred or more metres in height, and a myriad of walkways connected each to its neighbour. Small points of light glinted all around the city, and Sarik guessed that each was an anti-grav flyer of some sort, or perhaps one of those fiendish, thinking-machine drones.

Sarik tracked back from the city, locating the enemy troop build-up the Departmento Tacticae had reported on the western side of River 992. There it was, a dirty haze marking an area where the tau's grav-tanks were gathering, throwing dust up from the dry ground. From this distance, Sarik could make out very little of the gathering, other than suggestions of multiple armoured vehicles and the scurrying of infantry at the perimeters. No matter; he would soon be facing that force, regardless of its strength.

'Sergeant,' Brother Qaja said, nodding towards the extreme left end of the city. Sarik followed the gesture, tracking along the horizon and locating what must have been a star port, the skies above it clustered with hundreds of aircraft. Some were coming in to land, while others were departing, but all were travelling to or from orbit.

'Reinforcements?' Qaja said.

Sarik studied the scene for several moments as he advanced, noting as best he could from such a great distance the sizes and types of vessels. 'I don't think so,' he said. 'It looks to me like the tau are evacuating their city, brother.'

'Why would they do such a thing?' Qaja said. 'Why would not every citizen muster to defend his home?'

Sarik's eyes narrowed as he considered the situation. Qaja was correct, but only in so far as that was what most enemies would do. Rebels would man their barricades with men, women and children, while most aliens made no such distinction between the members of their population. Almost every foe Sarik had ever fought regarded the defence of hearth and home as sacrosanct, holy ground for which they would fight and die regardless of the chances of winning. Yet, here was a tau army clearly gathering to defend the city, while others were being evacuated rather than mustered to join the defence.

'They are truly alien,' Sarik said. 'We cannot know how they will fight or what drives them to do so. If they are evacuating non-combatants, then perhaps they believe they have already lost and their warriors intend to make a stand for the sake of honour.'

'You think they believe in honour, brother-sergeant?' Qaja said.

Sarik nodded as he walked. 'I will grant them that, brother,' he said. 'Until or unless they prove me wrong.'

Brother Qaja made no reply, though he appeared less then convinced at the notion of affording aliens anything akin to honour. The battle-brother merely hefted his plasma cannon, and fell back into the line of march.

The lead squad, another group of White Scars, had reached a cluster of boulders as the land ran down towards the distant river, and halted. With a gesture, Sarik ordered the entire force to halt, and with another to take up overwatch of the surrounding terrain. Crouching, he opened the vox-net and spoke to the squad's sergeant.

'Brother-Sergeant Cheren, report.'

'It's one of the tau stealthers, brother-sergeant. It appears that he died of wounds sustained before the rise and was left behind.' Sarik and Qaja shared a glance at the idea of leaving the fallen behind, a concept that was anathema to the Space Marines, and especially to the White Scars Chapter, whose people practised highly ritualised funerary rites and afforded the dead great respect.

'Hold position, brother-sergeant,' Sarik said, before leading his squad forwards from the column. He was painfully aware that the body might have been left there as a trap, to distract the Space Marines while a tau force deployed nearby. There was no honour in it, but he had seen such tactics used before, especially amongst the mortal followers of the Ruinous Powers.

His boltgun tracking left and right as he advanced, Sarik crossed the open ground, Brother Qaja at his back all the while, and soon stood over the alien body. He thought it was the stealther he had hit minutes before, but had no way of telling for sure.

'They were either fleeing, or it's a trap,' Sergeant Cheren said. 'Either way, there is no honour in it.'

'Aye, brother-sergeant,' Sarik replied. 'Or perhaps

both. These tau have proven tactically flexible. Even if the body was not left here to draw our attention they may take advantage of the distraction. Get your squad moving, we have a...'

Sergeant Cheren's body erupted before Sarik's very eyes. It happened so suddenly Sarik saw it almost in slow motion. An entry wound appeared in the centre of Cheren's chest armour, the ceramite actually rippling and distorting around the impact point. Then the sergeant's power pack shattered outwards as the projectile exited his body. So drastic were the forces exerted on the sergeant's body that it was liquefied inside his armour, reduced to a red gruel which sprayed outwards from the exit point like a burst in a high-pressure conduit. The Space Marine behind Cheren was standing directly in the path of that fountain of gore and his pristine white armour was turned deep red as he was covered head to foot in the sergeant's pulped remains.

'*Kuk...*' the blood-splattered Space Marine cursed, reverting instinctively to his native Chogoran tongue.

'Down!' Sarik bellowed, and the two squads of Space Marines nearby dived for cover amidst the boulders.

The air was ripped apart as two more hyper-velocity projectiles passed overhead in quick succession.

'Devastators!' Sarik said into the vox-net. 'What do you see? Report!'

'Stand by, brother-sergeant,' came back the voice of the Sergeant Lahmas, the sergeant of the Scythes of the Emperor Devastator squad. 'Tracking contact on Hill 3003.'

A deafening crack split the air and a hyper-velocity projectile slammed into the opposite face of the boulder Sarik was sheltering behind. It must have weighed ten tons, yet it visibly trembled and a jagged fracture appeared on the rock face right before Sarik's eyes.

'It's the same ordnance they use on their warships,' Sarik growled. *Come on Lahmas...*

'Sergeant,' Lahmas's voice cut in to Sarik's chain of thought. 'I have eyes on nine enemy heavy infantry. Each has twin shoulder-mounted weapons of unknown type. Range too great to engage.'

Another projectile struck the boulder that Brother Qaja was sheltering behind, razor-sharp spall spraying from the opposite face and catching the battle-brother across one cheek. Qaja gritted his teeth, one eye remaining closed and bloody as he hefted his plasma cannon and shouted something at Sarik.

The sergeant realised only then that the tremendous pressure wave of the impact had partially deafened him, but his hearing came back in a rush.

'...I said,' Brother Qaja repeated, 'Breakout?'

'Hold your fire, brother,' Sarik said, and risked a look around the edge of the boulder. Though he dared only expose his head for a couple of seconds, in that moment he located the crest of Hill 3003. Atop the hill's summit was a line of enemy warriors, clearly wearing some sort of heavy personal armour. The ground battle of Sy'l'kell came to Sarik's mind, at the height of which he had fought a tau commander wearing a battle suit of similar design. Yet these were even larger, and bore weaponry akin to that of a battle tank.

Sarik reached to his belt and un-stowed his battle helm, placing it on his head and re-opening the vox-link to Sergeant Lahmas. 'Seen. Lahmas, I want you to patch your sensorium exlink directly to my system. Keep eyes on, I'm calling this one in.'

The Scythes of the Emperor sergeant signalled his understanding, and a few seconds later Sarik's vision froze, then dissolved into static. A moment later a rune blinked into being, and then the view was replaced by the scene from the other sergeant's point of view.

'Machine communion established, brother-sergeant,' Lahmas said. Are you receiving?'

'Aye, brother,' Sarik replied. 'Stand by and hold still.'

Sarik had to focus his thoughts and concentrate hard to control the other's sensorium system, but after a moment he made the view magnify as much as it was able without the aid of magnoculars. The scene zoomed in on the summit of Hill 3003, where the enemy heavy infantry were clearly visible. Each was half as tall again as a Space Marine, their blocky armour reminding Sarik of one of the mighty Space Marine Dreadnoughts, though it was not quite so bulky. Like the Dreadnought, however, the battle suit was more piloted than worn, for the large torso must have housed the operator, who viewed the battlefield through the armoured sensor block mounted atop the body.

A flash of blue from further down the line of battle suits caught Sarik's attention, and Lahmas tracked across to it, guessing correctly that Sarik would wish to see more clearly. Before the movement was complete another boulder nearby was split in two, the Space Marine behind it only just managing to dive clear, and coming up near Sarik. Then the sound of the discharge rolled across the landscape, giving Sarik some idea of the speed the projectile must have been travelling to exceed its own report. He re-called the sensorium archive, re-playing the last few seconds at ten times slower speed, his eye on the timestamp as the projectile came in. He estimated that the enemy projectiles must have been travelling at between eight and ten times the speed of sound.

No wonder Sergeant Cheren's body had been liquefied inside his armour.

Sarik opened the crusade command channel. 'Sarik, beta-nine, zero-delta,' he said, the call sign and context routing his transmission straight through to the fighter command duty officer.

There was a brief pause, overlaid by machine-chatter as vox-exlink systems authenticated the identity of sender and receiver.

'Fighter command, go ahead, sergeant,' the duty officer replied. The channel was distorted, for the signal was being routed back to the more powerful vox-unit on board one of the nearby Rhinos, and then through hundreds of kilometres of atmosphere and orbital space to the *Blade of Woe*.

'I need a fighter-bomber fire mission, urgent, my authority.'

'Sergeant,' Sarik knew by the man's voice he was about to attempt to haggle. 'We have only...'

'Listen to me,' Sarik interjected. 'I know assets are scarce, but you can't keep them hidden away like your daughters at the victory feast, I need...'

'Repeat last, sergeant...' the duty officer said.

'Never mind,' Sarik said. 'I need a fire mission, right now, and if you can't process it I'll have to speak to General Gauge directly. Do you understand?'

There was a brief pause before the duty officer replied 'Understood, sergeant. Call it in.'

'Better,' Sarik growled. Before he could continue, the enemy battle suits opened fire again, blue pulses rippling up and down their firing line. Viewing the scene from another's point of view was faintly disconcerting, but Sarik focussed on the task at hand.

The channel clicked several times as the transmission

was shunted through multiple relay and encryption conduits. The background whine of powerful jets cut in, telling Sarik he was through to a fighter pilot. 'This is Silver Eagle leader, holding pattern east of your position. Go ahead, sergeant.'

'Good to hear you, Silver Eagle leader,' Sarik said. 'I have multiple hard targets atop Hill 3003. Heavy battle suits. I want a rapid-fire pass, full effect, from one-sixty, over.'

'Understood, sergeant,' the squadron leader replied, the background sound changing pitch as his fighter dropped five thousand metres in mere seconds. 'Splash two-zero,' the pilot said, his voice strained by the g-force inflicted on his body by the rapid dive. 'Keep your heads down, and good luck.'

Splash two zero. Twenty seconds to attack.

Sarik disengaged the sensorium link to Sergeant Lahmas, his vision locking for a moment before being replaced by a wall of static. After a few more seconds his armour's war spirit awakened and his vision was returned to his own perspective.

Craning his neck upwards, Sarik searched the eastern skies for the Thunderbolt ground attack squadron. Within seconds a distant roar filled the skies, but the fighters were travelling too low and too fast for Sarik to make them out.

The sound grew in volume, until it was almost upon the Space Marines. Four dark shapes appeared to the east, diving in low and following the undulating terrain, lines of bright shock diamonds trailing behind their engines. The tau heavy infantry turned towards the oncoming fighters, some raising their twin hypervelocity projectile weapons towards the oncoming threat. But none fired; there would have been no point with the fighters travelling in excess of fifteen hundred kilometres per hour.

In the final seconds, the tau battle suits took a ponderous step backwards, evidently lacking the short-burn jump jets that made the smaller stealthers so agile.

The roar of the fighters' turbofans became a deafening scream, and then the Thunderbolts opened fire. The first shots were from their nose-mounted lascannons, lancing out towards the tau in an incandescent blast.

One battle suit was struck square in the torso, vanishing in a pulsating explosion and leaving just shrapnel scattered across the ground. Another las-bolt struck its target a glancing blow to one of its arm-like appendages, its end terminating in a boxy weapons mount that must have been some sort of short-ranged, anti-personnel multiple missile launcher. The missiles in the weapon's tubes detonated spectacularly, causing the battle suit to stumble sideways as the one next to it was peppered with shrapnel. The last two beams split the air between two of the battle suits, setting the scrub behind them alight.

But the lascannon blasts were just the beginning. As the Thunderbolts screamed onwards they came within the range of their nose-mounted autocannons. The relentless hammering of multiple rounds split the air and the tau were caught in a storm of metal as thick as driving rain. Though many rounds churned into the ground around the battle suits' mechanical feet, so heavy was the torrent of fire that dozens struck their targets. Smoke and dust was thrown upwards, small white flashes of incandescence shining through, each sent up by an autocannon round striking its target and turning for a brief instant into a small, superheated ball of plasma. Sarik's helmet autosenses activated, momentarily darkening his field of vision so that his eyes were not damaged by the searing white lights that flickered up and down the entire crest of Hill 3003.

Before Sarik's vision had entirely cleared, he felt the sharp impact of a metallic object rebounding from his shoulder plate to patter to the dry ground at his feet. It was a brass shell casing, ejected from the first of the Thunderbolts as it screamed overhead, and it was followed by hundreds more raining down on Sarik and the other Space Marines. In a split second, all four Thunderbolts had passed overhead and were already gaining altitude as they banked east in the jade skies.

Sarik readied himself to issue the order to press on and assault the hill, for nothing could have survived that hail of autocannon fire. Sarik studied the distant crest as the smoke and dust was caught on a gust of wind and drifted clear, revealing the destruction the Imperial Navy fighter squadron had unleashed on the tau.

As the scene cleared, it became evident that somehow, at least three of the tau had survived. Sarik had seen even the fell war machines of the followers of Chaos reduced to smoking wreckage by such attacks and could scarcely believe that the tau battle suits, even as heavy as they were, could be so well armoured as to survive. Though each of the surviving battle suits was visibly damaged, the ochre yellow of their armour blackened and dented by numerous impact scars, two of them were regaining their feet and levelling their heavy, shoulder-mounted hyper-velocity weapons on the Space Marines.

'Silver Eagle leader to Sarik,' the squadron leader's voice came over the net. 'Report status, over?'

'Silver Eagle leader,' Sarik called back. 'Multiple effective survivors, over.'

There was a pause, then a crackle on the line before the squadron leader replied, 'Understood, sergeant. Remain in position. Returning to previous heading for full-effect bomb drop.'

The four Thunderbolts continued their wide bank towards the east, dropping low as they came about for a second pass.

A whip-crack report split the air not three metres from Sarik's position as the first of the tau opened fire again. Sarik guessed that whatever fire control systems they used must have been disrupted by the Thunderbolts' attack, for it was the first shot to have missed the boulders behind which the Space Marines waited. And a good thing too, for the huge boulder near Sarik was fractured in several places and would not provide cover for much longer.

Two more shots cracked the air, sounding like a steel cable at full tension suddenly cut. Sarik opened the vox-channel to address his force. 'All squads. The navy are going to flatten that hilltop. The second the bombs are down I want all units moving, tactical dispersion delta delta nine. I want that hill taken. Out.'

'Silver Eagle leader to Sarik,' the squadron commander's voice came over the vox-net again. 'Beginning attack run. Be advised, this is going to make a mess of everything within half a kilometre of that hill. Good lu...'

'Repeat last, Silver Eagle leader?' Sarik said.

'Stand by, sergeant...'

The squadron came in low across the eastern plains, then split into two pairs, one piling on the G's as it sped south, the other executing a tight turn that brought it on an approach vector back towards Hill 3003.

'...not falling for it...' the squadron leader's voice cut into the command channel. 'Half loop, execute!'

The group heading back towards the target rose suddenly into the air, the pilots executing one half of a loop. As one completed its manoeuvre and streaked back east, the other was engulfed by fire as its starboard wing was torn apart by a storm of gunfire.

'Silver Eagle leader is down,' a new voice filled the command channel. 'Eagle four, complete the run, I'll try to draw them off...'

As the squadron leader's Thunderbolt exploded across the sky shedding multiple smoking contrails behind it, his wingman dived towards the ground, the air rippling two kilometres behind. The other two Thunderbolts executed a rolling turn and came back on the attack vector, arrowing towards Hill 3003 at supersonic speed.

'All squads!' Sarik yelled into the vox-net. 'Brace for air strike, then follow me!'

The sound of the approaching jets increased to a deafening roar, doppler-shifting as they screamed overhead so low the backwash sent up plumes of dust from the ground.

'Payload deployed!' one of the pilots called, and Sarik went down on one knee beside the boulder as four 1,000 kilogram bombs dropped from the rapidly receding Thunderbolts, directly towards the crest of Hill 3003.

The hilltop erupted in such a devastating explosion that the entire rise was consumed in a plume of black smoke that blossomed rapidly into the air. An instant later the sound and pressure wave struck Sarik, showering his armour with grit and small stones pushed before it by the blast. Had he not been wearing his helmet the breath would have been torn from his lungs. Just a few hundred metres closer to the hill and his lungs might have been torn from his chest.

Then debris began to rain from the sky, large chunks of rock thrown up in all directions by the massive explosion. Sarik forced himself to his feet, still fighting the blast wave which continued to rage as the air pressure sought to right itself. He opened the vox-channel again, and bellowed, 'With me! If there's anything left on that hill I want it dead!'

Sarik burst out from the cover of the boulder, his squad close at his heels. The ground churned in front of him as debris rained down from the skies. The hilltop was now capped by a plume of black smoke rising ever higher into the air and blossoming outwards as it rose. Sarik pounded the ground, determined that any tau still alive on or near the hill would soon be struck down by his blade. Sarik's heart pounded and his blood rushed in his ears. He tore his helmet off and cast it to the ground without thinking, and unleashed a fearsome Chogoran war cry in the tongue of his people.

As he closed on the foot of the hill, the black cloud rearing high overhead, the ground became jagged and uneven with huge chunks of rock torn up by the explosion. Soon Sarik was climbing up the base of the hill, clambering over the uneven ground and shoving boulders aside as he powered upwards.

The cloud began to clear and the hill in front of Sarik became visible. Pausing in his climb, Sarik craned his neck to look upwards, to locate the foe he would soon be rending limb from limb.

Then it struck him. There were no enemies. They had been disintegrated. The entire crest of the hill had been disintegrated.

'They're gone, brother-sergeant,' Brother Qaja said as he came up beside Sarik, his voice ragged as he regained his breath. Qaja had kept pace with his sergeant as he had closed on the hill, despite the fact that he was bearing a weapon that weighed nearly as much as he did.

'No,' Sarik growled. 'There'll be more nearby. We take the hill.'

Qaja held Sarik's gaze for a moment, before nodding. 'By your command, brother-sergeant,' he said, bowing slightly as he spoke. As Sarik turned back to gaze up the rubble strewn slope, he heard Qaja bellowing commands as he strode off to muster the squads closing on the hill.

Leaving Qaja to organise the battle-brothers, Sarik unlimbered his boltgun and set off up the broken slope. His blood was still up, but he was thinking clearer now, and he scanned the skies for any sign of the surviving Thunderbolts or the stealthed tau fighter that had engaged and destroyed Silver Eagle leader. There was none; the jade skies were clear of all but the plume of smoke towering overhead.

It did not take Sarik long to reach the top of Hill 3003, for so much of its crest had been destroyed that it had lost half its height. As Sarik dragged himself up over the last chunk of debris, he found himself looking down, straight into a huge, smoking crater more resembling a semi-dormant volcano than a hill.

As Qaja led the Space Marines up behind him, Sarik started out around the crater rim, the view beyond it towards the river still obscured by thick smoke and drifting clouds of dust. Sarik pressed on, eager to gain the opposite side of the crater and the commanding view it would afford of the river and the city of Gel'bryn beyond. It took him another five minutes to work his way around the rim, and by the time he had reached the other side Qaja had directed the tactical squads to split into two groups and press around the rim.

Finally, Sarik stood on the opposite edge of the smoking crater, looking down at the opposite slope. Though it was as broken and jagged as the slope he had climbed, it was also wreathed in smoke and dust, and the view of the terrain leading down to the river was all but obscured.

'Your orders, brother-sergeant?' Brother Qaja said as he appeared at Sarik's side. 'Devastators are working their way around the base, they'll be in position to cover an advance towards the river within five. And, brother-sergeant?' he added.

'Yes, Brother Qaja?' Sarik said.

'You may have need of this,' Qaja said as he proffered Sarik the helmet he had discarded as he had charged across the open ground in the wake of the air strike. There was a note of reproach in the other's voice, and not without justification. Sarik nodded his thanks, knowing that he had committed a failing that a neophyte would have been punished severely for. Brother Qaja was an old friend, and only fate had placed Sarik as his senior; it could so easily have been the other way around. Qaja's unvoiced reproach was punishment enough for Sarik, but he would mount a vigil of prayer after the battle was over, and ask the primarch, honoured be his name, for guidance.

'Thank you, brother,' Sarik said as he took the helmet and clipped it to his belt. 'I'm not sure I would have...' Sarik stopped, turning his head sharply towards the smoke-wreathed downward slope. Qaja followed his glance, instantly alert.

'You hear it?' Sarik whispered low.

Brother Qaja nodded slowly, his eyes scanning the drifting smoke below. 'Sounds like...'

A dark shape appeared in the smoke. Qaja hefted his

plasma cannon and engaged its charge cycle. The rapidly rising whine of the plasma coils energising was shockingly loud.

'Get the squads forward, quickly!' Sarik said, now uncaring whether his voice was heard or not. He limbered his boltgun and drew his chainsword, thumbing it to life so that the monomolecular-edged teeth growled with sudden violence.

The shape in the smoke solidified as Brother Qaja beckoned the tactical squads forwards, and two more appeared at its side. It was tall, at least half as tall again as a Space Marine, and broad across the blocky, armoured shoulders. The first parts of the shape to become fully visible were the tips of the two long, rectangular hyper-velocity cannons mounted on its shoulders.

As the battle suit trod ponderously out of the drifting smoke, the cannons levelled out to point directly towards the crater rim where the White Scars, Scythes of the Emperor and Ultramarines tactical squads were taking position.

'No time,' Sarik growled. 'Cut them down!'

Brandishing his chainsword high, Sarik leaped from the crater rim onto the rubble-strewn slope below. The cannons tracked him, but he was moving too fast for the battle suit's targeting systems to get a solid lock.

As Sarik powered down the slope, small boulders cascading all around him, the sound of armoured boots striking the ground behind filled the air. Another three battle suits emerged from the smoke, and a detached part of Sarik's mind understood that the force that had held the crest of Hill 3003 must have been just a vanguard of a far larger group.

As Sarik closed to within thirty metres of the first of

the battle suits, the air was turned livid violet as Brother Qaja unleashed a blast from his plasma cannon. The roiling ball of pure energy spat downwards, its backwash burning a channel clear through the smoke before it engulfed its target.

The solid matter of the battle suit was consumed in an instant, its very stuff feeding the plasma ball. The energies expanded briefly, the heat so intense that the armour from the nearest battle suit was reduced to waxlike liquid. The entire roiling mass exploded outwards, burning the dusty ground and turning loose rocks into a liquid lava rain.

The heat and blast wave of the explosion struck Sarik as he closed on his target, and it felt for an instant as if he was running into the open hatch of a starship's plasma furnace. Then the energies disappeared and Sarik was upon his foe.

The battle suit Sarik had fought on Sy'l'kell came to mind again. That opponent had been similar in form, but equipped with lighter weaponry and short-burn jump jets similar to those used by the lighter stealthers. The enemy Sarik now faced was heavy and ponderous, made slow by the weight of additional armour and its heavy weaponry.

Knowing that the battle suit could not make use of its weapons at such short range, Sarik circled around it, chainsword raised in a two-handed guard position, looking for a weak spot in the tau's formidable armour.

The battle suit began to back away, its heavy tread crushing boulders to dust. Space Marines appeared all around Sarik, each following his example as they closed in on an opponent.

'Not so deadly now, are you...' Sarik growled as he pressed forwards. Locating what he judged to be a weak joint between leg and torso, Sarik feinted left, then swept his chainsword in low as the battle suit sought to avoid him.

The teeth of Sarik's blade howled as they struck the impossibly hard metal, grinding across the ball joint. The tau raised an arm terminating in a large multiple missile pod in an attempt to fend off another strike, and as it did so took a heavy step backwards. The damaged ball joint locked and the battle suit staggered as it fought for balance. Sarik pressed his advantage.

Sarik's blade lashed out and tore a ragged scar across the battle suit's torso, but the armour there was too heavy and solid to penetrate. Sarik bared his teeth in a feral snarl and brought the blade in a horizontal sweep that smashed the lens in the centre of the sensor block mounted atop the torso. Evidently blinded, the pilot of the battle suit tried to back away again, and toppled backwards as the ball joint failed entirely.

As the battle suit slammed into the ground, Sarik leaped forwards, his feet pinning his opponent's arms. He reversed his grip on his chainsword and raised it high.

The battlefield resounded with war cries and angry shouts, and the screaming of chainswords and the reports of bolt pistols fired at point-blank range. The Space Marines were laying into the battle suits, which were desperately outmatched and seeking to break away. But their enemies' armour was holding firm and the fight was far from won.

Sarik plunged his chainsword directly down into the centre of the battle suit's torso. The teeth ground against the hard armour, shrieking like some spirit from Chogoran legend. The blade slipped, gouging a wound across the face of the armour, and lodged in a recess between the plates. Redoubling his efforts, Sarik took advantage of the purchase he had found and put his whole weight into forcing the howling blade downwards. Smoke poured from the wound, the chainblade's teeth began to glow red, but the blade finally began to sink into the battle suit's torso.

Then the blade was through the outer armour, and it suddenly sank halfway up its length. Sarik growled and hacked the blade downwards, tearing off an entire panel of armour. He withdrew the blackened, smoking blade and cast it aside.

Consumed by battle rage, Sarik took a two-handed grip on the red hot edge of the wound he had torn, and forced it wide with his armoured gauntlets. A part of him was astonished at the armour's resilience, for rarely had he seen such strength on anything less than an armoured vehicle. Then the armoured plate gave and Sarik stumbled backwards as it came free in his hands.

Breathing heavily, Sarik looked down on the ruined battle suit. With the entire front torso armour torn away the pilot was visible within. The tau was compressed into an impossibly small, padded cockpit in an almost foetal position facing forwards. He wore a jump suit that resembled a glossy second skin, and numerous sensory pickups snaked from points on his body to terminals inside the suit. The pilot's face, spattered with his own purple blood, stared back at Sarik with unmistakable hatred.

'You fought with honour, foeman,' Sarik said, stepping forwards again to deliver the killing blow.

'Ko'vash,' the pilot coughed as he raised his fist out of the hole in the suit's torso. The pilot was holding some form of control device, and its thumb was raised above a flashing red stud. *'Tau'va. Y'he...'*

Even as Sarik brought his chainsword down, the dying pilot depressed his thumb on the control stud. Sarik's blade ground through the pilot's body as if it were not even there, a geyser of purple blood gushing upwards to stain Sarik's arms up to his shoulder plates.

'Brother-sergeant!' Qaja's voice penetrated Sarik's battle fury. 'The enemy are breaking off!'

But Sarik did not reply, for his gaze was fixed firmly on the blinking red control stud held in the pilot's death grip. The blinks were getting faster, and a sharp, electronic tone was sounding from within the gore-spattered cockpit.

Sarik's berserker rage lifted entirely and realisation dawned. 'Fall back!' he bellowed. 'Everyone back up the slope, now!'

Sarik's tone brooked no argument, and even if any of the Space Marines had sought to pursue the remaining battle suits as they backed into the smoke bank, their conditioning was such that it was all but impossible for them to ignore an order from a superior. Sarik turned, retrieving his chainsword, and pounded back up the slope, ensuring that his battle-brothers were all heading for cover.

As he climbed the last few metres Sarik overtook Brother Qaja, who despite his nigh legendary strength and the load-bearing mechanisms of his armour was impeded by the bulk of his massive plasma cannon. As he came alongside his battle-brother, Sarik hefted the weapon's snub barrel to share its weight and the two White Scars climbed the last few metres together and threw themselves over the crater rim.

For a moment, Sarik and Qaja were face to face. Sarik's battle-brother opened his mouth to ask the inevitable question, before it was answered for him.

The sky beyond the crater rim was consumed by a blinding white light and a staggering blast wave slammed into the crater rim behind which the Space Marines sheltered. The rim edge disintegrated, showering Sarik and Qaja with hot stone. The air burned and Sarik's multi-lung clamped its secondary trachea tightly shut so that he did not breathe in the searing atmosphere. Without his helmet's auto-senses to protect his eyes, Sarik was forced to screw them shut lest he be blinded. Even with his eyes tightly closed Sarik's vision boiled red as the light burned through.

Then all fell silent, and Sarik opened his eyes. Brother Qaja was on all fours, spitting blood from his mouth from a wound caused by flying debris. Further away, other battle-brothers were struggling to their feet, stunned by the sheer devastation of the explosion. The sergeants were restoring order, ordering battle-brothers to the crater rim and to cover all approaches an enemy might take.

As Sarik rose and looked down at the slope, he knew it was most unlikely that any more enemies would come that way. The entire slope had been scoured clean of everything but scorched black bedrock. Whatever device-of-last-resort the battle suit pilot had activated, it had afforded his companions the time they needed to break away from the Space Marines. With the smoke of the air strike blown clear by the explosion, the remaining battle suits were visible, half a kilometre away as they retreated back towards the river and the tau army that was even now mustering on the opposite shore. As he watched, the heavy battle suits reached another rise, where more of their kind had assumed a firing line with a commanding view of the surrounding landscape.

As Sarik surveyed his battle-scarred force, it occurred

to him that the Damocles Gulf Crusade might have far more vicious a struggle ahead of it than even its most bullish of leaders had anticipated.

'Qaja!' Sarik called. 'Gather the squads. We're far from done here yet...'

TWENTY KILOMETRES TO the north-west of Hill 3003, Lucian Gerrit was scanning his data-slate and considering his next move. As the crusade ground onwards towards Gel'bryn, the force mustering on the other side of River 992 launched a series of daring hit and run attacks. So accomplished were the tau mechanised forces at this style of warfare that the more ponderous units of the Imperial Guard were barely able to react. As the battles progressed, cadres of tau anti-grav tanks swept in towards the crusade's flank, disgorging up to a hundred warriors who unleashed a devastating volley of short-ranged fire before being carried away again by their transports. General Gauge fed more and more forces towards the river in an effort to overwhelm the tau defenders. Even as he did so ever-greater numbers of tau converged on Gel'bryn from the west, reinforcements sent from the other cities to stall the invasion.

The main advance split into three spearheads. The engines of the Deathbringers Legion gathered together into a formidable battle group that sought to push its way into the city's outer limits by brute strength alone. The Titans' initial assaults saw them destroy dozens of enemy armoured vehicles and hundreds of infantry. The fast-moving and agile Warhound Scout Titans made rapid gains in the first few hours of their advance. It was only several hours later, when the Warhounds had pressed so far forwards they had outrun the anti-air cover provided by the Hydra flak-tank companies of the

Imperial Guard, that they were engaged by heavy tau flyers. To the great surprise of the advisors of the Departmento Tacticae, these flyers proved to be the very same machines the tau utilised as gunships in space, revealing the hitherto unknown capability of operating in both deep space and planetary atmosphere.

The Space Marines had largely amalgamated into a single force, though Lucian noted with concern that his friend Sarik had encountered heavily armed and armoured battle suit infantry at Hill 3003 and his force was still engaged in that area. The remainder of the Space Marines, consisting of the Iron Hands, Scythes of the Emperor and Ultramarines, along with individual squads from a handful of other Chapters, had formed a single, large contingent under the direct control of Captain Rumann of the Iron Hands. That force had pressed towards the river, but had encountered large numbers of the jump-capable battle suit infantry. The Departmento Tacticae reported that the tau term for these particular battle suits, which the crusade had encountered a single example of, was '*hereks'vre*', which in their tongue meant the 'mantle of the hero'. Already, the Tacticae had bastardised that term to codify the battle suits as 'XV' class rigs, with various sub-classes already identified.

Even Lucian was surprised that the Space Marines were having such a hard time of it, for the XV-class battle suits appeared their equal in almost every respect. They were heavily armed, each carrying anything up to three weapons systems, some of which were capable of scything down a Space Marine in a single shot. Their battle suits provided at least as much protection as the Space Marines' power armour, and appeared to incorporate a number of additional systems such as advanced sensor and communication arrays. The XV-class battle suits were highly manoeuvrable too, for every one of them was equipped with a short-burn jump pack that made them as agile as an Assault Marine.

The numerous skirmishes the Space Marines had fought against the various types of battle suit infantry all pointed to a single weakness, details of which the Tacticae had disseminated to all commands. The tau were proving lacking in the field of all-in, hand-to-hand fighting. Many theories as to why this might be had been posited, from a biological deficiency that meant the tau could not focus on close-up and fast-moving objects as quickly as a human, to a fundamental moral weakness born of their alien philosophies. Lucian had his own ideas, which he knew would not find many sympathetic ears amongst the Tacticae and might even bring about the wrath of Inquisitor Grand were he to voice them too openly. Lucian was beginning to suspect that the tau regarded close combat as a brutal and dishonourable slaughter. They excelled in manoeuvre warfare, using speed and agility to dictate the terms of battle. When it was necessary to commit to a close-quarters assault, Lucian guessed the tau utilised the savage aliens his force had encountered the previous night. He wondered if they were the only alien allies the tau used, recalling how ready they appeared to be to subvert the human worlds on the other side of the Damocles Gulf.

Lucian's own battle group had performed well, pressing towards the outlying suburbs of the city on the eastern side of River 992. The Rakarshans had met and defeated more groups of the savage aliens, and for a while the two groups had fought on more or less equal terms. Both were adept at taking full advantage of cover, and a running battle had developed amongst the outlying settlements. The aliens had launched repeated ambushes, leaping from the tops of low buildings to engage the Rakarshans in brutal close combat. Having witnessed the aliens' despicable trait of devouring the corpses of the fallen, the Rakarshans' morale had initially suffered, for the superstitious riflemen believed their foe to be the mythical daemons of their world's dark legends. But Lucian had led them throughout the night, spearheading assault after assault and demonstrating that whatever else the aliens were, they were made of flesh and blood and could therefore bleed and die. The Rakarshans had learned that lesson well, and by morning the outlying suburbs were in their hands.

In the wake of Battlegroup Arcadius's assault came a huge force of Imperial Guard armoured and infantry units. As these gathered, the tau increased their hit and run attacks, and a front line had stabilised across the northern shore of the river where it looped around the flank of the city. The Imperial Guard had been forced to dig in, and it was only the aggressive and determined patrolling of the Space Marines into the no-man's-land between the two foes that kept the alien forces largely at bay.

Reaching the last of the latest batch of Tacticae updates, Lucian suppressed a curse. Concerned that the ground forces had reached an apparent impasse, Cardinal Gurney was shuttling down to the surface to imbue the warriors with his own particular brand of motivation. The cardinal's lander was due at the front within the hour. Leaving the battle group in Major Subad's command, Lucian left his warriors to head off whatever damage Gurney was no doubt intent upon inflicting on his own agenda, and that of his faction.

* * *

LUCIAN TOOK HIS place in the line of regimental commanders as the cardinal's lander swooped in on screaming landing jets and settled on the dry ground, throwing up a plume of dust as its landing struts flexed and touched down. Behind the commanders were gathered several thousand Imperial Guardsmen and hundreds of tanks, all lined up in parade ground formation to receive this most august of visitors. The vessel was one of the ubiquitous 'Aquila' landers, the name taken from the highly stylised swept wing configuration that gave it the appearance of an eagle. Lucian could not help but give a snort of derision, for the vessel was far from standard in appearance. It was painted gold, as if it had been chased in priceless leaf, and every flat surface was covered in line after line of spidery devotional script. The coffers of the Ecclesiarchy were deep indeed.

Ground crews rushed forwards to service the lander, and Lucian and his companions waited for the vessel's passenger pod to lower and its hatch to open. Lucian's eyes narrowed as the minutes dragged on, and he caught the furtive glances of those on either side. The minutes passed slowly, and Lucian's annoyance rose. What by the warp was Gurney playing at; did he really think the assembled warriors had nothing better to do than wait on his convenience?

Then the air was filled by the sound of chanting blaring out of a vox-horn mounted under the shuttle's blunt nose. The sound was amplified so loud that the horn was distorting, resulting in little more than a discordant racket and certainly not the heavenly chorus Gurney no doubt imagined it to be.

Then the passenger pod at the shuttle's rear engaged, accompanied by the sound of whining servos. The pod thudded to the ground, and a moment later the hatch lowered.

First to step out of the hatch was a robed and stooped attendant, an ornate censer held before him. A bluish cloud of sweet-smelling incense billowed from the orb, and the bearer voiced a loud imprecation, the gist of which was that the cardinal would not have to breathe the same air as the alien tau.

As the censer bearer marched forwards, the cloying cloud blossoming in his wake, three more attendants made their way down the hatch. Each was carrying a large book, the pages held open so that all about might gaze upon the wisdom of the saints and martyrs that had composed them.

Finally, Cardinal Esau Gurney appeared at the hatch and made his way down the walkway. The cardinal was regaled in the outrageous finery of his office, his robes the colour of ancient parchment lined with impossibly intricate, hand-stitched tracery. At his belt and around his neck Gurney wore dozens of holy relics, ranging from the smallest finger bones of saints to shining gold rings and other revered icons. He wore a cloak of deepest crimson silk, which trailed five metres and more behind him as he descended the ramp, and upon his head he wore a mitre bearing the sunburst skull of the Ecclesiarchy.

Gurney paused before stepping forth onto the dusty ground, and spat upon the earth. It was a clear message to all who saw it that the cardinal considered the entire planet cursed by the presence of the xenos tau. Then, he stepped from the walkway and made his way with his procession towards the gathered warriors.

Gurney halted in front of the gathered warriors, and stood there arrayed in his Ecclesiarchal finery, his dark gaze taking in the assembled ranks. Here was a side of the cardinal's personality that Lucian had not yet witnessed. He knew that Gurney was a firebrand, and it was by his sermons that much of the military forces of the crusade had been gathered in the first place. Many months previously, Gurney had preached first on the world of Brimlock and then across an entire sector, bullying, inspiring and cajoling the Imperium's leaders to contribute forces to the endeavour that became the Damocles Gulf Crusade. Many of those gathered here today would have heard those fiery sermons, and no doubt hold the cardinal in high esteem, regardless of what Lucian thought of the man.

'Warriors of the Imperium!' Gurney shouted, his voice so loud that even those warriors in the rear ranks would have no trouble hearing him. 'I salute you! Much blood has been spilled these last days, and many fell crimes committed by the foul xenos, but you are sons and daughters of the Emperor, and no vile xenos can possibly stand before you!'

The assembled Imperial Guardsmen were visibly moved by Gurney's opening words. Previously weary eyes came alight with faith, and stooped shoulders straightened as pride returned to warriors who had known little more than frustration at the tau's constant hit and run attacks and devastating ambushes.

'Today, you are blooded and weary, for the xenos foe is possessed of many forbidden technologies,' the cardinal continued. 'It uses tricks and treachery, and is devoid of honour and faith!'

The cardinal's eyes burned with the light of righteous zeal as he pressed on. 'But you are men of blood and faith! You bear the sanctified weapons of the Emperor, and all you need to conquer our foes is courage and cold steel, duty and honour!'

'Duty and honour!' the assembled Guardsmen repeated. 'Duty and honour!'

'Death or glory!' The cardinal bellowed.

'Death or glory!' the warriors repeated. 'Death or glory!'

LUCIAN STALKED AWAY from the impromptu rally, his mood darkening. He was forced to concede that Cardinal Gurney's sermon, which continued behind him, was certainly having a positive effect on the crusade's morale. He had discovered that Gurney would be touring the entire front, with the exception of the Space Marine positions, and repeating his words until every Imperial Guardsman in the crusade had heard them.

Lucian had no doubt that Gurney's presence on the surface would serve to rally the army and get the warriors inspired again. But Lucian's concerns were of a far more strategic nature. What happened afterwards, when Gurney returned to the crusade council with a string of victorious battles under his belt? That was what Lucian had sought to do, and it appeared to him now that Gurney was seeking to go one up on him, not by leading a force to victory, but by inspiring the entire army to slaughter the tau wholesale.

If that were allowed to happen, then Gurney and his ally Inquisitor Grand might take control of the crusade council, and nothing anyone could do would stop them doing things their way. The tau would be wiped from the galaxy, their empire cast down in flames. As a rogue trader, Lucian considered that a crime of unimaginable proportions, for it deprived the Imperium of so many potential resources. If the tau could be forced to a weak negotiating position, the Imperium could benefit from the natural resources their region harboured. At the very least, Lucian's clan could make a fortune in trade, but only if there were any tau left to force to the negotiating table and to actually deal with.

As he approached the lines of Battlegroup Arcadius, Lucian located his signalman and gestured him over.

'Patch me through to Korvane Gerrit Arcadius,' he ordered. '*Blade of Woe*.'

The signalman saluted smartly and set to work on his vox-set. After a minute, he had established the uplink and handed the headset to Lucian.

'Father?' his son's voice came through the static-laced channel. 'Father, are you well?'

'Well enough, son,' Lucian said. 'But Gurney's making a power play. What's the situation with the council?'

There was a pause as Korvane gathered his thoughts, during which Lucian could hear renewed cheering from the assembled Imperial Guard companies. Then Korvane's response came through. 'It's been quite anarchic here, father, but I've made inroads towards filling the vacant council seats.'

'Go on,' Lucian said impatiently. Even in the midst of a major planetary invasion, he could not entirely relinquish his role of patriarch of a rogue trader dynasty.

'Tacticae-Primaris Kilindini,' Korvane said. 'How well do you know him?'

'Not well,' Lucian said as he recalled the man his son was referring to. 'He's the head of one of the Departmento Tacticae divisions?'

'That's our man,' Korvane replied, warming to his subject. 'He's the overseer of codes and ciphers, but I've looked into his service record and I think he might be agreeable to our faction's agenda.'

'How so?' Lucian replied. 'Isn't he more concerned with breaking alien comms?'

'Yes, father,' Korvane said. 'But I've uncovered details of his serving alongside an Adeptus Terra diplomatic mission. The mission was to an eldar craftworld.'

'Interesting,' Lucian said, his mind racing ahead of him, aware that such contact was rare, but not unheard of. 'I take it this particular mission was especially out of the ordinary?'

'That it was, father.' Lucian could hear the smile on his son's lip's as he spoke. 'In that it did not end in mass bloodshed or planetary devastation.'

'Then you think Primaris Kilindini would be willing to back our intent. He'd be willing to enter talks?'

'He is willing, father,' Korvane replied. 'I've spoken to him already.'

'You've already...' Lucian bit back a stern reproach. He had after all left his son to deal with things. 'You've got his agreement? He'll join us?'

'He will, father. And both Gauge and Jellaqua will back him too. You'll have to speak to Sarik and Rumann though.'

'Agreed,' Lucian replied. 'And son?

'Well done.'

CHAPTER FIVE

Brielle gripped the railing as she looked down from the high gallery at the operations centre below. The whole chamber was shaped like the inside of a huge sphere, with row upon row of galleries working downwards towards the projector of a massive holograph in the very centre. Hundreds of tau officers manned stations all around the galleries, with each of the four castes of the tau race represented. Fire caste warriors coordinated ground operations, while air caste representatives controlled impossibly complex fleet manoeuvres like it was second nature. Earth caste leaders coordinated the logistics chain, while the water caste facilitated communications and the smooth operation of the entire endeavour. The tau war fleet was on the move again, a massive force heading in-system towards Dal'yth Prime.

'There's no way they'll do anything but accept your terms when they see the size of this fleet,' Naal said.

Brielle's response was to grip the white rail all the tighter, lest she make some remark she would later come to regret.

'The evacuation is ninety-eight per cent complete,' Naal continued, oblivious to Brielle's feelings on the matter. 'Ground forces are massing at Gel'bryn. The crusade has stalled before it's even got going.'

'Will you just…' Brielle started, but Naal interrupted her.

'Main viewer, Brielle,' Naal gestured towards the operations centre below.

As Brielle followed Naal's gesture, the holograph came to life. A huge, semi-transparent globe grew from a single blue point of light in the dead centre of the spherical chamber. It expanded to become a representation of local space the size of the entire chamber, so that even from the high gallery it filled Brielle's field of vision. A tau icon showed the location of Dal'yth Prime, and a cluster of smaller symbols indicated the position of the crusade's main ships of the line. A string of smaller icons showed the Imperium's supply vessels as they plied to and fro from the edge of the system, and, presumably, towards the Damocles Gulf.

Then the globe expanded still further, its outer surface almost within arm's reach, and Brielle was struck by how flawlessly the projection device operated compared to its equivalents in humanity's service. Her father's flagship, the *Oceanid,* had such a device on its bridge, but much smaller and far less reliable. The secret of the manufacture of hololiths, as the Imperium called them, was a closely guarded secret known only to a handful of Adeptus Mechanicus forge worlds, and Lucian's had been gifted to an ancestor of the Arcadius as reward for services rendered during the liberation of such a world from an ork invasion.

The globe stabilised, the individual icons representing the Imperium's warships amalgamating into a single, distant rune. At the edge of the blue globe there appeared a series of tau symbols that Brielle recognised as indicating alien naval battle groups. Naal was right. The fleet that Brielle was travelling on massively outnumbered the Imperium's force. Even if the crusade could summon reinforcements from across the Damocles Gulf, there was no way any would arrive in time to save it.

But, according to Aura's plan, the crusade would not need saving. It would need reasoning with, negotiating with. The tau still believed, despite all the evidence to the contrary, that the Imperium could be convinced to join the tau empire and sign up to the Greater Good.

The tau were nothing if not optimistic, Brielle thought, a state of mind rarely seen in the Imperium.

'Mistress Brielle,' the voice of the tau water caste envoy Aura sounded from behind her. She forced herself to appear unconcerned, despite the fact that she had not heard him coming. She was normally very good at detecting people creeping up on her...

'Aura,' Brielle replied, bowing as the envoy came to stand beside her at the railing. 'I trust all is well?'

Aura nodded back, his features set in the now familiar sadness they always showed. If it were not for the fact that the alien's voice sounded equally as melancholic Brielle might have concluded that he had some sort of condition, or had perhaps been dropped on his head when he had been hatched.

'All is very well, Mistress Brielle,' Aura replied. 'We are closing to within tactical communications range and a link with the troops on Dal'yth Prime is now possible. Such a link has been established, and is about to be displayed in the unit below.'

Brielle was instantly suspicious. Was Aura planning on showing her the tau gloriously defeating human troops? If so, why?

Aura's black, almond-shaped eyes held hers for a moment, and then he turned to the scene below. The representation of local space faded away, a mass of tau symbols scrolling through the air, before the projection flickered and was replaced by a monochromatic image that could only have been captured from a lens mounted on a warrior's armour.

'What am I seeing?' Brielle said, as much to herself as to the tau envoy.

'This is a real-time uplink from one of our glorious warriors, who even now is deploying against the invaders. His name is Cali'cha, which you might translate as "quick purpose", though the term has no exact analogue in your tongue. He is the leader of a crisis team, and he is closing on a group of the warriors you call Space Marines.'

'He'll be slaughtered,' Brielle muttered, causing Naal to cast a warning glance her way.

'Have no fear, Mistress Brielle,' Aura replied having overheard, but misconstrued her remark. 'Cali'cha is a warrior of great experience and skill. He has served the Greater Good with peerless dedication and knows well the ways of human warriors.'

'Has he ever fought Space Marines?' Brielle said.

'His battle suit is well equipped to counter their armour, Mistress Brielle, of that you may be certain.'

'Space Marines are more than armour...' Brielle started, but Aura had turned his attentions to the holo projection.

It was night, and the tau were moving out from the outskirts of Gel'bryn city, moving in graceful, bounding leaps powered by the thrusters mounted on the suits' backs. Cali'cha set down at the western shore of a river, and his two companions appeared in his field of view. Each wore one of these 'crisis' battle suits, boxy missile launchers mounted at their backs and stubby energy weapons on their arms. The team exchanged what Brielle took to be ritualised, pre-battle words, each touching the tips of their weapons to a representation of a ceremonial blade painted onto their armoured torsos. In the background, the night sky flickered with distant explosions and tracer fire rose with seeming laziness high into the air.

'The Imperium have moved their anti-air assets forwards, Mistress Brielle,' Aura said, having seen her following the tracers as they arced high overhead. She merely nodded, and Aura turned back to the projection.

Their ritual complete, the three warriors moved out, gathering speed as they approached the river. At the very shore, they leaped high into the air, soaring through the night sky with a grace Brielle had only seen amongst the alien eldar. As they reached the height of their bound, the land ahead was revealed. Distant artillery boomed and flashed, and insect-like gunships swept in low over the shadowed terrain. A huge flash lit the entire horizon, and for a second, Brielle saw the towering silhouette of what could only have been a war Titan of the Adeptus Titanicus.

'They have commenced a bombardment of the city's outer limits, Mistress Brielle,' Aura said. That was not good, Brielle thought, knowing that her father would have objected to such a course of action had he the power to affect it. Clearly, the more hawkish elements of the crusade council were gaining the ascendancy.

The crisis team set down on the opposite edge of the river, splashing down in the shallows before making its way past a cluster of dome-shaped buildings at its edge. Evidence of war was all around, from the scorched surfaces of the nearby structures to the wounded tau warriors being evacuated by teams of earth caste medics. It struck Brielle how well the tau treated their combat wounded, each individual casualty being tended by an entire team of medical staff as they were rushed away on anti-grav stretchers towards waiting medical vehicles. In the Imperium, especially in the Imperial Guard, the wounded were often treated at best as an inconvenience and at worst as malingerers. They would be treated, most certainly, but not through compassion or sympathy, but more to get them back in the fight as soon as possible so that their duty to the Emperor might be done.

The crisis team passed quickly through what must have been a forward assembly area, and came to rest in the lee of a dense fruit tree formation. A group of gangly aliens rushed by, squawking and whistling as they disappeared into the trees and were gone. The view panned left and then right, and Brielle saw that the team had joined a larger force, consisting of at least five more groups of battle suit warriors.

'Flawless,' Aura said to himself. 'Mission commences in four...'

Now every tau in the chamber focussed their attentions on the huge projection, an expectant silence settling across the scene. The crisis teams turned towards the east, the sound of a heavy weapon pounding away nearby filling the chamber. Then they were leaping forwards and the fruit trees were rushing past below, the shadowy forms of the rangy aliens weaving through the plantation.

Tracer rounds scythed upwards towards the battle suits as they powered through the air, at first appearing to move as if in slow motion, but speeding up as they closed. Brielle knew that only one in four or five of the heavy bolter rounds would be filled with the chemicals that made them burn bright red, and that the air must have been filled with a storm of shots far greater than the eye could see.

As the crisis team came in to land, the source of the firing came into view. In the ruins of an outlying agricultural building the heavy bolter sprayed death in a wide arc. The stream of tracers followed the tau as they bounded forwards, several rounds clipping the battle suits. The command centre resounded to the harsh metallic thuds and clangs, but the tau pressed on, unharmed.

The next sound was that of Cali'cha issuing last-second orders to his teammates. Brielle could not understand his words, although their meaning was universal.

The view from the battle suit as it closed towards the enemy position jolted and swung crazily as the tau evaded incoming fire. Then the crisis team was in range, and a targeting reticule appeared in the centre of the projection, hovering just above and behind the sputtering muzzle flare of the heavy bolter.

A missile streaked out from behind the crisis team leader's field of vision, and rose rapidly into the air. Within a second it was streaking downwards, its predicted trajectory etched in the glowing line through the air of the command centre. Then it struck, and the gun position disappeared in a blinding flash. Seconds later the heavy bolter's ammunition started to cook off, filling the ruins of the building with whip-crack flashes.

The crisis team pressed onwards, swooping in amongst the ruins as the last of the heavy bolter's rounds crackled and fizzed across the ground. The view point tipped downwards as Cali'cha looked down at the dead gunner, evidently keen to afford the command staff a view.

The breath caught in Brielle's throat as the gunner's ruined body resolved in the air in front of her. He wore power armour, painted white with red detailing in what could only have been the livery of the White Scars Chapter. His face was almost entirely gone, just blood-smeared bone and hair visible as dead eyes stared upwards at the Space Marine's executioner.

'You see, Mistress Brielle?' Aura said sadly. 'The Space Marines are far from undefeatable...'

The envoy's words were cut off as the air was filled with the unmistakable sound of massed boltguns being fired from nearby. Rounds clattered loudly from Cali'cha's battle suit and sparks danced across the field of vision. The view point swung across to the left towards a second ruin, where a line of white-armoured figures was advancing on the tau, weapons blazing.

The battle suit pilot issued a calm order, and the team leaped backwards, the energy weapons mounted on their rigs' arms spitting incandescent beams of blinding blue fire towards the enemy. One went down, and several others appeared to have been wounded, but still the line came on, the night air filled with rapid-fire death.

Then the command centre was filled with a savage war cry, several dozen of the tau manning the control stations visibly flinching before the terrifying sound. Cali'cha panned further left, in time to see a chainsword-wielding, white-armoured figure emerging from the darkness. The warrior's screaming blade lashed outwards and severed the arm from the battle suit of one of Cali'cha's team mates, before leaping forwards to drive the weapon straight into the square sensor block atop the armoured torso.

The channel howled with the sound of the chainsword's teeth grinding through the battle suit's systems, and an instant later the death scream of the pilot joined it. Then the channel went abruptly silent. Brielle could not tell whether the pickups had been destroyed or the tau below had severed the connection in order to spare the viewers from the terrible sound.

'Savages…' Aura said, glancing sideways towards Brielle. 'So callous, and brutal.'

Brielle made no reply, her eyes fixed on the projection. The crisis team had been caught in an anarchic melee, and were desperately seeking to back away from their enemy. The field of view swung back to the right, showing the first line of white-armoured Space Marines charging in to join the fray. A second member of Cali'cha's crisis team was pulled down as he attempted to engage his suit's thrusters, one Space Marine gripping a mechanical leg while another used a bolt pistol to hammer shot after shot into the jet's innards.

The battle suit's propulsion system erupted in seething energies as a bolt-round bored through to its generator. The Space Marine pulling the suit downwards towards the ground was thrown clear by the explosion, though his armour was visibly damaged by the energies, his left shoulder plate torn off as he came upright again. The second Space Marine backed away, but continued to pump rounds into the writhing battle suit until finally its torso split wide open under the relentless barrage and the pilot inside was pulped to a bloody mess.

'*Mon'at...*' Aura said sadly, as Cali'cha finally broke clear and the scene of devastation receded below him.

'He is alone,' Naal said. 'His team is reduced to one. It is a sad fate indeed for a servant of the Greater Good.'

Brielle nodded, though in truth she had no sympathy for the surviving warrior. His commanders had drastically underestimated the Space Marines if they thought them so easily defeated. She had even tried to warn them...

'Reinforcements,' Aura said, and the projection was filled by the scene of a dozen more battle suits swooping in to join Cali'cha. The air filled with the Space Marines' war cries and the deafening report of boltguns, and battle was joined again.

SERGEANT SARIK LOOSED a feral grunt as he yanked his screaming chainsword from the torso of the ruined battle suit, bracing an armoured boot against its groin as he pulled the weapon clear. The blade was coated in purple fluid and its teeth almost clogged with small chunks of the pilot's flesh. Raising the chainsword to a guard position, Sarik looked around for another foe.

A sharp explosion sounded from nearby as Sarik's battle-brothers finished off the second of the battle suit team, and a third was lifting high overhead on hissing blue jets.

'Regroup!' Sarik bellowed. 'On me!'

Within moments, Sarik's warriors had gathered at his side and Sergeant Tsuka's squad was inbound, loosing a hail of fire at the retreating battle suit as they came. The scene was one of utter devastation, the Imperial Guard's bombardment of the settlement on the nearside of

River 992 having ruined every structure and cast flaming debris over a wide area.

'We'll need more squads moved up fast, brother-sergeant,' Tsuka said when he reached Sarik's side. 'It appears the enemy are attempting to probe the Guard lines.'

It was only by repeated Space Marine combat patrols throughout the area bordering the northern loop of River 992 that the tau had been held at bay. General Gauge knew that the Imperial Guard's possession of the area beyond the river was by no means secured, and it would take only a determined enemy thrust to disrupt the entire area of operations. Captain Rumann had approved the patrols, which had been in action throughout the night. Significant progress had been made, the patrols keeping the enemy away from the Guard as they moved their heavier units forward.

'Sergeant Rheq,' Sarik said into the vox-net as he opened a channel to the Scythes of the Emperor contingent leader. 'Sarik. What is your status?'

Sergeant Rheq's reply was half drowned out by the sound of gunfire in the background, the Space Marines' bolt-rounds competing with the tau's energy rifles. Then the hissing streak of a missile cut across the channel, a muffled explosion sounded, and the tau weapons fell silent. 'Grid three-alpha-nine secure, Sarik,' the Scythes of the Emperor squad leader replied. 'Enemy probe neutralised.'

'Good,' Sarik replied. 'Sergeant Rheq, can you spare two or perhaps three squads?' Although technically Sergeant Rheq's superior under the terms of the Space Marines' contribution to the Damocles Gulf Crusade, Sarik knew diplomacy would get him a lot further than rank in multi-Chapter operations.

'I can spare two tactical and two Devastator combat squads,' Sergeant Rheq replied. 'That's including three heavy bolters and two tubes. Is that sufficient, brother-sergeant?'

Sarik's eyes scanned the dark skies above the river, where he caught sight of another group of battle suits zeroing in on his position. 'I am sure it will be, Rheq,' Sarik said. 'My thanks.'

Closing the channel to the Scythes of the Emperor leader, Sarik opened a transmission to all Space Marine squad leaders in the area. 'All commands,' he said. 'Enemy heavy infantry multiple inbound on grid seven-theta-nine.'

A ream of acknowledgements came instantly back from the Ultramarines and Iron Hands squad leaders operating in adjacent grids, each promising immediate reinforcement of Sarik's section of the front.

There was time for one last batch of brief orders to Sarik's squads before the enemy battle suits touched down in the lee of a ruined building one hundred metres to the south-east. Bitterly won experience had taught Sarik that the tau battle suits preferred to keep their distance, bounding into weapons range, unleashing a torrent of fire and then retreating to cover before a counter-attack could be staged. But they could be beaten, as Sarik had discovered. The tau were highly accomplished technically, but they displayed an almost paralysing fear of close assault that could be used to blunt their advances and counter their technological trickeries.

Leaving a Devastator squad to cover the dead ground, Sarik led his warriors into a wooded area that ran down to the river, passing the ruin the battle suits had touched down behind.

'The third moon at the false dawn,' Sarik said. Both of the squads accompanying him were of the White Scars Chapter, meaning he could use the battle-cant to impart information far more efficiently, and secretly, than he could with the larger, composite force.

Following Sarik's battle-cant order, the White Scars spread out into two long columns. Such a formation afforded rapid movement through the dark, dense terrain within the plantation, and allowed for superior arcs of fire. Though the White Scars were born of the nomad tribes of the plains of Chogoris, they were superior warriors even in the dense, wooded plantation. Their white-armoured forms took on the aspect of ghosts moving implacably through the dark woods, backlit by the occasional explosion or streak of tracer fire from beyond.

The sounds of artillery and gunfire receded as the White Scars pressed into the plantation, though the vegetation caused the sounds to echo unpredictably. Something caused Sarik to slow down, some inkling that something was not quite right. He halted, and gestured for the silent order to be passed down the line. Within seconds, the two squads had stopped moving, each Space Marine stood motionless against the night.

Then Sarik realised what it was that was niggling at his subconscious mind. To his enhanced senses, the complex but entirely natural aromas of the fruit trees tasted somehow... tainted, as if some other substance had been mixed in with them. Or, he realised, as if the juices of the fruit were being used to mask something else...

Sarik made a hand-gesture warning to alert the battle-brothers of a potential ambush. He took another deep breath, and this time he was sure. The fruit scents were being deliberately employed to mask something entirely different, something oily and alien.

Sarik raised his bolter and scanned the ground up ahead. The plantation was well tended, so there was very little in the way of ground cover in which an ambusher could conceal himself. Sarik tracked first left, then right, seeing no sign of an enemy using what little cover the tall tree trunks would offer. Then a gentle gust of wind sighed through the plantation, carrying with it a cocktail of smoke, cordite, blood and...

Sarik froze, forcing every muscle in his body to remain still. Though he kept his eyes locked on the path ahead, he knew that his enemy was directly above, suspended in the canopy.

Sarik breathed again, and this time there was no mistaking the oily scent of alien skin. It could only have been the alien savages his friend Lucian had reported. His gorge rising, he recalled the promise he had made himself when he had first read of these aliens' repulsive practices. Not a single one of his warriors would suffer such a fate.

Not wishing to give the alien ambusher any clue that he was aware of its presence, Sarik continued tracking his raised weapon across the ground up ahead, but his eyes were not scanning the ground, but the tree canopies. It was only when an air-bursting explosion half a kilometre distant cast the entire scene in a brief, flickering glow, that he caught sight of a mass of bodies suspended high up in the trees to the right.

Guessing the alien in the canopy directly above him was a sentry for the larger ambush group up ahead, Sarik made his decision. In a single, fluid motion he bent his arm at the elbow and fired a burst directly into the air. The bolts struck flesh, and exploded an instant later, showering Sarik with a fine rain of oily gore.

Proceeded by the snapping of branches and the rustling of leaves, a ragged mass of limbs and quills slammed to the ground in front of Sarik. He had no time to waste with an examination, but a brief glance confirmed that this alien was not a tau. It must be one of the carnivores Lucian had faced the previous night.

'The night-howler!' Sarik bellowed in battle-cant. 'Swooping from the peak!'

He had never used that particular phrase before, but the beauty of using battle-cant was that his warriors could infer his meaning with reference to the culture of Chogoris. Night-howlers were creatures of legend. According to the old tales, they had once lurked in the equatorial mountains, waiting for passing travellers whose bodies they would drag away to consume in their caves.

Sarik was up and firing as his warriors pounded forwards to his side. His shots slammed into the canopy up ahead, and without needing to be told his warriors followed his example, adding the weight of their fire to his own. The throaty *thump thump thump* of a heavy bolter opened up from the right flank, and an entire tree was torn to shreds, along with the three aliens that had waited in its canopy.

A piercing shriek filled the air, sounding to Sarik like some wailing banshee from nomad myth. Shadowy figures dropped from the trees all around, landing silently and bounding forwards on whiplash-muscled legs.

And then the Space Marines and the aliens were upon one another. Curses and oaths clashed with screeches and hisses, and both groups loosed a final volley of fire before clashing in the brutal mass of hand-to-hand combat. The aliens fired their musket-like rifles from the hip as they closed, livid bolts of blue energy slamming into white power armour. A battle-brother of Sarik's squad was struck square in the chest, a chunk of his chest armour torn away to reveal the flesh beneath. Another was struck a glancing blow to the helmet, the entire left side of his faceplate shorn away.

But the Space Marines' weapons were far more deadly, for the aliens wore no more armour than the occasional shoulder pad. Sarik fired his bolt pistol at the closest alien as it screamed in towards him. The bolt buried itself in the rope-like tendons of the creature's hip, lodging in amongst the flexing musculature. Then the mass-reactive round detonated, and the savage's entire leg was shorn off to cartwheel through the air trailing a comet-like plume of blood. The alien crashed to the ground at Sarik's feet, but still it came on, screeching hatefully as it used its barbed rifle to pull itself upwards.

Sarik put a bolt-round into the alien's head, and it went down for good.

Then the entire plantation seemed to erupt in savage fury as the two groups merged into one another. A spiked rifle barrel swung in towards Sarik's head and he ducked, the spike catching on a vent of his back-mounted power pack. That was all the opening he needed, and he pistol-whipped his attacker, staving in its bird-like skull with the butt of his bolt pistol.

Another creature leaped in from the right, its spiked rifle held two-handed like a stave. The alien came in high, feet first, and before Sarik could reach his chainsword it had slammed into him, one foot on each of his shoulder plates. The savage was surprisingly heavy, and its muscles so powerful that Sarik was pushed backwards under the weight and power of the impact. Instead of resisting the weight, Sarik rolled backwards with the alien's momentum, his back striking the ground as his opponent was suddenly forced to struggle for balance. Then Sarik brought his legs up sharply, his knees striking the alien in the back and powering it overhead to strike a nearby tree. Sarik was up in an instant. The alien was stunned, struggling to regain its feet. Sarik made a fist and unleashed such a pile-driving punch that the alien's head was pulped into the tree trunk.

A brief lull in the melee allowed Sarik to draw his chainsword and thumb it to screeching life. The fight was finely balanced. The aliens were no match for the Space Marines on a one-to-one basis, but they outnumbered Sarik's force three or four to one. Sarik looked around for a means of tipping the odds in the White Scars' favour. Then he saw it.

Twenty metres away, beyond the swirling combat, stood an alien that Sarik knew instantly must have been their leader. It was tall, and robed in a long cloak of exotic animal hide. Its olive green skin was daubed with swirling patterns of deep red war paint, applied, Sarik guessed, from the blood of the fallen Rakarshans. The alien was screeching loudly and gesticulating wildly as it issued its shrill orders to its warriors.

'You!' Sarik bellowed, pointing his chainsword directly towards the alien leader and gunning its motor so that its teeth wailed a high-pitched threat. The alien heard him and turned, its beady, bird-like eyes narrowing as they focussed on him. It seemed for an instant that the swirling mass of the raging close combat parted between Sarik and his foe, affording a clear path between the two.

The alien ceased its racket, and turned fully to face Sarik, the dreadlock-like quills sprouting from the back of its skull bristling with evident challenge.

'You hear me,' Sarik called mockingly. 'Face me!' Knowing the alien would not understand his words, Sarik put as much symbolism into his tone and body language as possible, so that even a brain-damaged gretchin would get the message and understand he was being issued a one-to-one challenge.

To Sarik's surprise, the alien nodded. It might have been coincidence, but Sarik was struck by the impression that the savage somehow understood his tongue, though he could not see how. It screeched again, and every one of its warriors nearby leaped backwards, disengaging from the Space Marines. Several of Sarik's warriors pressed instinctively after their foes, but Sarik stilled them with a curt order, and silence descended on the plantation as both groups of warriors eyed one another grimly.

Sarik stepped forwards, and the alien leader strode to the centre of the clearing to meet him. Another air-bursting shell exploded high overhead, and for the first time Sarik was afforded a clear view of his enemy. The alien was tall, taller even than a Space Marine, who were counted giants compared to the bulk of humanity. Its muscles were like steel cables, and it appeared not to have an ounce of fat on its lean body. The leader wore its ragged animal-skin cloak as if it were a stately robe of office. Apart from that it wore no other garments, but numerous leather belts and bandoliers hung with pouches and fetishes were wrapped about its torso.

As it came to a halt, the alien threw one side of its robe back over its left shoulder, revealing a sword scabbard at its belt. Sarik's eyes narrowed as he saw that the blade was obviously a power sword, its guard worked into the form of the aquila, the Imperial eagle and icon of humanity's faith in the Emperor. It appeared then to Sarik that the alien was actually boasting of its possession of the weapon, as if the Space Marine was expected to respond in fear or admiration.

'I've seen a power sword before, bird brain,' Sarik growled.

The alien's beak opened and it issued a sibilant hiss. Its warriors repeated the sound until it echoed around the entire plantation.

Sarik decided to play along. 'I come in the name of the primarch,' he called.

'Honoured be his name!' his gathered warriors responded, drowning out the aliens' hissing.

Energised by his brothers' proud war cry, Sarik raised his chainsword high and rushed in towards the alien. He expected his opponent to reach for the power sword and attempt to parry the attack, but to his surprise the alien made a casual gesture with its clawed hand, and Sarik's blade rebounded as if from an invisible barrier.

'Psyker...' Sarik spat, raising his chainsword to a guard position. That changed things.

'So the power sword's just for decoration,' he said, seeking to distract his foe and buy time to engineer an opening. The alien hissed in response, its worm-like tongue writhing in its beaked mouth.

'The Librarians will hear of this,' Sarik said, as much to himself as to the alien. 'Even should I die.'

As he spoke, Sarik worked his way around his opponent, then circled back the other way, all the while seeking to gain the alien's measure. He feinted to the left and the alien gestured again, invoking its invisible psychic shield. He feinted right and it did so again. A third feint further to the left told Sarik all he needed to know.

Sarik gunned the chainsword to maximum power and raised the weapon high for an obvious downward strike. The alien raised its hand and as the blade descended its screeching teeth were deflected once again. But the ruse had worked. Even as the chainsword came down, Sarik was drawing his bolt pistol with his left hand. The alien never saw the pistol coming, and Sarik had correctly surmised that the shield was a highly localised effect only able to protect the alien leader from one quarter at a time. The bolt pistol spoke, and a mass-reactive round penetrated the alien's chin, lodging deep inside its skull.

Amazingly, having a large-calibre micro-rocket slam into its head barely registered with the alien. It stepped backwards beyond Sarik's reach, and screeched its anger at the Space Marine, its eyes wide.

Then the bolt-round detonated, and the alien's headless body toppled heavily to the ground.

'Take them!' Sarik bellowed, and twenty boltguns levelled on the aliens. Within seconds, the ground was littered with shattered and burned alien corpses, trampled beneath the armoured boots of the rapidly redeploying White Scars.

BRIELLE SEETHED INSIDE, drawing on every ounce of her noble-taught discipline to remain outwardly calm. She was standing in a ceremonial robing chamber belonging to the water caste, and it was lined with rail after rail of garments of office. Having been disrobed by water caste attendants, Brielle was being fitted for the finery of an envoy such as Aura.

Aura had not joined the spectacle, leaving it to a group of more junior members of his caste. The first time she had sworn at one, Brielle had learned that none of them spoke her tongue.

Everything was happening too fast. The tau had fallen for Brielle's gross exaggeration of the crusade's strengths, and that had without a doubt bought her time and saved lives on the ground. But the tau empire was small and concentrated, and its fleets were able to respond to local threats far quicker than would be the case in the Imperium, where populations were separated from their neighbours by huge gulfs of space. The tau fleet, of which the *Dal'yth Il'Fannor O'kray* was now a part, was inbound for Dal'yth Prime in massively overpowering strength.

'Ow!' Brielle spat with unconcealed irritation as one of the attendants manhandled her ankle. He was trying to get her shoe off, but he was unfamiliar with the human ankle arrangement, for the tau's lower legs were reverse jointed. She flicked her foot and the shoe came off, the attendant scurrying off after it.

That was another thing that annoyed her. Though the tau were treating her with politeness, they had no idea of personal space. She had submitted to the ritual disrobing, though only grudgingly, and the attendants had treated her more like a mannequin than a living being. It occurred to her that the tau's collective philosophies were probably the cause, the needs of the individual being secondary to the needs of the many. At first she had been reticent to stand bare before the attendants, but they had proven entirely disinterested in her body. She told herself that was a good thing, but it just served to annoy her even more...

Another attendant approached, carrying in his arms a folded shimmering, silver robe. It was made of the same material as the robe worn by Aura, though Brielle noted its embroidery was not quite so intricate. The attendant came to stand in front of her, and with a gesture he ordered her to hold her hands out to either side. Another attendant joined the first, and together they draped the silver robe over her shoulders so that it covered her body from neck to feet. The material felt cool, and although it covered her entirely, Brielle was nonetheless pleased with the way it draped across her form and accentuated her curves. Her thoughts were not rooted in vanity, however. Even as a second layer was being lifted over her head and fastened around her waist, she was calculating which of the Imperium's merchant families might be interested in acquiring such fabrics, and how much they might be prepared to pay.

More of the attendants closed in, the idiot who had had such trouble with her shoes lifting one of her feet gingerly. She looked down and saw the monstrosity that he was about to place on her foot. 'You've got a lot to learn,' she told the uncomprehending alien. 'No way am I wearing those... hideous things. I'll go barefoot, thank you.'

The water caste attendant looked up at her as she spoke, and seemed to get the message, backing off and taking the ugly, tau-made shoes with him. Others closed in from behind, and a fine array of interwoven braids was applied around her waist and neck, cinching the silver fabric and completing the costume.

Brielle regarded herself in the wide mirror. Her robes glinted in the white overhead light and her dark, plaited hair tumbled down her shoulders and across her back. The costume resembled nothing she had ever seen a human noble wearing, and she felt a deep unease at the sheer alienness of her reflection. Then a soft hiss sounded from behind as a door slid open, and she saw in the mirror the envoy Aura step into the chamber.

'Mistress Brielle,' Aura said as he came to stand beside

her. 'Your transformation is almost complete. Soon, you shall not only wear the trappings of a senior water caste envoy, but you shall wield the power of one too.'

Almost complete? Brielle turned towards the envoy, her mind racing but her expression congenial.

'This,' Aura reached towards Brielle's neck and pulled aside the robe's collar. 'I bring you a gift; a far more appropriate adornment for one of your station.'

Brielle looked down and saw that Aura was holding the aquila pendant she still wore on a slender chain about her neck. In his other hand, he held the tau equivalent, a bisected circle, with a smaller circle within the first.

Her gorge rose as Aura's alien hand closed around the eagle, the symbol of humanity's faith. Despite all she had done in turning aside from her family and the crusade, she had nonetheless never abandoned her faith. And now, that was exactly what the tau expected her to do.

It was too much.

Brielle stood stock still, staring at her own reflection as Aura removed the eagle and passed it to a water caste attendant. Then he took the chain of the pendant, and placed it over her head, the symbol of the tau empire settling on her chest.

'Now, you are one of us,' said Aura. 'The fleet closes on Dal'yth Prime, and your duty awaits.

'The Greater Good, awaits.'

'I'M GOING ALONE, Naal,' said Brielle. 'This is complicated enough already.'

Naal turned his back on her, stalking to the opposite side of Brielle's quarters to stand at the wide viewing port. Dal'yth Prime glinted in the distance, and the blue plasma trails of a hundred tau vessels formed a blazing corona around the planet.

'You won't be coming back,' said Naal.

Brielle forced down a blunt reply. He was right, but she had to make him think she was sacrificing herself for the Greater Good, and not thinking of her own future.

'I may be,' she said softly. 'If I am able, I will.'

'They won't let you, Brielle,' said Naal. 'Grand will have you in his excoriation cells the instant you step foot on the *Blade of Woe*.'

Brielle sighed, knowing that the possibility was all too likely. 'Not if my father is willing to protect me. He wields the Warrant of Trade. That still means something.'

'And Grand wields the Inquisitorial rosette,' Naal replied. 'As well you know.'

'We are beyond the borders of the Imperium,' said Brielle. 'The rosette grants no formal power here, just influence.'

Naal turned his back on the viewing port as he replied. 'How much influence?' he said bitterly. 'You're counting on your father carrying the will of the council. That's a pretty big assumption to make, given the charges Grand will level on you, and on anyone who supports you.'

Brielle closed on Naal and took his hands in hers as she replied. 'I have faith, Naal. I have to do this.'

'For the Greater Good?' he said, his eyes locked on hers.

Brielle held his gaze, but hesitated to answer.

'Or for your own, Brielle?'

She let go of his hands and walked back to the centre of the living area. 'Perhaps both,' she said finally. That was as much as she would give him, though she knew inside that he deserved more. Since the two had met on the Imperial world of Mundus Chasmata, they had gone from co-conspirators to lovers and eventually to friends. But Brielle knew enough of herself to see how this would all end. Naal had sought, through genuine conviction, to show her something different from the Imperium. He served the Greater Good even though it made him a traitor to the entire human race. He sincerely believed that humanity could change, could embrace the Greater Good and stand side by side with the tau and others, rather than simply exterminating any race it could not enslave.

She knew he was wrong. She was leaving, but not on the shuttle the tau were even now preparing for her diplomatic mission.

'I'm to leave soon,' Brielle said. She turned, a coy smile at her lips. 'That gives us just enough time...'

She was in his arms before she had finished speaking, his kiss stealing the words from her mouth. The tau would have to wait a little longer.

LUCIAN STOOD IN the midst of his battle group's command post, Major Subad nearby poring over a large map while the voice of Sergeant-Major Havil bellowed in the background. A gaggle of Departmento Tacticae specialists had joined the Rakarshans and were busy attempting to disseminate the reams of intelligence the crusade had gathered, and learn what they could of the aliens from those who had fought them. The Rakarshans had done a lot of that recently.

Putting some distance between himself and the anarchic command post, Lucian brought the vox-set to his mouth. 'Go ahead, Korvane.'

'Father,' Lucian's son replied. 'Would you prefer the good news, or the bad?'

Lucian scowled, knowing that his son rarely joked about such things. 'Give me the good news, son. Sugar the pill.'

'I have two more candidates for the council, father. It looks like they'll be accepted at the next sitting.'

'Who?'

'The first is Pator Ottavi. He found me in fact. He's been pronounced Pator Sedicae's successor by his House, making him the senior Navigator in the crusade.' Sedicae had been killed when the *Regent Lakshimbal* had been destroyed by tau warships, and it made sense that his successor would desire a seat on the crusade command council. Well enough, thought Lucian, so long as he showed a little more interest in the running of the crusade than his predecessor, who was almost entirely concerned with predicting the currents of the warp.

'He'll support us?' Lucian said, lowering his voice and moving further away from the command post.

'I believe so, father,' Korvane replied. 'He seems to agree that this region should be exploited, not put to the torch.'

'Well done, son,' said Lucian. 'And what of the other?'

'The Explorator, Magos Gunn,' Korvane said. 'I sounded him out and eventually discovered that he's a member of a Mechanicus faction that seeks to study the type of technology the tau use. He doesn't care if they all die, but he wants something left behind to study, and that puts him on our side as far as I can make out.'

'I know the man,' said Lucian. 'Something of an outcast amongst the wider Mechanicus, but not so much for an Explorator. Make it happen, then.'

'Did you want to hear the bad news, father?' said Korvane.

'Not really, son,' said Lucian. 'Give me it anyway.'

There was a pause, during which Lucian guessed that his son was checking the channel was secure and the conversation was not being listened in on. 'Something's happening,' Korvane said.

Lucian glanced back at the command post, and the Tacticae advisors busying themselves at their temporary cogitation-stations. 'Go on.'

'I think the fleet is preparing to face another force, father,' Korvane said. 'I think it's a big one.'

'The tau?' Lucian said, though he knew it could be no other. 'They're reinforcing?'

'More than that, father,' Korvane replied. 'I think the Tacticae are in the process of re-assessing the tau's capabilities.'

'Re-assessing?' Lucian said. 'As in, voiding themselves because they're coming to realise the tau aren't dirt-grubbing primitives that can be rolled over with a single crusade?'

'Well, I wouldn't put it quite like that, father,' Korvane replied. Lucian wouldn't expect his son to, for he had been raised in the Court of Nankirk, one of the most refined in the quadrant. 'But essentially, yes.'

'Have they informed the general?' Lucian asked.

'No, father,' Korvane replied. 'I don't think they've told anyone yet. Perhaps at the next council sitting...'

'Leave this with me, Korvane,' Lucian said, his mind racing as a hundred possibilities sprang into being. 'See about calling a council session as soon as possible, even if we have to conduct it remotely. Understood?'

As Korvane signed off, Lucian walked back to the command post, his eyes on the Tacticae advisors all the while. There was certainly something... furtive about them. It was as if they were desperately trying to piece together a puzzle they really didn't want to complete.

It all made a kind of sense, Lucian thought as he stepped back into the post. The crusade had already met far greater resistance than any had thought possible, first in space, and then here on the surface of Dal'yth Prime. The landings had started off well, but the advance had all but ground to a halt along the northern bank of River 992. Tau reinforcements were by all reports flooding east from the world's other cities, and now it appeared that a new fleet was inbound for Dal'yth Prime.

Things were just about to get interesting...

CHAPTER SIX

'LUCIAN,' SAID SARIK as the White Scar strode into Battle-group Arcadius's bustling command post. The staff were preparing for a session of the Damocles Gulf Crusade command council, with each councillor attending from a remote station. Large pict screens were being erected in the centre of the tented command post, each connected by snaking cables to a central field-cogitation array.

The rogue trader turned from the tacticae-station he was leaned over, and grinned when he saw his friend. With a last word to the Rakarshan trooper manning the station, Lucian crossed to the Space Marine, and the two clasped hands.

'How goes the war?' asked Sarik.

Lucian's expression darkened before he replied. 'We've been ordered to dig in,' said Lucian. 'The whole operation's grinding to a halt.'

'Aye,' said Sarik. 'It's the same along the whole front.

The tau have evacuated non-combatants and their reinforcements are flooding in. We've been fending off probing attacks all night.'

Lucian nodded, and leaned in conspiratorially. 'Have you spoken to any of Gauge's staff?'

Sarik noticed that the command post was manned by a large number of Departmento Tacticae staff, and guessed that the rogue trader was not entirely happy about the fact. 'Indirectly. Talk plainly, friend.'

'Well enough,' Lucian replied quietly. 'I think something's up. I think the Tacticae are reassessing the strategic situation.'

'To what end?'

'I think they're coming to realise that the crusade is overextended,' Lucian said. 'My son reports that the fleet is struggling to protect the supply trains, and if things get any worse dirt-side will be hard pressed to support orbital and ground operations together.'

'It's only a matter of time before Gauge receives this information, then,' Sarik said. 'And when he does?'

'Hard to say,' Lucian said. 'If I read Gauge right, I think he'll press for a breakout, but something will have to be done quickly. My son believes there is a substantial tau war fleet inbound, so time is at a premium.'

'Is this to be the crux of the council session?'

Lucian grinned. 'Possibly, but there is other business too. My son has been busy, finding prospective replacements for the vacant council seats. I aim to propose three new members, all of whom are sympathetic to our faction's agenda.'

Something inside Sarik stirred, for he disliked being dragged into the crusade's politics. Far better to leave such things to Chapter Masters and their peers, he believed, and leave sergeants such as himself to lead the troops. Still, he had accepted the responsibility of a seat on the command council, and could scarcely expect to avoid such things, no matter how tedious he found them.

Before Sarik could answer, one of the Tacticae staff called out, reporting that the pict screens were all in place and the council session ready to convene. Sarik and Lucian strode to the centre of the command post, the screens arrayed in a circle around them. 'Ready?' Lucian asked.

'Ready,' Sarik replied. The advisor gestured to a technician, and the screens burst to life as one.

A respectful quiet descended on the command post, and the static on the screens resolved into a dozen images of the face of the council's convenor. The man's expression looked distinctly stern, and he was obviously unhappy with the nature of the session, which was being conducted with each of the councillors widely separated rather than together in the council chamber aboard the *Blade of Woe*.

After a brief moment of silence, the convenor spoke. 'This extraordinary session of the Damocles Gulf Crusade command council is hereby convened. In attendance are Inquisitor Grand of the Most Holy Ordos of the Emperor's Inquisition, General Wendall Gauge of the Imperial Guard, Admiral Jellaqua of the Imperial Navy, Captain Rumann of the Adeptus Astartes Iron Hands, Lucian Gerrit of the Clan Arcadius, Veteran Sergeant Sarik of the Adeptus Astartes White Scars, Logistician-General Stempf of the Adeptus Terra and Cardinal Esau Gurney of the Adeptus Ministorum. Cardinal Gurney has the chair.'

With that, the convenor slammed his staff of office against the deck, and his face disappeared from the pict screens, to be replaced by the councillors. Four of the screens remained blank.

Cardinal Gurney now addressed the council, the scene behind him indicating that he was near the front line, his attendants gathered around him. 'It is my honour to chair this session of the council at this most auspicious of junctures. The first order of business is to answer the petition of Korvane Gerrit Arcadius regarding the election of three new councillors to our august body. I call Korvane Arcadius to address the council in this matter.'

Now one of the previously blank screens showed Korvane's face. Lucian's son was stood on the bridge of his vessel, the *Rosetta*.

Something occurred to Sarik, and he leaned in to speak to Lucian. 'Was that too easy? Would we not expect the cardinal to place obstacles in the path of this petition?'

Lucian appeared to be thinking the same thing. 'Aye, Sarik,' he replied in a low voice. 'Something isn't right here...'

'Honoured members of the command council,' Korvane said. 'It is my intention to propose Tacticae-Primaris Kilindini of the Departmento Tacticae, Explorator Magos Gunn of the Adeptus Mechanicus and Pator Ottavi of the Navis Nobilite be called to serve the council. I would like to–'

'The council thanks you, Korvane Gerrit,' Cardinal Gurney interrupted Korvane's petition. 'Given the urgency of the situation I call upon those in attendance to cast their votes.'

Now Sarik knew that something was definitely awry. Gurney had sidestepped procedure and gone straight for a vote, as if he was not even concerned that those proposed for council seats might be sympathetic to his rivals' agenda. Within a minute, each of the councillors had cast their votes and the three were elected, their faces appearing on the three remaining screens.

'Welcome, then,' Gurney continued. 'With that settled, I call upon General Gauge to appraise the council of the strategic situation.' Sarik could not help but read a note of smugness in Gurney's voice, as if he looked forward to his rival being forced to recount bad tidings.

'Thank you, cardinal,' Gauge scowled, his flint-hard eyes narrowing as he spoke. 'I have this hour received a full report from the Departmento Tacticae, presenting a reappraisal of our enemy's strengths and capabilities. Needless to say, I have not had the time to fully assimilate the report, but I can summarise what I have read simply enough.'

Sarik glanced around the screens, gauging the reaction of each of the councillors. Admiral Jellaqua looked as dour as Gauge, while Captain Rumann was as unreadable as ever. Gurney still looked smug, while Inquisitor Grand looked downright triumphant. 'He knows already,' Sarik whispered to Lucian, nodding towards the screen showing the inquisitor's face. Lucian nodded slightly in reply.

'It now appears that the tau are a substantially more established race than previous intelligence maintained,' Gauge continued. 'Their domain is larger by a factor of ten than initially estimated, and their technology far more dangerous.'

'And what do you propose, general, to overcome this situation?' Cardinal Gurney interjected. 'Given the evident perniciousness of our foe, how shall we defeat it?'

It was obvious that Gurney was attempting to bait the general, to force him to admit that conventional military tactics would not prevail. Sarik doubted the veteran warrior would rise to so crude a tactic, and was pleased to be proven correct.

'My staff have been busy preparing a new plan, cardinal,' Gauge replied, his voice dry and dangerous. 'I propose Operation Hydra.'

'I don't think–' Cardinal Gurney began, before he was interrupted by Lucian.

'I would hear the general's plan,' Lucian said.

'So too would I,' said Sarik.

Admiral Jellaqua and Captain Rumann added their ascent, and Gauge continued. 'I propose a rapid breakout across River 992, crossing using the bridge at the settlement designated Erinia Beta. By massing the Titans and the armoured units of the Brimlock Dragoons, we can take the city's star port and push the enemy back against the southern coast.'

'And what then?' Inquisitor Grand spoke for the first time. 'When the star port is in your hands and the tau beaten back, what would be your next course of action?'

General Gauge's cold eyes swept the screens in front of him, evidently measuring carefully his next words.

'Having taken the star port, we will have reached a tipping point,' Gauge said. 'The tau will not be able to bring in any more reinforcements, and the city will be ours for the taking. In fact, we can use it to bring in our own, without the need to bring units through the desert from the landing zone.

'But there is this,' Gauge continued, his voice suddenly low. 'The reinforcements we were promised at the outset of the crusade have not materialised. Without these, we may have to consider–'

'There are to be no reinforcements, general,' Inquisitor Grand interrupted.

Silence descended on the council and in the command post, all eyes now focussed on the inquisitor.

'Explain,' Gauge said, his eyes glinting with murderous incredulity. 'What do you mean, inquisitor?'

'This crusade is over,' Grand said, pulling back his hood as he spoke. His features were twisted and scarred, the result of Lucian's daughter attacking him with a flame weapon before she had fled the crusade and disappeared. In amongst the scars, Grand's face was decorated by a swirling mass of tattoos, describing esoteric runes and symbols. His eyes had no lids, a deliberate message that his gaze would see all and never falter. At his neck was the red-wax seal of the Inquisitorial rosette, the irrefutable font of an inquisitor's power and authority.

The message was quite clear.

'The tau are to be exterminated, one world at a time. I have heard all I will of pride and honour. They are xenos, and they deserve no mercy. Exterminatus shall commence in precisely twenty-four hours, by which time any ground units not evacuated will be left to their fate.'

A stunned silence followed, before Admiral Jellaqua spluttered, 'The council must vote–'

'There is no council!' Grand boomed, the first time he had raised his voice above a sibilant whisper in all the council sessions Sarik had attended. 'I hereby invoke the authority invested in me by this rosette. My orders are to be obeyed as if they came from the High Lords themselves.'

The Inquisition had such power throughout the Imperium that in theory, its servants could do as they pleased, enacting every possible sanction from summary execution all the way up to planetary devastation, for the survival of humanity. In practice, however, the extent of an inquisitor's power relied on his standing within the Inquisition, and the broader strategic and political situation. To Sarik's mind, Inquisitor Grand was on anything but firm ground, dealing as he was with highly placed officials and far from the Imperium's borders.

Sarik reached a decision, and was on the verge of speaking when Lucian gripped his forearm, and subtly shook his head. Anger welled up inside the White Scar, a feeling that honour and duty were being set aside for the aggrandisement of the inquisitor and his pet firebrand cardinal. The thought of the inquisitor unleashing a virus bomb and enacting Exterminatus filled him with seething fury, for where was the honour in reducing every last scrap of biological matter on Dal'yth Prime to a rancid gruel?

He took a deep breath, and Lucian redoubled his grip on his forearm. 'Sarik!' Lucian hissed. 'We'll deal with this, but not now, not like this…'

Sarik forced himself to calm, and nodded back at Lucian. The rogue trader was correct; Sarik knew that. Then his attention was turned back to the screen that showed Gurney's smirking face as the cardinal addressed the council.

'So there it is,' Gurney crowed. 'I suppose it falls to me as chair to close this convocation. Each of you shall be receiving his orders in due course, and these will be obeyed without question, on the authority of the Inquisition. That is all.'

'THAT IS ALL?' Sarik fumed as he and Lucian stalked away from the command post. 'How dare he speak like–'

'Friend,' Lucian said, coming to a halt and placing a

hand on the Space Marine's shoulder armour. 'You are a warrior of great renown, and I have nothing but admiration for your battlefield skills...'

'But?' Sarik interjected. It was obvious there would be a 'but'.

'But,' Lucian smiled as he went on. 'The council is not your native battleground. I don't mean that–'

'I know, Lucian,' said Sarik, smiling himself. 'You are going to say that around the council table, my skills are no more deadly than those of a neophyte.'

'Well, I wasn't going to go quite that far,' Lucian said. 'But essentially, yes. There is far more going on here than we just witnessed.'

'What else is happening?' asked Sarik, frustrated once more by petty politicking. 'What did I miss?'

Lucian looked back towards the command post, where several dozen staff officers and Tacticae advisers were already starting to break down the tacticae-stations and pict screens.

'I think we need to speak with Gauge and Jellaqua, Sarik. I fear there's a lot more fighting ahead of us yet.'

QUIETLY, SO THAT she did not wake the slumbering Naal, Brielle pulled the glittering water caste robes around her body and made for the door of her living quarters. She made no attempt to arrange the formal attire in the intricate manner it had originally been arrayed in; she had no intention of taking part in Aura's plan, and would not be playing the role he had ordained for her.

Pausing at the hatch, Brielle looked back into the chamber. Naal stirred, but did not awaken. She was leaving, not just Naal, who she had shared her life with these last few months, but the tau and the Greater Good. On the dresser beside the bed was the pendant

Aura had given her, the symbol of the tau empire. She was leaving that too.

Brielle took a deep breath, knowing that she once again stood upon the precipice. She had been here before; the last time when she had made the decision to leave Clan Arcadius and follow Naal into the service of the tau empire. Now all of that seemed like a dream from which she was slowly waking. The tau, she now knew, were no different from the clan or the Imperium. They expected her to play her part in their great games, to subsume herself within the greater ideal. How was that any different from her former life? The only difference she could discern was that the tau offered her no way to forge her own destiny, while her life as a rogue trader at least allowed her some control of her fate.

Her hand hovered above the hatch control rune, and for a brief moment she considered rejoining Naal and accepting her fate. But the notion passed as quickly as it had come, and her mind was made up. She blew the sleeping Naal a last kiss, and opened the hatch.

The door slid open silently, and in an instant she had slipped through into the brightly-lit passageway outside. As the hatch closed behind her, she took a second to straighten her robes and brush down her dishevelled, plaited locks. She doubted the tau would notice the state of her hair, but they had taken great care in the arrangement of her ceremonial robes, and she did not want a stray glance to raise suspicion. Barefoot, for there was no way she was wearing the hideous shoes the tau had given her, she strode forth along the passageway, her mind racing as she formulated a plan.

She knew that she had to return to the crusade and throw herself upon her father's mercy. That much was clear, for Inquisitor Grand would try to execute her the instant he discovered she was still alive. During their last encounter Brielle had assaulted him, burning him almost fatally with a burst of the micro-flamer secreted in one of the ornate rings she wore. She still wore that xenos-crafted ring, but it contained only enough fuel for one more burst. Hopefully, she would not have to use it.

She continued along the passageway, passing several earth caste technicians going about their business with typical efficiency. None appeared to pay her any notice. She was headed along the vessel's central spine, making towards the shuttle bay she knew to be located amidships in one of the huge modular sections slung beneath the ship's backbone. Several possibilities came to mind as she padded along the hard white floor.

The first possibility she had already discounted. She could have played along with the whole charade, playing her role as envoy to the crusade. Instead of delivering the tau's message that the Imperium should surrender itself to the Greater Good, she could simply have told the truth. But that would not work, because Inquisitor Grand was sure to be amongst those she addressed, and there was no way the mind-thief psyker would let her live after what she had done to him.

The next possibility was to steal a shuttle and make for the crusade fleet. Again, that was extremely dangerous, for not only would she have to penetrate the shuttle bay and force a pilot to ferry her to the fleet, she might simply be blasted by the first picket vessel she encountered. Still, stealing a shuttle could work, if she could find a way of getting to the fleet or to her father without appearing in the crosshairs of a trigger-happy naval gun crew.

That left the third option, which Brielle was rapidly

deciding was the only way to come through this alive. She would head to the shuttle bay and commandeer an interface craft. She would make for the surface, and from there try somehow to rejoin the crusade's ground forces. Perhaps agents of her father were down there, or even her father himself. Even if they were not, she could find a way of infiltrating the staff and from there make her way back to the fleet.

Her mind resolved, Brielle arrived at a junction. There were more tau here, technicians and soldiers busying themselves with preparations for making orbit. The *Dal'yth Il'Fannor O'kray* was approaching Dal'yth Prime from the opposite side to the Imperial war fleet, in the hope that the tau would gain the element of surprise when they revealed themselves and demanded the crusade receive their envoy. As large as a warship was, it was still a speck of dust compared to the bulk of a planet, and there was a lot of orbital space. Brielle calculated the odds, and came to the conclusion that even if the tau were discovered on their final approach it would still take several hours for the crusade fleet to deploy into a battle stance.

Then Brielle turned another corner, and the sight she saw her made her halt. The passageway opened up into a long processional chamber, banners hanging from the tall walls. The entire ceiling was transparent, affording a breathtaking view of space. It was not only the black of the void that was visible, but the upper hemisphere of the planet Dal'yth Prime.

The tau war fleet had arrived in orbit around the embattled world. Brielle knew that she had mere hours to escape, if even that.

The sound of a thousand boots stamping the deck resounded through the hall, and Brielle lowered her gaze from the sight above. The chamber was filled with tau warriors arrayed in such precise ranks that the sternest of Imperial Guard commissars would have been proud. They wore the distinctive, hard-edged armour plates protecting shoulders, torsos and thighs, as well as the blank-faced, ovoid helmets. The armour was painted a mid tan colour, which Brielle knew from her talks with Aura to be the most appropriate scheme for the dry worlds that the tau favoured.

The warriors stood perfectly still for several minutes, and Brielle was considering pressing on along the hall, through their midst towards the exit at the other end. Then a swirling blue light appeared in the air over the warriors, cast by projector units set flush into the walls of the hall. The light resolved into a face, and with a start, Brielle realised it was the face of the water caste envoy, Aura.

Brielle took a step backwards, her back pressing against the wall of the long chamber. Every tau in the hall was looking towards the face of the envoy, which towered high above. Aura appeared to be looking down at the assembled warriors, making Brielle curse the fact that tau buildings and vessels were so starkly lit there were no shadows she could retreat into.

Then the envoy started to address the warriors. Brielle was far from fluent in the tau language, but she had been taught its basics and picked up more as she had interacted with the race, especially those of the water caste. Aura appeared to be briefing the warriors, informing them of the plan to use Brielle as an envoy to the human fleet and to demand its surrender. The whole scene struck Brielle as odd, for Aura was a diplomat, not a military leader. She could think of no case where an Imperial diplomat would even think of explaining an operation to the rank and file. Certainly a military leader might give the troops a rousing speech to get their blood up, but briefing them on the behind-the-scenes intricacies appeared to Brielle almost a complete waste of time. It only served to remind her how alien the tau were from the human mindset, and how out of place she really was.

After something like ten minutes, Aura concluded his address, and the massive projection of his face appeared to sweep the ranks, something akin to pride in his glassy, oval eyes. Then he said a phrase Brielle knew well from her time amongst the tau. *'Tau'va'*: *'for the Greater Good.'* The thousand assembled fire warriors repeated the phrase in unison, a thousand clenched fists striking a thousand rigid chest plates. To Brielle's great relief, the image of the envoy faded, and the warriors filed out of the hallway.

After another five minutes, the warriors had left the hall, leaving only ship's crew passing along its length. Brielle cast another glance upwards through the transparent ceiling, where Dal'yth Prime's northern pole was still visible. So too were several dozen other tau warships, the blue flare of their plasma drives telling her they were assuming a station-keeping formation in high orbit. A swarm of small motes of blue light clustered around each vessel and plied the space between them, each the drive of a small picket, tender or dispatch boat.

Clearly, the tau were readying for what they saw as their victory over the Imperium. Brielle suppressed a snort of derision as she recalled her conversations with Aura about the extent of human held space. No matter how she had tried to convince him that the Emperor's domains spanned two thirds of the known galaxy and had stood for ten thousand years, he had refused to take her seriously. He had talked often about how the peoples of the Imperium would be welcomed into the tau empire, how they would willingly throw off the oppressive regimes of despotic planetary governors when the truth of the Greater Good was revealed to them. Eventually, Brielle had stopped trying to convince him otherwise.

But out here, beyond the borders of the Imperium, the crusade was isolated and exposed. The tau war fleet could certainly destroy it, though not without great losses. All the more reason to get back to her father, Brielle knew, and turn a potential disaster into an opportunity for gain.

Brielle smiled slyly as she hurried along.

THE PROCESSIONAL HALLWAY several minutes behind her, Brielle was padding along another starkly-lit passageway when she was forced to duck into a recessed portal. Up ahead, she had seen a group of junior water caste envoys, and they were heading in her direction.

The seconds dragged on as Brielle waited for the envoys to pass. She could not be sure whether Aura had been amongst the group, for even though she was well used to his features, tau faces still appeared to her far more homogenous than those of humans. Several technicians strode past, followed by a fire warrior in light armour carrying a long rifle across his shoulder. Just when she thought the envoys had turned off, she heard their voices getting nearer, and she simultaneously shrank back into the recess whilst straining her ears to catch their conversation.

She thought she caught something about armed escorts, and then her own name was mentioned. A moment later the envoys passed by the recess, and she held her breath. Then they were gone, their voices receding down the corridor, and she could breathe once again. Aura had not been amongst the group, but they had been talking about her...

Gripped by a sudden sense of urgency, Brielle straightened up and stepped from the recess as if she had every right to be there. She continued along the passageway towards the shuttle bays, knowing that time was rapidly running out.

EVENTUALLY, BRIELLE CAME upon the *Dal'yth Il'Fannor O'kray's* cavernous shuttle bay. Sensing danger ahead, she had ducked into a technical bay as soon as she had entered. Whatever intuition had made her do so, she was grateful indeed, for Aura, a number of his water caste juniors and a group of at least two-dozen fire warriors were waiting on the hardpan in front of the shuttle she was expected to be taking to the crusade fleet.

The shuttle bay was huge, at least a hundred metres tall and three hundred long. In common with the interiors of so many tau buildings and vessels it was brightly-lit and constructed of the ubiquitous hard resin material. Unlike most other areas, the bay showed some small signs of wear and tear, though even these were as nothing compared to the uniform state of decay and disrepair an Imperial facility of the same type would display. Small burn marks scuffed the hardpan, the only evidence of the coming and going of countless shuttles and other small vessels, at least a dozen of which were sat upon its surface. The far wall was open, the cold void beyond held at bay by an energy shield which glittered with dancing blue motes of light as a small lighter passed through and settled on hissing jets to an area indicated by tau ground crew waving illuminated batons.

Through the open bay Brielle could see the surface of Dal'yth Prime. At least two-thirds of the visible surface was land, and most of that dry and arid. Nonetheless, there were patches of green dotted regularly across the land, which Brielle guessed were belts of arable land surrounding each of the planet's cities. The seas were especially eye-catching, for they were a deeply serene turquoise, sparkling with the light reflected from the Dal'yth system's star.

From behind a row of fuel drums, Brielle strained her ears to catch what Aura was saying to the group. Such a thing would have been impossible in a shuttle bay on an Imperial vessel, which would have resounded with screaming jets, shouting deck crew, the thuds and scrapes of cargo being dragged about, the tread of lifters and a thousand other raucous sounds. The bay in front of her was eerily quiet compared to that, with little more than a background hum audible.

Aura was speaking in the tau tongue, but Brielle was by now well used to his manner of speech and could pick out a fair amount of what he was saying. He was telling the assembled tau to be ready to depart soon, for he was to return to the vessel's command centre from where he would be transmitting a communiqué to the human fleet. Aura's message was to inform the crusade that their lost daughter was returned, that she served the Greater Good with all her heart, and that she was to go before them in the spirit of peace. Brielle's heart sank, for she knew that such a message would damn her. Even her father would find it next to impossible to protect her from Grand, and then only if he did not reject her and abandon her to her fate.

Brielle's options were rapidly narrowing. It was too late to return to the tau, and if that message got out to the crusade she would be doomed. Her earlier notion of commandeering a lander to take her to the surface was looking increasingly impracticable, for it appeared that the tau warriors assembled in front of the shuttle were to be her honour guard.

Events were moving fast, but Brielle's mind even faster.

Hunkering down in her hiding place, Brielle considered her priorities. First, escape the tau vessel, then later, worry about getting a message to her father. She had to get moving before Aura could deliver his message, to somehow contact her father before the envoy ruined everything. She just had to get to the surface...

Then it struck her. She did not need a lander to get to the surface. Her heart raced as she leaned out from behind the drums and scanned the shuttle bay's outer bulkheads. Surely, there must be a...

There it was! A row of small hatches in the vessel's outer skin, each edged with yellow. It was what she had been looking for. All she had to do to get to the surface was to reach a saviour pod, an emergency life raft designed to ferry crew from a crippled vessel and if possible, to land them safely on the nearest world.

The shuttle bay's pods were out of the question, for she would have to skirt the brightly-lit space in full view of her honour guard. But she knew there must be others nearby, and so she hoisted her silver robes and padded off, back to the bay entrance and the corridor beyond.

Once back in the passageway Brielle assumed an erect stance and forced herself to walk at a normal pace. It became all but impossible for her to maintain her composure as she saw in the middle distance another row of yellow-edged hatches. She just had to pass a wide, open portal into a technical bay, and she would be away.

Her head held high, Brielle walked past the entrance, hearing as she passed the chatter and hum of the tau's advanced, the Imperium would say heretical, communications systems... the systems that Aura would soon be using to transmit his damning message to the Damocles Gulf Crusade command council.

Brielle halted as she passed the entrance to the communications bay. Aura would be on his way to the command centre at the vessel's fore, but the transmission systems were here, right in front of her. She turned her gaze from the row of escape hatches not twenty metres away, and looked into the communications centre, a sly grin curling her lips...

CHAPTER SEVEN

LUCIAN'S COMMAND POST was all but abandoned, the fleet staff having dismantled the majority of the tacticae-stations. It was dark outside, the cool night air gusting in through the open portal as Lucian and Sarik entered. A trusted cadre of Rakarshan staff officers manned those tacticae-stations that had not yet been removed, and these stood up and left as Lucian dismissed them with a curt gesture. Most of the remaining screens were blank, but two were not: those showing the faces of General Wendall Gauge and Captain Rumann.

'Are you with me or are you not?' the general growled, his face looking to Sarik even more craggy than normal. He swore he had seen Chogoran qhak-herders in their eightieth year with fewer lines.

'You ask much, general,' Captain Rumann said, his voice metallic but harbouring within it something of the raw furnace heat at the heart of the forge. The Iron Hand's voice was hard to read, but his features were even harder, for both eyes and much of his face were made of metal, the weak flesh replaced with infallible steel.

'I know, captain,' Gauge said. 'But I repeat. Operation Hydra must go ahead regardless of the inquisitor's proclamation. We can take that star port and scatter the tau before us, and within the twenty-four hour limit he has imposed. If we do that, he'll have no choice. We'll have got the crusade moving again, and he'll have to call off his Exterminatus.'

'And if we take the star port,' Lucian added, 'we still have the option of using it to transport our own troops. In whichever direction.'

Sarik's eyes narrowed as he considered Lucian's words. The general and the rogue trader were right; capturing the star port would put the crusade's ground forces in a powerful position, and force Gel'bryn's defenders up against the southern coastline. Sarik did not want to countenance using the star port to evacuate, for there was little honour in doing so, but the plan opened up more possibilities than simply going along with Grand's order.

'I agree,' Sarik said, his mind made up. 'There is no honour to be found in evacuating now, and even less in enacting Exterminatus.'

General Gauge nodded his thanks, and Sarik and Lucian looked towards the pict screen showing Captain Rumann.

The Iron Hands Space Marines were in many ways the polar opposite of Sarik's Chapter, and they measured such things as honour and duty according to a different standard. Sarik's people were the savage, proud children of the wild steppes of Chogoris and much of their home world's wildness flowed in their veins. The Iron Hands, however, were often held to be aloof and distant, a seemingly contradictory mix of emotionless, cold steel and the implacable, burning heat that forged it. Sarik knew such a view point was overly simplistic, but as with most stereotypes did contain a kernel of truth. Even though he had served alongside Rumann for several months now, Sarik still had great difficulty reading the captain's intentions.

'Exterminatus is without doubt the most efficient means of defeating our foe,' Rumann said. 'But much has been committed to the ground offensive. Veteran Sergeant Sarik is correct; there is no honour in evacuating as per the inquisitor's proclamation.'

'Then we are all in agreement,' General Gauge said. 'Operation Hydra is to go ahead, regardless of the inquisitor's orders.'

Sarik nodded gravely. As Space Marines, he and Captain Rumann were at least partly insulated from the wrath of the Inquisition. Lucian's standing and his rogue trader's Warrant of Trade afforded him, in theory at least, some protection. The general, however, was taking a great personal risk.

'You are a man of great honour, general,' Sarik said, nodding his head slightly towards the pict screen displaying the general's face. 'You alone of our number have much to lose. I shall not allow that to happen.'

'Nor I,' growled Captain Rumann.

Perhaps for the first time in the long months since the Damocles Gulf Crusade had been launched, General Wendall Gauge looked genuinely speechless, perhaps even moved. Sarik grinned, keen to avoid embarrassing the old veteran any more, and pressed on. 'Friends, I move that this session of the command council be wrapped up.' Lucian laughed out loud at that, and

Gauge's normally cold eyes twinkled with amusement.

'Let our next meeting be convened at the Gel'bryn star port,' Sarik concluded. 'No more than twenty-four hours from now.'

Several hundred kilometres overhead, in orbit around Dal'yth Prime, death incarnate was slowly awakened from a timeless slumber. Deep in the bowels of the Blade of Woe, *in a section of the mighty warship given over to the use of Inquisitor Grand and his staff, ancient and all-but forbidden devices were being activated. Inside a huge and lightless vacuum-sealed chamber sat a sleek, black form, enveloped within a stasis field and blessed by the wards of a thousand exorcists. A secret word of command had been uttered, and a cipher-sealed communication heeded. The stasis lock was opened, and that which had been held within stirred once more.*

The stygian darkness was pierced by a wailing klaxon, an apocalyptic forewarning of the end of a world. Flashing red lights penetrated the dark, their illumination sliding across the black form like oil mixed with blood.

Within that sleek form, a billion viral slayers were freed from aching stasis. Suspended in a blasphemous medium of hybrid cell nuclei, the slayers set about the one and only task they were capable of doing. They replicated, and with each reproduction tore in two their hapless cell-hosts. In a living being, such catastrophic cell damage would lead to death within minutes, sometimes seconds, as the host's cells were literally torn apart and their body reduced to a writhing sludge.

The process set in motion, death was inevitable. Either the viral slayers must be unleashed upon a world, to infect the nuclei of every living thing, or they would expend the artificial gruel they were suspended in, and potentially break free of their prison. At that point, the slayers would have to be slain, jettisoned into space or scoured by nucleonic fire lest a single one remain.

A deep, grinding moan echoed through the chamber, and the sleek black form was in motion. The deck beneath it sank on well-oiled gears and jets of superheated steam spurted from release valves. With a final mournful dirge of sirens, the deadly payload was swallowed whole, inserted into the transport conduit that would carry it to the launch bay.

The countdown to Exterminatus had begun.

AS THE SUN rose, Operation Hydra got under way. Sergeant Sarik was at the speartip of a mighty war host, and the sight of it filled his savage heart with pride as he rode south in his Rhino.

AHEAD LAY THE settlement codified Erinia Beta, and its strategically vital bridge. Behind Sarik was the crusade's entire contingent of Space Marines, the livery of their Rhinos proudly proclaiming the colours of the White Scars, Ultramarines, Scythes of the Emperor, Iron Hands and several other Chapters. The Rhinos were accompanied by Predator battle tanks, Whirlwind missile tanks, land speeder grav-attack vehicles and mighty Dreadnoughts. The skies above the column were filled with the whining of jump packs as Assault Marines advanced in great, bounding leaps towards the enemy.

As impressive a sight as the Space Marines were, they were merely the smallest fraction of what followed in their wake. Nineteen entire front-line Imperial Guard regiments surged forwards as one. First came the armoured regiments, each consisting of dozens of battle tanks, their huge cannons levelled at the distant settlement with unequivocal threat. Behind the armoured spearhead ground forwards the Chimera-mounted regiments of the Brimlock Dragoons, scores of armoured personnel carriers throwing up a storm of dust into the air overhead.

The host's right flank was made up of the lighter regiments, including the Rakarshan Rifles and the Brimlock Fusiliers. These would move forward on light trucks, then fight on foot, following in the wake of the armoured thrust and consolidating its victories whilst guarding the flanks and rear against enemy infiltration.

But it was towards the army's left flank that Sarik looked as he rode high in his transport's cupola. There was to be seen the most impressive sight of all. Even through the haze thrown up in the host's passing, the distant figures of the crusade's Titan contingent were visible. Gauge had massed the gigantic war machines into a single force, which even now strode forwards towards its position at the head of the advance. The first Titans to move forwards were six Warhounds, their characteristic stooped gait and back-jointed legs giving them the appearance of loping dogs of war. Behind the Warhounds strode the even larger, upright Reaver-class Battle Titans. Each of these was half as high again as a Scout Titan, with huge banners streaming from their turbo-laser destructors proclaiming the symbols of the Legio Thanataris. High atop the carapace shell of each Reaver was an Apocalypse missile launcher, each carrying as much destructive potential as an entire Imperial Guard artillery company.

Yet even the mighty Reavers were small in comparison to the single Warlord-class engine that followed in its companions' wake. As the Warlord strode forwards, it broke through a drifting bank of dust, parting it as a huge ocean-going vessel emerging from a seaborne fog.

Even at a distance of several kilometres, the ground shook as the Warlord advanced. Its head was wrought in the image of a long-dead Imperial saint, its gold-chased features ablaze in the white morning light. The Warlord's right arm was a gatling blaster, each one of its multiple barrels many times larger than a tank's main weapon and capable of rapid-firing a storm of shells. Its left arm was a volcano cannon, one of the most powerful weapons in the Imperium's ground arsenal, and capable of obliterating even another Titan in a single shot. A pair of turbo-laser destructors was mounted on its shell-like armoured carapace above each shoulder, in all probability making the Battle Titan the single most lethal combatant on the entire planet, if not the whole region.

As the Titans strode in from the flank, the Chimera-mounted Brimlock Dragoon regiments took position behind them. Gauge intended to use this mighty armoured force to smash through the main body of the tau forces and press into the city itself without even stopping. Aside from the tau destroyers, the Departmento Tacticae had not identified anything in the enemy's arsenal heavy enough to confront a Titan. On the evidence gathered so far, the tau did not utilise Titan equivalents, as so many other races did. That scrap of good news had been disseminated throughout the army, and was very welcome indeed.

As the tread of the Titan force shook the entire landscape, a deep roar passed high overhead. Squinting against the harsh morning light, Sarik saw the massed formation of the crusade's fighter and bomber force streaking south. Gauge and Jellaqua had committed the crusade's entire sub-orbital air force to a single, vital mission. The force was tasked with intercepting the tau's destroyers and bombing their airfields, protecting the Titans from their super-heavy weapons. Both leaders knew that they were asking the veteran aircrews to embark on a nigh suicidal endeavour, and the crews themselves knew it too. Nevertheless, the men and women of the Imperial Navy tactical fighter wings were amongst the most dedicated servants of the Emperor in the crusade, and every one had vowed to undertake the task given to them so that not a single Titan would be lost. Most of the aircrews had already received the last rites from Gurney's army of Ecclesiarchy priests.

As the massed fighter and bomber wave plied south on miles-long white contrails, the Imperial Guard's artillery opened up. Several hundred Basilisk self-propelled artillery platforms lobbed their shells high into the air from the army's rear, the first strikes blossoming amongst the pristine white structures of the tau city. The outer suburbs on either side of River 992 had already been relentlessly bombarded, and these were targeted for yet more devastation so that the enemy infantry defending them would be driven to ground. Missiles streaked overhead from Manticore launchers alongside the Basilisks. These fell amongst the defended ruins and sent up vast mushroom clouds as they exploded. What little cover the tau might have found amongst the ruins was blasted to atoms, reducing the settlement to a scarred wasteland.

'Five hundred metres to phase line alpha,' Sarik's driver reported.

The sergeant turned his attentions from the vast spectacle of the crusade army going to war, back to his own small part in the mighty endeavour. Sarik's objective was to take the bridge over River 992 at the Erinia Beta settlement. Though the mission sounded simple enough, the success of the entire operation would hang on that single bridge being taken intact, and without delay. Without that happening, nineteen regiments of Imperial Guard would be forced to bridge the river individually, an operation that could not possibly be completed in the face of enemy opposition and within the brief window before Inquisitor Grand carried out his threat of enacting Exterminatus upon Dal'yth Prime.

Sarik's grip tightened on the cupola's pintle-mounted storm bolter as he tracked the weapon left and right to test its action. The terrain grew denser as the Space Marine column neared the river, and Sarik trained his weapon on every potential hiding place he passed in case enemy spotters were concealed within.

Where were they? Sarik raised his magnoculars to his eyes and tracked across the ruins up ahead as best he could with the Rhino bucking and shaking as it ground forwards. Smoking ruins filled the viewfinder, and fresh craters were visible across the road leading towards the bridge. Still, no enemy troops were to be seen.

Had they fallen back in the face of the crusade's advance? The tau had displayed such an ability at the tactical level, when individual squads would pull back and re-deploy with well drilled precision and often-deadly effect. But for the tau to enact the same doctrine at the operational level was not something the crusade had anticipated.

'Two fifty, sergeant,' the driver reported.

Sarik's Rhino was now passing through the outer limits of the wrecked settlement, the scorched, dome-shaped structures clustered near the river.

* * *

'Slow down to combat speed,' Sarik ordered, before he opened the command channel. 'I want all Predators and support units forward, now.'

Sarik's driver steered the Rhino to the left of the road, its tracks grinding over a low wall and crushing it to a powdery residue. Three Predator battle tanks prowled past, one belonging to the White Scars and two to the Ultramarines. Their turret-mounted autocannons and sponson-mounted heavy bolters tracked back and forth, while the tanks' commanders rode high in their cupolas in order to spot any enemy that might lurk in the ruins armed with short-ranged but devastating tank-busting weapons.

As soon as the three Predators had ground past, three Rhinos followed close behind, two of the Scythes of the Emperor Chapter and one of the Black Templars. Each of these would shadow one of the battle tanks, ready to deploy the squads it carried to counter-attack any enemy infantry that approached through the cover of the ruins.

As the column pressed forwards, the bridge over River 992 came into view. It was an impressive structure, a hundred metres across and twenty wide. It was by far the largest bridge across the river, and far larger and sturdier than anything the Imperial Guard's combat engineer units could have erected even had there been time to do so. The bridge was pristine white, unmarked by the devastation that been unleashed on the buildings of Erinia Beta. Even a single stray artillery round or rocket could have rendered the bridge unusable, but the bridge was perfectly intact.

But that in itself raised further questions. The reason the Space Marines were ranging ahead of the main crusade army was to ensure that the tau did not have time to destroy the bridge should they fall back. Clearly, the tau had gone, but why then had they not undermined the bridge?

The lead Predator, a venerable Ultramarines vehicle with the title *Son of Chrysus,* edged towards the ramp of the bridge, its autocannon tracking left and right threateningly. Sarik's vox-bead clicked, and the tank's commander came onto the channel.

'Phase line reached, veteran sergeant,' the commander reported. 'Your orders?'

From his position further back in the column, Sarik had only a limited view of the bridge. He needed to know more before he committed his force.

'Choristeaus,' Sarik addressed the commander of the *Son of Chrysus*. 'Can you see any evidence of demolitions being set?'

There was a pause as the vehicle commander scanned the base of the bridge and the supports that were visible from his vehicle. 'Negative, sergeant,' the commander reported. 'No evidence at all. Request permission to proceed.'

Sarik had no time to consider the implications of the commander's request, for the crusade army was following hot on the heels of the Space Marine column. To delay the crossing of the bridge and the securing of the far shore would impose an intolerable bottleneck on the army, and the momentum of the entire advance would be lost. The consequences should that occur were too dire to ponder.

'Proceed, sergeant,' Sarik answered. 'But with caution. All other units, follow on when *Son of Chrysus* is halfway across.'

Dozens of acknowledgements came back over the vox-net as the Ultramarines tank powered up the bridge's ramp. The next two Predators edged forwards, their weapons tracking protectively back and forth, covering any scrap of cover that a tau spotter could be using to train a laser designator on the *Son of Chrysus*.

His Rhino halted by the side of the road, Sarik raised his magnoculars again, and trained them on the far side of the river. More ruined domes lined the shore, palls of smoke drifting lazily upwards. Dotted all around the ruins were stands of fruit trees, reduced to little more than splintered skeletons by the relentless bombardments. Sarik increased the magnification, his view almost entirely obscured by banks of smoke and darting cinders. He tracked left, towards the great loop in River 992 that led south around Gel'bryn. Seeing nothing but wreckage, he tracked the magnoculars right, his view temporarily obscured by the blurred mass of the *Son of Chrysus* as the Predator ground inexorably forwards. The shore five hundred metres to the right of the opposite end of the bridge was even more obscured, a pure white bank of smoke sizzling with inner turmoil making it impossible to see anything more.

Something about the white cloud made Sarik pause. He reduced the magnification so that the entire right side of the bridge was visible. With the view widened, Sarik could see what had raised his suspicions. The area of white was an anomaly, for the smoke rising from the rest of the ruins was grey or black. Where the banks were lit by orange fires deep in their innards, the white area seemed to shiver and pulse, as if charged by some unknown energetic reaction.

Then the wind changed, and the sharp taint of bleach filled Sarik's nostrils. Ozone.

'Choristeaus!' Sarik called into the vox-net. 'Ambush right, six-fifty, the white patch of smoke!'

Sarik did not need the magnoculars to see what happened next. The Predator's turret tracked right as sergeant Choristeaus located the area Sarik had indicated. 'My thanks, sergeant,' the tank commander replied. 'Standby.'

Then the white smoke was parted by the passage of an invisible, hyper-velocity projectile. It left no trail or wake, and struck the Predator's glacis plate at an oblique angle. The entire front left section of the tank was vaporised, tearing a ragged wound in the prow, peeling back layer upon layer of armour and exposing the Predator's mangled innards. The driver was killed instantly, his body directly in the path of the projectile. No trace of it was ever found.

'Power loss,' the tank's commander reported, his voice calm and steady even as death closed in on him. The white smoke that had parted when the projectile had been fired now drifted clear, revealing that it had been generated by some hybrid gas/distortion charge device mounted on a grav-tank. The tank prowled forwards threateningly, lining up a second shot with its massive, turret mounted gun.

'Choristeaus!' Sarik bellowed over the vox-net, though loud enough that the tank commander probably heard him with his own ears. 'Bail out, brother, now!'

'Negative,' the sergeant replied calmly. 'Engaging capacitor surge.'

With its power systems crippled, the Predator was unable to traverse its turret to fire on the enemy vehicle. But the tank was not dead yet, as Choristeaus knew. By activating the capacitor surge device, every ounce of power remaining in the Predator's machine systems would be flooded to the turret actuators. Enough power would be provided to turn the turret and line up a single shot, even as every fuse in the entire vehicle blew out. It was a last resort, and Choristeaus grasped it.

A dozen angry sparks went up from various points on the wounded Predator's hull as the capacitors were squeezed dry and the vehicle's fuses blown. Then the turret tracked right, and the autocannon lowered. The *Son of Chrysus* opened fire even as the tau grav-tank found its mark. The Predator's first shot struck the enemy's left thruster pod, the cannon shell slamming right through the slatted armour protecting the intake and exploding within.

Sarik fought the unseemly urge to punch the air in celebration. Before the second autocannon round could cycle into its chamber, the tau grav-tank fired. The alien gunner's aim must have been spoiled when his vehicle's thrusters had been struck, for the shot clipped the rear of the Predator, tearing through the armour protecting its rear section. The hyper-velocity slug was transformed into plasma as it impacted against the solid mass of the Predator's armour, which in turn burned its way through one of the tank's ammunition hoppers. A hundred shells detonated as one, and blow-out panels intended to protect the crew against such catastrophic damage were automatically jettisoned from the rear, a great gout of fire and burning debris erupting forth.

Less than a second passed between the projectile striking the Predator and the second autocannon shell cycling into its chamber. Even as the ammunition hoppers detonated, sergeant Choristeaus fired the last shell, which boomed from the cannon mouth and struck the tau grav-tank a metre to the left of the first shot. The joint between the grav-tank's thruster unit and its main hull was shattered, and the entire pod split off to slam to the ground.

The enemy tank slid sideways through the smoke, its pilot struggling in vain to control his vehicle now it was bereft of the thruster. He failed spectacularly, the solid bulk crashing into a nearby dome, slewing sideways and then flipping over entirely. At the last, the upturned tank ploughed into the ground, kicking up a spray of dirt as flames spouted from its wounds.

But that was not the last of the engagement. The rear of the Predator blew outwards as more of its ammunition detonated, its failsafe systems unable to contain the extent of the damage the hyper-velocity weapon had inflicted. Sergeant Choristeaus braced his arms against the rim of his cupola and pulled himself upwards, even as gouts of flames erupted around his waist. Then the rear of the Predator blew apart, the over-pressure escaping via the open wound at the tank's prow and the open hatch through which the tank commander was attempting to escape. The blast propelled the sergeant from the hatch and he was hurled through the air. He slammed to the ground hard ten metres behind his now furiously burning tank, and miraculously, rose to his feet.

Sarik had seen enough. He opened the vox-channel and bellowed, 'All commands, I want that bridge taken, now!'

Tank engines gunned to life and the Space Marine column ground forwards towards the bridge, dozens of weapons trained on the far bank lest any more ambushers show themselves. The two Predators that had followed the *Son of Chrysus* forwards powered up the bridge's ramp and sped towards the wreckage of their fellow. Then the three Rhinos that Sarik had ordered to support the Predators powered forwards, the first one slowing and dropping its rear ramp so that Sergeant Choristeaus could board.

As THE FIRST of the Predators approached the wreckage in the centre of the bridge, Sarik's Rhino started moving. The sergeant stood tall in his cupola, his magnoculars trained on the banks of drifting smoke on the far shore. He zoomed in on the scene of the destroyed tau grav-tank, the view jumping wildly as his Rhino pressed on. Flames were guttering from the tank's flank where its thruster unit had been blown away, and they were spreading, greasy black smoke spouting from several vents across the vehicle's hull.

Then the grav-tank's commander clambered out from the vehicle's rear hatch. He was obviously wounded, his entire left side blackened and his chest armour shattered. As the commander staggered from the wreck, several figures appeared behind the tank. Within moments, a squad of fire warriors was surrounding the wreck while two of their number dragged the wounded commander to safety.

At a shouted order from the aliens' leader, another warrior clambered under the grav-tank's upturned prow, risking the flames to reach the driver's hatch.

'I have a clear shot. Engaging...' the voice of a Predator vehicle commander came over the vox-net. It was Sergeant Larisneaus, the commander of the Predator called *Wrath of Iax*. The Ultramarines battle tank was aiming its autocannon directly at the fire warriors, its commander keen to avenge the destruction of the *Son of Chrysus*.

'Negative, Larisneaus!' Sarik snapped. 'They recover their fallen. Let them do so.'

'Sarik,' the tank commander replied. 'They killed my kin. It is my–'

'Negative!' Sarik shouted. 'They honour their fallen, as we do our own. You will obey my order, Sergeant Larisneaus.'

The other tank's autocannon lingered on the scene of the fire warrior dragging the unconscious or dead tau pilot from the burning grav-tank. The Predator pressed forwards at combat speed, its turret tracking to the right as its commander kept the object of his wrath in his sights.

The *Wrath of Iax* slowed as it passed the smoking wreck of the *Son of Chrysus*, forced to manoeuvre through the gap between the bridge's edge and the ruined Predator. Sarik's Rhino mounted the bridge and he was afforded a clear view across the shimmering waters of River 992 to the devastation beyond. He trained his magnoculars on the wrecked enemy tank, seeing that the pilot and commander had been dragged clear. The alien squad leader was shouting orders, gesturing for his fire warriors to re-deploy.

Then the scene in the viewfinder exploded in purple blood and orange flashes. With the wounded tau clear, Sergeant Larisneaus had opened fire. The Predator's turret-mounted autocannon and its two sponson-mounted heavy bolters opened fire as one, unleashing a terrible storm of explosive metal that caught the tau in the open. Rounds tore through alien bodies, ripping them apart in a welter of blood as limbs were sent cartwheeling through the air. The flank of the grav-tank erupted in sparks as stray rounds hammered into its armour, gouging huge ragged chunks out of the alien material. Within seconds, the fire warriors were reduced to smoking meat scattered around the upturned grav-tank, their blood splattered across its side.

'Honour is settled,' Sergeant Larisneaus said flatly over the vox-net. Sarik could scarcely argue.

'Contact front!' another voice yelled over the vox-net. It was Sergeant Jhkal, of the White Scars Predator *Stormson*. An instant later the sound of the tank's autocannon and heavy bolters opening fire rang out.

On the far side of Bridge 992, the tau were counter-attacking.

BATTLEGROUP ARCADIUS, LUCIAN Gerrit and his officers at its head, charged through the ruined settlement on the nearside bank of River 992. Explosions erupted all around and deadly bolts of searing blue energy whipped through the air. The Rakarshans were at the army's extreme right flank, guarding against the possibility of the enemy launching rapid strikes against the host's otherwise exposed edges. Five minutes earlier, such a strike had been launched.

Lucian threw himself against a mass of burned-out machinery as a volley of energy bolts scythed through the air not a metre from him. The air sizzled as the bolts zipped past and he felt his skin tingle at their passing. Looking back along his path, Lucian saw that a platoon of Rakarshans were following close behind, Sergeant-Major Havil at their head.

'Havil!' Lucian called out, but the warrior ignored him, running past his position with his power axe raised two-handed and his beard trailing behind him. More shots whined past and Lucian momentarily lost sight of Havil.

'Well enough,' Lucian growled. 'We'll do it the Rakarshan way.'

Lucian propelled himself to his feet, his plasma pistol instantly raised as more of the riflemen ran forwards. He tracked the pistol left, then movement from the right caught his eye and he brought his weapon to bear on it. A tau warrior had risen from a previously concealed position, a short, stubby carbine braced against his shoulder and pointed straight at the charging sergeant-major.

Lucian fired, and the roiling blast of raw plasma took the tau's right arm off at the shoulder, the backwash of lethal energies spraying across his blank faceplate. The alien screamed horrifically as he fought with his one remaining hand to tear the rapidly melting helmet away before the liquid energies melted through.

For an instant, Lucian felt a stab of guilt for inflicting such a grisly death upon another sentient being. He was just about to fire again, to end the alien's obvious suffering, when Sergeant-Major Havil did it for him. Voicing a shrill, ululating war cry that drowned out the alien's pain-wracked wailing, Havil stormed in and brought his power axe in a wide, horizontal sweep that scythed the tau's head clean from his shoulders. The decapitated head flew in one direction, while its helmet spun away in the other.

Lowering his plasma pistol, Lucian glanced around, scanning the ruined buildings for more targets. Furtive movement further ahead suggested the tau he had just shot was not alone, but no solid targets showed themselves. The sergeant-major's maddened voice sounded a second time, and Lucian saw an arc of purple blood spurting outwards from behind a shattered dome. He started forwards, the platoon of Rakarshans at his side. As they closed on the cover where Lucian had seen movement, the riflemen drew their blades and uttered their own chilling war cries.

Lucian and the riflemen pounded forwards after the sergeant-major, rounding the corner to see Havil standing over the bodies of three more tau. These wore lighter armour that the main line infantry, suggesting they were scouts or spotters of some sort. And where there were spotters, Lucian knew, there was inevitably something to be spotted for.

Lucian turned to find the platoon commander, seeing the officer running towards him in the midst of his men. He opened his mouth to order the man to get his men to cover, when he saw a red light paint the ground at his feet.

'Get–!'

It was as if lightning struck the ground not ten metres from Lucian. An instant before, the air became charged and his skin stung, then everything went white. He was propelled backwards to crunch painfully into the side of a building, though his power armour absorbed the worst of the impact.

Temporarily blinded, Lucian had little idea what had struck the Rakarshans. The air had crackled as a deafening wail had screamed in from somewhere to the south, and it sounded as if the air itself had been ripped in two.

Even after the explosion, the air was filled with crackles and buzzes, not unlike the sounds that dominated a warship's generatorium.

Then, just as Lucian's vision began to clear, the screaming began.

'What the...' Lucian started. The surface of the road along which the Rakarshan platoon commander had been running was a blackened crater, seething with arcs of bright energy. Inside the crater was scattered the charred remains of the officer and at least five of his riflemen, every single bone of their bodies pulled apart, their flesh burned away by whatever had struck them.

The screams were coming from those riflemen not caught in the blast's full effect, but who had been close enough to suffer from its blast wave. Men writhed upon the ground, arcs of what looked like electricity sweeping up and down their bodies and burning their flesh wherever they passed.

'Medics!' Lucian bellowed into his vox-link. 'All commands, I need immediate–'

Lucian stopped, the channel howling with interference that popped and crackled in time to the energies spitting from the crater. He looked around, and located his signalman, who had only recently returned from treatment for the wounds he suffered at the hands of the alien savages what seemed like many weeks ago.

The vox-officer was furiously working his vox-set, desperation written clearly on his face.

'It won't work,' Lucian said as he grabbed the man's shoulder. 'Go get help. Find Subad and tell him to get some anti-tank up this way too. Now!'

The signalman nodded, hoisted his vox-set onto his back and dashed back through the settlement towards the battle group's rear. As he ran he passed another platoon pushing forwards, grabbed the command section's medic, and pointed towards the crater. The medic followed the gesture, nodded grimly, and in an instant was at the side of the nearest wounded rifleman.

Lucian's skin tingled, and this time he took the warning. He dived across a low, ruined wall and rolled into cover just as a seething ball of energy crackled overhead. He did not see where the shot impacted, but he heard the detonation, and guessed that it had been aimed at the second platoon pressing forwards through the settlement.

'Damn it…' Lucian spat. 'Havil!'

When he heard no response, he raised his head above the ruined wall and looked about for the sergeant-major. It was no wonder the man had not heard his call, for he was up and running already, a handful of Rakarshans at his heels. Then Lucian saw what the sergeant-major was charging towards. It was a tau grav-tank, its turret surmounted by the previously unknown weapon that had unleashed the devastating energy ball. The tank was moving down the far end of the street, several dozen tau infantry flanking it as they passed quickly through the ruins on either side.

'Mad bastard…' Lucian growled, stepping out from the ruins. 'Rakarshan!' he bellowed, drawing his power sword and raising it high so that every rifleman nearby would see him and have no doubt as to his meaning. 'Rakarshans, forward!'

'Rakarshan!' dozens of voices repeated, accompanied by the metallic ringing of ceremonial blades being drawn from jewel-encrusted scabbards. Seconds later, scores of Rakarshans were charging headlong down the street, and Lucian was caught up in the ferocious charge, carried forwards by its inevitable momentum.

The Rakarshans discarded all notion of tactics and subtlety as they closed on the tau. Though expert stealthers and mountain troopers, when it came to the charge the Rakarshans fell back on the atavistic nature of their ancestors. The tau unleashed a desperate fusillade as the Rakarshans closed, felling at least a dozen in the last seconds. The rifleman to Lucian's left was felled by a gut shot, doubling over as he grasped his stomach to keep his innards from spilling out of the smoking wound. The rifleman to Lucian's right was shot in the knee, his entire lower leg blown away as he collapsed to the ground. Lucian bellowed along with the Rakarshans as he closed on the tau warrior only twenty metres ahead.

The alien raised his carbine and brought it to bear on Lucian's head. For one awful second which felt to Lucian like an eternity, he felt the alien's crosshair settle right between his eyes. Then an alien voice called out an order, and the alien lowered his weapon to the ground. He pumped the action of an underslung launcher, and a projectile spat from a secondary barrel. It slammed into the ground between the aliens and the charging humans, and Lucian's vision was filled with flickering motes of energy.

He kept going, as did the Rakarshans. Everything around him swam as the air distorted and perspective slewed out of kilter. Colours bled into one another and the spectrum abruptly reversed. Then he was through the bizarre effect, which was evidently intended to disorientate an assaulting foe, and upon his enemy.

The tau in front of him raised his carbine instinctively as Lucian swept his power sword downwards. The energised blade scythed the weapon clean in two, and then did the same to the alien's torso, spilling its internal organs across the ground at Lucian's feet before the two halves fell apart. Lucian continued forwards, and the next tau warrior died as its head was split in half by a high strike.

On either side of Lucian, the Rakarshans were butchering the tau infantry. What little resistance the aliens had been able to mount was rapidly turning into a rout as the enemy sought desperately to break off. The melee swept into the ruined buildings on either side of the road, and for a moment, Lucian found himself alone in the open, his power sword smoking in his hand as he took a great gulp of air and looked around for another enemy to slay.

A high-pitched whine assaulted Lucian's senses, and he looked up. Thirty metres ahead, the grav-tank was advancing, its huge main weapon lowering towards him.

'Sir!' the voice of Lucian's signalman rang out. 'Down!'

Lucian dived to the right and an instant later a hissing roar thundered down the street. He came up in a roll as the missile streaked overhead, and flung himself into the cover of the nearest ruin.

Less than a second later, the missile struck the grav-tank with a deep, resounding wallop. Then something detonated within, and the entire tank blew itself apart. The blast wave vaporised the road surface, throwing up an instant curtain of dust within which flames danced. The grav-tank's turret was thrown directly upwards into the air, the barrel of its weapon shearing off and spinning away into the distance. Then the turret crashed down into the ruins of the building Lucian was sheltering in, showering him with shrapnel and embers.

Lucian's power armour took the worst of the shrapnel, though its livery would have to be lovingly reapplied much later, and triple-blessed by a confessor. Though the skin of his face felt singed and bruised, Lucian was alive.

The jade sky above darkened as a figure was silhouetted against it.

'Sir?'

Laughter came unbidden to Lucian's throat as he focussed on the signalman standing over him. He let it out, giving voice to a deep, booming laugh that must have sounded to the officer like that of a madman.

'Sir?' the signalman repeated, bright cinders dancing around him.

'Glad to see you, lad,' Lucian said when the laughter had passed. 'Now help me up.'

The signalman took hold of Lucian's power-armoured forearm with both hands, and put all his weight into hauling Lucian up. As he stood, dust and ash fell away from Lucian's armour, the dark red and gold trim of his clan's colours almost entirely obscured by debris and burns.

The street outside the ruin was wreathed in smoke and a driving rain of glowing embers thrown up by the burning wreckage of the tau grav-tank. Riflemen were rushing past, firing into the ruins as they drove off the remnants of the tau counter-attack. Major Subad was striding towards him, another signalman hurrying behind him. Lucian was relieved when he heard the booming voice of Sergeant-Major Havil further ahead, pushing the riflemen onwards against the remaining tau.

'My lord,' said Major Subad as Lucian stepped outside into the street. 'What happened to you?'

'Never mind me, major,' Lucian said as he looked back down the street towards the scene of the grav-tank's first attack. Company medics were already getting to work on the wounded. 'Call in a medicae lander,' Lucian said. 'I want those men evacuated.'

'Yes, of course, my lord,' Subad replied, gesturing to his signalman to enact Lucian's order. 'But...'

'What?' Lucian said. It was obvious that the major had bad news.

Subad hesitated. 'What?' Lucian repeated, on the verge of losing his temper.

'I have just received word straight from General

Gauge's a.d.c,' Subad said. It was going to be very bad news.

'What did he say?' Lucian pressed. 'Out with it, man.'

'He wished that you be informed that Cardinal Gurney has just left the front line, and is returning to the *Blade of Woe*.'

'He's what...?' Lucian started. But he was interrupted by the sight of a shining gold shuttle streaking overhead. A moment later a deafening sonic boom rolled across the ruins, and the shuttle was gone.

'Bastard...' Lucian growled. 'Subad? Pass me that vox-set.'

WORD OF THE Space Marines' assault upon River 992 was disseminated quickly through every level of the crusade's ground army, the command echelons of the nineteen front-line combat regiments passing it down to their line companies, who informed the platoons. The Titans, now in position at the army's head, strode forwards, ready to support the Brimlock Dragoons as their massed armoured transports raced towards the bridge. As the army advanced, enemy counter-attacks gathered momentum, and soon it was not only Battlegroup Arcadius that was fighting to keep them at bay, but every light infantry unit at the army's flanks.

But the Space Marines were forcing their way across the bridge, and the order was given. Cardinal Gurney himself had been at the head of the force, bellowing his battle-sermons and filling the hearts of tens of thousands of Imperial Guardsmen with resolve and courage. When the first of the tau counter-attacks struck at the army's flanks, Gurney redoubled his efforts, ordering that his words were relayed through the command-net and amplified through the vox-horns on each signalman's set so that every warrior would hear them and take heart.

Gurney's sermons drove the beleaguered flank units to superhuman efforts, his furious imprecations ringing in the ears of the combatants, lending strength to the arm of the Guardsman, succour to the wounded and dying, and even planting fear in the hearts of those tau warriors close enough to hear them. Enemy units mounted in fast-moving grav-effect carriers looped wide around the Imperial army, the passengers disembarking to unleash fusillades of withering fire at the flank companies. At one stage the fastest of enemy cadres threatened the army's mobile artillery concentrations at the rear, which were moving forward in great, bounding advances while keeping up a storm of supporting fire for the front-line regiments. The Brimlock Light Infantry moved swiftly to counter the sudden threat, redeploying seven companies and holding the enemy at bay long enough for the heavy weapons companies to set up their field pieces and drive the enemy off completely. The fight was bitter and intense, but Gurney's words rang out across the battlefield as the sun reached its zenith in the jade sky, pushing the warriors of the Emperor to ever-greater feats in the service of their lord and god.

Then something happened. It would never be known who sent the original transmission, but as quickly as word of the Space Marines' assault across the bridge had reached the lowest levels of command, so this new piece of information spread equally as fast. Cardinal Gurney, so the message stated, had quit the field of battle to return to orbit. Yet, how could this be? The cardinal's voice boomed out of every vox-horn on the battlefield. Surely, Gurney was at the very leading edge of the army, only waiting for the Space Marines to take the bridge before he would lead the faithful across, into Gel'bryn and on to victory.

Then where was he? Concerned that this rumour would undermine morale, commanders and commissars alike hounded their vox-officers to seek clarification. But every channel was filled with Gurney's sermons, and no other transmissions could penetrate.

The rumour spread far and wide, sowing confusion in its wake. Where Guardsmen had fought with righteous fury, now doubt gnawed at the edges of their courage. Where previously las-rounds had flown with vengeful and unerring accuracy, now they wavered. Where men had stood firm in the face of overwhelming odds, now they cast wary glances backwards. Where the order to fix bayonets and charge into the very teeth of the enemy had been obeyed without question, now men hesitated.

And still, none could locate the cardinal.

Runners were sent from regimental commands, intelligence cell liaison officers seeking out their opposite numbers in the other units. Where is Gurney? Is he with the armour? The infantry? The artillery?

He was nowhere to be found, for he had indeed quit the field of battle. His transmissions were recorded phono-loops, broadcast by a vox-servitor left at the landing zone while Gurney sped away in his gold-liveried personal shuttle towards the waiting *Blade of Woe*. This fact took longer to discover and disseminate than the previous rumour, but despite the best efforts of the Commissariat, it could not be contained for long. As the runners returned to the regimental commands and informed their superiors of what they had heard, others overheard and repeated the tale.

Gurney was gone, so the initial rumours stated.

Gurney was dead, so others said, but that could not be so for his voice still rang out from the vox-horns, dominating every channel. Gurney had fallen hours before, others said, and his sermons were being looped over and over so that none would ever know. Gurney was dead, still others claimed, and was preaching to the faithful from beyond the grave!

Regardless of the exact rumour men heard, the effects were universal. The advance lost momentum even as the Titans closed on the nearside shores of River 992 and prepared to wade across. First the armoured and mechanised units slowed, the gap between them and the Titans increasing all the while. Then the infantry faltered as first confusion, then panic swept through the ranks. Men refused to advance, and the commissars were forced to execute dozens.

As the advance stalled, the tau redoubled their attacks on the army's flanks, and men previously galvanised by the cardinal's presence were suddenly terrified by his absence. Those platoons at the battle's leading edge began to fall back, and soon entire companies were retreating in the face of an enemy they had previously had no fear of whatsoever.

It was midday, and Operation Hydra hung in the balance.

SARIK YANKED HIS screaming chainsword from the torso of a tau warrior, the screeching teeth back-spraying a torrent of purple blood as he used his armoured boot to force the body down. The far end of the bridge was less than thirty metres away, but the tau were making his force bleed for every metre the Space Marines took. Already, over a dozen battle-brothers lay slain on the once-pristine, now bloody and scorched surface.

'Missile launcher!' Sarik bellowed as yet another battle suit dropped out of the air, coming to a smooth landing thirty metres in front of him. Sarik was learning to recognise the tau's weapons, and their capabilities. This one's arms were twinned fusion blasters, each capable of melting a fully armoured Space Marine to bubbling slag.

'Ware the fore!' a battle-brother yelled, and Sarik pushed himself sideways, right to the edge of the bridge. He turned his head, and for an instant looked directly down into the glistening waters of River 992. Then the missile screamed overhead, and Sarik gritted his teeth against the imminent explosion.

But none came. He rolled over, raising his boltgun as he looked back towards the end of the bridge. The battle suit had leaped high, the missile streaking beneath it and off into the roiling smoke beyond the bridge. It was coming down to land right in front of Sarik, its deadly blasters locking onto him.

Sarik squeezed the trigger of his boltgun, unleashing almost an entire magazine of mass-reactive explosive bolts directly into the enemy's torso. The first shots sent it reeling off-balance and it stumbled backwards on its claw-like mechanical feet. As more shots impacted against its armour, detonating with furious staccato flashes, it swivelled around again, bracing itself against the fusillade as it raised its blasters.

Then a crater appeared in the centre of its torso armour, and Sarik concentrated his last few rounds on that exact spot. Round after round buried themselves in the wound, and detonated as one. The battle suit quivered as its systems sought to respond to the nerve signals coming from the dying pilot's mind; then it shook violently as a jet of purple blood and gristle spurted out of the wound.

The battle suit collapsed in a still-quivering heap in front of Sarik, and in an instant he had leaped upon it and was brandishing his chainsword high. Utter savagery filled Sarik's heart, his conscious mind struggling to maintain control over his battle-rage. That part of him that was a supremely trained, genetically enhanced, psycho-conditioned warrior-champion of the Emperor of Mankind was fighting a constant battle against the other part, perhaps the greater part, that was a wild, untamed, undisciplined son of the windswept steppes of the feral world of Chogoris. No amount of conditioning or training could entirely rid a son of the steppes of that warrior spirit; indeed, it was the very heart of all that the White Scars were.

At times such as these, it was the savage that won the battles.

Sarik swept his chainsword down, pointing it directly towards another squad of enemy warriors rushing forwards in a desperate, last-ditch attempt to hold the far side of the bridge. He snarled an incoherent oath, and leaped forwards as his warriors joined him. As Sarik and his battle-brothers closed the last thirty metres of the bridge, the tau opened up with a fusillade of energy bolts so dense it felt as if he were charging through raging sheet lightning. A brother went down, his head split in two; Sarik could not see who it was. He bounded over the body even before it came to rest, gunning his chainsword to full power as he closed the last few metres.

Then he was in amongst the tau. His chainsword hacked left and right, and aliens died with its every stroke. Purple blood sprayed in all directions and stringy gristle threatened to jam the blade's action. He roared with savage battle lust as enemies fell at his feet to be crushed to paste beneath them. The white-armoured forms of his battle-brothers pressed in, and behind them came warriors bearing the deep blue of the Ultramarines and the black and yellow of the Scythes of the Emperor. Bolt pistol fire rang out from all about and combat blades flashed in the midday sun. The white of the bridge's surface was stained purple with tau blood and the air was filled with the mingled sounds of the Space Marines' battle cries and the aliens' terrified screams.

Quite suddenly, there were no enemies within Sarik's reach. Those not slain in the charge were fleeing headlong towards the ruins of Erinia Beta. Sarik bellowed in frustration and denial, and sprang forwards after them, cutting the closest down from behind with a horizontal sweep of his chainsword that hacked the alien's legs from out beneath it.

Not breaking stride, he powered onwards, the remaining tau fleeing before his wrath. The first aliens to reach the ruins turned to raise their weapons to cover their companions' retreat, but upon seeing Sarik's fury abandoned the notion and fled deeper into the wreckage and out of his sight.

As the last of the tau disappeared into the smoking ruins, Sarik came to a halt. His breath came in great ragged gulps. He spat, surprised to see blood in the spittle, and wiped his bloody face with the back of his gauntlet as a hand settled on his shoulder plate.

'It is done, brother-sergeant!' shouted Qaja.

Sarik stared his battle-brother in the eye, but it took him a moment to recognise his old friend. Then reason dawned on him and the red mist lifted. Qaja's face was stern, his eyes dark and unreadable. After another few seconds, Qaja nodded back across the river, and Sarik followed his gesture.

The Warlord-class Battle Titan was striding through the ruins of eastern Erinia Beta, every tread of its huge mechanical feet crushing an entire building. The settlement, already reduced to ruins by the crusade's bombardment, was now flattened to rubble as the engine strode forwards towards the edge of River 992.

The ground trembled with the Titan's every step, the waters of the river quivering as crazy patterns sprang into being across its surface. Its sculpted head gleamed blindingly bright in the harsh noon sun as its gaze swept across the scene on the far side of the bridge. It looked to Sarik as if that beatific face was casting its benediction on the battle fought to capture the bridge, granting its approval of the alien blood spilled in the Emperor's name.

The Warlord came to a halt at the river's eastern shore, its Reaver-class consorts stepping to its side, three on its left and three on its right. The seven Titans halted, forming a towering line along the river as solid and massive as a fortress's curtain wall. An odd stillness settled upon the scene as the Titans stopped moving, the only sound that of pulsing plasma generators and sizzling void shields.

Then the sirens spoke. The Warlord's voice was deep and resounding, its war horn filling the air with a slowly rising and falling dirge that sounded to Sarik like the dying cries of a gargantuan beast. But this was no mournful lamentation; it was a warning, and a dire one at that.

Friend or foe; be warned. I am the God-Machine, and I am your doom.

'All commands,' Sarik was forced to shout over the terrible drone. 'Heed their warning and get your heads down!'

Then the six Reaver-class Titans added their own voices to the Warlord's, and now it sounded like the end times were truly come to Dal'yth Prime. Space Marines boarded their Rhinos, which made for the one place nearby they knew the Titans would leave untouched – the bridge. As the apocalyptic chorus wailed on, the Space Marines formed up in a long column along the bridge, the vehicles packed closely for mutual cover. The assault squads, who did not have their own transports, swept down amongst the armoured vehicles, each Assault Marine taking what cover he could find.

Then the sirens powered down, the pitch and volume falling to the subsonic. A brief moment of utter silence stretched out, and then the line of Titans opened fire.

The first weapon to fire was the Warlord's gatling blaster. Rounds the size of men were cycled into the weapon's chamber, and fired with explosive force before the next barrel rotated around to fire the next shot. If a man-portable assault cannon sounded like a bolt of silk being torn in two, then the Titan's equivalent sounded like the air, the sky, the very fabric of reality being torn apart.

Round after round hammered from the rotary weapon in impossibly fast succession as the Titan swept its fire from right to left across the far bank. Each round was as powerful as a heavy tank shell, blowing out the already damaged structures across the river one by one as the line of fire swept along their length in seconds. Sarik had only previously seen such devastation from a low-level bombing run conducted by an entire wing of fighter-bombers, each successive explosion coming microseconds after the last as the detonations walked across the line. It was an impressive sight, even through his Rhino's vision block, and his transport shook violently with successive blast waves.

As each shell pummelled into its target, a blinding white blast preceded a rapidly expanding cloud of dust and rubble. Seconds later, shrapnel and debris began to fall on the Space Marine vehicles, some pieces razor-sharp fragments that zipped through the air and pinged on armoured plates, others large chunks that clanged heavily upon upper hulls.

Within seconds, the entire line of buildings on the Gel'bryn side of the river were reduced to dust. The Titans' sirens started up again.

The Warlord stepped forwards first, one foot setting down into the waters of River 992. As its armoured shin sank, the waters churned, huge waves crashing around. The tidal effect caused the waters to surge up and over the riverbanks, flooding either side of the settlement and dousing many of the fires with a billowing of white steam. The waters rose up the bridge's pilings, but the bridge was just high enough over the river to avoid being swamped.

The engine's leg sank down to its knee, and then it set its other foot down and set out across the river. A moment later, the six Reavers waded in too, the waters coming right up to their waists and completely swallowing the heraldic pendants slung between their legs. The Warhounds appeared on the shore at the formation's flanks, their torsos swivelling left and right as they maintained overwatch for their far larger companions. The river was too deep for the Scout Titans to wade across safely, for the waters would swamp their arm-weapons. They would have to cross via the bridge, once the Space Marines were clear.

Though the warning klaxons still howled their

doom-laden song, Sarik judged that it was time to get moving. As the Titans passed the midway point of the churning river, he opened the vox-net to order his units forward. 'All commands, Predators forward. Column, advance.'

As his driver gunned the Rhino forwards, Sarik hauled open the hatch above his head and took position at the cupola's storm bolter. In the open, the Titans' klaxons were all but deafening, drowning out the roar of the Space Marines' armoured vehicles. The Titans passed the middle of the river, huge bubbles and gouts of steam churning from the waters all around. Then the air was filled with multiple howling shrieks as the Apocalypse launchers atop each Reaver's carapace shell unleashed a salvo into the settlement. So dense was the smoke enveloping the shore Sarik could not see their targets, but the Titans were gifted with arcane sensorium systems capable of detecting a target in the most adverse of conditions. With each salvo, distant buildings erupted in seething explosions and defenders died by the score.

Sarik's Rhino rolled forwards, picking up speed as it cleared the end of the bridge, a dozen others, as well as Predators, Whirlwinds, Dreadnoughts and land speeders, following close behind. Sarik ordered the grav-attack speeders to range forwards, to scour the ruins for any sign of surviving tau, while the vehicle column formed up into an advance pattern before plunging into the ruins.

'All squad leaders,' Sarik said into the vox-net. 'We need to get clear so the main body can cross the bridge. Spread out as soon as you are across.'

There was a brief pause, then Sergeant Lahmas of the Scythes of the Emperor came on the channel.

'Brother-sergeant,' Lahmas said. 'I'm at the rear. I have no visual contact with following forces, over.'

'What?' Sarik said as he turned in his cupola towards the column's rear. Through banks of drifting smoke and dust he could just about make out Lahmas's carrier at the far end of the bridge, but virtually nothing beyond it for the smoke was too thick.

'Confirmed, brother-sergeant,' the pilot of one of the circling land speeders reported. Sarik glanced up and located the speeder. 'I have visual contact on the approach. There are no Imperial forces visible at all, over.'

'Where the hell are they...?' Sarik growled. If the army did not cross River 992 at Erinia Beta and take Gel'bryn before Grand's ultimatum expired, they would all be dead.

SEVERAL KILOMETRES EAST of Sarik's position, Lucian pushed his way through a crowded regimental muster. Grumbling Chimeras filled the air with acrid exhaust fumes and the shouts of hundreds of Imperial Guardsmen assaulted his ears. Hospitaller staff in a hastily erected medicae station did their best to succour scores of wounded troopers, and winding processions of Ministorum preachers threaded their way through the masses, dispensing the Emperor's blessings to all and sundry. Haphazardly parked armoured vehicles and knots of exhausted troopers spread out across a wide expanse of land, and evidently, they were going nowhere in a hurry.

By the time Lucian had located Colonel Armak, the commander of the Brimlock 2nd Armoured and brevet-general of the ground force, Gurney's transmissions had abruptly cut out. The cardinal's vox-servitor had been discovered and deactivated, and the Imperial Guard's command channels were finally clear of the incessant phono-looped sermons.

'Why aren't you moving?' Lucian bellowed as he crashed the colonel's orders group. Armak and his subordinates were clustered around the flank of the colonel's command tank, a huge map suspended from its side. A dozen heads turned towards him as he approached.

'I said–'

'Lord Gerrit,' the colonel interrupted, removing his peaked cap with one hand and sweeping back his stark white, sweat-plastered hair with the other. 'It's a miracle we're here at all and the entire army isn't hightailing it for Sector Zero. You were saying?'

Lucian forced his way into the throng of commanders and aides, coming to stand in front of the colonel. 'Good answer, colonel,' he grinned. 'But we need to get this force moving again, or we're all f–'

'Thank you for your astute observation, Lord Gerrit,' Colonel Armak said, a wry smile touching his lips. The distant roar of a Titan's gatling cannon thundered across the land from the south, and Armak continued. 'This is a mess, Gerrit, but I'd appreciate your input.'

'Well enough,' Lucian replied, coming to stand by the tactical map hanging from the command tank's side. He consulted his chrono, then looked to the map to locate the phase line the army should have reached. 'We're well behind...' he said.

'And the Space Marines and Titans are pushing forwards,' the colonel replied. 'Word's just come in that they've taken the bridge and are pushing towards the city.'

'Then we have some catching up to do,' Lucian said.

The commanders exchanged surreptitious glances. 'Well?' Lucian continued. 'What's the problem?'

Colonel Armak sighed as he replaced his battered cap. He looked around at his subordinates, before answering 'Morale is the problem, Lord Gerrit.'

'Gurney,' Lucian said flatly, noting that many of the assembled officers were now looking at their feet, the ground, or anywhere other than their commander. 'His departure.'

'Yes,' Armak replied. 'His sermons bolstered the advance, got it going, kept it going when the enemy counter-attacked...'

'But now he's gone,' Lucian finished for the colonel. 'And without him, the men have lost their spirit.'

Colonel Armak held Lucian's gaze for a moment, then nodded. Lucian understood then the colonel's problem. The Brimlock commander and all of his staff knew that Gurney's departure had caused the advance to falter and stall, yet they could not bring themselves to say as much. These men were from the same world as Gurney himself, had in all likelihood grown up with his planet-wide sermons. It had been his words of fire and brimstone that had instigated the Damocles Gulf Crusade. He had been the Brimlock regiments' totem, and they had been his favoured sons and his praetorians. When their home world's planetary forces had been raised to the Imperial Guard, they had been proud to pledge themselves to his service, and follow him into the xenos-pyres across the Damocles Gulf.

Now, he had left them.

Cardinal Gurney's departure had left behind it a vacuum. A grin split Lucian's face, for politics, as with nature, deplored a vacuum.

'Then we need to resurrect that spirit, Colonel Armak,' Lucian said.

The officer remained blank-faced, his eyes darting around the group to meet the gazes of several of his subordinates. 'How?' he said finally.

'Someone needs to speak to the men,' Lucian said. 'Whatever it was the cardinal gave them, they need to get it back.'

The colonel's eyes narrowed. 'Who?' he said.

Lucian recognised the officer's disquiet, and trod gently. 'You?' Lucian said. 'A commissar? That's what they're trained for…'

'Or you,' Armak said flatly. 'Is it command you seek here? You're known as an ambitious man, Lord Gerrit.'

Lucian forced himself not to appear too triumphant as he answered, 'That's been said, I'll grant you that. But I know my limits. I have no desire to take over your command, Colonel Armak. And none to preach against the cardinal.'

'Then what do you propose, Lord Gerrit?'

The scream of a mighty salvo of missiles being fired by the Titans rolled across the land and receded into the distance. Lucian turned towards the battle, marked as it was by a column of black smoke where Erinia Beta burned. He fancied for a moment he saw the dark shapes of Battle Titans moving amongst the dark stain.

'That we follow the example already set us,' he answered, gesturing with a nod towards the battle. 'You command, and I'll lead.'

Colonel Armak nodded, at first a slight gesture as if he were considering Lucian's words. Then the motion became more resolute, and he held his hand out towards Lucian.

The rogue trader took the proffered hand, and the two

men shook on it. 'Let's get things moving then,' Lucian said, casting a glance heavenwards as he imagined Inquisitor Grand's gnarled hand hovering impatiently over the command rune that would doom them all.

BRIELLE HELD HER breath as another tau technician walked past the recess that had become her hiding place. She had infiltrated the communications bay with the intention of disabling its systems so that Aura could not contact the human fleet, but getting in had been the easy part. Carrying out her plan, which in truth she had not entirely thought through, was proving far harder. She glanced back along the service passage, the bay entrance through which she had come now impossibly distant. At ten metre intervals, the passageway's walls were inset with a recess like the one she was hiding in now providing access to machine systems, and it had taken her far too long to penetrate as far as she had. But now she was committed, for she was nearer to the communications control system than she was to her escape route.

Not for the first time in the last few months, Brielle questioned her seemingly unerring ability to get herself into the most ridiculous of situations...

The technician was gone and the passageway was clear again. Brielle peered cautiously along its length. No more crew were in sight, so she carefully eased herself out of the recess, keeping her back to the wall and her eyes on the far end of the communications bay. She darted forwards silently on bare feet, and ducked into the last recess.

Peering from her hiding place, Brielle confirmed that the communications bay was empty. As she had proceeded along the service corridor she had noted the comings and goings of the tau. It appeared that regular checks were made on the bay's systems, but it was not permanently attended. Such a location on an Imperial vessel would be staffed by dozens of crewmen, and its systems maintained by even more man-machine servitors, many hard-wired directly into the machinery. The tau utilised what they considered to be highly advanced technologies, reducing the reliance on living and breathing, and fallible, crew. The Imperium warned against the folly of relying too heavily on machine intelligence, many considering it a blasphemy capable of bringing about the doom of the entire human race. Indeed, Brielle had read texts that claimed that such a thing had come about in humanity's pre-history, texts that ordinary men and women had no access to whatsoever. She shook the apocalyptic visions that text had described from her mind, offering thanks to the God-Emperor of Mankind that the path ahead was clear.

Taking a deep breath to steady herself, Brielle checked the charge on the compact flamer hidden in the workings of her ring. It read the same as it had the last dozen times she had checked – one shot left. She had not used the weapon in months, not since the deed that had forced her to flee from the crusade into the all-too-ready arms of the tau. She had been cornered by Inquisitor Grand, who had been intent upon probing her mind for signs of the traitorous thoughts he, quite correctly, suspected that she harboured. She had unleashed a blast from the disguised flamer, immolating the inquisitor almost unto death, and fled in the aftermath.

Judging that the way ahead was clear, Brielle slipped from her hiding place and entered the communications bay. It was a circular area, a good twenty metres in diameter, the ceiling a solid white light source. The circular walls were lined with large screens, across which endless streams of tau text scrolled. The characters meant very little to her, though she had learned a little of the aliens' script. Five narrow access ways led from points around the wall, and Brielle could see that each led into the bowels of the communication bay's systems. Picking one at random, she made towards it, then came suddenly to a halt.

The slightest of movements had caught her eye, and she slipped sideways, ducking into the next access point along. As she sank into the shadows, she watched as a small, disc-shaped drone, floating two metres from the deck, emerged. The tau, Brielle had learned, made extensive use of such machine-intelligent devices, some for basic security tasks, but many more for maintenance and other menial jobs. The heaviest examples carried weapons underslung beneath an armoured disc. Fortunately, this one must have been a maintenance drone, for while it was equipped with a jointed appendage beneath the disc, it carried no obvious weapons.

The drone floated on its anti-grav field into the centre of the bay and stopped. Its single, red-lit eye blinked slowly as it revolved on the spot, its machine gaze lingering on each of the access points.

Brielle looked behind her, desperately seeking any implement she could use as a weapon should the need arise. She cursed the tau's efficiency, for there were no loose objects to hand. As the drone completed its scan of the bay, its lens-eye turned on her, and the blinking turned into a slow pulse.

She made a fist, ready to activate her concealed flamer, though she was loath to use its last charge. But how else could she defeat the drone if no other weapon was to hand?

* * *

Two million, three hundred thousand kilometres was impossibly far from a safe distance from a planetary body for a vessel to break warp and translate back to real space. Not even the most legendary of Navis Nobilite master Navigators would attempt such an operation, for in all likelihood their vessel would be smeared across interplanetary space, and every soul on board smeared across the depths of the empyrean.

Nonetheless, at a point in space two million, three hundred thousand kilometres coreward of Dal'yth Prime, a wound was ripped in the flesh of reality. Were it not for the vacuum of space, the gibbering of ravening, hungry monsters and the wailing of every damned soul ever to have lived and died might have echoed from that wound, and driven any mortal that heard it utterly insane.

Writhing aetheric tentacles quested forth from the wound, some impossible leviathan sensing the lush feeding grounds on the other side of the gate. Then, as by a surgeon pulling tight on the sutures around an incision, the wound was drawn shut, the tentacles, if they were ever really there, slurping back inside.

The blackness of the void reasserted itself once more. But the starry backdrop of space was somehow darker than before, a patch of stars missing. Stars do not simply go missing, of course, but they can be obscured.

A black patch of space started moving, slowly at first, but rapidly gaining speed. Whatever systems propelled the sleek black form, they cast no signature on any spectrum the human race could read, though several older races might have detected them. It angled towards the distant globe that was Dal'yth Prime, and speared silently through space towards its destination, two million, three hundred thousand kilometres away.

CHAPTER EIGHT

AFTER TAKING THE bridge over River 992, the Space Marine column pushed rapidly through the ruins of the settlement designated Erinia Beta and was soon fighting its way into Gel'bryn proper. Prior to their entry into the city, the Space Marines had fought amongst the low agri-domes and service habs of the small settlements surrounding Gel'bryn. Now, the true character of tau construction revealed itself as the smoke clouds of burning Erinia Beta parted.

The city was built on a grand scale, yet it was wholly different from the sprawling hives of the Imperium. Gel'bryn had obviously been planned with meticulous precision, its wide thoroughfares and graceful, almost organic structures arrayed according to some grand, unifying scheme. Where humanity's cities continued to grow for centuries, even millennia, buildings often constructed in layer upon layer of rockcrete sediment, the tau built their cities according to need, and built another when that need was exceeded. It was a process of continuous dynamic expansion, but one that could only lead to confrontation with other races as space and resources dwindled.

As the Space Marines pressed on, it became evident that their assault had achieved some measure of surprise. Either the tau had not expected the Space Marines to defeat what forces had defended Erinia Beta, or they had fatally misunderstood the crusade's capabilities and intentions. Much later, Tacticae savants would postulate that it was the presence of the mighty war machines of the Legio Thanataris that caused the initial disintegration of the tau defence, the sight of the huge god-machines striding along the wide streets striking awe and terror into the defenders' alien hearts. The Titans, however, did not move as fast or penetrate as far as the Space Marines, for speed was of the essence. Besides this, the central areas of the city were ill-suited to Titan combat, and the Legio was relegated to a support role, for the time being.

And all the while, Sarik was keeping an eye on the column's rear, hoping he would see evidence of the Imperial Guard's armoured units following on in the Space Marines' wake. So far, there had been none.

The column passed through the wide-open spaces between rearing structures that resembled gargantuan fungus made of the ubiquitous white resin. The buildings were interconnected by walkways hundreds of metres in the air, along which the Space Marines could make out defenders moving hastily to pre-designated strongpoints.

The Space Marines smashed aside all opposition, the column becoming the very tip of the spear blade that plunged into the heart of the tau city. The manner of the defence made it clear that the tau had not expected any enemy to ever penetrate so deep. The lead Predators gunned down lone squads of the enemy's fire warriors. Many were attempting to re-deploy when they were forced to make a desperate last stand, their bodies crushed to pulp beneath the tracks of the Space Marines' armoured vehicles.

Individual tau snipers took position on the high walkways, their pinpoint fire striking a number of the Assault Marines from the sky. One Space Marine, the sergeant of the single tactical squad contributed by the Subjugators Chapter, was shot clean through his helmet's eyepiece while riding in his Rhino's hatch by a sniper at least two kilometres distant. Even as they had raged against the loss of such a valuable warrior, Sarik and his battle-brothers had saluted the enemy's obvious skill at arms.

As the column penetrated the city, pressing ever onwards towards the star port, the enemy's defence became more organised. Where before there was little coordination between defending units, soon the defence took on an altogether different character. Isolated groups of defenders were quickly and efficiently brought into a coherent command and control structure. Some defenders fell back towards more defensible positions, while others provided them with deadly accurate fire support.

But still the Space Marines had the upper hand, for they were able to bypass enemy strongpoints and render them entirely ineffectual. The column was within ten kilometres of its objective when General Gauge's chief of staff came on the vox-net to issue Sarik a warning.

'Be advised, sergeant,' the officer said, the channel interlaced by pops and crackles. 'Fleet augurs have detected a pattern of destroyers moving to and from the star port. Tacticae believes the enemy is ferrying rapid deployment units to defend the objective.'

'My thanks,' Sarik replied. 'What type of units?'

'Unknown at this time, sergeant. But tactical analysis would suggest battle suits.'

'Understood,' Sarik said. 'Interceptors?'

'All but expended neutralising enemy airfields,' the officer replied, sadness evident in his voice. 'The tau air force is now so hard pressed they are forced to use their remaining destroyers to ferry reinforcements to the star port.'

'Well, at least that keeps them off the Titans,' Sarik said. He looked to the column's rear, before asking, 'What word of the Guard?'

There was a pause while the officer consulted his tactical readout, then he came back on the channel. 'Brimlock 2nd Armoured is now across River 992,' the officer said. 'As are the Rakarshan Light Infantry.'

Sarik's brow furrowed at that – how had a tank and a light-role infantry unit crossed at the same time? 'Explain last?' he said.

'The Rakarshans are riding the tanks, sergeant.'

'Lucian?' Sarik said, smiling.

'Indeed, sergeant,' the officer replied. 'By all accounts, Lucian had a few choice words for the rank and file, and he got them moving again. The Dragoon regiments are close behind the 2nd Armoured, and the rest not far behind them.'

Sarik performed a quick calculation, then saw movement amongst the buildings up ahead. 'So we can expect to link up by what, plus eight hours?'

'Give or take thirty minutes, yes, sergeant,' the officer replied. 'Your intention?'

'Enemy inbound,' he said. 'We'll attempt a breakout, and I want it coordinated with the Guard. We'll hold the enemy off until the 2nd and the Rakarshans reach us, then we break out for the star port, regardless.'

'Understood, sergeant,' the officer said. 'Good luck. Out.'

Sarik closed the channel and turned his attentions back to the road up ahead. Two huge structures towered overhead, interconnected by a dozen precarious walkways up and down their length. He tracked along the walkways, left and right, to the points where they joined the towers. There, lurking in the shadows of portals at the end of each walkway, were the now familiar shape of tau battle suits.

'All commands,' he said into the vox. 'Enemy heavy infantry concentration, twelve high. Assume static defensive posture and hold them here.'

Acknowledgements flooded back as the armoured vehicles ground to a halt on the roadway, forming up into a ring with Predators covering every angle and Whirlwinds in the centre. The last voice on the channel was that of Brother Qaja, who was in the troop bay of Sarik's own transport. 'We're holding, brother-sergeant?'

'Aye, brother,' Sarik said as he lowered himself through the hatch, grabbed his bolter and located the heavy weapons specialist in the cramped bay. 'The Guard are delayed, but inbound, and we have a large tau concentration closing from the front. We link up here, and then break out together.' Sarik braced himself against a bulkhead as the Rhino came to a halt, the entire vehicle swinging forwards on its suspension before settling. Qaja nodded his understanding, then bellowed, 'Hatch open! As the hunter in the dawn mist!'

Sarik smiled at Qaja's use of the White Scars battle-cant, for he had barely heard it amongst the mixed Space Marine force. The battle-brother was a highly capable second in command, and the members of Sarik's squad were out and deployed around their transport in double quick time.

Sarik was the last to exit the Rhino, his armoured boots clanging on the ramp as he strode down and stepped on to the white road surface.

The buildings of the tau city reared all around and stretched upwards to dizzying heights far above. The squads were deploying exactly according to his orders. Sarik strode to the centre of the circle as the spearhead's missile tanks raised their boxy launchers ready to engage the enemy. It was relatively unusual, though not unheard of, for such a mixed force to operate together. Sarik had served alongside other Chapters before, most recently the Harbingers Chapter at the Battle of Sour Ridge. But in that action, the white of Sarik's battle-brothers had remained distinct from the deep purple of the Harbingers livery, and their chain of command uninterrupted. Yet here, the White Scars livery co-mingled with the blue of the Ultramarines, the black of the Iron Hands and the Black Templars, the black and yellow of the Scythes of the Emperor, the jade green of the Subjugators, and a handful of other colours. Sarik realised that he found the sight quite inspiring.

Silhouettes appeared on the walkways above and to the fore. Sarik judged he had less than a minute before combat was joined.

'Battle-brothers!' he bellowed.

The warriors, who had taken up defensive positions on and around the laagered vehicles, kept their weapons trained to their front, but turned their heads to heed his words.

'We stand this day, together, united!' Two-dozen bulky silhouettes dropped from the nearest walkway, bright white jets flaring as they descended.

'Our primarchs watch our every deed!' The air was split by a searing blue fusillade of energy bolts as the silhouettes found their range and opened fire on the nearest of the Space Marines. Shots whined in to slam against the armoured glacis plates of Rhinos and Predators. The battle-brothers simply waited, listening for Sarik's order.

'For the primarchs!' Sarik bellowed, raising his boltgun one-handed and tracking the nearest of the dropping battle suits as it neared the ground, its jets flaring to slow its final descent.

'Honoured be their names!' Brother Qaja bellowed.

'Honoured be their names!' three hundred voices repeated as Sarik opened fire. A moment later, the entire force followed suit as more battle suits appeared at the walkways all around and began their descent. A Dreadnought bearing the blue and white of the Novamarines Chapter, mere metres from Sarik, engaged its rotary assault cannon, the multiple barrels spinning faster and faster as it prepared to fire. The cannon raised as the venerated pilot of the ancient suit expertly selected his first target. The weapon locked onto a rapidly-dropping battle suit, and opened fire.

The burst of fire lasted only three seconds, but in that brief period, several hundred rounds were cycled through the six barrels from the huge hopper at its rear. The sound of those rounds leaving the barrel was a continuous, deafening scream. The battle suit was caught in the torso at a range of eighty metres and a height of thirty, and it simply disintegrated before the Space Marines' eyes. One moment the armoured opponent had been descending of jets of white flame, its weapons spitting seething blue balls of energy, and the next it was a rapidly expanding ball of flame and vapour. Tiny chunks of debris rained down on the Space Marines, not one of them larger than a man's thumb so thoroughly was the target destroyed.

From every walkway, scores of battle suits now dropped down on the Space Marines' position. The jade sky was filled with the yellow-tan forms, each spitting round after round of livid blue energy down upon Sarik's warriors. The tau were dropping down all around the laager, unleashing devastating bursts of fire and then taking to the air once more with bursts of their jets. The tactic was designed so that the Space Marines could not concentrate fire on one target before the battle suit was gone, leaping through the air to repeat the process elsewhere. There was no point moving squads around, for to do so would be to fall for the enemy's ploy. Sarik ordered the sergeants to direct the fire of their squads as best they could, concentrating their fire on the targets in their fire arcs with ruthless efficiency.

Meanwhile, Sarik concentrated on the larger picture, reading the ebb and flow of battle and predicting every probing attack the tau made. When a large horde of the olive-green-skinned alien carnivores appeared in one quarter, he ordered the Whirlwinds to open fire. Two-dozen missiles streaked from the launchers atop the tanks on boiling black contrails, sweeping high into the air before plummeting down on the aliens. The resulting explosion engulfed the entire horde, slaying a hundred or more as missile after missile detonated in their midst. When the smoke cleared, the surface of the road the enemy had advanced along was a mass of black craters, several hundred aliens blown to charred meat scattered across the whole area.

When the arcane sensors of the Novamarines Dreadnought detected the presence of tau stealthers working their way around to what they assumed was a weak point, Sarik ordered the column's land speeder squadron forwards from the holding pattern the flyers had been engaged in overhead. The five two-man craft descended on the invisible enemy like predatory razorwings swooping on a defenceless prey, unleashing a solid wall of fire from their assault cannons and heavy bolters. As the smoke cleared and the land speeders climbed back on screaming jets, the now visible remains of at least twenty enemy stealth suits could be seen, scattered across a wide area. The flank of the structure the stealthers had been sneaking around was splattered by great arcs of purple blood.

But the Space Marines were surrounded until the Imperial Guard caught up with them, and casualties were inevitable. The hated tau battle suits carried a fearsome range of weaponry, from rapid-firing burst weapons similar to the Dreadnought's assault cannon, to short-ranged but devastating fusion blasters designed to cut through vehicle armour as if it were not even there. Some carried flame projectors, but these were short-ranged and of limited use against the Space Marines' ceramite power armour, while others used longer-ranged missile systems to fire warheads fully capable of slaying a Space Marine or cracking open a tank with every shot.

The Dreadnought attracted a heavy weight of enemy fire, leading Sarik to the conclusion that the tau had never seen its like and were concentrating upon it out of fear and awe. The mighty war machine shrugged off missile after missile and its intricately engraved sarcophagus was reduced to a mass of smoking scars by round after round of energy weapon fire. Every time a missile exploded against its armour, the iron beast would stride through the smoke to return fire, earning cheers of adoration from Space Marines of every Chapter, not just its own.

Then the Dreadnought shuddered, swaying back and forth for a moment. With a crash like a granite column toppling, it struck the ground, sending up a plume of pulverised resin roadway. The Dreadnought was down, but Sarik mouthed a prayer of thanks that it appeared still intact.

'Overhead!' Brother Qaja yelled, and Sarik looked up to see a line of the heavy battle suits arrayed on the highest walkway. They were the same type the Space Marines had encountered at Hill 3003, their three-metre-long, shoulder-mounted main weapons angled almost straight down towards the Space Marines.

This time, Sarik knew there were no Imperial Navy Thunderbolts on station, and no 1,000 kilogram bombs to be dropped on the heavy battle suits.

'Land speeders,' Sarik ordered. 'Work your way around the heavy suits, but do not get too close.'

As the pilots acknowledged Sarik's order, he opened the channel to the commanders of the Whirlwinds positioned in the centre of the laager. 'How many Hunter missiles do you have?'

There was a pause as the commanders shared load-out manifests, then the answer came back, 'Twenty-eight Hunter missiles, brother-sergeant. But if you mean to use them against–'

'Duly noted,' Sarik interjected. Each of the Whirlwind

missile tanks carried a load of anti-air missiles called Hunters, in addition to their regular, anti-personnel ordnance. The Hunters were effective against air targets, but whether or not they would be any use against the heavy battle suits was unknown. There was only one way to find out, and no alternative.

Another of the hyper-velocity projectiles hammered down from above, striking an Iron Hands Predator battle tank square in the commander's hatch. The tank was buttoned up, its commander ensconced within, but the shot penetrated easily. The projectile turned to superheated plasma as it impacted on the armoured hatch, and the jet went straight through the commander, the tank's innards and out through its belly armour. The entire tank seemed to be pushed down as if by an invisible fist, as far as its suspension would allow. Then it sprang back up as its systems reversed the impact, but not before something deep inside detonated. There was a sharp explosion and a fountain of crackling flames erupted from the top hatch. Another three seconds later, the entire tank exploded, shunting sideways the Rhinos on either side, killing three Space Marines outright, and slamming a dozen more to the hard ground as the blast wave overtook them.

A chunk of blazing armour scythed through the air, forcing Sarik to throw himself aside as it passed less than a metre overhead. The projectile was as dangerous as any weapon. It carried on, striking a Black Templars Space Marine from behind and severing both of his legs at the knees. The warrior collapsed to the ground, but even as Sarik watched, retrieved his bolter and continued firing into the mass of enemy battle suits his squad was defending against.

'Whirlwinds!' Sarik bellowed as he pulled himself to

his feet. Those heavy suits needed to be shut down, right now. 'Target the suits with Hunters, full spread, now!'

The twin launcher boxes atop each Whirlwind whined as they traversed, elevating almost to their maximum angle. The augur dishes between the boxes tracked their targets, pinpointing coordinates and calculating trajectories. The war spirits in each missile tank communed silently as the firing solutions were communicated and the shots plotted. Then the missiles fired, one after another, until all twenty-eight were streaking upwards on hissing contrails.

The missiles banked and climbed, the machine-spirit in each warhead homing in on its designated target. The heavy battle suits saw their peril as the missiles rose in a wide spread, climbing towards, and then past, the walkway. Sarik saw the battle suits tracking the missiles as they reached their maximum ceiling, some of the tau taking a step backwards on the narrow, rail-less walkway.

Then the missiles dived directly downwards, and slammed into the line of heavy battle suits. As each impacted against its target it unleashed a blinding white burst of light and the suits disappeared in a devastating line of explosions that sent fragments of burned armour shooting off in all directions. The staccato *crump* of the explosions came a second after impact, and rolled out across the artificial valleys of the alien city.

'Land speeders,' Sarik said into the vox-net. 'Close and engage any survivors, now!'

As the grav-attack flyers banked high and dived down upon the smoking walkway, Sarik turned his attentions back to the tau attacking the laager, just in time to see a trio of battle suits closing from the east. A Devastator squad of the Scythes of the Emperor unleashed a fusillade of heavy bolter fire at the fast-moving suits, but the enemy came on regardless, seeking to close the range.

Then Sarik saw why the enemy were prepared to brave the storm of mass-reactive bolt-rounds. All three of them were carrying twinned weapons that Sarik had learned were the tau's equivalent of meltaguns, fusion effect blasters capable of reducing an armoured vehicle to slag in a single shot.

If the battle suits got close enough, they could open a breach in the laager. Sarik would not let that happen.

'Squad!' Sarik called to his battle-brothers. 'With me!'

Sarik limbered his boltgun and drew his chainsword, gunning it to screaming life as he charged towards the Devastators and the Razorback armoured fighting vehicle they were using as a makeshift fortification. The twin lascannon turret on the back of the vehicle spat a double lance of searing white light towards the enemy, striking the lead battle suits full in the torso. But amazingly, the blast, which was amongst the most powerful armour-piercing weapons in the column's arsenal, did not penetrate. At the last possible moment, a bubble of blue energy sprang into being, and the lascannon blasts were absorbed.

As Sarik reached the Devastator squad, he bellowed 'Weapons down! Chainswords and pistols!'

The Devastators obeyed without question, disengaging quick-release weapons couplings and discarding their bulky heavy bolters. Each Devastator carried a bolt pistol as a personal sidearm, for just such a necessity. As the Scythes raised their pistols, Sarik charged past, vaulting over the glacis of the Razorback and pounding towards the battle suits with a feral snarl on his lips.

The nearest of the battle suits raised its twinned

fusion blasters towards Sarik as he charged in towards it. The pilot hesitated, the suit actually taking a step backwards. The tau might be inexperienced in the realities of a galaxy at war, but they were fast learners, that much was clear. They were quickly learning to keep the Space Marines at arm's length, though doing so was easier said than done.

The berserk fury descended on Sarik again as he closed the last few metres. The fusion blasters powered up, nucleonic energies pulsating through their vents as they prepared to fire. The blasters zeroed in on Sarik, and he dived forwards as they fired. As he struck the ground, the twinned blasts turned the air above him into a roaring inferno. The heat caused the skin on the back of his head to blister and cook, and the hair of his topknot to melt and sizzle. So immense were the tightly contained energies that he could feel their effects even through his power armour, the war spirit within flooding his system with combat drugs to negate any pain that might otherwise have slowed him down.

As the blast dissipated, Sarik came up with his chainsword in both hands. He was right in front of the battle suit, too close for it to bring its fusion blasters to bear. He bellowed and brought his screaming blade directly upwards, seeking to damage the vulnerable ball joint between leg and pelvis. But as the chainsword swept in, the energy shield activated again, sheathing the battle suit in pulsating blue energies for but a moment, and repulsing Sarik's blade.

Sarik was pushed back by the forces unleashed by the energy shield. He ducked to the left as the battle suit brought its fusion blaster to bear, and as he did so he saw the first of the Devastators closing on another of the suits. Sarik shouted a warning as the other suit raised its twin blasters, but his words were drowned out by the furnace roar of the weapons discharging at close range.

The two blasts converged on the nearest Space Marine, turning his entire body into a seething lava-orange mass. In an instant, his armour was reduced to slag, great gobbets of liquefied ceramite blowing backwards and splattering across the battle-brothers following close behind. In less than a second, the Devastator was gone, nothing but a long smear of rapidly cooling, bubbling liquid marking his passing.

Bolt pistol shots rang out at close range, successive blasts driving the battle suits back one step at a time. Through his rage, Sarik saw that his opponent's jets were powering up, ready to leap into the air and redeploy nearby, so that he could fire from outside of Sarik's reach. Sarik needed to disable the battle suit so that he would have the time to drive his chainsword through its armour, but the energy shield was making it impossible to find a weak point.

Frustration and anger raging inside him, Sarik made a crude upwards thrust. The energy shield sprang into being again, rebounding the attack, but this time, Sarik saw that the energy was being projected from a small, disc-shaped device mounted at his opponent's shoulder.

Throwing caution to the wind, Sarik sprang forwards, grabbing hold of the battle suit's sensor unit head with one hand while he gunned his chainsword with the other. Bracing himself, he set his armoured boots on the battle suit's thigh panels, and hauled himself forwards to grapple his foe, or otherwise embrace it in a furious death grip. There was no way the pilot could have anticipated such a reckless move, and the energy shield generator activated half a second too late.

Sarik was inside the shield.

Hauling himself onto the battle suit's upper torso, Sarik fought for balance as his weight caused the pilot to all but lose control. The jets fired, but encumbered by the combined weight of the Space Marine and his power armour, the tau could only rise three metres. Sarik roared in utterly incoherent savagery, and forced the sensor block backwards as if it were the head of a living enemy and he was baring its throat to sever its jugular. He brought the chainsword down, its teeth grinding into the armoured joint between head and torso, sending a fountain of sparks arcing upwards into his face as if from an angle grinder. The battle suit crashed back to the ground, the pilot barely able to keep it upright under Sarik's weight. It bent almost double, whether through a deliberate attempt to throw Sarik off or simply as a desperate random reaction the Space Marine could not tell.

The chainsword shrieked, then its monomolecular teeth were through the neck joint's armour and Sarik sheathed his weapon. Using both hands, he tore the head from the torso, and threw it savagely to the ground.

Blinded, the pilot attempted to raise the suit's fusion blaster arms towards his tormentor. Sarik dodged back, his one hand grasping the wound in the torso for purchase while the other alighted on the shield generator. He grabbed the disc-shaped device and yanked it back with all his might at the exact moment that the pilot tried desperately to fire his blaster at the Space Marine, at perilously close range.

The heat blast turned the air to nuclear fire, half a metre from Sarik's face. He turned away, putting his left shoulder plate between his head and the impossible heat. The livery of the entire left side of his armour blistered and was scoured away in a second, leaving only the bare, dull metallic surface beneath, charred and blackened by the fusion blast.

The fire died, but the weapon was cycling up for another burst. Pulling himself up on top of the bucking battle suit, Sarik rolled over the upper surface of the torso and reached downwards to grab the weapon's barrels, one in each hand.

The weapon's systems had shed much of the heat, but it was still impossibly hot. Even through his armoured gauntlets, Sarik felt the flesh of his hands cooking. His power armour pumping ever more palliative elixirs into his system, Sarik strained, hauling the weapons around as the feed chambers peaked at full capacity.

The pilot could not possibly have known Sarik's intentions, and in truth, neither did he, for he was acting on pure instinct, his body flooded with adrenaline and potent combat drugs. The fusion blasters discharged, the furnace-beams enveloping a second battle suit, towards which Sarik had tracked the weapons' barrels.

The other battle suit's energy shield cast a shimmering blue bubble. Sarik bellowed as he held the weapons on target, forcing the fusion beams to burn through the shield. Overwhelmed by the titanic energies, the shield pulsated, before collapsing in upon its projector.

The battle suit's armour withheld the raging sun storm for all of three seconds before the panels peeled back, one laminate at a time, each layer disintegrating into billowing black gas. The instant the armour was gone, the rest of the suit was turned to liquid fire which scattered on the hot winds stirred up in the wake of the devastation.

Finding that his gauntlets were fused to the barrels of the weapons, Sarik hauled with all his strength to tear them free. The battle suit bucked and kicked beneath him, but could not dislodge his bulk. Then one hand tore free, pain flaring until his armour systems administered yet another dose of elixir. Though he could barely feel his free hand, he made a fist and powered it down into the open wound atop the battle suit's torso. It crunched through a layer of internal systems, before striking something soft. The battle suit went immediately limp and as it crashed to the ground, Sarik finally tore his other hand free and rolled clear.

As Sarik braced himself to bound upright and engage the last of the three battle suits, he heard a voice bellow, 'Sarik! Keep down!' Bolt-rounds tore overhead, followed by a missile streaking in from a position further behind. He was barely able to hold his berserker fury in check, the urge to spring to his feet and charge the last enemy almost overcoming the danger of the gun and missile fire.

He rolled sideways, and saw the last battle suit enveloped in a roiling mass of flames and smoke as the missile struck its energy shield and detonated. The shield defeated the missile, but the battle suit's pilot was retreating and was outside of the effective range of its fusion blasters. As the smoke cleared, the suit's back-mounted jets flared to life and it sprang up and backwards in a great bounding leap.

Sarik was overcome with the desire to tear the battle suit's pilot from the infernal machine, and surged to his feet with a snarl on his lips.

'Sarik!' he heard from behind.

He started forwards, his chainsword raised, before his

name was called again, this time from closer behind. 'Sarik!'

Something in the voice caused him to pause. It was Brother Qaja, his old friend, who he had known since both had served as scouts in the 10th Company. For a brief moment, he was back on Luther McIntyre with his fellow neophytes. Qaja was wounded and Kholka cornered by the mica dragon...

...Sarik drew his bolt pistol and threw himself forwards, determined to save his fallen brother from the beast's rage. Qaja called his name and tackled him to the ground, pushing him away from the creature's snapping maw. The beast distracted, Kholka darted clear, helping Sarik as he dragged the wounded Qaja from the cave. Only Qaja's shouted intervention had saved him from a fool's death...

Reality crashed back in on Sarik, and he realised he was standing in the open twenty metres beyond the laager. Brother Qaja had hold of his blackened, fused shoulder plate and was dragging him around to face him. Shots whinnied all around and savage explosions rent the air.

Sarik turned and looked his fellow White Scar in the face. For a moment, it was not *Brother* Qaja that stood there before him, his face a latticework of honour scars. It was *Scout* Qaja, his face untouched and unlined.

'Never do that again!' Scout Qaja had said as the three neophytes had cleared the mica dragon's cave.

'You said you would never do that again!' Brother Qaja said angrily. 'There is honour, and then there is foolhardiness... I thought you understood the difference!'

Sarik's rage lifted as his battle-brother's words sank in, and he allowed himself to be pushed towards the laager. The Devastators were falling back in pairs with disciplined precision, one covering the other with his bolt pistol as they fought their way back to the vehicles. A lull seemed to have settled on the scene of the battle, the tau pulling back to regroup after their failed attempt to breach the Space Marines' defences. In less than a minute, Sarik and Qaja were back within the circle of armoured vehicles.

'This time, brother,' Sarik said as he caught his breath. 'This time, I mean it.'

Qaja's face was grim as his dark eyes bored into Sarik's. Then he nodded, and said, 'This time, I believe you. You are master here, you must rein in your battle-lust, but you know that already, I am sure.'

'Aye, brother,' Sarik said, looking around the laager and noting the casualties suffered in the first wave of assaults. 'Too many rely upon me for me to indulge in such things.'

'Not unless you truly have no alternative,' Qaja said. 'I shall say no more on the matter.'

But Sarik was not content with that. 'No, brother,' he said. 'If you need to do so, you must. I shall seek the counsel of the Chaplains later, but in the meantime, you must be my confessor.'

'And if you do not heed my words?' Qaja said, a wry grin creasing his scarred face.

'Then you can strike me down,' Sarik smiled, 'just like you did on Luther McIntyre.'

'I promise it, brother,' Qaja replied. 'I–'

The air shuddered as the Whirlwinds opened fire again, three-dozen missiles streaking overhead to detonate amongst another wave of the savage alien carnivores surging towards the laager. Sarik clapped his battle-brother's shoulder, then bellowed orders as he strode to the nearest squad, ready to man the defences.

Qaja hoisted his plasma cannon and checked its power cycle, then followed after his friend and commander.

'Repeat last, Korvane!' Lucian shouted into the vox-horn, one hand clamping the phones around his head. 'You're breaking up!'

Lucian was hitching a ride in a Chimera belonging to the 2nd Armoured's regimental intelligence cell, and the transport bucked and jolted as it hurtled at top speed along the road to the Gel'bryn star port. The passenger bay was cramped, filled with staff officers working field-cogitation stations and yelling into vox-sets. Lucian could barely hear himself think, let alone what Korvane was saying.

'I said,' Korvane's voice cut through the burbling static, 'I'm going to try to rally the council against the inquisitor. I've got to do something. I can't just stand by and watch him go through with this!'

'I understand, Korvane,' Lucian said. 'But there's nothing the council can do. It's been dissolved, as well you know–'

'Only because he says it has, father,' Korvane interjected. 'And only because the councillors accept his authority.'

'He's an inquisitor, Korvane,' Lucian hissed, trying not to be overheard by the other passengers of the command Chimera. It was practically impossible, but it seemed the staff officers had their own concerns and none were at all bothered with his. 'He can do what he wants.'

'Father,' Korvane said, his tone almost chiding. 'You know as well as I that his authority beyond the Imperium relies on others acknowledging it. His rosette holds no more inherent authority than your warrant, or the council's charter. The council only accepts its dissolution because its members are scared of him.'

'And with good reason, son,' Lucian said. 'You're right; we're all peers out here, but what happens when we get back to Imperial space? If we make an enemy of him, a real enemy, we make an enemy of the entire Inquisition.

'And besides,' Lucian continued, 'he has a damned virus bomb.'

There was a pause, punctuated by popping static and low, churning feedback. Then Korvane answered, 'Father, I'm going to try to stop him. I don't know–'

'You cannot!' Lucian growled. 'Son, you're the sole inheritor of the warrant. There is no second in line!' Not since Brielle had disappeared, presumed dead. There was a third in line, but he was a pampered imbecile, and aside from a few distant cousins Lucian had no desire to see the Clan Arcadius go to anyone but his son on his own death.

'Leave this to me, father,' Korvane replied, his tone resolved. 'I have to do something, and I will. You are needed at the front; I am needed here.'

'Well enough, Korvane,' Lucian said, his words belying what he felt inside. He looked across the command Chimera's transport bay, towards the glowing map displayed on a nearby tacticae-station. The 2nd Armoured was coming up on ten kilometres from the star port, and would soon be linking up with Sarik's Space Marine force. Five other regiments were close behind, and the Deathbringers moving in support. If the combined force could push through the tau and take the star port, Inquisitor Grand might call off his insane plan to virus bomb Dal'yth Prime. If not, Lucian might be able to return to orbit and stop his son getting himself killed.

'Good luck, son,' Lucian signed off. 'Damn fool offspring...'

* * *

Brielle held perfectly still as the drone approached, its slowly pulsing, red-lit lens-eye closing on her as she waited in the shadows of the recess off the communications bay. She pressed backwards into the shadows, feeling her way behind her with her left hand while with the other she prepared to unleash the last, precious load of her digital flamer. As she ghosted back, the drone came on – surely, it had not discovered her presence, for it would have raised an alarm had it done so. Perhaps it had just glimpsed movement and was following some pre-programmed imperative to investigate. Or perhaps it had raised a silent alarm, and a squad of armed warriors was rushing to detain her even now.

A small, levered arm unfolded from beneath the drone's disc-shaped body, an unidentified tool clicking at its end. It was less than three meters away, level with the end of the shadowed recess, and still it had not seen her. From her hiding place, Brielle studied the drone, deciding that it must be some low-level maintenance machine, with a correspondingly low level of intelligence or will.

The tool levered out in front of the drone, and touched a piece of wall-mounted machinery. Brielle's eyes followed the movement, and she saw that the drone was more interested in the communications subsystems lining the recess than in her. In fact, she saw with a small smile, it was straightening up a piece of looped cabling she had disturbed as she had pressed backwards.

A thought struck her. Keeping her eye on the drone's pulsing eye-lens, she stepped backwards still further, the recess becoming all the more narrow and cramped as she penetrated deeper into the communication bay's innards. Her hand behind her tracing the wall, she located another cable run, and took it in her grip. Then she looked around slowly, careful not to make too sudden a movement in case she drew the drone's attention, and found another. She knew enough of the tau script to understand the meaning of the characters stencilled across a junction box the second set of cabling led to: danger.

Last chance, she thought as she flexed the finger on which she wore the concealed flamer. Use the last charge, or take a risk on the cabling. She had never shied away from risk, and would not be starting now.

The hand that gripped the first loop of cabling tightened, and Brielle committed herself. She pulled hard, and yanked the cable from its terminal, darting backwards beyond the second cable's junction box as she did so. A sharp, bright discharge filled the dark recess, and Brielle was blinded for a brief moment. She felt her way along the walls, and crouched down. As her vision returned, she saw that the drone had closed on the damaged cable, its tool-arm re-seating the ripped-free cable even as she watched.

Knowing it was now or never, Brielle reached up and gripped the second cable. This time, she closed her eyes as a bright arc of power leaped from the end. Raising the spitting cable high, she stabbed upwards, and plunged its end into the drone's exposed underbelly.

With a high-pitched, electronic screech that sounded disturbingly organic, the drone's systems erupted in sizzling lightning. Small arcs of power seethed around its body, up and down its levered tool-arm and along the cable it was holding. The drone hovered there, shaking violently as smoke begun to belch from vents around the upper facing of its disc.

It hovered there for another ten seconds, Brielle watching from the very end of the recess. Then it shuddered one last time and exploded, white-hot, razor-sharp fragments of its body scything in all directions. When the smoke cleared, a dozen small fires had sprung into being amongst the systems hidden in the recess, but Brielle was unscathed.

Brielle suppressed a wicked laugh as she realised that the drone's destruction might be the perfect way of crippling the communications bay. Then she heard a hissing sound, and glanced upwards. Some manner of fire suppression system, mounted in the recess's ceiling. It hadn't yet kicked in, but it would, within seconds. She guessed that whatever gas would spring forth would starve the fire of oxygen, hence there would be an in-built, if slim, delay to allow crew the chance to get clear.

Brielle's eyes tracked the pipework emerging from the suppression vent, across the ceiling, down the bulkhead, along, to a junction box three metres away. She crossed to it quickly, intently aware that she might only have seconds before the lethal gases erupted from directly overhead. The box was stencilled with a line of unfamiliar characters… she ripped the front off, and stared into a mess of cables and blinking control studs, three blue, one red.

'Never press the red one…' she said, her fingers hovering over the blue control studs.

The fires were taking hold, and the hissing overhead was increasing as the fire suppression system prepared to pump oxygen-starving gases into the communications bay. She pressed the red one.

The hissing immediately died. She turned, and saw that the fires were now engulfing the recess, and spreading towards her. A small explosion *crumped* from somewhere nearby, followed an instant later by the sound of glass shattering across the floor of the main bay. The damage was spreading faster than even Brielle could have expected.

Time to be somewhere else.

THE SPACE MARINE armoured column was once more advancing through the thoroughfares of Gel'bryn City, smashing the tau defence aside as it speared towards its ultimate objective, the star port. As the spearhead advanced deeper into the city, the structures became ever more imposing until the Space Marines and their vehicles were dwarfed by the towering buildings. The tau had disengaged soon after Sarik's slaying of the battle suits, though the sergeant suspected the two events were not connected. More likely, the tau had detected the Brimlock 2nd Armoured moving to link up with the Space Marines and quite sensibly determined they were outnumbered and outmatched.

The instant the tau assaults lessened, Sarik ordered the laagered Space Marine vehicles to assume an attacking formation once more. Within minutes, several hundred Space Marines of a dozen different Chapters were aboard their transports again, which moved out in a long column punctuated by Predator battle tanks, Whirlwind missile tanks and stomping Dreadnoughts. Space Marine assault squads moved forwards in great bounding leaps, guarding the column's flanks against enemy counter-attack. The Assault Marines engaged dozens of the laser-designator-armed spotters, slaughtering the aliens before they could bring indirect missile fire onto the armoured vehicles. The assault squads were by now well-practised in locating the spotters' hiding places, and what mere days ago had been a lethal threat was now expertly countered.

Land speeder squadrons soared overhead on screaming jets, providing Sarik with a continuous reconnaissance of the tau defences further ahead. Several times, the land speeders were intercepted by heavy gun drones. Two speeders were lost in the first engagement, one belonging to the White Scars and one to the Iron Hands, though two of their crew survived, to be rescued by an Ultramarines assault squad and join the ground forces. Later engagements saw the land speeders avoid dogfighting with the heavy gun drones, and call in ground-to-air Hunter missile fire from the Whirlwinds stationed along the length of the column.

The advance was a stop-start affair, for the tau forces were highly mobile and well able to mount localised defences at key points in the city. Sarik soon realised that the tau were either falling back to the star port, or they had guessed that it was the Imperium's objective. As the column pressed on, it encountered hastily mounted defence positions from which the tau would attempt to ambush the Space Marines before falling back in their on-station anti-grav carriers. Sarik's orders were clear – such defences were to be bypassed, and engaged where necessary by the trailing forces of the Imperial Guard. In most cases, the positions were abandoned long before the Imperial Guard reached them, the tau re-deploying to the next ambush point ahead.

As the sky darkened with the approach of evening, the combined advance of the Space Marines, Imperial Guard and Adeptus Titanicus developed into a series of running battles against a seemingly piecemeal defence. While the Space Marines spearheaded a focussed assault, the Imperial Guard spread out onto multiple axes as they pressed on, the better to take advantage of their numbers. Entire regiments of tanks rolled aside any opposition they encountered, though only the heavy battle suits even dared make a concerted stand against such forces. Dragoon regiments moved forward rapidly, armoured fist squads using their Chimera transports as mobile bunkers and fire support bases as they dismounted and cleared enemy-held positions with bayonets fixed. While the Rakarshans rode forwards on the backs of the 2nd Armoured's tanks, other light infantry units followed on foot, using their skills in fieldcraft to move rapidly through the urban terrain.

The Titans of Legio Thanataris split into smaller formations, each moving out to support the advance on its far flanks. The Titans unleashed holy hell on every tau defence point they encountered, flattening structures hundreds of metres tall and striding through the high walkways, causing hundreds of defenders to plummet to their deaths in the streets far below.

With their remaining destroyers committed to ferrying troops to the star port, the tau were unable to oppose the Titans, though they made repeated and numerous attempts to do so. Tau stealth suits launched desperate and often suicidal attacks against the Titans, leaping from high structures in an effort to board the mighty war machines.

Using fusion blasters, the stealthers attempted to cut through the Titans' ceramite armoured shells and disable the systems within. One group swarmed over a Reaver Battle Titan in an attempt to overwhelm its armour and inflict death by a thousand cuts. At first, the Reaver's princeps was dismissive of the threat, determined to ignore the attackers as beneath his notice and deserving of no more than contempt. Only when his Titans' Apocalypse launcher was disabled did he take the threat seriously. His answer to the boarding attempt was to smash his Titan through a nearby building that was taller than his war machine. The entire structure burst apart as the Reaver strode through it, the collapsing debris scouring the stealthers from its body and leaving the Titan coated in a layer of bone-white dust that lent it the aspect of a gargantuan apparition.

Soon after, the Warlord Battle Titan was assaulted by at least sixty tau stealth suits deployed from the bowels of an armoured transport that soared high overhead. The battle suits descended on their target like drop troops onto a bastion, and immediately turned their fusion blasters on the turbo-laser destructors. The Warlord's princeps was not so fast to dismiss the threat, yet his war machine was too tall to repeat the Reaver's act of smashing through a building. Instead, the princeps ordered three nearby Warhound Scout Titans to turn their Vulcan mega-bolters on him.

The Warhounds' princeps were loath to fire on their commander's sacred engine, but were ordered to do so on threat of disciplinary action. The three Warhounds opened fire, and the Warlord's entire upper body was stitched with thousands upon thousands of rapid-firing, mass-reactive explosive shells. Though the Warlord suffered multiple minor systems damage, the enemy attackers were utterly wiped out. Their purple blood was smeared across the Titan's upper hull in garish patterns that would stain its livery for years to come despite the best efforts of legions of artificers.

The battles did not go entirely in the Imperium's favour. Inevitably, some units became separated as the advance penetrated deeper into the city and became encircled and destroyed entirely by rapidly counter-attacking enemy units. One of the 4th Brimlock Dragoons heavy weapons companies was engaged by a wing of extremely agile tau skimmers, their Chimeras outflanked and torn to shreds as the squads attempted to deploy their heavy weapons against a foe they could not get a fix on. The 4th Storm Trooper company turned back from its advance to attempt a link-up with the dragoons, but was outflanked and pinned down by the skimmers. A Warhound Titan was in turn ordered to aid the stormtroopers, but by the time the skimmers were driven off by the war machine's sustained Vulcan mega-bolter fire, the dragoons were all but wiped out.

As nightfall approached, it became evident to the Departmento Tacticae advisors, on the ground as well as in orbit, that something was awry with the tau's command and control systems. While many individual tau units mounted a competent and disciplined retreat in the face of their enemy, a feat considered amongst the hardest of manoeuvres to accomplish, coordination between the tau units became notably degraded. It was Sarik who noted this phenomenon first, as he witnessed two tau battle suit groups falling back as one. In previous engagements the two groups would have coordinated their retreat, one covering the other as it redeployed so that a constant fire-and-movement was kept up. Before Sarik's very eyes, both groups fled, neither offering the other any fire support. As a consequence, both battle suit groups were cut down as the Space Marines forced their advantage, punishing the tau for their tactical error.

And that error was being repeated all over the front. Sarik communicated his observation to Colonel Armak of the Brimlock 2nd Armoured while the Tacticae ensured it was disseminated to all other commands. Fleet intelligence turned its efforts to uncovering the roots of the degradation, and the elite Codes and Ciphers division under Tacticae-Primaris Kilindini reported that command and control signals between the tau ground forces and off-world contacts had become garbled and weak. It was soon discerned that the tau defending Gel'bryn had been coordinated by a higher command echelon in space nearby. It appeared that the tau's much vaunted and feared technology was turning against them, though none amongst the Tacticae could offer a plausible explanation as to the cause.

As darkness engulfed the city, the battlefield was illuminated by strobing explosions, the glowing contrails of missiles streaking high overhead and a thousand lasguns and boltguns gunning down the tau wherever they were encountered. The only sound audible was that of the engines of the Space Marines' armoured transports and the tanks and carriers of the Imperial Guard. The air was filled with the stink of exhaust fumes, ozone and fyceline. The sky was etched with tracer fire and the flaring jets of hundreds of battle suits and anti-grav transports as they fell back in a long stream towards the star port.

Three hours after nightfall, the advance elements of Sarik's column were within five kilometres of the star port, and the tau's defences appeared to have collapsed entirely. The column paused while Sarik sent his land speeder squadrons forwards to undertake a reconnaissance of the objective. Minutes later, the land speeders reported that the traffic around the star port was now entirely in one direction: outwards. At some point during the closing hours of the day the tau had ceased ferrying reinforcements into the city and were now ferrying those same troops out as fast as the destroyers could carry them. The land speeder crews relayed images of masses of alien troops and machines flooding towards the star port's multiple landing pads. The activity was disciplined, but the intent was clear: the tau were retreating.

The Tacticae advisors passed word to the Commissariat, who approved the dissemination of a simple communication to the troops. Word that the tau were in full flight was welcomed with cheers and celebration, but the morale officers were sure to impress upon the men that there was much fighting yet to be done.

Higher up the chain of command, a debate was set in motion. Some commanders pressed for the advance to continue without delay and the tau to be slaughtered even as they fled. Others counselled that there was scant honour to be earned in slaying a retreating enemy, even the xenos tau who, it was largely accepted, had fought thus far with honour and tenacity.

A brief operational pause set in as high command considered the next phase of Operation Hydra. And all the while, unknown to most of those on the surface of Dal'yth Prime, the countdown to Exterminatus ticked inexorably down to zero...

GENERAL GAUGE STOOD calmly in the midst of the controlled chaos that had engulfed his command centre aboard the *Blade of Woe*, his arms folded across his chest. He was the calm at the centre of the storm, his razor-sharp mind the cold focus of the entire invasion of Dal'yth Prime. His expert eye took in the reams of information scrolling across a dozen pict screens. First-hand accounts and tactical updates streamed in from the surface, Tacticae officers rushing to and fro as they collated the data and entered it into cogitation banks. Maps and charts were updated on a minute-by-minute basis, the information becoming obsolete within moments of being entered. Staff officers yelled into vox-horns as they sought clarification from their opposite numbers on the ground, desperately trying to piece together a coherent picture of exactly what was happening as the crusade army advanced.

Gauge glanced to his chron. It was almost an hour since his last vox conversation with Colonel Armak, and it would soon be time for another. He was just about to order his aide-de-camp to patch him through to the colonel when the officer appeared at his side and handed him a data-slate coded for his personal attention.

His eyes narrowing, Gauge entered his personal cipher and scanned the message header. It was from Tacticae-Primaris Kilindini and penned by the man's own hand.

My lord general. My division has traced the enemy's command and control net to a node in high orbit on the far side of Dal'yth Prime. My staff conclude that enemy ground forces are being coordinated via a tight-beam conduit from a high command element off world. Back-trace cogitation reveals that this node has been controlling enemy ground forces for at least twelve hours, but the signal has been steadily degrading. At zero-nine-nine, the signal cut out entirely. My conclusion: enemy operational command and control capacity has been severed and is at this time defunct. Recommend this intelligence be acted upon as best you see fit.

Gauge allowed himself a ghost of a smile as he closed the message and handed the data-slate back to his aide. He checked his chron again, his mind performing a hundred calculations and filtering a thousand possibilities all at once. Inquisitor Grand's deadline would expire before the sun rose over Gel'bryn, and the ground forces were within five kilometres of their objective. They could take it, he knew. If they pushed on, driving the tau ahead of them, they could take it. The enemy would be forced to abandon the star port, and trapped en masse against the sea to the south of Gel'bryn.

'Get me Sarik, Armak and Gerrit,' Gauge said to his aide. 'I want the advance moving again and that star port taken.'

'ALL COMMANDS,' SARIK said into the vox-net as he rode in the cupola of his Rhino. 'Objective in sight. Repeat, star port in sight, five kilometres. Form up on me and advance like your primarchs are watching! Out.'

Sarik's driver gunned the Rhino's engine and the transport gained speed. Sarik's blood was up, but he had finally mastered the raging berserker fury that had consumed him earlier. In fact, he now felt as if that fury had been lurking within him for years, and he had only just acknowledged its toxic presence. He felt as if he had passed through some form of trial, one that he had come perilously close to failing. He had walked the precarious line between control and unfettered rage, and he had seen, with his battle-brother's assistance, how close he had come to stepping over an invisible threshold. The previously hidden delineation was now entirely clear to him, and he knew himself, his limits and his capabilities, as he had never done before. He would harness this newfound realisation, nurture the wisdom he had uncovered, and turn it to the execution of his duty and the pursuance of honour above all things.

Sarik swept his pintle-mounted storm bolter left to right, tracking the buildings on either side of the road that led as straight as an arrow towards the star port. The buildings were growing closer together, and every portal and window harboured deep shadows within which an enemy might be lurking. The Assault Marines bounded alongside the column, ensuring that no tau spotters waited to call in the lethal, indirect-firing missiles that had accounted for so many armoured vehicles, and even a mighty Titan, since the opening of Operation Pluto. No spotters had been encountered for several hours, yet the Assault Marines still carried out their task, for even a single spotter left undiscovered could wreak havoc amongst Sarik's force.

Sarik reviewed his force's disposition as the Rhinos, Razorback, Predators and Whirlwinds advanced. Though many squads of the crusade's Space Marine contingent were engaged in detached duties elsewhere, the bulk of the battle-brothers were under his command. His heart swelled with fierce, martial pride as he watched the column on its final advance towards the objective. The white and red livery of his own Chapter was but a small proportion of the colours displayed by the vehicles of the dozen Chapters, and it was the greatest honour of his service to act as their force commander. Though many had fallen in the advance, untold acts of individual heroism had earned every Chapter represented untold honour. The histories of a dozen Chapters would record the name of Operation Hydra and the Battle of Gel'bryn as a prized battle honour, and the chronicles of the White Scars would recall his own squads' actions for all time.

The lights of the star port were now coming into view. Sarik recalled the surveillance images captured by the fleet's orbital spy-drones, mentally comparing them to what little he could see in the darkness up ahead. He knew that the star port was a sprawling complex of raised landing platforms, each served by a grav-dampener that both cushioned an incoming craft's final approach and aided the launching of outgoing ones. The crusade's Adeptus Mechanicus greatly coveted those generators, for while their construction was known to them, they were eager to learn how the tau had come about knowledge of a technology considered arcane by their order. The star port was lit by intense arc lights that cast their stark illumination upwards into the night sky, creating six square kilometres of bright day in the midst of Dal'yth Prime's night. Control towers speared the sky, warning lights chasing up and down their flanks, and the entire complex was ringed by what the Departmento Tacticae advisors warned were probably automated gun turrets.

Sarik's vox-bead came to life. 'Ancient Mhadax to Sergeant Sarik,' the machine-modulated voice of a Scythes of the Emperor Dreadnought said. Sarik spun the cupola around one-eighty degrees, and saw the hulking walker containing the mortal remains of the celebrated Captain Mhadax striding along two hundred metres behind. To the White Scars, internment in the sarcophagus at the heart of the mighty war machine was anathema, for the Chapter far preferred to let its mortally wounded heroes die, their spirits to return to the wide open steppes of Chogoris, than to keep them alive indefinitely in such a manner. It was always a trial to contain such notions when confronted with Dreadnoughts from other Chapters.

'Sarik,' he replied. 'Speak, honoured one.'

'My prey-sense augurs are detecting movement

amongst the structures up ahead, sergeant. Be warned.'

'My thanks, Captain Mhadax,' Sarik said, deliberately using the ancient's rank, though the vast majority of those interred in the iron body of a Dreadnought relinquished their right to command. Sarik was technically Mhadax's commander, but it would be hubris of the worst kind not to accept his words.

'All commands,' Sarik said in the vox. 'Prepare for contact, minus twenty to plus twenty.'

Sarik's driver allowed the Rhino to fall back slightly as two Predators growled forwards, one bearing the black and yellow livery of the Scythes of the Emperor, the other the jade green of the Subjugators. Both trained their heavy weapons on the structures on either side of the road as they pressed on, their commanders riding high in their cupolas so as to spot any sign of movement in the shadows.

'Sarik!' Ancient Mhadax's machine voice cut in urgently. 'Zero-seven high, twenty metres. Beware!'

Sarik spun the cupola round to the position the Dreadnought had indicated, tracking the storm bolter up the side of a tall structure. The barest hint of movement caught his eye and he swung the weapon upwards sharply...

With a blink of muzzle flare, something fired from a shadowed recess high on the side of the rearing structure. An instant later, an energy bolt zipped past Sarik's head, so close it made his scalp sting. The round impacted on the Rhino's rooftop hatch.

'Contact!' Sarik bellowed, but he had no need to issue any more orders, for his force was already reacting. Bolt-rounds were stitching through the air, tracing death across the shadows of the building's flank. Another enemy shot whined past, only missing him because the

Rhino had bucked sharply at the last possible instant. This time Sarik caught the exact location of the firer, and zeroed his storm bolter on the shadows.

More energy bolts rained down on the Space Marine vehicles, and Sarik knew that multiple firers were engaging the Space Marines. Settling the storm bolter on the patch of shadow where he knew his assailant to be hiding, he squeezed the trigger and loosed a rapid-fire volley.

The rounds exploded as they plunged into the target's position, the backwash of their detonations casting hellish, strobing illumination on the sniper's nest. A body was flung backwards against the wall behind, then flopped forwards over the edge to plummet the twenty metres to the ground below. Sarik saw instantly that the body was not that of a tau, but of one of the savage alien carnivores he had encountered in the plantations what seemed like a week before.

As the alien's gangly body crunched to the hard surface below, Sarik brought his storm bolter around, seeking other enemies lurking in similar hiding places. The Predators were already passing the building, and slowing slightly. Their sponson-mounted heavy bolters coughed to life as the commander of the Subjugators tank came on the vox-net. 'Brother-sergeant, multiple xenos carnivores ahead. Engaging.'

'Carnivores' was the term by which these savage aliens were becoming known amongst the crusade's army, and it described them well. From his position, Sarik could not yet see the targets of the Predators' fire, but he could well picture the vile creatures as they threw themselves onto the tanks' guns. While he had come to afford the tau with a certain amount of respect and ascribe them something akin to honour, these other aliens were something else entirely. They were possessed of a fearsome degree of fieldcraft, Sarik granted that, but their habit of consuming the flesh of the fallen cast them beyond redemption.

'Kill them, sergeant,' Sarik growled to the Subjugators tank commander. 'Show them no mercy.'

As the Predators' fire redoubled in fury, Sarik opened the channel to address the entire column. 'All commands, heavy contact ahead. All squads dismount to repel enemy infantry, but do not allow yourselves to get bogged down. Out.'

As Sarik's Rhino closed on the two Predators, he got some idea of how many carnivores must be inbound. The tanks' turret autocannons were belching round after round of explosive shells, tracking back and forth as they gunned down the alien horde's front ranks. The heavy bolters mounted on the flanks of each tank were keeping up a constant, thunderous fire, a continuous stream of spent shell casings ejecting from side ports to clatter across the hard white road surface.

Still, Sarik's view of the horde was obscured by the tanks and the fyceline haze thrown up by the heavy weight of weapons fire. 'Brother Kjanghis,' Sarik addressed his driver over the transport's internal vox. 'Halt here.'

'Yes, brother-serg–' the driver began, before a sound like a piledriver hammering into the side of the Rhino cut him off. The Rhino lurched violently under the impact, throwing Sarik forwards in the cupola. A sharp metallic clatter sounded from the right-side track nacelle, and Sarik knew instantly the transport had been struck hard on its tread unit and thrown a track.

As Sarik righted himself, the driver brought the Rhino to a halt, the right-side track unfurling behind and the foremost road wheels grinding into the road surface with an ear-rending squeal.

Sarik dropped down inside the vehicle. 'Brother Jek,' Sarik nodded to one of his warriors waiting in the troop bay. 'Aid Brother Kjanghis with the track. The rest of you, with me.'

The warrior nearest to the Rhino's rear punched a bulkhead-mounted command rune and the rear hatch thumped downwards to form an assault ramp. The squad was out in seconds, Brother Qaja's plasma cannon sweeping left and right as the Space Marines secured the immediate area.

The air roared as a solid round sheathed in blue energy thundered from the smoke up ahead and passed directly through the Space Marines' formation without striking one of them. Sarik traced the shot's trajectory back towards its source, offering a silent prayer as he did so that the huge round had not struck any of his battle-brothers. The round had been of a type the Space Marines had not yet encountered, some kind of solid projectile encased in the seething blue energies fired by many of the tau's weapons.

As the following Rhinos ground to a halt behind Sarik's squad, Space Marines pounding down assault ramps to take position around their vehicles, Sarik waved his warriors forward. He kept his gaze fixed on the arc the projectile had come in from as he ran forwards into the smoke, his battle-brothers close behind.

The squad plunged into drifting banks of stinking smoke, made all-enclosing in the dark night. The thunderous report of the Predators carried weirdly through the dense smog of battle, and the ringing of brass casings pattering across the ground was almost louder than the sound of the weapons firing. Then Sarik heard another sound – a gruff snuffling. A low, birdlike chirrup followed, and the first sound ceased. The bird sound was undoubtedly that of a carnivore, but Sarik could not place the other.

He raised his hand to indicate a cautious advance to contact, allowing Brother Qaja to come level with him. The squad moved forwards with weapons raised to shoulders, spread out with each battle-brother covering a separate arc.

Then a gust of wind ghosted across the scene, and the haze thinned for just a moment. Sarik and Qaja both saw the beast at once as it reared on stumpy hind legs, its apelike forearms raised high overhead.

For an instant, both battle-brothers took the creature for a *rokchull,* a demonic beast of their home world's most ancient legends. Its body was grossly muscled, its face low between massively humped shoulders. That face was grotesquely akin to that of the alien carnivores, as if the two were but strains of the same xenos genealogy. Its face was dominated by a huge, beak-like mouth, the lower jaw protruding so its jagged edge formed an underbite. Its beady eyes were aglow with dumb malice and it opened its mouth wide as it reared on its hind legs.

As Sarik and Qaja brought their weapons up as one, they saw that the beast had a rider. A single carnivore was clinging onto the creature's back, manning an overlarge, crudely manufactured projectile weapon lashed to the mount's shoulders by strips of cured hide. It was that weapon that had fired the solid round at the Space Marines.

Sarik had no need to issue Qaja the order to fire on the beast with his plasma cannon while he targeted the rider with his boltgun. Qaja's weapon completed its power cycle an instant after Sarik's boltgun spat a full auto burst that thudded a line of rounds into the rider's torso. The alien was torn apart in a welter of gore as the mass-reactive rounds detonated, its arms still flailing as its limp, broken body toppled backwards from its saddle.

A high-pitched whine announced that the war spirit within Qaja's plasma cannon was ready and eager to slay its foes. The weapon's containment coils blazed a livid violet, and then the blunt nose erupted as a concentrated ball of super-heated plasma cascaded forth. The beast was so close it had no chance to avoid the shrieking ball of energy. It was engulfed in seething arcs of raw plasma, its beak gaping wide as it threw its arms out as if in denial of its imminent death, roiling energies spilling across its muscular form.

Then it exploded. The beast was torn apart as the raging power of the heart of a sun transformed the solid matter of its body into another state entirely. Sarik and Qaja were blasted by a wave-front of black ash, all that remained after the hideous transformation. The air was filled with the flash-stink of body fluids turned to super-heated steam and the blast wave scoured away the smoke of battle.

Sarik and Qaja looked to one another in the wake of the explosion. Each saw that the other was a blackened mess, his face streaked with bloody soot. Both warriors' proud white and red livery was almost entirely obscured, and Sarik's armour was blistered and deformed down one side.

'You look like a ghak-sifter, Brother Qaja,' Sarik grinned, his white teeth bright in the midst of his blackened face. 'You're a disgrace.'

'And you look like a midden-herder, Brother-Sergeant Sarik,' Qaja replied. 'If I may be so bold.'

Sarik's brow creased as he considered Qaja's words. 'A midden-herder?'

'Aye, brother-sergeant.'

'Hmm,' Sarik said, as he turned towards the horde of at least a thousand screeching carnivores thundering towards the Space Marines.

'Glad we've got that settled.'

LUCIAN SAW STACCATO lightning a kilometre up ahead, and lowered his prey-sense goggles to get a better idea what was happening at the head of the advance. He was riding in the turret of the Chimera, the vehicle lurching and jolting so hard he could barely keep the image through the goggles steady.

Activating the goggles, Lucian's world became a grainy, green wash, but he could now see something of the Space Marine column where before all that had been visible was smoke, shadow and muzzle flare. Advanced elements of the 2nd Armoured were pushing through the middle distance, and beyond them, the Space Marines' Rhinos were formed up and stationary, their rear hatches down. The battle-brothers were spreading out and forwards while the column's support vehicles ground to a halt behind the Rhinos.

Guessing that the Space Marines had dismounted to deal with some threat they could not either bypass or smash straight through, Lucian shouted down to the vehicle's commander. 'Slow down! The Space Marines are engaging on foot, we need to give them space.'

The commander nodded, and relayed the information to the company officers of the Brimlock 2nd Armoured. The Brimlock tanks up ahead slewed off the road to either side and ground to a halt, and a moment later, the Chimera that Lucian rode in did the same.

Behind, the entire regiment was strung out in a line of tanks, transports and support vehicles three kilometres in length. And that was just the first regiment of nineteen, all of which were pushing hard for the star port at the heart of Gel'bryn.

Tracking his goggles from the view up ahead to the nearest tau buildings, Lucian saw a cluster of luminous blobs moving across the flank of a tall, sail-shaped structure. With a twist of a dial at his temple, he increased the magnification. The side of the building was swarming with long-limbed and nimble figures, scuttling across the surface like insects.

Lucian activated his vox-link at the same moment as he swung the pintle-mounted heavy stubber around. 'Contact right, high.'

The turrets of two dozen nearby tanks and armoured transports swung around to the right in response to Lucian's warning. He squeezed the stubber's trigger plate with his thumbs, thumping off a three second burst that would tell the gunners exactly where the enemy were. Tracers streaked towards the enemy, and Lucian was surprised to see several of the carnivores blown to bloody chunks as his un-aimed fire thundered in. Realising they had been detected, the remainder of the carnivores redoubled their speed as they crossed the surface, jumping down to the ground as soon as they reached a safe height to do so.

Then C Squadron opened fire. Twelve Leman Russ battle tanks fired as one, the flaming discharge from their battle cannons turning night into day. The shells slammed into the side of the building the carnivores had been scaling, blowing out the entire façade in a mass of blossoming explosions. Clouds of pulverised resin swelled upwards, illuminated by raging inner fires, and then the whole face collapsed, burying the aliens beneath tons of debris.

'Contact left!' a tank commander from B Squadron called.

'Contact right!' D's squadron sergeant-major called.

'Movement rear!' B Echelon's commander reported.

•

'ALL UNITS,' THE voice of Colonel Armak cut into the channel, his code overriding the transmissions of his subordinates. The colonel's tone was measured and calm, exactly what his men needed at that moment. 'We're surrounded on all quarters by large numbers of xenos carnivores. We can't push forwards until the Space Marines get going again, and I'm sure as hell not going to be the first commander in this regiment's history to order a retreat. All units, prepare to address! Don't stop firing 'til they're right on you, then up and at 'em!

'Good luck.'

'Battlegroup Arcadius,' Lucian said into his command-net once the colonel had finished his address. 'Dismount. Keep well clear of the tanks while they fire, then address as the enemy close. Out.'

Closing the channel, Lucian tracked the heavy weapon back and forth, seeing movement in the darkness. He magnified the view through his goggles, penetrating the thick banks of smoke drifting across the scene. What at first appeared a blurred, undulating mass resolved into the front rank of a thousand-strong horde of alien carnivores. The gangly xenos were bounding forwards in great leaps, their dreadlock-like head spines erect like the hackles of an attack canine. They bore their long, primitive rifles, firing from the hip as they advanced, though not with any accuracy. Their beaks were open wide as they hissed and screeched, their vile war cries filling the air.

'Enemy at three hundred metres!' Lucian called down to the Chimera's crew. 'Prepare to–'

'Father, this is Korvane,' the voice of Lucian's son came over the vox. 'Father, do you receive?'

Settling the heavy stubber's aiming reticule over the front rank of the advancing aliens, Lucian replied, 'Korvane? This isn't a good time. Can it wait?'

'No, father, it cannot!' Korvane replied. There was no mistaking the urgency in his voice. Lucian's son had been raised in the rarefied atmosphere of the high court, and was not given to inappropriate shows of emotion. If he was spooked, there was a damn good reason.

'Go ahead,' Lucian said, as the aliens surged forwards, his fists tightening on the stubber's twin-grips.

'Father,' Korvane continued. 'You have to get off the surface, right now...'

'What?' Lucian said as the vehicles on either side opened fire, their deafening reports drowning out Korvane's voice and flooding the channel with interference. 'Repeat last!'

'I repeat,' said Korvane. 'You must evacuate, now. All of you... everyone!'

'Why?' shouted Lucian over the sound of heavy gunfire. 'Calm down and tell me what's happened.'

There was a pause as Korvane got a grip, then carried on. 'Father, Grand has brought forward the deadline. The Exterminatus is–'

'What?' Lucian cursed. 'And he was going to tell us when...?'

Another pause, before Korvane replied, 'He wasn't, father.'

'Understood, son,' Lucian replied as the alien horde closed and he opened fire with the heavy stubber. The thump of the weapon firing and the bloody ruin it inflicted on the aliens' lanky bodies drowned out the rage rising within him...

A gnarled, scarred hand caressed a sleek, black form, its owner cooing words of power that penetrated the armoured housing and reverberated through the cell-hosts. Death heard those words, and heeded their meaning. A trillion murder-cells quivered with hungry life, as if each and every one tasted the scent of their prey, far below.

The vessel of death, the Exterminatus torpedo, waited, held securely in a cantilevered launch cradle. The hand receded, and the words of power fell silent. Wait... death was told. Wait, and soon you shall feed...

CHAPTER NINE

BRIELLE PULLED THE hatch closed behind her, the hiss of the saviour pod's life support systems engaging filling the small space. The sound of alarms and the shouts of emergency response crews receded behind the armoured panel, and everything was suddenly very quiet.

The interior of the pod was sparsely appointed and illuminated with a blue light that Brielle assumed was the equivalent to the low, red glow the Imperium's vessels utilised in similar circumstances. The bulkheads were covered in crash padding, and the deck consisted of an arrangement of ten grav-couches radiating from a central command terminal.

Now what? Brielle stepped over the couches and peered out through a porthole. The glowing orb of Dal'yth Prime filled the circular viewer, the arid surface clearly visible. It was day below, but Brielle knew that the battle at Gel'bryn was currently being fought at night. That meant she was half a world away from where she wanted to be.

She studied the world's surface for a moment, half entranced by the intricate patterns of mountain ranges, coastlines and the sparkling reflections of Dal'yth's star cast from the pristine turquoise oceans. The other half of her mind was committing the world's topography to memory, tracking trajectories and calculating the flight path she would have to take to reach the Imperium's forces at Gel'bryn.

There were so many other risks and variables there was simply no point worrying about them all. What if the pod would only take one path, directly to the surface below? What if it was programmed to make for tau territory? Even if she could control the descent, what if it landed her in the midst of a battle instead of near friendly forces?

She cast all such things from her mind and lowered herself into the nearest grav-couch.

As she settled into the couch, the padding expanded to grip her body, holding her firmly in position. Only her bare feet were left loose, for they were too different from the tau's reverse-jointed lower legs to be accommodated. As she leaned back, giving in to the unfamiliar loss of freedom of movement, a command terminal lit up on the bulkhead above her. Its screen displayed a single, flashing word in the angular tau script.

She struggled to decipher the text, recalling the lessons Aura had conducted weeks ago as she had been transported across the Damocles Gulf. Tree? No, that made no sense. Nostril? Come on, concentrate... Propel, perhaps... Launch!

But she did not want to launch, not yet at least. She

wanted to enter a flight plan, to ensure the saviour pod took her where she wanted to go. If it took her to the surface by the most direct route, she would be dumped in the middle of the desert, to be picked up by the tau, or starve to death in the arid wastes. She hated arid wastes. They played havoc on the pores.

There must be some way to…

A voice outside the hatch, raised in question.

Brielle's breath caught in her throat. She was trapped in the grav-couch, barely even able to move her head. She looked down the length of her body to the access hatch, and heard the voice again. What she had taken for a question was in fact a statement. Something like… 'Safe to come out.'

Whoever was out there, he thought that Brielle was a tau crewman who had fled to the saviour pod at the sound of the alarms, assuming the fire raging through the communications bay would engulf the entire deck, perhaps the entire ship, and necessitate escape.

The voice came again, this time more insistent. She was being *ordered* out of the pod.

She looked back to the blinking text on the screen above as a thud sounded against the hatch. Whoever was out there was now pounding on the outside, evidently losing patience. She knew it was only a matter of time before a crewman with the sense or authority to override the lock arrived and dragged her out.

She had no choice. She would have to worry about plotting a course to the crusade's ground forces once she was in transit.

'Launch,' she said out loud, as it occurred to her that there was no lever or command rune to activate to set the pod in motion. The terminal over her head beeped loudly, and the text changed.

Confirm launch order.

So it was voice activated, she realised. Another thud came from the hatch as she struggled to recall the pronunciation of the tau word for 'confirm'. Then she realised that she had said 'launch' in Gothic, and the pod's systems had understood her. Clearly, the tau had extensive knowledge of the Imperium, and had disseminated that knowledge throughout their empire.

'Confirm,' she said.

The blue illumination inside the pod dipped, then came back, assuming a pulsating rhythm. A siren started up as the pod's systems cycled into life, the air pressure change causing her ears to pop.

There was a grinding sound as an unseen launch cradle disengaged, accompanied by suddenly frantic knocking at the hatch. A low, subsonic machine hum started up, rising through the audible range to a high-pitched whine that made the hairs on the back of Brielle's neck stand on end.

With a jolt, the saviour pod propelled itself from the launch tube. The grav-couch enveloped Brielle's body even tighter, pressing in around her so that only the extremities of her legs, torso and arms were visible. Then a dampening field powered up around her, entirely cancelling out any sense of acceleration. The view through the porthole changed as the globe of Dal'yth Prime swung away, to be replaced by the white, cliff-like flank of the *Dal'yth Il'Fannor O'kray*. The now-empty tube that the pod had launched from was revealed as one in a line of dozens, and yet more were visible on every deck of the vessel.

A plume of silent flame, flaring as if in slow motion from a black wound on the warship's side, drew Brielle's attention. She smiled wickedly, proud of her work in wrecking the communications bay. She guessed that the flame was the result of the entire bay being voided, so as to starve the fire of oxygen since she had disarmed the suppression systems.

The pod's manoeuvring jets flared, the hissing sound especially loud in such a small vessel. The tau warship spun around as the pod changed attitude, and Brielle caught sight of a point defence weapons blister nearby. The blister sported a twin-barrelled weapon, which swivelled around to fix on the pod. Brielle's heart almost stopped beating as she fixed on the gun turret, willing it not to fire. Now would be a damn stupid time to die, she thought... Please, don't fire.

It didn't, the weapon lingering on the pod for a moment before tracking back in the opposite direction.

The manoeuvring jets flared again and the pod swung around so that its base, which consisted of one, huge retro jet, was pointing directly towards the planet below.

The terminal above Brielle's head bleeped and the display changed from the tau text, to a graph plotting the craft's insertion, descent and landing. The three stages were shown in simple graphics, each labelled with the time it would take to complete. The chart showed a direct descent, lasting twenty-two minutes from now to landing. The craft would be in position to begin the descent in less than six minutes.

'No you don't...' Brielle said under her breath, another manoeuvring jet firing.

Repeat instruction, the text blinked, superimposed over the trajectory chart.

'What?' Brielle muttered.

Repeat instruction, the text flashed again.

'Erm...' Brielle said, feeling at once foolish and guilty. She had grown accustomed to the tau's use of thinking machines, but actually talking to one dredged up the teachings of the Imperial Creed in no uncertain terms. 'Alter, er... landing point?'

Input new landing point, the screen flashed. A moment later the text was replaced by a flat representation of the surface of Gel'bryn, overlaid with a fine grid. Brielle understood the system straight away, and recognised it as intended for use under the considerable pressures of an emergency evacuation from a stricken spacecraft. She searched her memory for a rough idea of the location of Gel'bryn, and scanned the area where she estimated it would be found. That stretch of the main continent's eastern seaboard contained a dozen cities. She recalled the conversations with Aura, and the scenes she had witnessed in the command centre. It must be the eastern-most of the twelve cities, the one nearest the ocean.

There it was. 'Nine, nine, seven, zero two, er...' she read off Gel'bryn's coordinates from the grid, 'by, er, two, nine, two, five, zero.'

The graphic changed, the flat grid replaced by an image of the globe. A line traced the course from the pod's current position to its interface point, then almost straight downwards towards the surface.

Confirm course change, the text blinked.

'Confirm,' Brielle said, swallowing hard at the finality of the statement. The manoeuvring jets flared again as the saviour pod came around to its new heading. Brielle forced her breathing to a calm rate, and tried to relax her body, but she could not rid herself of the mental image of the vessel being transformed into a streaking meteor as it plunged towards the surface of Dal'yth Prime.

* * *

THE VOYAGE TO the interface point took less than an hour, and Brielle watched through the porthole as the saviour pod crossed directly over the terminator line where day turned into night. Throughout that time she was gripped by a feeling of helplessness; that her life was in the hands of a machine that appeared to be able to think and hold, albeit rudimentary, conversation. She was entranced by the patterns of light glinting from the serene seas far below, and the faint, wispy cloud formations gracefully whirling over them.

Several times throughout the journey to the interface point, the pod's vox system had blurted into life, only to cut out after delivering several seconds of distorted garbage. She had no doubt that the *Dal'yth Il'Fannor O'kray's* main communications banks would be out of action for quite some time, and guessed that these transmissions were coming from vessels further away, or from less powerful, secondary transceivers on the warship. She could just imagine the confusion and concern the tau must have experienced as the saviour pod cleared the ship. Perhaps they imagined it to contain an over-reacting crewman convinced the ship was crippled. After her failure to make any attempt to reply to the hails, they had probably concluded that the pod had malfunctioned and been fired in error, and would just let it slip away. After all, they had far more pressing concerns.

The pod had been over Dal'yth Prime's dark side for twenty minutes when its manoeuvring jets fired for the last time. The view through the porthole shifted, the world gliding out of view to be replaced with the star-speckled blackness of the void. The pod's interior lighting dimmed, then started to pulsate as it had when it had first launched from the *Dal'yth Il'Fannor O'kray*.

Brielle looked straight up at the pict screen, and guessed that the descent to the surface was due to begin.

Again, that feeling of utter helplessness came over her. She had made planetfall countless times, but always, she had been in command. Although she had only rudimentary piloting skills and was no drop-ace, she had always been in charge. The pilot of whichever vessel she had rode had invariably been her servant, and that, she realised, was the root of her unease. She hated not having someone she trusted to rely upon, or if it came to it, boss around.

As the saviour pod began its descent, Brielle realised that she did have someone to rely on. She closed her eyes, not wishing to watch the blinking icon on the screen above her as it rode the trajectory line in a hell-dive to the surface of Dal'yth Prime. Someone very far away. Forty? Fifty thousand light years? Certainly, half a galaxy at least...

'Imperator,' she began, sacred words she had not spoken in years coming unbidden to her lips as a shudder ran through the pod. 'From the cold of the void, we beseech your protection. From the fire of re-entry, we implore you to shield us, from the...'

The saviour pod began its dive, surrendering to the inexorable pull of gravity. For the first few minutes, not a lot seemed to happen, but Brielle could feel the slow build-up of gaseous friction on the outside of the pod. Then she realised she was sweating, and not from the tension of her situation. The temperature inside the pod was rising, even with the life support systems cycling at full power. A foolish notion appeared in her head: what if the tau's biology was more resistant to the trauma of re-entry than a human's, and the pod's tolerances designed with that in mind? Nonsense, she told herself.

Those of the air caste might be more comfortable in zero-g, while tau of the earth caste were better suited to hard work, but the pod would have to accommodate them all.

A fluttering tremble passing through the hull cast the thought from Brielle's mind. She looked towards the porthole, and saw ghostly flame dancing across the black void beyond. In any other circumstance the effect would be quite entrancing, she thought, but being strapped into a lump of alien tech plummeting at Emperor-knew-what speed through the sky above a warzone took the edge off it.

Another tremble, and the whole pod started to vibrate. The craft was entering Dal'yth Prime's upper atmosphere. While still incredibly thin, the air was still dense enough to cause friction on the pod's outer hull, though the energy shield projected below was absorbing the majority of it. The Imperium's military drop-pods and emergency saviour pods were only rarely fitted with such a feature, the utilitarian planners regarding it as a luxury in most cases. By all accounts, planetfall in one of those junk buckets was almost as dangerous as taking your chances on a burning assault ship.

Despite the energy shield protecting the pod from the worst of the turbulence, the whole interior was shaking. The effect increased to a violently quaking crescendo as the pod neared terminal velocity and the heat in the interior rose still further. Brielle squeezed her eyes tightly shut, wishing only that she could free her arms to clamp her hands over her ears to deaden the screaming rush of burning air consuming the pod.

Then, the pod's retro thruster kicked in. The grav-couch cushioned the worst of the violent arrest in downward momentum, but every cell in Brielle's body felt as if it were being squeezed, flattened and compressed, all at once. Brielle felt at that moment that the pod really was a small compartment bolted onto a huge jet thruster, which belched and roared just below her supine form. She could feel the incredible energies being unleashed in that terminal burn, and abandoned herself to them.

Quite suddenly, the roaring inferno that had raged outside was replaced by a shrill whistling. Brielle opened her eyes and looked towards the porthole. The view outside was of the dark-jade, night-time skies of Dal'yth Prime.

In the last few minutes of the descent, the manoeuvring jets kicked in one final time, and the pod altered attitude. The stars swung upwards and the distant horizon hove into view. An anti-grav generator powered up, guiding the pod towards its final crashdown.

ACCORDING TO IMPERIAL Navy doctrine, as well as sound military principle, a fleet undertaking offensive operations should maintain an extensive counter-penetration defence screen. A network of picket vessels, of every displacement from interceptor to frigate, should provide three hundred and sixty degree, three-dimensional surveillance before, during and after any engagement. The fleet of the Damocles Gulf Crusade was not particularly large by naval standards, especially given its losses at Pra'yen, and its carrier capacity was woefully short, but nonetheless, no enemy vessel should have been able to get within five thousand kilometres of its flagship, the *Blade of Woe*.

Thus, it was something of a surprise when Admiral Jellaqua's vessel was hailed by an unknown vessel from less than a thousand kilometres away, and well within its picket screen.

'*Blade of Woe*,' the unknown sender said, his voice relayed through the vox-horns on Jellaqua's bridge. 'This is theta-zero. Requesting immediate dock, over.'

'Who the *hell* is it?' Jellaqua scowled at none of his bridge officers in particular. 'Who the hell *dares*...?'

'Augur scan collating now, admiral,' a crewman called out. Jellaqua crossed to the station, his eyes scanning the reams of scan data scrolling across the flickering pict screen.

'Run it again,' Jellaqua said. 'That makes no sense. Run it again.'

'Erm, admiral,' the officer stammered. 'I have, sir. This is the third run. Whatever that vessel is, it matches nothing in the registry.'

Jellaqua turned from the augur station and crossed to the comms station, half a dozen aides trailing in his wake. 'Well?'

Jellaqua's Master of Signals was as much machine as he was man, a dozen snaking cables running from grafted terminals in his cranium to the cogitation array in front of him. The Master of Signals nodded, as if listening to something very far away, before replying. 'A sub-carrier wave, admiral.'

'What seal?' Jellaqua said, guessing the answer before it came.

'Magenta, my lord.'

'Confirm docking and alert all commands,' Jellaqua said, two-dozen staff officers rushing off to enact his orders as others started yelling into vox-horns. 'Prepare to receive Inquisition boarders.'

* * *

The light infantry companies of Battlegroup Arcadius were advancing on foot through the streets of Gel'bryn, and Lucian could see the lights of the star port visible mere kilometres ahead. The tau were disengaging across the entire city, the last of their units falling back on the star port to be evacuated by huge, wallowing transports. The tau were still mounting a defence, but it was poorly coordinated and piecemeal, and the crusade armies were pushing them back on every front. By all accounts, the enemy's command and control network had completely collapsed, and the tau leaders on the ground had proven ill-prepared to adapt. Lucian had no idea what had caused the collapse, and Gauge had claimed that it was none of the crusade's doing. Whatever had caused it, Lucian and the other commanders gave silent thanks for this one nugget of good fortune.

It seemed to Lucian now that the tau were suddenly the lesser of two enemies, and that it might be Inquisitor Grand that defeated the entire undertaking.

The last hour had seen the tempo of Operation Hydra attain a new urgency, which Lucian impressed upon his subordinates as the other regimental commanders did on their own. Unlike the vast multitudes of the rank and file, the commanders knew the reason for the sudden haste. An operation that had previously been allowed an extremely tight twenty-four-hour window to achieve its objective now found even that deadline brought forward. The problem was, not even General Gauge knew exactly when that deadline would expire.

Lucian seethed inwardly as he moved along the street. The elite patrols platoon of the Rakarshan Rifles were ranging ahead of him, while two rifle platoons was close behind. What the hell was Grand playing at? The inquisitor's initial threat to enact Exterminatus within twenty-four hours had been extreme enough, but the remnants of the crusader council had thought themselves able to call Grand's bluff and make the devastation of the entire world unnecessary. Lucian was coming to suspect that Inquisitor Grand had intended to bring the Exterminatus forward all along, and Lucian and his allies had played right into his hands in pushing towards the star port, well beyond their capability to return to Sector Zero and evacuate.

'Warp take him…' Lucian cursed, for the tenth time in as many minutes. The madman was prepared to slaughter thousands upon thousands of Imperial Guard and several hundred Space Marines just to prove a point…

'Excuse me, sir?' Lucian's signalman said from close behind as a barrage fired by a troop of Manticore missile tanks streaked through the night sky overhead.

'Nothing, son,' Lucian growled, bitterness rising inside as he recalled his actual son, and the risks he had taken to discover and communicate the fact that Grand had brought forward the Exterminatus order. The Manticore barrage walloped into a tau position a kilometre distant, setting off a staccato burst of secondary explosions that lit the edge of the star port with a hellish orange glow.

Lucian was torn, his duty to the crusade conflicting violently with his duty to his dynasty. He could leave within the hour, he knew, by calling a lander from the *Oceanid* to return him to the fleet. He could confront Grand and ensure his son's safety, though he suspected doing so might cost him his life. But to abandon his duty now, as his battle group closed on the objective it had fought and bled so hard to capture, would be the act of a self-serving coward.

No, Lucian knew that the only course of action open

to him was to lead Battlegroup Arcadius forward in glory, and take that cursed star port as soon as possible. Korvane would have to do what he could, as would General Gauge and his staff, though that was precious little. As dire as his own predicament seemed, Lucian did not envy Gauge. The general was faced with an apparently insane inquisitor, an individual who wielded authority to all intents and purposes equal to that of the High Lords of Terra themselves, as well as the pressing need to win a major victory and evacuate tens of thousands of troops.

'Sir?' the signalman said again.

'Nothing,' Lucian repeated, distracted by his train of thought and not really paying attention to his surroundings.

'Sir!' the man said, the urgency of his tone snapping Lucian back to the here and now. The signalman was pointing up ahead, and Lucian slowed as he followed the gesture. Patrols platoon had disappeared, and the street was empty.

No, it was far from empty. The elite scouts and trackers of patrols platoon had simply melted into the shadows on either side of the wide street, and that could only mean trouble.

'Tell the column to stand by,' Lucian said, and the signalman passed the order along.

Cautiously, Lucian advanced along the street, lowering his prey-sense goggles to pierce the smoke and darkness beyond patrols platoon. Whatever the scouts had spotted, he could not yet see it, but his goggles would detect what even the elite trackers could not see.

Lowering the brass headset over his eyes, Lucian tuned the viewfinder. The smoke appeared to lift like a morning mist dispelled by the rising sun, revealing a group of boxy vehicles at the far end of the street. After a moment, Lucian realised that the vehicles were Space Marine Whirlwind missile tanks, and that his battle-group had almost caught up with Sarik's spearhead. Lucian knew that the Rakarshans would have to slow their advance so that the two groups did not become mixed up, frustrating given the haste to reach the star port, but that could not have been why patrols platoon had gone firm.

'Signals,' Lucian hissed, waving the adjutant to his side while keeping his gaze fixed upon the vehicles up ahead. He heard the signalman speaking low into his vox-horn, and the hushed, distorted chatter of return traffic. Then he saw...

'Carnivores, sir,' the signalman reported, passing on the report from the Rakarshan captain leading patrols platoon. 'They're just about to–'

'I see them,' Lucian hissed, not taking his eye off the dark shadow moving towards the rearmost of the Space Marine vehicles.

Then the boxy twin-launchers atop that vehicle angled upwards on whining servos, and a flaring jet of flame belched from the rear vents. A missile spat out-wards from one of the launchers, and the scene at the end of the street was fully illuminated in the sudden flare.

Something big was moving towards the Whirlwind, something so large the carnivores around it seemed little more than scuttling vermin. It was some type of beast, its long body supported on massive hind legs. Its front legs were little more than vestigial claws, while its head was dominated by a jagged-edged beak and quills sprouting from the crown. As the light cast by the mis-sile guttered away, Lucian saw that the beast carried some form of oversized howdah or saddle, and that two or three more carnivores were mounted on its back, manning some kind of primitive, crossbow-like heavy weapon.

'Get some tubes forward,' Lucian ordered, then activated his own vox-link, cycling through the channels until he found the one reserved for the Space Marine commanders. Ordinarily, the channel would be locked out to anyone other than the Adeptus Astartes, but Lucian had friends in high places. The channel burst to life, curt orders cutting back and forth as squad sergeants called targets and coordinated fire and movement between their units. He waited for an opportunity to cut in, but the beast was closing on the Whirlwind too fast to stand on ceremony.

'Rearmost Astartes Whirlwind,' Lucian said. 'This is an urgent transmission, over.'

The voices went silent, the tinny sound of gunfire bleeding in. 'Last sender, identify yourself,' a gruff voice said.

'Stand down, Sergeant Rheq,' the familiar voice of Sergeant Sarik came over the channel. 'Make it quick, Lucian.'

'Carnivores closing on your rearmost launcher. And they have something big,' he said. 'I'm moving up anti-tank, so I suggest you get your vehicles clear.'

'Understood, Lucian,' Sarik replied. 'My thanks. Out.'

As Lucian closed the link, three two-man missile launcher teams came level with him, one man in each carrying the shoulder-fired tube while the other bore a case of three reloads. Sergeant-Major Havil followed in their wake, his long-hafted power axe slung over his shoulder. Havil immediately set about bullying the missile launcher teams into setting up their tubes in double time, and soon they were ready to fire.

Meanwhile, the Whirlwinds' engines were gunning to life, thick smoke belching from their side-mounted exhausts. Lucian saw the carnivores react, halting as they crept forwards, their primitive, spiked rifles raised. The beast was reined in, its vile face glowering at the source of the sound.

Yet, while Lucian could see the scene clearly thanks to the arcane systems of his prey-sense goggles, the smoke was obscuring it entirely from the missile launcher teams.

The carnivores were gesturing towards the nearest Whirlwind as it juddered forwards. The heavy weapon on the back of the huge beast was turning around to engage the missile tank from almost point-blank range. Even such a primitive weapon could cause damage at close enough range, especially against the tank's rear armour.

Realising the beast-mounted weapon was about to open fire, Lucian made up his mind. He rushed towards the nearest of Sergeant-Major Havil's missile-launcher teams, and grabbed the tube from the grip of the stunned Rakarshan. The man was about to voice a protest, when Havil thumped the non-lethal end of his power axe into the back of his head. The Rakarshan hefted the weapon from his shoulder and passed it to Lucian.

Raising the tube to his shoulder, Lucian realised that he would not be able to sight using the weapon's onboard system, for it could not penetrate the smoke. Steadying the tube with his right hand, he used his left to pull a cord from his goggles, which he jacked into a port on the side of the launcher's sighting unit. Lucian prayed that the war spirits within the two devices would achieve communion, and not reject one another as often happened. A moment later the vision through his goggles was overlaid with the launcher's targeting reticule, the two devices operating as one.

His thumb closing on the firing stud, Lucian took a moment to still himself, breathing out as the reticule settled on the beast. He played the aim across its body, rejecting the sure kill, but possible miss of a headshot for a sure hit, but less likely kill, body shot.

'Clear!' Lucian called, issuing one last warning to anyone behind him that he was about to fire.

'Clear!' he heard Sergeant-Major Havil confirm.

He pressed the firing stud, and the missile streaked from the tube. The backblast blew hot, sharp-smelling gases into his face, before the main charge ignited ten metres out and propelled the missile along the length of the street and into the smoke.

The missile struck the huge beast square in the howdah, exploding the heavy weapon which had been preparing to fire on the Whirlwind. The two carnivores manning the weapon were enveloped in a white flash, leaving only their legs, fused to the wreckage on the beast's back.

'Missed,' Lucian spat. 'Reload!' he said to the Rakarshan beside him.

'No need, my lord,' Sergeant-Major Havil said, a broad grin splitting his black-bearded face.

Lucian lifted his goggles to see that the missile's explosion had blown away the smoke at the end of the street, exposing the carnivores to the Rakarshan's view. Though Lucian's missile had not struck the huge beast square as he had hoped, in winging it and killing its riders he had caused it to go berserk. The beast was enraged, lashing out with its beaked head and stomping the ground hard with its huge, taloned feet.

The beast spun around as the carnivores scattered. Several were too slow. One was bitten in half at the waist by the beast's snapping, razor-edged beak while another was pounded flat by a crushing foot. Some of the carnivores dashed into side streets, but the majority backed off along the main thoroughfare, towards Lucian's force.

Seeing his opportunity, Lucian stood, and bellowed, 'Rakarshans, address!'

Then he realised the Rakarshans probably had no idea what 'address' meant. He turned to the sergeant-major, who was still grinning. The whip-crack ripple of coordinated section fire sounded from patrols platoon's position, and the street lit up with white, strobing light.

Dozens of carnivores were cut down as the veteran riflemen of patrols platoon rose up from their concealment, unleashing rapid-fire death on the foe. The enemy were caught in the open and in the crossfire of the two halves of the platoon, one on either side of the street. Gangly bodies danced and spun as las-rounds lanced into them, and within seconds the ground was littered with smoking, twitching, alien bodies. The Rakarshans had a debt of honour to settle, and the carnivores had much more to pay.

The enraged beast roared, its savage face whipping left and right so fast its head-quills rattled loudly. The Rakarshans held their fire, knowing that to shoot the beast would probably draw a charge. Then it roared again, and stomped off down a side street, the pounding of its heavy tread receding into the distance.

'Get patrols platoon forward, sergeant-major,' Lucian ordered, passing the missile launcher back to its original owner. 'Secure the area, but let the Adeptus Astartes press forwards.'

'Understood, my lord,' Havil replied, before striding off down the street to pass Lucian's orders to the captain in charge of patrols platoon.

Lucian looked up into the night sky as Rakarshans dashed past. The eastern horizon was touched by the merest hint of green, the first visible sign of the coming dawn. Hardly believing that the night had almost passed, Lucian checked his chron, and cursed. Time was running out.

A fiery light streaked overhead, another missile barrage, Lucian assumed. He glanced up, but saw that the light was travelling north-east to south-west, so could not have been a missile fired from the Imperial Guard's lines.

The light passed almost directly overhead, casting a flickering luminescence over the scene, and Lucian saw that it was not a missile, but a small craft making a controlled crashdown following planetfall. The air beneath the craft seethed with burning atmosphere, the heat absorbed and simultaneously shed by an energy shield projected below it.

No Imperial lander that Lucian knew to be in orbit employed such a device.

The object disappeared from view as it sped past one of the city's hundred-metre-tall structures. The sky flashed white behind the tower, and the sound of the craft's violent crashdown rolled down the street. Whatever it was, the battle group would be passing it soon.

Seeing that the path ahead was secured and the rearmost vehicles of the Space Marine column had ground ahead and were out of sight, Lucian looked around for his executive officer.

'Major Subad!' he called.

A moment later, Subad was running towards him from further down the street. 'My lord?' he said as he came to a halt and saluted.

'Get the companies moving, major,' Lucian said. 'The objective is in sight.'

CHAPTER TEN

SARIK PULLED HIS shrieking, gore-streaked chainsword from the broken torso of the barbarous alien carnivore, and brought it up into a guard position as he sought another opponent. The only enemy left were the dead and the dying, the Space Marines pushing forwards with boltguns raised as they secured the area.

A muffled *thump-crack* rang out as a battle-brother put a bolt pistol shell through a wounded alien's head.

'Clear!' Brother Qaja shouted, and a dozen similar acknowledgments flooded over the command net.

'Transports forward,' Sarik ordered, the roar of several dozen engines revving to life sounding from behind as his order was enacted. The Space Marines had reached a junction, and the outer limits of the Gel'bryn star port lay around the next turn in the road. The ground was strewn with the spilled blood and severed limbs of the alien carnivores, which crunched and split under Sarik's armoured tread as he walked forwards towards the corner.

The aliens had fought like nightmarish creatures from Chogoran legend, though why, Sarik could not tell. The tau themselves had almost entirely evacuated the city, and none had been reported for an hour at least. It seemed that the tau had deployed the carnivores as a rearguard, but one that they must have regarded as expendable given the imminent fall of Gel'bryn and its star port. Perhaps the carnivores were bound to the tau by some unknown blood oath. Perhaps they had simply been paid so handsomely they considered the nigh suicidal defence worth attempting. All that really mattered was that they were xenos, and their mindset quite literally alien.

Sarik cast such thoughts from his mind as he approached the turn. He skirted the wall of one of the massive tau buildings, and as he came to the corner, edged around to get his first look at the star port complex.

A huge, flat expanse of ground formed the bulk of the star port, with numerous circular pads raised on fluted stilts providing the launch terminals. Control and sensor towers soared high overhead, and arc lights shone down from others, bathing the whole scene in a cold, white light. The nearest of the landing pads, a mere three hundred metres from Sarik, was the scene of bustling activity as tau ground crew rushed to and fro in preparation for a fat, vaguely ovoid lander with four huge thruster units swivelled downwards and spitting a backwash of flame. As the lander neared the pad, its engines cut out, and Sarik thought for a moment its systems had failed. But no, the vessel had been caught in the anti-grav sheath projected by the pad's systems, and was being carried safely downwards towards its docking station.

As the lander came in, Sarik saw a stream of tau warriors emerge from a structure near the landing pad's base, and make their way across the dry ground, towards the elevators inside the structure's supports. These must be the very last of the tau, Sarik thought; the last shuttle out of Gel'bryn.

A squadron of sleek tau flyers rose from a landing pad further away, and moved in towards the lander, assuming an overwatch formation, hovering as their multiple-barrelled heavy weapons scanned the star port's edges. That changed things, Sarik thought. While he might have been prepared to let the lander go unharmed, the presence of the heavily armed escorts made it a matter of military necessity to engage it. The star port had to be captured without delay, and the enemy flyers were an obstacle to be overcome.

'Your orders, brother-sergeant?' Qaja said as he appeared at Sarik's side.

Sarik thought a moment, a plan forming in his mind. His gaze tracked downwards from the rearing landing pad, and across the flat expanse of the complex. The entire area was ringed with a line of low bunkers, and behind them a ring of shield projectors, exactly the same as the one his force had broken through at the very beginning of Operation Pluto.

'No delay,' Sarik told Brother Qaja. 'Grand's deadline may already have passed, so this finishes, now.'

'Agreed, brother-sergeant,' said Qaja. Sarik had no need of his agreement, but he valued Qaja's opinion nonetheless.

'Those bunkers appear to be configured for anti-personnel work.' Qaja nodded his confirmation as he studied the bunkers' low gunports, seeing the multiple-barrelled cannons pointing out threateningly. 'We advance on foot behind the Predators and Rhinos, then use krak and melta on the shield projectors beyond,' Sarik continued. 'After that, we take the landing pad. The enemy surrender, or they die.'

'More likely they die,' said Qaja. 'None of them have surrendered yet.'

'We haven't yet given them the chance, brother,' said Sarik.

'Understood,' said Qaja, understanding well that Sarik was referring as much to his own previous losses of control as to the breakneck speed of the advance. 'I'll pass the order along. Ten minutes?'

Sarik smiled grimly as he took one last look at the line of bunkers. 'Ten minutes.'

THE INSTANT THE Predators and Rhinos moved out, the bunkers opened fire. Twinned cannons spat an incandescent rain of energy bolts from the dozen or so bunkers that had the range and arc to target the Space Marines, hammering the frontal armour plates of the vehicles. Even as dawn edged the horizon a deep jade, the air was lit by livid blue pulses that chased the shadows from the streets.

Sarik had deployed his lascannon-equipped Predator battle tanks and Razorback armoured transports to the head of the formation. Six tanks from four different Chapters ground forwards across the open ground leading to the bunker line, Rhinos fanning out on either side. Energy rounds spat across the two hundred metres between the bunkers and the tanks in constant streams, every round as bright as a tracer, washing back and forth across the tanks. Where the energy rounds struck, they produced a dull wallop and gouged out a lump of armour the size of a clenched fist, but none could penetrate the tanks' forward plates.

The tanks moved at a stately pace, cautious not to advance too rapidly for Sarik's squads were following on foot. While Sarik judged the tanks to be all but impervious to the bunkers' fire, he was less certain about the power armour his warriors wore. What the energy bolts lacked in armour penetration capability, they more than made up for in raw ballistic force, meaning they could wreck a Space Marine's armour systems and cripple the warrior even without cracking open his protective suit.

Striding along behind the lead Predator, Sarik rued the fact that the crusade's Terminators were being held in strategic reserve. All of the heavy-armoured veterans belonged to the Iron Hands Chapter, and Captain Rumann had made it quite clear they were being held back for boarding actions should the fleet find itself engaged in orbit. Sarik conceded that he would have done the same thing, though a squad or two of Terminators teleporting into the bunker line would have made the current advance unnecessary.

'Fifty metres!' Brother Qaja called out over the roar of the tanks.

'Proceed,' Sarik said into the command-net.

Every armoured vehicle that was armed with a lascannon opened fire on its prearranged target. Searing white lances of focussed energy speared the air, slamming into the bunkers and blowing three to atoms within seconds. The weight of fire immediately lessened, but the remaining bunkers swung their fire across to the tanks that had fired, hundreds of energy rounds scything into them with relentless ferocity.

The tanks ground on, their frontal armour plates soon

transformed into cratered slabs of smoking ceramite by the constant fusillade. One Predator, the *Executioner* of the Scythes of the Emperor Chapter, sustained three successive shots to the armour plate immediately fore of the driver's station, and a fourth shattered the whole glacis. The round passed through the wrecked armour and struck the driver a glancing blow to his left shoulder, rendering the arm limp and useless. Despite his wound, the stoic driver continued with his duty, keeping the *Executioner* steady while its commander directed round after round of lascannon fire, taking revenge on the enemy in lethal fashion.

As the vehicles closed on the bunker line, a clear breach was opened where three ruined structures smoked and spat fire into the dawn air.

'Squads forward!' Sarik bellowed. He had no need to use the vox-link for the Space Marines were pressed in behind the armoured vehicles, ready to move forwards and smash aside any resistance that still stood.

Squads deployed in pairs, one group using their boltguns to cover the other as it rushed forwards to storm the bunkers with bolt pistols and grenades. Sarik drew his chainsword with one hand, and took up a melta bomb in the other. While Qaja and the rest of his squad covered him, Sarik joined an Ultramarines assault squad deploying on foot rather than by jump pack, and joined the charge.

As he stepped out from behind the cover of a Rhino, Sarik located the nearest operational bunker and gestured for the assault squad to follow him towards it. The bunker was low and dome-shaped, with the twinned energy burst weapons sweeping left and right from the fire port. The Space Marines came in at the extreme edge of the bunker's firing arc, but still the gunner saw them, sweeping his fire in a wide fan that pulverised the ground and sent up fountains of dust. The charge took only seconds, though Sarik was intensely aware of every single energy bolt as it buzzed through the air towards him and his warriors. Seething blue points of strobing light passed by, etching a trail of vapour where they passed. One bolt struck an Assault Marine square in the chest, gouging a deep wound, its edges flickering blue as the warrior went down. Sarik knew instantly the Ultramarine would fight again.

Seconds before Sarik reached the bunker a final burst of defensive fire spat directly towards him, and he dived to one side. The Assault Marine behind him was not so fast to react. A dozen energy bolts slammed into the Ultramarine's helmet, the first handful destroying the armour, the remainder vaporising the head. The warrior's body continued to run for several seconds, his nervous system locked on the last imperative it had received. Or perhaps the body was driven even beyond the point of death to serve. Perhaps it was just the armour's actuators failing to register that the wearer was slain.

The dead Ultramarine only stopped moving when he slammed into the side of the tau bunker, the headless body finally realising it was slain and toppling to the ground in a heap. Sarik was the next warrior to reach the bunker, followed within seconds by the eight remaining Ultramarines. The twinned cannons continued to spit their blizzard of energy bolts, homing in on more distant targets now that Sarik and the Assault Marines were too close to engage. The stream of fire split the air in a thunderous barrage almost within arm's reach, charging the air and creating small crackles of energy that played across the Space Marines' armour plates.

Sarik edged around the curved form of the bunker, gesturing for the three closest Assault Marines to follow him. The warriors carried bolt pistols in one hand and frag grenades in the other, ready to storm the enemy fortification the instant Sarik's melta bomb had cracked it open.

Aware that enemy infantry might be guarding against an attempt to penetrate the bunker, Sarik moved fast. As he cleared the bunker's rear he looked for an entry hatch, but to his surprise, found none.

'Thinking machines,' Sarik growled, realising that the turrets were automated, controlled by the same heretical machine intelligences that animated the tau's gun drones and other such hated devices. He activated the melta bomb, set it to a three second delay and clamped it to the base of the bunker wall, praying that the charge would be sufficient to penetrate the armour.

The charge set, Sarik retreated back around the wall. He turned to the Assault Marines, and nodded to the frag grenade the nearest was carrying. 'Krak grenades,' he ordered, and a second later the melta bomb detonated.

A ripple of nucleonic fire spread outwards from the bomb, eating the bunker's outer shell and reducing the material to streams of superheated lava. The reaction lasted only seconds and was accompanied by a nigh deafening roar and an instant pressure change as the air was consumed and more rushed in towards the vacuum. When the reaction ceased, the entire rear of the bunker was a blackened mass, a great bite taken out of it to reveal machine systems within.

Sarik had been correct; there were no tau gunners within, merely an automated, machine-controlled gun system. 'Go!' he ordered, and three Assault Marines stepped past him and lobbed their armour-piercing krak grenades inside. The charges detonated with the ear splitting report that gave them their name, and the sound of the twin cannons instantly stopped. Thick black smoke belched from the wound, and the line was silenced.

Now the breach in the bunker line was sufficiently wide for the entire Space Marine force to break through. The Predators ground forwards and assumed overwatch positions, their turret weapons tracking back and forth ready to engage any enemy that counter-attacked from the star port. Rhinos and Razorbacks followed, while the first eight dismounted tactical squads formed two assault groups that pressed left and right along the bunker line to suppress and destroy any bunkers that had the arc and range to harass the force's flanks. Within minutes the sound of melta bombs and krak grenades being brought to bear on more bunkers filled the air, and the bunkers fell silent.

'Brother Targus,' Sarik addressed a Techmarine of the Red Hunters Chapter. The warrior was studying the line of energy shield projectors that lay beyond the bunkers, his articulated servo-arms stretched out from his backpack, the sensors at their ends blinking. 'Mines?'

The Techmarine's sensors tracked back and forth for a moment, before the warrior answered, 'None detected, brother-sergeant. But the xenos may have some method of hiding them from the gaze of the Omnissiah.'

'Understood, Brother Targus,' Sarik replied. 'Please continue your vigil.'

'Predators forward,' Sarik then ordered. 'Breaching duty to positions.'

Five of the battle tanks not standing overwatch moved

forwards through the breach, their dozer blades lowered. Behind each, a tactical squad took position, the battle-brothers equipped with extra supplies of krak grenades.

Sarik moved up to join a squad from the Aurora Chapter, the green-armoured warriors in position and ready to advance. 'Be advised,' he said into the vox-link. 'If this is a minefield, it does not register. Advance.'

The Predators gunned their engines and lurched forwards, and immediately a torrent of burst cannon fire rippled through the air overhead. The flyers overseeing the extraction of the last tau warriors had opened fire, but were remaining protectively close to their charge.

'Your status, brother?' said Sarik.

Brother Qaja's voice came back straight away, 'Enemy infantry have reached the landing pad, brother-sergeant. Crossing towards the lander now.'

'Let's get moving then!' Sarik bellowed, and the Predators began their advance. The tanks moved slowly but surely across the flat expanse of ground between the bunker line and the shield projectors, their dozers lowered and scraping across the packed earth in order to trigger mines that might be waiting just below the surface. Sarik studied the ground at his feet as he strode behind the Predator, looking for tell-tale signs of booby traps amongst the tilled soil.

More rounds screamed in, thudding into the ground behind the Space Marines. The enemy flyers were increasing the volume of their fire, sensing that the tau warriors would soon be overtaken. But the angle was poor and the shots whined harmlessly by over the Space Marines' heads.

It was only when the breaching group was exactly half way across the open ground that the first mine detonated. The ground a mere three metres behind Sarik erupted in a geyser of dust and a mine spat directly upwards. It exploded at a height of two metres, a blinding pulse of booming energy radiating outwards.

One of the Aurora Chapter Tactical Marines was almost directly beneath the explosion. He was slain in an instant, his armour transformed into a deadly wind of razor-sharp shrapnel that tore into a battle-brother nearby. The fragments buried themselves in the warrior's armour, penetrating it in a dozen places and passing straight through in several locations. Another Tactical Marine further out from the blast wave was blown clear, his helmet and half of his face torn from his head by the raging energy pulse.

Sarik had time to turn his shoulder into the blast and brace himself against the wave-front. He felt the hot, actinic energies wash over him, his already ruined shoulder plate absorbing the worst of the damage. As he straightened up again, a second detonation sounded from further along the line, right in the midst of Sergeant Rheq's Scythes of the Emperor tactical squad.

Realising that the mines must have been command operated, Sarik opened the vox-net to address all commands. 'All overwatch units. Locate enemy spotters. Someone must be calling in the detonations.'

The weight of incoming fire redoubled as the tau flyers sought to pin Sarik's force down in the open. Ordinarily, an assault group exposed in such manner would be forced to take cover or retreat in the face of such overwhelming odds. But the Adeptus Astartes rarely began an assault they could not complete, and there were precious few such missions.

The advance continued, not one of the vehicle or squad commanders even contemplating halting unless issued with a direct order to do so. Energy bursts *spanged* from the Predators' frontal armour and hammered into their turrets, then another mine sprang from the ground and exploded directly above an Iron Hands tactical squad further down the line. The explosion sounded like a sonic boom, the rapidly expanding ball of energy casting a luminous blast wave in a wide circle. Three more Space Marines fell, one of them having sustained a fatal wound.

'Lahmas to Sarik,' the voice of the Scythes of the Emperor Devastator sergeant came over the vox-net. 'Enemy spotter located. Engaging.'

The air above the Space Marines was lit by a hail of heavy bolter fire as Lahmas's Devastators hammered the position from which the enemy had been observing the advance. But Sarik was not taking any chances. 'Breaching duty!' he yelled. 'At the double!'

The Predators' engines roared as they lurched forwards at combat speed, the Space Marines behind them increasing their own pace to keep up. Sarik glanced behind him, noting sadly that the broken forms of at least five fallen battle-brothers littered the open ground. He made a silent promise to avenge their sacrifice now, and return for their bodies later.

A sharp explosion halfway up the side of one of the landing pad's supports drew Sarik's attention back to the assault. The entire side of the structure was peppered with ugly black scars, the unmistakable sign of massed heavy bolter fire.

'Spotter neutralised, brother-sergeant,' Lahmas reported curtly. 'Resuming overwatch.'

Sarik's force crossed the remainder of the open

ground without incident, weathering the constant hail of fire incoming from the prowling tau flyers. Within minutes, the breaching duty squads had planted dozens of krak grenades on the nearest three energy shield projectors, and the way into the Gel'bryn star port was at last clear.

SARIK DIVED TO the left as a wave of energy bolts screamed in, rolling across the hard white surface of the landing pad and coming up in a kneeling position, boltgun raised. With a flick of his thumb he set his weapon's shot selector to full auto, and squeezed off a rapid-fire burst at the three tau warriors.

The bolts hammered through hard shell armour and detonated in soft flesh. The first tau was blown backwards into the warrior behind by the impact, then exploded as the bolt-rounds detonated inside his chest, showering his companion with purple gore. The second tau took a round to the throat between helmet and chest armour, his hands grasping the wound instinctively. When the round exploded the warrior's head was torn right off, and sent spinning across the hardpan.

The third tau tried to fall back, firing as he went, but the last of Sarik's burst stitched across his shoulder armour and down his right arm, the detonations blowing the limb away in a shower of vaporised blood, and the weapon it had carried clattered to the ground. The warrior turned to run, and two shots to the back took him down for good.

'Hunters!' Sarik called into the vox-net as he glanced upwards at the circling tau flyers. 'Bring them down!'

The Whirlwinds' commanders acknowledged Sarik's order, and two seconds later a wave of a dozen missiles streaked in from below the raised landing pad, their engines bright in the dawn sky. The tau flyers saw the danger and began to turn, but not before the wave of missiles had split into two, each group arrowing in on one of the nearest two targets. The two flyers were struck simultaneously. The first was hit square in the flank, spinning crazily around as its pilot fought for control. Its engines screamed as they fought for lift, and the craft was soon lost to view. The second was hit directly in the cockpit, the entire front of the vessel exploding outwards and showering the landing pad with white-hot debris. What little was left of the airframe appeared suspended in the air as its anti-grav systems remained online a few seconds more, then it simply dropped, like a boulder, straight down as its systems failed. The wreck struck the edge of the landing pad and sheared in two, touching off a secondary explosion before disintegrating.

Only two flyers remained, one circling back and around the opposite end of the landing pad, its chin-mounted cannon sweeping back and forth. Sarik judged it had been ordered to hold back to protect the lander when it finally launched, which Sarik was determined it would never do. The other was moving forwards towards the hatch, its nose dipped as its multiple-barrelled cannon cycled up.

'Ancient Mhadax to Sergeant Sarik,' the mechanical-sounding voice of the Scythes Dreadnought came over the vox. 'Engaging.'

The entire front section of the flyer erupted in pin-point explosions as the Dreadnought opened up with its assault cannon. So heavy was the fusillade that the craft's forward momentum was arrested, a thousand solid rounds hammering into it in seconds. The armoured nosecone splintered under the relentless assault and was eaten away in an instant. The Dreadnought focussed its fire on the penetrated segment, a hundred more rounds chewing into the flyer's exposed innards.

The flyer disintegrated in mid-air as the assault cannon rounds hollowed it out from within, the rounds now passing straight through its ruined frame. The flyer did not even explode – it literally disappeared before Sarik's eyes, reduced to fragments that scattered wide and fell as hard rain across the entire landing pad.

'Go!' Sarik called to the Space Marines pouring out of the access hatch. Then he was up and running towards the next group of tau backing across the landing pad towards the open rear hatch of the lander. At least thirty tau warriors were at the top of the ramp, keeping up a constant rain of fire intended to suppress the Space Marines and keep them at bay as the last few squads dashed for safety.

Sarik and his squads were halfway across the pad when the four huge, downturned thrusters mounted at each corner of the lander cycled deafeningly to full power. The air rippled as the thrusters powered up and anti-grav projectors thrummed into life with a rolling, sub-acoustic drone.

The Space Marines fired from the hip as they pounded across the hardpan, gunning down the last group of tau left on the pad. The shuttle bounced as the anti-grav cradle took hold, and the thrusters reached full power with a deafening wail.

'Rapid fire!' Sarik bellowed over the howling of the quad thrusters, raising his boltgun to his shoulder and squeezing off a staccato burst right into the gaping rear hatch. Two of the tau warriors were slammed backwards, and the fire of the rest of the Space Marines took down three more and peppered the bulkhead with explosions.

With a tortuous wail, the shuttle wallowed, then began to lift. The last surviving tau flyer banked protectively overhead, its chin-mounted cannon pulsing blue as it opened fire.

The surface of the landing pad was chewed up as burst cannon fire swept in towards Sarik and his warriors.

But Sarik stood his ground. 'No mercy,' he growled, and reached for the melta bomb at his belt. Twisting the plunger, Sarik set the fuse to three seconds, and hurled the charge in an overhead throw that sent it sailing upwards straight towards the lander's open rear hatch. The flyer's fire scythed in towards Sarik, but only when the melta bomb was clear did he dive to one side.

Sarik hit the surface hard, rolling over to look directly upwards as the melta bomb arced through the air and disappeared into the shuttle's hatch.

Time slowed to an impossible crawl as Sarik awaited the melta bomb's detonation. The shuttle laboured upwards, its thrusters at full power as the anti-grav cradle kicked in. The shuttle was twenty metres up and climbing when it suddenly trembled, its progress abruptly arrested. The underbelly swelled grotesquely as nucleonic energies distended the airframe, like a dead thing bloated by corpse gas. Fierce energies raged inside the distended hull, visible through the taut fabric of the distorted armour. The illumination grew, spreading outwards until the entire swollen underside was aglow, the air distorted in a baleful shimmer.

The doomed shuttle shook again, and a mass of flame coughed outwards from the open hatch, followed by a rain of debris and the flailing, flaming bodies of several dozen tau warriors.

Even as blackened body parts slammed down all around, the shuttle exploded. Sarik turned his head away as the sky was turned orange. He screwed his eyes shut, feeling the nuclear wind tearing at his armour and exposed skin. The landing pad shook violently as fragments of the lander hammered downwards and a million red-hot pieces of shrapnel scoured its surface.

Then there was quiet. Sarik rolled over and opened his eyes, the dawn sky lightening overhead. Painfully, he came up onto one knee and scanned the landing pad. Not a single square metre of the surface had been left untouched by the explosion, the pristine white turned to scorched black. Flames licked the hardpan and fragments of debris were scattered all about. Some were just about recognisable as parts of the tau lander, while others, Sarik guessed, belonged to the smaller escort flyer, which must have been caught in the devastation. Most of the debris was so distorted it could have been anything.

A curse sounded from nearby, and what Sarik had at first taken as a mass of debris rose up, revealing itself to be a battle-brother of the Scythes of the Emperor Chapter. The warrior's formerly black and yellow armour was now simply black, its every surface caked in dust and debris. The Scythe reached up and unlocked the catches at his neck, removing his helmet. His face looked startlingly white compared to the condition of his armour.

'Your orders, brother-sergeant?' the brother said dryly.

A burst of laughter rose unbidden to Sarik's throat, and he grinned widely despite himself as he looked around. The rest of the battle-brothers that had charged at his side across the hardpan were slowly regaining their feet, bolters raised as they tracked back and forth across the scene of utter devastation.

'My orders?' said Sarik, wiping a gauntlet across his blackened face. 'Inform crusade command,' he said.

'Operation Hydra primary objective secure.'

WHEN THE TOP of the raised landing platform had been engulfed in flame, Lucian had thought that everything and everyone up there must surely have been slain. Battlegroup Arcadius had been closing on the wrecked bunker line when the dawn sky had been consumed by the destruction of the tau shuttle, and the hot shrapnel had rained down on bodies nowhere near as well protected as a Space Marine's. Three riflemen had been injured by the shrapnel, one severely, and the tanks of the 2nd Armoured, engaging bunkers the Space Marines had bypassed, had been peppered with potentially lethal fragments.

It was only as Lucian was climbing over the ruined fortifications that his vox-bead burst to life, the news not only of Sarik's victory, but of his survival filling every channel. The 2nd Armoured had secured the minefield between the bunkers and the shield projectors, and Lucian had made his way to the landing pad.

'A great victory, my friend,' Lucian said to Sarik as the two stood upon the platform looking out at the aftermath of the destruction. 'A truly great victory.'

'Aye,' Sarik replied, his gaze sweeping outwards past the still-burning hardpan to the city beyond. The sun was rising and the eastern skies were a blaze of luminescent turquoise, their tranquillity marred only by the scores of black, smoking columns rising kilometres into the air. 'I only pray it achieves the desired outcome.'

Lucian glanced upwards into the sky, thinking of the Exterminatus which might rain down upon Dal'yth Prime at any moment. Then he thought of his son, Korvane, who was up there now, on the same vessel as the murderously insane Inquisitor Grand.

'We'll soon find out,' said Lucian. 'Gauge wants a conference, right away.'

'Where?' Sarik said.

'Armak's command vehicle,' said Lucian. 'Coming?'

'Aye, I'm coming,' said Sarik, turning his back on the wreckage-strewn landing pad and the burning city beyond.

SARIK STOOD ASIDE as Colonel Armak's adjutants and subalterns tramped down the ramp of the Brimlock command Chimera, then ducked inside. The interior was cramped, especially for a Space Marine in full battle plate, and lit solely by the illumination of two-dozen flickering readouts.

Sarik seated himself as best he could, and Lucian and Armak followed him in. The colonel of the Brimlock 2nd Armoured and Gauge's chief officer on the surface hauled a lever on the bulkhead over the rear hatch, and the ramp rose up with a hiss of pneumatics. Only when the hatch had slammed shut and the vehicle's overpressure systems sealed it entirely from the outside did the colonel speak.

'Gentlemen,' said Armak, then he paused as he looked towards Sarik. 'Brother-sergeant, can I get you some water?'

Sarik snorted in amusement, though he appreciated the sentiment. He nodded, and Armak tossed him a half-full canteen. Instead of drinking from the vessel, he sluiced it over his face, ridding himself of just a small portion of the grime and dried blood caking his features.

Sarik set the canteen down on a nearby tacticae-station, and Armak reached across to a command terminal and entered a code into its keyboard. 'I'm opening the most secure link I can, one normally reserved for Codes and Ciphers.' The terminal lit up as reams of data script scrolled across its surface.

Sarik and Lucian exchanged dark glances, the rogue trader raising his eyebrows to indicate he had no idea what Armak was about.

'How secure a link do you need?' asked Sarik. 'And why?'

'You'll see, brother-sergeant,' said Armak. 'One moment, please.'

The terminal droned and chirped for another ten seconds, then it chimed to announce its system had achieved machine communion with another. All of the tacticae-stations in the Chimera's passenger bay burst into life as one. Half of them showed General Gauge seated in a chamber equally as dark as the Chimera's interior, while the other half showed Captain Rumann, standing at the command pulpit of the *Fist of Light*.

The Iron Hands captain was entirely immobile, his augmetic features unreadable. General Gauge appeared gaunt and washed out, though his eyes still shone with the cold, steely light that was so familiar to Sarik and Lucian.

'Veteran Sergeant Sarik,' Gauge said. 'Please accept my congratulations on your victory, and my commiserations on your losses.'

'Both are welcomed,' said Sarik. 'Though neither is necessary.'

Gauge nodded, expecting the response, then addressed Lucian. 'Lord Gerrit. Your rallying of the ground forces in the aftermath of Cardinal Gurney's... withdrawal, contributed greatly to the capture of Gel'bryn, and averted a rout of catastrophic proportions. Your deeds shall be remembered.'

Lucian made a dismissive gesture with his hand, but Sarik knew better. The rogue trader was rightly proud of his actions.

'Colonel Armak?' said Gauge.

'Sir?' Armak replied, as if he had not expected to be addressed by his commanding officer.

'You have been serving as brevet general. That rank is confirmed. Congratulations, General Armak.'

The officer's expression told of his genuine surprise, but Gauge continued before the officer could reply. 'Now, to the real reason I have called this gathering.

'The Damocles Gulf Crusade has reached a critical juncture. We are faced not with one enemy, but two. Though the tau have fallen back from Gel'bryn, a massive war fleet is in orbit already, and Grand might unleash his Exterminatus at any moment.'

Gauge allowed his summary of the strategic situation to sink in, then continued. 'I propose we muster all forces at Gel'bryn star port, and evacuate.'

Sarik took a deep breath, the blood and sacrifice of the last few days flooding his mind. Then, Captain Rumann spoke for the first time, his machine-wrought voice sounding all the more metallic across the clipped and distorted channel.

'No,' Rumann stated coldly.

General Gauge nodded sadly, evidently expecting the captain's reaction. Then Lucian cut in. 'Wait,' the rogue trader said. 'All of you, just wait. Wendall,' Lucian used the general's first name, 'tell us the truth. How bad is it?'

Gauge nodded his thanks towards Lucian. 'When the tau were first encountered, by Lucian and other rogue traders, they were deemed a low-level threat. They were found only in small groups, coreward of the gulf, and usually acting as mercenaries or advisors to planetary governors who had... strayed, to a greater or lesser extent, from the rule of the Imperium. But that was uncovered as a ruse. They were acting as fifth columnists, infiltrating system after system in an effort to expand their sphere of influence. The crusade was raised to put that threat down. Every shred of intelligence and analysis available to us indicated they could hold no more than a handful of worlds. When they were first catalogued, millennia ago, they were no more than over-evolved dromedaries with no technology more advanced than sharp sticks.'

Gauge let that hang for a moment, then continued grimly. 'Yet here they are, in control of an entire star cluster, possessed of a substantial fleet capable of interstellar travel, unheard-of tech, and weaponry that, frankly, outguns most of our own.'

'Sedition,' Captain Rumann said flatly. 'No inferior xenos can stand before us...'

'But that's it!' interjected Lucian. 'Quite clearly, the tau are not inferior, and they *are* standing against us.'

'We've given them a bloody nose,' said General Gauge, smiling wryly at his unintentionally ironic turn of phrase. 'But their reinforcements are here already, and despite previous promises, ours are not. We pull out now, or we spend the rest of our lives as their prisoners.'

'No Astartes will allow that to happen, general,' said Sarik. 'As well you know.'

'We all know you'll never surrender,' said Lucian. 'But

is it not true that all your doctrines teach that futile expenditure of life is as great a sin as surrender?'

'Do not presume to preach the *Codex Astartes* to us, rogue trader,' Captain Rumann growled. The captain's anger was expressed as much by distortion and feedback as by any change in his mechanical voice patterns.

Sarik could no longer contain his annoyance. 'Let him speak.'

'What?' said Captain Rumann.

'Lucian is correct,' said Sarik. 'Our doctrine states that a tactical redeployment to muster for further action is preferable to a hollow last stand, if at all possible.'

'You intend, *Sergeant* Sarik, to stand by them in-'

'I do,' growled Sarik, aware that the others appeared uncomfortable to be witnessing the confrontation. He was also aware, painfully aware, how divergent the views of his Chapter and the captain's were. The White Scars' methods of war were born of the noble savages who had made war across the steppes of Chogoris for millennia, masters of the lightning strike that was reflected in the Chapter's very symbol, which he wore proudly on his shoulder. When facing a larger foe, the Chogorans would strike, then pull back, then strike again, until the enemy was bled to death one drop of blood at a time.

Captain Rumann on the other hand was a product of the Iron Hands Chapter. Their determination and resilience was born of their own beliefs about the frailty of the flesh, which they replaced with iron by augmenting their bodies with bionic components. Within each burned a heart as fierce as molten iron. But now, the Iron Hands' legendary determination was, to his mind, in danger of turning into blind stubbornness.

'What sense is there, what *honour* is there, in the

crusade overstretching itself and being cut off?' said Sarik. 'I propose that we do as the general says: evacuate, consolidate, and return with a war fleet capable of fulfilling the bold promises made at the outset of the crusade.

'That way,' Sarik concluded, 'will we find honour.'

A tense silence descended, disturbed only by background static churning from the vox-horns. Then Rumann answered. 'I will not order my forces to retreat.'

'Then order them to re-deploy, brother-captain,' said Sarik. 'A great victory may be won here. But not now, not like this.'

Captain Rumann simply nodded.

'Then we are in agreement on this?' said General Gauge.

'We still have the issue of the Exterminatus,' said Lucian. 'If that goes ahead, even after we've evacuated, all of this will have been for nothing.'

'That, gentlemen,' said Gauge, 'is another matter, which forms the basis of the reason for Admiral Jellaqua's absence from this conference.'

'Explain,' said Rumann.

'Right now, I cannot,' said Gauge. 'Not even on this channel.'

'Why can you not…?' said Sarik, but his words trailed off as every pict screen at every station in the Chimera's passenger bay flickered with static, went blank and then returned. The faces of General Gauge and Captain Rumann had been replaced by that of another.

'Because,' said Inquisitor Grand, 'he is a traitor... As are you all.'

IN THE HOURS after its capture, Gel'bryn star port came rapidly to resemble a makeshift Imperial Guard muster point. The 2nd Brimlock Armoured quickly established a cordon around the entire complex, their tanks and support vehicles acting as bunkers with their weapons trained on any approach a counter-attack might develop from. The Rakarshan Rifles of Battlegroup Arcadius were the next regiment to move in. Major Subad dispatched the light infantry companies to secure the complex's many buildings, towers and storage facilities, in case the tau had left their carnivore allies as stay-behinds.

The Brimlock regiments poured into the complex after the Rakarshans had spread out, the flat expanse of ground beneath the raised landing platforms soon filling with grumbling armoured vehicles. Hydra flak tanks tracked their quad-barrelled autocannons back and forth across the skies, anticipating a tau air strike at any moment. Thankfully, the sacrifice made by the aircrews of the Imperial Navy at the very outset of Operation Hydra had severely punished the tau flyers, and none appeared.

As the regimental provosts set about marshalling the huge numbers of men and machines flooding into the star port, attached tech-priests invaded the control towers. Ostensibly, the adepts of the Machine-God were tasked with fathoming the operation of the star port's anti-grav cradles, which would speed up the landing and liftoff of the hundreds of troop transports that would soon be in operation immeasurably. It took the tech-priests less than an hour to master the anti-grav generators, and another for them to begin disassembling at least one of the devices for later study.

The mighty god-machines of the Legio Thanataris dispersed to form a wide ring around the star port, their crews vigilant for signs of tau activity. Wherever they trod, the Titans caused as much damage as an Imperial Guard artillery bombardment, and they had soon cleared a rubble-strewn killing ground around the complex, over which they stood silent sentinel with weapon limbs scanning the horizon.

The Space Marines spread out into the surrounding areas too, coordinating their actions with the princeps commanders of the Battle Titans. Sarik ordered his force to ensure that no enemy infantry were lurking in the ruins around the star port, and the squads soon drove off several groups of carnivores that attempted to ambush them amongst the shattered habs. These skirmishes were tiny in comparison to the scale of Operation Hydra, but Sarik ordered the savage aliens hunted down and slaughtered, so vile was their habit of eating the flesh of the fallen.

It was as the first of the troop transports were descending on the star port on boiling pillars of flame, that Lucian, walking towards the Rakarshans' lines to take his leave of the bold mountain fighters, received a transmission from Sergeant Sarik.

'Lucian?' Sarik began, the rogue trader sensing something unusual in the Space Marine's tone. 'What is your present position?'

Lucian halted, looking around for a landmark. Imperial Guard troopers, battered and bloody, trudged past him in long files, many fully laden with what weapons and equipment they could evacuate with them. An entire heavy weapons company was passing through the breach the Space Marines had made in the bunker line, which had been widened and made safe by Munitorum pioneers. 'I'm at phase point nine-zero,' he said, using the term the Tacticae planners had coined for the outer perimeter of the star port. 'Why?'

'I'm five hundred metres north east of your position,' said Sarik, ignoring Lucian's question. 'Get here, now.'

What now, Lucian thought, drawing his plasma pistol and checking the charge. It was down to ten per cent. His power armour was scratched and scored, much of its surface black with carbonisation and soot. He was fatigued and thirsty, and well in need of rest, yet he loosened his power sword in its scabbard as he pushed through the lines of the Imperial Guard troopers flooding in the opposite direction. Many cast him irritated glances as he forced his way on, but many others wore vacant and shell-shocked expressions that spoke of the ferocity of the battle they had just faced.

Clearing the breach in the bunker line, Lucian located the direction Sarik had indicated, and hurried towards it as fast as he could manage. His power armour lent him some strength at least, though not much more than it took to bear its own weight. The suit had served him well, but it would need much attention to restore its war spirit to its full vitality once this was over.

He passed along a wide boulevard, its surface caked with a dried paste made from the blackened remains of the alien carnivores. To one side he saw a pair of Space Marine Apothecaries, one from the Novamarines, the other from the White Scars, recovering the scattered body and armour parts of a slain battle-brother. He could not tell which Chapter the dead warrior was from, for the armour was so encrusted with gore and ash its colours were entirely obscured.

Lucian gave the two medics a wide birth, leaving them to their sad duty out of respect.

After another few minutes crunching through the corpse litter, Lucian saw the white-armoured forms of a group from Sarik's Chapter gathered up ahead. Around twenty White Scars were gathered about a ruined, smoking dome, the rubble of its destruction strewn all about.

As he approached the White Scars, Sarik turned and waved him over.

'Lucian,' said Sarik. 'She'll talk only to you.'

'Who?' said Lucian as the White Scars parted to make way.

The dome had not been ruined by ordnance or the tread of a Battle Titan, but by the impact of a small craft of tau origin. That craft protruded from the cracked eggshell structure, and a figure was sat languidly upon its upper surface, clad in the tattered remains of tau water caste finery.

'I thought you'd never get here, father,' said Brielle.

LUCIAN APPROACHED THE downed saviour pod, for that was what he judged the craft to be, in silence. Sarik clapped Lucian on the shoulder as he walked past, then the Space Marine led his warriors away a respectful distance.

As Lucian approached the pod, Brielle pushed herself off and slid down its rounded surface, coming to rest, barefoot, in front of him. Lucian's eyes narrowed as he met his daughter's gaze.

'Well?' he said.

Brielle's lop-sided grin faded, and she cocked her head, her plaited locks a dishevelled mess.

'Well what...?' she muttered petulantly.

'You are dead,' Lucian said flatly. 'You assaulted an agent of the Holy Orders of the Emperor's Inquisition and disappeared.'

'I never *said* I was dead...' she started.

'You never said *anything*!' Lucian bellowed. For some reason he could not begin to fathom, he was not the slightest bit surprised to find his daughter, who he had every reason to believe dead, standing here, in a burning tau city, light years away from where he had last seen her. He fought back the urge to strike her, so maddening was her manner.

'I didn't get the chance,' said Brielle. 'And I'm sorry, father. I'm really sorry.'

'What happened?' said Lucian. 'Why all this?' he gestured to the downed saviour pod, but both knew he meant a whole lot more.

'I'll tell you everything, father,' Brielle stepped closer as she spoke. 'But first, I have to tell you about the tau fleet...'

'The tau fleet in orbit on the far side of this world?' Lucian cut in. 'We're not stupid, Brielle.'

Her expression darkening, Brielle ploughed on. 'The tau intend to demand the crusade's surrender,' she said. 'They wanted me to be their envoy, and that's how I got out. I tricked them, I...'

Lucian raised an eyebrow, well aware that his daughter was only telling him part of the truth, the part that suited her the most.

'...but they have no idea of the crusade's true strengths,' Brielle continued. 'They don't know about the reinforcements.'

Lucian barked out a bitter laugh, and his daughter assumed a crestfallen expression.

'There aren't any reinforcements,' she said, a statement rather than a question.

'We're pulling out,' said Lucian flatly. 'But I imagine you guessed that. If you'd left it any later to enact your cunning plan,' Lucian smirked, 'you'd have had to stay behind.'

'I didn't want to go in the first place,' Brielle said, her

pout making Lucian laugh despite himself. 'Grand attacked *me*. I didn't mean to kill him...'

'Well, you can apologise in person,' said Lucian.

Brielle stopped dead in her tracks. 'He's alive?'

'No thanks to you, yes,' said Lucian. 'Though he sustained serious wounds.'

'If he's still alive,' she stammered, 'he'll–'

'Grand has lost it, Brielle,' Lucian interjected. 'He's insane and he'll kill us all if he can.

'You're hardly the top of his list.'

'ALL WILL RISE!' the convenor bellowed, his metal-shod staff of office striking the deck of the council chamber with a resounding thud. Korvane Gerrit rose from the council seat normally occupied by his father, and the remainder of the gathered councillors rose from theirs.

The chamber seemed empty, with several seats around the circular, black marble table unoccupied. Korvane's father, as well as Veteran Sergeant Sarik, was still on the surface, while Captain Rumann was engaged on the *Fist of Light*. Those not present in person would nonetheless witness the session, by way of the images transmitted by a score of servo skull spy-drones hovering discreetly in the shadows, their multiple lenses whirring and clicking as they tracked the scene. General Gauge had not yet arrived either.

Inquisitor Grand sat across the table from Korvane, his black robes seeming to draw him into the shadows, or perhaps to gather the darkness towards him. What little of the inquisitor's flesh was visible was covered in a chaotic mass of scar tissue, the result of the flamer attack unleashed by Korvane's sister months before. Thinking about Brielle made Korvane's skin crawl, for he too had suffered at her hands. While he could never prove it, he harboured the suspicion that the accident aboard his vessel had been caused by her. Korvane had drawn on the resources of the Clan Arcadius to ensure his wounds were treated, and while they had largely healed, they still pained him greatly.

It appeared to Korvane that the inquisitor wore his wounds proudly and overtly, allowing the scar tissue to enshroud his limbs as nature intended. Perhaps he was making some point about the ascendancy of the human form and the purity of its function, Korvane thought, for the Inquisition was riven with hundreds of different doctrines and philosophies that sometimes set its members violently at odds with one another.

Cardinal Gurney sat to Grand's right, glowering at Korvane. No doubt word of Lucian's rallying of the troops following Gurney's untimely departure had spread. It was now obvious to all gathered that the cardinal had left the surface having been forewarned of Grand's intention to bring forward the Exterminatus, but something had happened to forestall the devastation that hovered over Dal'yth Prime like the executioner's axe.

No one knew why the disbanded council had been reconvened, or why Grand had not overridden the convocation. The atmosphere was tense, and the council chamber noticeably colder than usual.

'Admiral Jellaqua, of the Imperial Navy,' the convenor intoned, 'and…'

Jellaqua leaned in to whisper into the convenor's ear, then the man announced, '…Interrogator Armelle Rayne, of the Holy Ordos of the Emperor's Inquisition.'

The air in the council chamber grew colder still. Another figure appeared at the door behind the admiral and his companion.

'General Gauge,' announced the convenor, striking the deck once more. 'Admiral Jellaqua has the chair. Let the council convene.'

General Gauge took his seat three places to Korvane's right, nodding to him as he did so. The portly Admiral Jellaqua sat himself next to Gauge, gifting Korvane a surreptitious wink as he settled into his chair. The individual who had been introduced as Interrogator Rayne took the seat between Jellaqua and Korvane, and as she sat, she pulled back the hood of her outer robe.

The interrogator was a striking woman, her head bald and her skull subtly elongated, as if nature or augmentation had sculpted her into a new form. Her eyes too were ever so slightly altered and the irises were mirrored. Her features were sharp, almost angular, and her lips full. The side of her bald cranium was tattooed with an intricate tracery of arcane symbols: the aquila, the 'I' of the Inquisition, and many other glyphs worked into dazzling patterns.

Rayne noted Korvane's scrutiny, and turned towards him. She inclined her head in greeting. 'Korvane Gerrit of the Clan Arcadius,' she said, her voice like the purr of a felid. Korvane realised she must have been casting some psyker's glamour to subtly manipulate the councillors' perceptions, and forced his attentions towards the gatherings.

Rayne caught Korvane's eye the instant that thought crossed his mind, the ghost of a wry smile touching her lips.

'Fellow councillors,' said Admiral Jellaqua. 'I have called this extraordinary session of the crusade council...'

'This council is dissolved,' Inquisitor Grand growled,

his voice low and threatening. 'By the authority of the Seal.'

Jellaqua's eyes narrowed as he dared meet those of Inquisitor Grand. 'Nonetheless,' the admiral matched Grand's tone, 'there is much to discuss.'

'There is nothing to discuss!' Cardinal Gurney growled as he rose to his feet. Jellaqua smirked slightly at the spectacle of the firebrand preacher performing the role of the inquisitor's attack hound, but otherwise kept his gaze fixed squarely on Inquisitor Grand.

'As I said, there is much to discuss,' said Jellaqua, then inclined his head towards the interrogator at his side. 'I present Mamzel Rayne,' he paused, the air growing colder as he spoke. 'Envoy of Lord Inquisitor Kryptman.'

Korvane's breath formed a cold, billowing cloud as he breathed out. Mere days had passed since the astropathic communication informing the council that Kryptman's envoy would be joining them. None had expected the envoy to arrive so quickly, for the crusade itself had taken long weeks to cross the Damocles Gulf. Korvane had heard the whispered spacer's tales of the archeotech vessels the highest servants of the Inquisition had access to – perhaps they were not mere tales at all.

Interrogator Rayne stood, her black outer robe sliding from her bare shoulder to fall across the chair behind her. She was adorned in a long, flowing, off-the-shoulder gown made of the finest black void-silk Korvane had ever seen. She appeared more a noble of a high court than an agent of one of the most feared institutions in the Imperium.

'My thanks,' Rayne nodded to the admiral, before her gaze swept over the gathered councillors. Gurney was lowering himself back into his seat, his face a mask of righteous, yet impotent fury, while Inquisitor Grand had visibly stiffened in his chair, his spindly body coiled as if ready to strike at any moment. Logistician-General Stempf would clearly rather have been anywhere else than at the council table, and he studiously avoided the interrogator's gaze as it swept over him.

The three new councillors, who Korvane had recruited, seemingly futilely for the council had been disbanded by Grand straight after, met Rayne's gaze confidently. Korvane knew that he had chosen the three well, that they were men of principle who had nothing to hide from the interrogator's scrutiny.

'I come before this council as the emissary of my master, Lord Kryptman. The missive I have to impart comes directly from him, and he has sanctioned me to act in his name, in all things.'

Korvane could not help but feel that the last statement was aimed directly at Inquisitor Grand. The air grew colder still. All of the councillors knew that Inquisitor Grand was the source of the drop in temperature, and several cast wary glances around the table, yet none dared show any overt sign of discomfort or fear.

Interrogator Rayne reached to a pouch at her waist and withdrew a small, circular device with a glassy orb on its upper surface. Activating a command stud, she slid the device across the surface to the centre of the table, and stood back with her arms folded.

The orb flickered to life and then cast a column of harsh white light into the space above it. The shaft danced with motes of energy, which resolved into a figure. It was a stooped, old man, clothed in the robes of an inquisitor, and he was possessed of such power and authority that all in the chamber felt utterly cowed.

Then, the glowing, transparent figure spoke, his rich, low voice filling the chamber.

'I am Inquisitor Lord Kryptman,' the projection began. *'And I come before you with the full authority of the High Lords of Terra themselves. There is scant time for explanations and none for debate, so I will get straight to the point.*

'All commands receiving this message are hereby ordered, by the authority of the Senatorum Imperialis, to cease all military operations and set course for the Macragge system in the Realm of Ultramar. Every possible asset is to be mustered and no resource expended except in the execution of this order.'

The flickering projection of Inquisitor Lord Kryptman paused, as if gathering his thoughts.

'Fellow subjects of the God-Emperor, I shall not lie to you. A threat the likes of which the Imperium has not faced since the dawn of this age is descending upon us. I do not know if this is the beginning or the end, but I tell you this. If we do not defeat it at Macragge, the entire Imperium may fall.

'Heed the words of my envoy as my own, and obey what orders you are given as my own.

'That is all.'

Profound silence descended on the council chamber, only the faint whirring of the servo-skulls' spy-lenses audible as they hovered in the shadows. The projection faded to nothing, and Interrogator Rayne stepped forwards, placing her hands at the table's edge and leaning in hawkishly to address the councillors.

'The Damocles Gulf Crusade,' Rayne began haughtily, 'though a righteous and noble undertaking, is ended.'

A thin skein of ice appeared on the surface of the marble table, spreading outwards from Grand's gnarled hands where they gripped its edge. A sense of primal dread settled on the chamber, and Korvane knew that dread was the inquisitor's ire, made manifest by the agency of his formidable psychic potential. Rayne's glance settled on Inquisitor Grand for a moment, before she continued without comment.

'All available forces are to answer my master's call and muster at Macragge.'

'What threat?' Cardinal Gurney stammered. 'What could possibly–'

The interrogator went from haughty calm to banshee rage in a heartbeat. 'You will be silent!' Rayne screamed, her rage so focussed and sharp it was as if she had drawn a power sword and plunged it directly into the cardinal's heart. 'By the authority vested in me by my master, I *order* you to be silent.'

Cardinal Gurney looked like he had been bodily assaulted, his face draining of its colour as he visibly shrivelled before the interrogator's anger. Korvane knew that the cardinal, as an officer of the Ministorum, could claim to be outside of Kryptman's authority. But then again, the lords of the Inquisition relied not on rule-books to impose their will, but on influence, and Gurney was well outranked in that regard. Korvane glanced towards Inquisitor Grand, who had remained silent throughout. Grand was rigid, but now a frosting of ice coated his flesh.

Several of the councillors swallowed hard, as much through fear of the inquisitor as dread at the envoy's words. What could possibly threaten such a vast expanse of the mighty Imperium of Mankind? Even the most widespread rebellion, the mightiest ork incursion or the most ferocious crusade of the arch-enemy rarely afflicted more than a sector of Imperial space. To threaten an entire segmentum, an enemy would have to be of a scale not witnessed since the Imperium's darkest days.

'The enemy of which my master speaks is a previously unknown xenos-form, which he has codified *tyranids*,' Rayne continued, satisfied that Gurney's interruption was at an end. 'Already, they are classed *xenos terminus*, but serious consideration is being given to creating a new threat rating, just for them.'

'What are these... tyranids?' said Korvane. 'What is their nature?'

Rayne turned her head to look down at Korvane, before replying, 'They are beasts of nightmare.' Her gaze became distant as she spoke, as if recalling sights she would rather not describe. 'They take a million forms, from gargantuan, world-razing monstrosity to flesh-eating parasite. They are teeth, claw, tentacle and maw.' The interrogator stopped there, and Korvane had little desire to learn more, though he knew he would.

'How were they discovered?' Korvane pressed.

'Initially, when outlying worlds surveyed long ago by the Exploratus, fell silent.'

Korvane nodded, reminded of the misfortunes that had overtaken the Clan Arcadius in recent years, as ancient hereditary trade routes to the galactic east had run dry, seemingly without cause. Worlds that generations of his dynasty had traded with had gone silent, the once ceaseless flow of exotic goods slowing to a mere trickle. The clan's fortunes had suffered so badly that Lucian had pinned all of his hopes on the Damocles Gulf Crusade, aiming to establish exclusive trade deals with the tau once they had been put firmly in their place. Grand's Exterminatus had threatened all of that, but Rayne's news spoke of something far worse than a threat to a single world.

'Having perceived a pattern in reports of worlds once catalogued as sustaining life being reduced to barren rocks, my Lord Kryptman received dispensation to investigate. At the Explorator base at Tyran Primus, he found evidence of a xenos abomination so virile and ravenous its organisms can strip an entire world of its biomass in days.'

'To...' Logistician-General Stempf stammered, '...to what end?'

'That is under investigation,' Rayne answered. 'Certainly to feed, presumably to reproduce, but we do not yet understand why they need so much biomass or to what use they put it. But they descended on Thandros like a swarm of voracious locusts, like a beast rising from the depths of the ocean. Then it was Prandium.'

'And after Prandium,' said Jellaqua, 'comes Macragge, fortress home world of the Ultramarines.'

'Surely,' said Tacticae-Primaris Kilindini, speaking for the first time at council, 'an entire Chapter of Space Marines can hold this species at bay. To assault Macragge is suicide on a racial scale...'

Interrogator Rayne studied the Tacticae for a moment, as if he were a curious morsel on a sample dish laid out before her. 'No,' she said flatly. 'Let me make this quite clear.'

'The tyranids are more than a species. They are a blight, a swarm. They are a storm of teeth and claws and chitin and saliva, and they hunger to consume us all. They are a billion billion ravening organisms bred for one purpose and one purpose alone: to kill. Each organism is but a single cell in a mass that is spread across light years of space. Where that mass travels, its thoughts drown out the light of the Astronomican and cast the warp itself into impassable turbulence. Astropaths caught in that 'shadow in the warp' would rather scratch their brains out than endure the chittering of a trillion voices that all speak as one.'

'So no, Tacticae-Primaris. The Ultramarines alone cannot hold this foe at bay. It will take every Chapter, regiment, Legio and fleet on the Eastern Fringe to afford even the slightest chance of survival, yet alone victory.'

There was a drawn-out pause, before Korvane spoke up. 'How long.'

'In truth,' sighed Rayne, 'we have no way of knowing. Every unit of every arm we can reach is being recalled to Macragge, whatever their status. We may have months, or just days, but should Macragge fall, nowhere will be safe.'

'I have already briefed Interrogator Rayne as to our ground forces' status,' said General Gauge. 'Most of our units are at or closing in on the Gel'bryn star port. The evacuation is already under way.'

Now the temperature in the council chamber was dropping towards sub zero, and Rayne turned her gaze on Inquisitor Grand.

'You have a statement to make, inquisitor?' Rayne said haughtily. 'An objection, perhaps?'

Grand's hold on the side of the marble tightened, his knuckles turning white. Frost crept up the glass drinking vessel in front of Korvane, and he knew that should he touch it his skin would adhere to its surface. Though little of Grand's face was visible beneath his hood, his scarred mouth scowled as he answered.

'The Writ of Exterminatus has been cast upon this place called in the base tongue of the xenos *Dal'yth Prime*,' the inquisitor growled, his disgust at using the tau's name for their world plain to read. 'I have pronounced my sentence upon the xenos of the world below, and that sentence shall be enacted.'

Interrogator Rayne tipped her regal head back and

looked down her nose at the inquisitor. For one of her rank to display such open contempt for a superior would ordinarily have provoked the most lethal form of censure. But Rayne was speaking with the authority of an inquisitor lord, and all present in the chamber knew it.

Inquisitor Grand knew it.

'The Writ of Exterminatus is hereby revoked,' said Rayne, her eyes boring into the shadows within Grand's hood. 'By authority of my Lord Inquisitor Kryptman.'

A sharp groaning echoed through the chamber, the sound of metal and wood distorted by the cold.

Something dropped suddenly from the shadows above the conference table, smashing to a thousand shards and causing all except Grand and Rayne to pull back sharply and several to utter curses and exclamations. Korvane's heart thundered as he saw that the icy table surface was now covered in bony splinters. One of the servo skulls had frozen solid and plummeted from the air, shattering on impact with the cold, hard marble.

'To leave an enemy at our backs is–' Grand began.

'Entirely the point,' interjected Rayne, her tone low and as cold as the air in the chamber.

'It is decided,' said General Gauge. 'On Kryptman's authority.' At a nod from the interrogator, Gauge went on. 'If these tyranids are the threat they appear, then the tau are more use to us alive than exterminated.'

'Blasphemy!' Cardinal Gurney spat. Rayne shot him another dark glance, and he looked to the inquisitor at his side, but said no more.

'I think I see it,' Korvane spoke up. 'If the incursion is dire enough to imperil the entire segmentum, then the tau will likely have to face it too. It is not unheard of for humanity to stand side by side with xenos against a mutual foe. Have our forces not taken to the field along-side the eldar, against the arch-enemy?'

'Indeed,' said Rayne. 'And if the tau will not cooperate in this, they will face the tyranid swarm alone. Either way,' she reiterated Gauge's words, 'they are more use to us alive.'

'As a backstop,' said the Tacticae-Primaris, nodding. 'Better the invaders expend their energies against the tau's worlds than against our own.'

Interrogator Rayne looked around the table to each of the councillors, allowing her words to sink in. She ended her sweep on Inquisitor Grand, her gaze lingering on him along with that of every other councillor present.

Slowly, the inquisitor rose to his feet. He turned without a word, and stalked from the council chamber, frost billowing in the air behind him.

LEANING BACK IN the seat in the passenger bay of his Rhino, Sergeant Sarik exhaled slowly. The pict-feed showed the council breaking up. The councillors each had a myriad of tasks to undertake, for the crusade fleet would be disengaging as soon as practicable. Sarik and the rogue trader had watched the proceedings in grim silence, barely able to conceive of the scale of the xenos incursion the interrogator had described. With a flick of a control rune Sarik deactivated the command terminal, the pict screen fading to grainy static.

'Well?' said Lucian.

'Any misgivings I had about evacuating are now entirely assuaged, friend Lucian,' Sarik replied. 'The storm rises, and soon worlds shall burn, of that I am sure. Honour demands the Astartes answer the call to war.'

'And Dal'yth Prime?' pressed Lucian.

'Honour is satisfied,' said Sarik. 'You are troubled?'

Lucian paused before answering, then nodded. 'Sarik, you are a mighty warrior, and a noble man...'

'But?' said Sarik, a hint of amusement glinting in his eye.

Lucian smiled, though his own eyes showed no amusement at all. 'But, your battles are fought in the open, against foes you can see and understand and kill.'

'And yours are not,' said Sarik.

'Aye,' Lucian sighed. 'They are not.'

'How then must you win your own battle?' Sarik said. 'Tell me this, and I offer you what aid I may provide.'

'This is not over,' said Lucian flatly.

'Explain, please,' said Sarik, judging that Lucian referred to something more than the crusade and its battles against the tau.

'Grand won't let it end like this,' said Lucian. 'Since the earliest days of the crusade council's formation, I've suspected that he had something more than conquest in mind. The fact that he concealed his possession of an Exterminatus device suggests to me he never intended to suppress the tau, or to conquer them, or to contain them on this side of the Gulf.'

'Lucian,' sighed Sarik. 'The fact that an inquisitor demands the extermination of a xenos species is hardly outside of his remit.'

'True, but he was prepared to sacrifice the ground forces, including your own, in the execution of his Exterminatus. He's a radical, Sarik, I'm sure of it.'

'The internal politics of the Inquisition are no concern of mine, Lucian,' said Sarik. 'But I believe you are correct. Whatever his agenda, it is clearly a danger to us all. What do you think he will do next?'

'I don't know,' said Lucian, his expression pained. 'But I need to be there, to stop him.'

Sarik nodded slowly, weighing up the consequences, for his Chapter as well as himself, of what he was about to say.

'Then I too must be there,' he said solemnly. 'Your Warrant of Trade is a powerful totem, Lucian, but so too is the Inquisitorial rosette. You will not face Grand alone, on that I swear.'

CHAPTER ELEVEN

KORVANE PRESSED HIS back against the cold, iron bulkhead, listening intently to the sound of Grand's footsteps receding further down the shadowed, red-lit passageway. The metal of the bulkhead was cold because Grand was exuding billowing clouds of frost in his wake as he prowled further from the council chamber. As Korvane readied himself to move on again, the frost under his hand turned to liquid as normal temperature returned, thin, oily runnels streaking down the walls.

When the inquisitor's footsteps were almost too distant to hear, Korvane pressed on again. His heart pounded with barely suppressed terror as he considered for the hundredth time turning back. This was insane, he told himself. In going after the inquisitor, he was putting himself in mortal danger, for Grand was known to be a powerful psyker and as well an accomplished torturer.

Nonetheless, this had to be done, Korvane thought as he felt the now familiar weight of the ring his father had given him. The gift was far more than an object, far more even than the contents of the stasis tomb it would unlock. It had given Korvane strength and courage, even as it had loaded him with the responsibility of the heir of Clan Arcadius. That was why he was trailing an insane inquisitor through the bowels of an Imperial warship.

Because he had to, because honour and duty demanded nothing less. Korvane had always assumed that being at or near the head of a rogue trader dynasty should remove one from the action, with legions of underlings to get the dirty work done. He now understood that the reverse was true. He could understand exactly why his father had desired to participate in the ground war, and it was nothing so prosaic as ego.

Some things you just had to do yourself.

With the *Blade of Woe* preparing to take thousands of passengers on board and getting ready to make warp, the subsidiary passageways through which Korvane passed were virtually empty. Every available crewman was at his station, attending to the myriad tasks required of him prior to departure. Korvane wished he were back in the command throne of his own vessel, the *Rosetta*, pursuing the fortunes of the Clan Arcadius, not engaged in internecine political wars with parties who should count one another allies against a common foe.

Inquisitor Grand.

Korvane tried to keep his footfalls as silent as possible as he stalked the passageway, knowing that such sounds had a habit of reverberating in odd, unpredictable ways in the bowels of a starship as large and venerable as the *Blade of Woe*. Even with the ever-present throb of plasma conduits and the distant whine of the drive banks cycling to idle, his footsteps might betray him to the inquisitor.

More likely, however, Korvane's own thoughts would betray him. Grand was a psyker of prodigious power, and while Korvane did not know if the inquisitor was an empath, he must assume that he was. He had to keep his distance, in case Inquisitor Grand heard not just his footsteps but his mind.

Korvane realised that the air was getting colder, meaning Grand must have slowed or come to a halt. He glanced around to get his bearings, but the red illumination of ship's night cast the entire scene in stark shadows. He followed a conduit feeding into a purge manifold, and squinted to read the text stencilled on its corroded outer casing. *Sub-deck delta twelve, sector D.*

Korvane processed the coordinates, comparing them to what he knew of the *Blade of Woe* and other vessels of its class. It was hard, for the vessel was ancient and had been added to, renovated, overhauled and rebuilt numerous times over the millennia. The stencil told him that he was amidships, eighty-three decks below the secondary mycoprotein vats that turned the crew's waste solids into edible tack. He should have known that from the low-level stink that permeated the whole deck. Another half a kilometre fore of his position would be the vast cryo-chambers in which slain crewmen awaited reconstitution, and twenty more levels below him was the low deck sump in which entire communities of mutants lived without ever crossing paths with a crewman. Recalling what he could of the *Blade's* impossibly complex internal arrangement, Korvane realised that there was a tertiary docking bay not far away. Could that be Grand's destination?

Slowing as he approached a junction, Korvane drew his laspistol and loosened his power sword in its scabbard. All men and women of his background were required to master such weapons, but he had rarely had cause to use them in anger.

Coming to the junction, Korvane peered around to the passageways beyond. Grand's trail was unmistakable, the glistening skein of ice on the bulkheads marking his passing towards the hangar Korvane knew lay to the right. Perhaps the inquisitor was planning to escape by lander, Korvane thought, before dismissing the notion. Somehow, he knew that the truth would be far worse.

'Indeed it is...' a rasping voice whispered from the hangar portal.

'...much worse.'

'COME, SCION OF the Arcadius,' said Inquisitor Grand. 'And you shall reap what you have sown.'

Every shred of Korvane's being screamed at him to turn and flee; yet he could not. One leaden step at a time, he passed through the open hangar portal and into the cavernous launch bay. Though only a minor facility compared to the *Blade of Woe's* main bays, the space was so large it rivalled the interior of a mighty Ecclesiarchy cathedral.

The hangar was cast in the bright, turquoise light reflected from the surface of Dal'yth Prime. The world filled the view through the open hangar, the air held within by an invisible energy shield. Serene seas framed the arid continental masses, the scene so pristine it belied the devastation Inquisitor Grand had sought to work upon it. How quickly the glowing orb would have been transformed into a black, shrivelled wasteland if the inquisitor had not been countermanded by one of the few in the galaxy with the authority to do so…

Korvane felt his legs stop moving as he reached the centre of the hangar. Before him, held firmly in the cantilevered arms of a ceiling-mounted launch cradle, was a matt-black, elongated form five metres in length. It reminded Korvane of an ocean-borne predator, its prow blunt, with numerous angular fins protruding from its length. The object's rear section was a compact plasma drive with a single thruster, ready to power it through the atmosphere on the hell-dive of Exterminatus that would spell its death, and that of every living organism on the world below.

'You are correct, Arcadius,' said Inquisitor Grand as he emerged from behind the torpedo. As he moved, he ran one hand along the torpedo's flank, fingering each sharp fin as his wizened touch passed over it. Where that hand caressed the matt-black skin of the torpedo, the kiss of frost was left in its wake.

Korvane's heart thundered as he forced himself to stand erect before the traitor. He would die, of that he was sure. But he would do so on his feet, with his head held high, like a true son of the Arcadius.

Inquisitor Grand reached his gnarled hands up to his hood, and lowered it, so that his face was visible. His entire head was a single, badly healed wound, with clumps of silver hair poking out between knots of scar tissue. His ears were mere stumps, his eyes lidless slits between folds of wizened, twisted skin. His nostrils were ragged flaps of skin above his mouth, which was all he normally allowed others to see. His lips were formed into a bitter, feral sneer.

'You're going to do it…' said Korvane. 'You're going to defy Lord Kryptman…'

Grand's sneer twisted further as his hand came to the end of the torpedo, his touch lingering on the flared plasma thruster. 'Please accept my apologies, Arcadius,' Grand leered. 'You really aren't worthy of an extended valedictory diatribe. I think I'll just kill you...

'That,' Grand added with a twisted grin, 'will really piss your father off.'

Grand brought his right hand up, the sleeve of his robe falling back to reveal yet more ravaged scar tissue. Korvane's breath came in laboured gulps, and his limbs froze solid as wracking cramp gripped his muscles. Slowly, one gnarled finger bending back at a time, Grand made a fist.

As Grand's little finger folded back, Korvane felt an icy flare of pain in the centre of his chest. As the ring finger curled around, the ice crept into his heart. When the middle finger folded inwards, a dozen icy daggers speared into Korvane's heart.

Grand paused, bringing his thumb and index finger together slowly. Korvane felt his heart falter, his pulse becoming weak. The strength was rapidly draining from his muscles as ice spread through his veins. Blackness pressed in at the edges of his vision, and he tore his eyes from his leering executioner so that the last sight he saw might be that of the serene world for which he had given his life.

His vision swimming, Korvane struggled to focus on the scene beyond the hangar bay portal. The turquoise orb of Dal'yth Prime was suddenly white and angular and entirely out of focus. With the last of his strength, Korvane struggled to resolve the scene, which made no sense to his oxygen starved brain.

Then, the view beyond the hangar portal swam into focus, and Korvane's lips formed into a weak grin.

The serene globe of Dal'yth Prime was all but obscured by the sight of a Thunderhawk gunship rising on flaring manoeuvring jets, veering slightly as its pilot brought it in towards the void-sealed portal.

Inquisitor Grand spun where he stood, turning to face the gunship. The instant his attention was turned elsewhere, Grand's icy hold was relinquished. Korvane dropped to the hardpan, his limbs screaming with the pain of frostbite. Gasping for breath, he rolled onto his side as Inquisitor Grand stalked around to the opposite side of the torpedo, the inquisitor watching calmly as the gunship pierced the void-seal and set down nearby on screaming retros.

With a last burst of gas, the gunship settled on flexing landing struts. Even before it was fully down, the hatch at its blunt prow lowered on hissing hydraulics, and slammed to the deck with a resounding clang. A group of figures tramped down the assault ramp. Korvane's eyes struggled to bring them into focus.

The first of the figures to set foot on the hardpan was a Space Marine, his formerly pristine white power armour scorched black and smeared with gore. A flowing topknot capped the Space Marine's head, and his face was traced with an intricate pattern of honour scars. Veteran Sergeant Sarik of the White Scars.

When Korvane saw the next figure, his heart leaped. It was his father, resplendent in his heirloom power armour that was almost as battered and dirty as Sarik's. Lucian wore his hair in a style not unlike the sergeant's, a hint at the fact that the Clan Arcadius had long-established links to the Chapter's home world of Chogoris. The Space Marine and the rogue trader both drew their blades as one, spreading out as they approached the waiting inquisitor.

As the two parted, a third figure was revealed behind. It was a woman, ragged strips of silver fabric flowing around her body and long, plaited hair streaming madly behind.

'No...' Korvane gasped. 'You bitch...'

A rasping chuckle echoed through the cold air of the hangar, audible even over the sound of the gunship's engines powering down. Korvane realised the sound was coming from inside his own head, and the voice was Grand's.

Korvane's joy at the arrival of his father was dispelled in an instant by the sight of his stepsister, still alive, and at Lucian's side. Bitterness and hatred welled inside his heart, causing stabs of pain far worse than those inflicted by Inquisitor Grand. She had tried to kill him months before, but Korvane had thought her dead, as had everyone else. Now she was back, and it would all start again.

But not if Inquisitor Grand killed her, Korvane thought as he slumped backwards on the deck, allowing the pain of the psychic assault to wash over him, to carry him away on the waves of a bitter, cold ocean of hatred.

SARIK DREW HIS chainsword as he stepped onto the deck of the hangar bay, his gaze settling on the wizened form of Inquisitor Grand. The floor all around the inquisitor was slick with ice, and beyond it lay the barely conscious form of Lucian's son, Korvane.

Behind the traitor, for that was what Grand surely was, waited the unmistakable form of the Exterminatus torpedo, sleek and black and held in place by the claws of its launch cradle.

Sarik moved to the right as Lucian stepped to the left,

aiming to encircle the calmly waiting inquisitor. Lucian's daughter came behind, and beyond her at the head of the gunship's assault ramp came Major Subad and Sergeant-Major Havil of the Rakarshan Rifles.

'You named us traitors,' Sarik called out, shouting to be heard over the Thunderhawk's whining jets. 'I name *you* traitor, Inquisitor Grand, and you will face my judgement.'

Inquisitor Grand simply smiled grotesquely, and raised his wiry arms to his sides. The air temperature plummeted and a patina of ice crept across the decking towards Sarik's armoured boots. He gunned his chainsword, but held his ground. Grand was no fighter, Sarik judged, but would be deadly nonetheless.

'It is not within your power to judge me, Astartes,' Grand sneered, his rasping whisper carried over the powering-down jets and directly into the minds of all those present.

'I issue you this one, simple warning,' Grand continued. 'Depart this place now, before I freeze your blood in your veins.' Glancing towards Brielle, Grand added, 'But she shall stay, and face punishment for her assault on my person and her consorting with xenos.'

Sarik growled, a curse forming on his lips. Lucian swore, but before either could intervene, Brielle had stepped forwards and was pointing directly towards the traitor.

'You remember this, gak for brains?' she spat.

Grand froze, staring at Brielle's outstretched hand.

'Yes you do,' Brielle sneered. 'Now shut the hell up.'

A sheet of liquid fuel surged out from the miniature flamer unit disguised as a ring on Brielle's index finger.

The jet speared through the cold air and ploughed into Grand's chest, but truly the fates mocked Brielle as the chemical failed to ignite.

The inquisitor grinned cruelly as he took a step towards Brielle, his arms rising to unleash a lethal blast of psionic force.

As Brielle backed away from Grand, terror writ large on her face, Sarik drew his bolt pistol. He fired, the bolt plunging into Grand's form and finally igniting the flamer's fuel.

In an instant, the inquisitor was completely engulfed in flames, the promethium fuel clinging to his body as it burned through his flesh. The robes were seared away, their remains smouldering on the deck at his feet. Grand had become a naked torch, his limbs wreathed in dancing fire, yet somehow, he was still alive.

The human torch spun towards Sarik and threw a flame-licked arm out in a violent gesture. The bolt pistol was struck from Sarik's grip by an invisible force and sent spinning across the deck.

'Abomination!' Sarik cursed, bringing his chainsword up to the guard position. Others moved in around him, Lucian from the inquisitor's rear, Subad and Havil not far behind.

Seeing Lucian drawing his plasma pistol, Sarik bellowed 'No!', but too late; Grand spun the other way and with another gesture sent a piledriver of invisible psyker-force into Lucian's chest. The armour buckled as Lucian was propelled backwards. Brielle dashed towards her father's prone form, and Grand tracked her, girding his flaming, twisted body to leap forwards with supernatural force.

A figure appeared between the inquisitor and Lucian's daughter, a power cutlass raised high. It was Major

Subad. He moved with the lightning speed of years of training with his blade. Subad darted in, delivering a vicious slash to Grand's stomach that should have spilled his guts across the deck. By sheer force of will, Grand was defying death even as the raging flames consumed his flesh.

Sarik took advantage of the distraction Major Subad was providing, working his way around behind Inquisitor Grand. Subad dodged aside as Grand lashed out with flaming claws, searing a smoking wound across the Rakarshan's right arm.

Subad tossed the blade to his other hand without breaking stride, and lunged forwards again.

The curved sword scythed towards Grand's head, but the inquisitor moved left, a tail of flame and roiling embers trailing behind him like a ragged cloak. He swept around the torpedo, moving in towards the launch cradle's command terminal hanging down on a sheaf of cables.

Sarik saw what Grand intended and moved in, his chainsword screaming. Rounding the launch cradle, Sarik closed on Grand, and saw that his body was disintegrating in the heart of the conflagration that still engulfed him. Slivers of smoking, charred meat were sloughing from his bones with his every step, yet still, his bitter, indomitable will drove him on well beyond the point of death.

Grand was bent over the command terminal, and as Sarik approached he turned, his charred face a black coal in the heart of a furnace. His eyes, mouth and nostrils were lit from within, the fire so consuming him that he was no more than a hollow skeleton of blackened bone.

The inquisitor brought his flaming, skeletal hand

down and punched the command rune. A klaxon wail started up, low at first, but rising to the banshee dirge that announced the death of worlds. The illumination in the hangar suddenly changed to strobing red as the alert lumens flashed into life.

Through the crackling of flames and the howling of sirens, Sarik heard distant, echoing laughter. Grand stumbled backwards, away from the launch cradle, as hydraulics engaged and white gases hissed from purge vents.

Grand lurched, what was left of his body losing form and stability in spite of the staggering power of the mind that sustained it. As the traitor fell, Sarik charged in, his chainsword ready to deliver the killing blow.

An arm looking more like the blackened branch of a lightning-struck tree was raised. The air rippled and an invisible hammer pounded into Sarik's chest, driving the air from his lungs and cracking the plate wide open. He staggered back, fighting to remain standing as the rapidly failing systems in his war-ravaged power armour flooded his body with combat drugs and stimms. He rose on one knee, to see Sergeant-Major Havil appear behind the inquisitor, his massive ceremonial power axe raised in a double-handed grip.

The sirens reached a deafening crescendo, and the torpedo's plasma thruster ignited. The launch cradle lurched violently, and the cantilevered arms depending from above flexed and shivered as the thruster built power.

Havil's blade swept in across the horizontal, as sure and true as the executioner's axe... then melted into splattering lava mere inches from Grand's blazing form, orange gobbets scattering across the deck. Grand struggled to his feet as he turned fully to face the sergeant-major, who was joined a moment later by Major Subad.

Sarik forced himself to his feet as the inquisitor raised both hands towards the two Rakarshans. The air twisted and distorted around him, the fabric of reality sucked into a swirling maelstrom centred on the inquisitor. Havil raised the haft of his ruined weapon before him, while Subad made ready for one final lunge with his curved blade. The air seethed and screamed, as if the universe were drawing breath, then exploded outwards in an unstoppable tsunami that propelled both Rakarshans backwards and out of Sarik's line of sight.

The torpedo's thruster reached full power, and the launch cradle's arms let it go. Instead of dropping, the torpedo hung in the mid-air for a moment. Like a predator scenting its prey, the torpedo blasted forwards, through the void-seal, and began its hell-dive towards Dal'yth Prime.

Sarik was consumed by grief. He had failed.

Grand's back was still turned on the White Scar. Even through the pain and rage threatening to consume him, he saw his opening, and took it.

Sarik drew the chainsword back over his shoulder, then swept it down hard. The whirring teeth shattered Grand's hollow, flaming skull and cleaved downwards through his torso, shattered ribs exploding outwards along with a fireball of foul gas.

The swirling psychic maelstrom still raging in the air exploded outwards, unleashed and unchannelled without the inquisitor's fearsome will to focus its impossible energies. The air twisted around itself, turning reality inside out as dimensions converged and lines of psychic power burned through the aether.

Sarik threw himself clear as the vortex expanded, rolling across the hard metal deck towards Brielle, who was kneeling over the barely conscious form of her father. He rose to his knees as the vortex buckled the deck panels behind him. He grabbed Lucian's armour by its neck collar with one hand, and Brielle's arm with the other and hauled them both backwards towards the inner hatch, the maelstrom chasing them all the way.

At the last, Sarik pounded the hatch release, and the blast door crashed down behind him as the vortex engulfed the hangar. Witch-fire ravaged the bay, bolts of aetheric vomit splashing through the void-seal in a slow-moving fountain of impossible energies.

The maelstrom churned outwards from the portal, spewing across the void in a rapidly expanding aetheric blast wave. The *Blade of Woe* slewed and listed slowly as the energies spat from her midsection, a thousand klaxons sounding as emergency retro thrusters coughed into life to correct the sudden and drastic course deviation. The very void of orbital space rippled and buckled, the globe of Dal'yth Prime appearing like a reflection in rippling water.

Then the leading edge of the maelstrom overtook the Exterminatus device as it plummeted downwards, hungry to consume the cells of every living thing of an entire world. The torpedo quivered, its shark-form length elongating as if caught at the event horizon of a black hole. Black ripples passed along its length, and then it detonated, a million shards of metal streaking through the heavens trailing searing white contrails behind.

A trillion murder-cells died in the furnace of re-entry, seared from existence by the elemental nucleonic fires.

On the surface of Dal'yth Prime, a new sun appeared briefly in the jade skies, then winked out of existence once more, its passing marked by a slowly descending shower of meteors.

EPILOGUE

'QUESTIONS?' SAID LUCIAN, slowly scanning the crowded council chamber.

The crusade council had convened for one last session, but such a weight of business lay before it that the conference had ground on throughout the night. A million details had to be thrashed out, from the embarkation of thousands of ground troops to the distribution of millions of tons of capital munitions. Several hundred motions had been proposed, debated and passed in an effort to tie up every possible loose end. The treacherous, insane Inquisitor Grand had been replaced on the council by a Munitorum Plenipotentiary Delegatus by the name of Captain Palmatus. Lucian had never met Palmatus before, but found him capable and shrewd, and the council's business had been conducted with a speed and efficiency not seen throughout the entire crusade.

With all of the council seats occupied for the first time in what seemed like months, the chamber had filled with other officials, many of whom had a statement or request to make. Master Karzello, the crusade fleet's senior astropath, came before the council and told of the alien snarls and screeches resounding through the minds of the astropathic choirs, driving some insane and others to take their own lives. Interrogator Rayne confirmed the phenomenon as the gestalt echo of a trillion xenos minds, howling their hunger into the void. Pator Ottavi, the Navigator Korvane had brought into the council, described the shadow that had settled over the warp, even blocking out the light of the sacred Astronomican which shone from distant Terra and guided the Imperium's vessels through the benighted void.

Others too had spoken. The Ultramarines sergeant Arcan had told of his urgent need to return to his home world, and requested the aid of his brother Chapters. Arcan was scarcely recovered from the wounds inflicted on his body when his Rhino had been struck by fusion blaster fire, and both of his legs had been replaced by heavy augmetics. Despite his injuries, the Ultramarine's words had stirred the hearts of those present, and all who had the authority to do so had pledged their aid in the defence of Ultramar.

Then, the tau had come before the council. Few of those crowded into the council chamber had even laid eyes on their foe; in fact most had never before confronted any type of sentient alien. When Aura and his fire caste honour guard had entered the chamber, utter silence had descended. The Space Marines had watched impassively, not acknowledging the aliens' presence but at least refraining from pumping a magazine full of mass-reactive explosive rounds into their heads. The Adeptus Astartes had far larger concerns than the tau, Sarik had told Lucian before the session, concerns that made these comparatively benign aliens pale into utter insignificance.

The initial discussions had been stilted and difficult, with the tau envoy making all manner of veiled threats. Yet, Lucian had brought into play every ounce of his diplomatic skill, drawing on a lifetime's experience of trading with all manner of societies and races the length and breadth of the Imperium. With Rayne's blessing, Lucian had imparted something of the coming tyranid swarm, though he had twisted the truth to suggest that the tau were actually in more danger than the Imperium. It was hoped that in doing so the tau would allow the Imperium to depart unopposed while they fortified their worlds against the coming storm, and cause them to focus all of their efforts against the tyranids. Whether or not the envoy had entirely believed him, Lucian could not be sure; but regardless, face was saved and honour maintained, and the tau had not only agreed to allow the fleet to disengage, but the seeds of future cooperation had been sown.

Most importantly, from Lucian's own perspective, he had forged a number of highly lucrative, exclusive contact treaties with the tau, securing the fortunes of the Clan Arcadius for decades to come. His mind had wandered as the council session had dragged on into the early morning, Lucian calculating the profit his dynasty stood to make. Perhaps he would rebuild the family manse in Zealandia Hab on Terra, or purchase a paradisiacal garden world for the same outlay.

When the council had finally come to vote on the ceasefire motion, only Cardinal Gurney had objected. It appeared to all that Gurney's career in politics was as good as over, yet he planned, by all accounts, to accompany the fleet to Macragge, to use his fiery rhetoric to drive the ground troops forward in the glory of the Emperor. Lucian grudgingly accepted that was the best role for the cardinal, but silently hoped he went and got himself eaten by some slavering alien monstrosity.

At the last, Brielle had been summoned to address the council. Lucian's daughter had given a detailed, if somewhat truculent account of her dealings with the tau, in which she had justified her actions by claiming she had sought all along to bring the aliens to the negotiating table for the benefit of all. Lucian had to admit, Brielle had given an impressive performance, playing the innocent victim to Grand's hostility and the selfless servant of the Imperium in her crippling of the enemy's command and control system that had caused the tau armies to lose coherence during their retreat from Gel'bryn. Most of the council had lapped it up. Lucian was nowhere near so gullible, but propriety was maintained, and his daughter returned to his side.

As Brielle sat back down, Lucian repeated, 'Does the council have any questions?'

Most of the councillors appeared too weary to query anything of Brielle's statement. Lucian was about to call for the motion to dismiss his daughter, when Cardinal Gurney stood.

'I call for a motion of censure,' Gurney scowled. 'For the crime of conspiring with xenos.'

Lucian sighed inwardly, though outwardly he maintained his composure. 'And who will second this motion?'

Gurney looked to the Logistician-General to his right. Ordinarily, Stempf would have toed the line of his council faction. But with the demise of Inquisitor Grand and the settlement of the ceasefire, that faction had to all intents and purposes ceased to exist.

Stempf stared at the black marble table in front of him, suddenly very interested in the lines of deep maroon flashed through its polished surface.

'It appears, cardinal,' said Lucian, 'that none here will support your motion.'

Gurney's eyes flashed with impotent rage, and he sat back down, casting a vengeful glance at his former ally by his side.

Brielle was trying hard to disguise a dirty smirk by fiddling with a lock of plaited hair.

'Then if there are no objections,' Lucian announced, 'I propose this final session of the Damocles Gulf Crusade command council is closed.

'Thank you, gentlemen.'

WITH A CURT gesture, Lucian dismissed the crewmen tending to the sensorium terminals of the observation blister high atop the *Oceanid's* spine. Turning to his son and his daughter, he spread his arms wide. 'Welcome back,' he grinned, 'the pair of you.'

Brielle and Korvane refused to acknowledge one another, addressing only Lucian. Brielle stepped up to one of the arched, leaded ports and stared out at the mass of activity in Dal'yth Prime's orbit. She muttered something, which Lucian could not quite hear.

'Brielle?' said Lucian.

His daughter turned, and Lucian saw an unfamiliar hint of sadness in her eyes. 'I was saying a prayer,' she said. 'For them.'

Lucian followed her gaze, towards a trio of huge troop transports that hung in formation ten kilometres to the

Oceanid's starboard. Each carried an entire regiment of ground troops, and Lucian knew that one might be carrying the noble Rakarshans.

'They're all going to die,' Brielle said flatly.

Korvane grimaced, evidently unconvinced by his stepsister's uncharacteristic show of empathy.

'All of them,' she said with grim conviction. 'And billions more.'

Lucian felt a cold shiver pass up and down the length of his spine, as if Brielle's words were somehow prophetic; as if she were gifted some insight denied to others. He suddenly felt the weight of his own mortality, for the span of his life had been extended beyond the normal measure by the application of rejuve treatments few in the Imperium had access to. As he pictured entire sectors stripped to bare rock by a species of ravening alien abominations, the thought struck him; perhaps the ancient and noble line of the Arcadius would end with him. Who then would remember his deeds and honour his name?

At Lucian's side, his son closed his hand around the ring his father had given him, the ring containing the cipher matrix of the stasis-vault on Terra, where rested the most valuable asset in the dynasty's possession: the Arcadius Warrant of Trade.

SERGEANT SARIK WAS knelt in prayer in the *Nomad's* chapel. Through an armoured portal wrought in the form of the White Scars lightning-bolt Chapter icon he could see the crusade fleet mustering for war, scores of tenders and service vessels swarming around the wallowing capital ships as crews and supplies were ferried back and forth. Most of the ground forces were already embarked, though it appeared that at least one

Brimlock unit would be left behind, from the initial deployment at least.

The chapel represented a small part of Sarik's home world, the pelts of huge Chogoran beasts adorning its walls lending it the aspect of the interior of a chieftain's yurt. Mighty curved horns adorned the walls, many inscribed with the names and the deeds of the warriors who had slain them in glorious battle. In the centre of one wall was mounted a massive, reptilian skull, taken from the mica dragon that Sarik and his fellow scouts Qaja and Kholka had slain together on Luther McIntyre when all three were but neophytes. The scent of rock-rose hung heavy in air, the dense smoke drifting upwards from an incense bowl set in the centre of the chapel. Upon the altar beneath the lightning-bolt portal was laid a sacred stone tablet bearing ten thousand-year-old script hewn by the hand of the White Scars' primarch himself, the proud and wild Jaghatai Khan.

Sarik was in the chapel to recite aloud the name of every battle-brother that had fallen in the battle for Dal'yth Prime. Each would be honoured later, he knew, according to the customs of each Chapter represented in the crusade force, but Sarik had been their field commander, and he owed them that much. The tally had been great, for the tau had proven a fearsome, yet ultimately honourable adversary. He felt no ire towards the aliens, and accepted the necessity of the re-deployment to Ultramar. Sarik was a warrior of the Adeptus Astartes, a son of Jaghatai Khan, who was himself a son of the Emperor. His duty was to a higher calling.

As Sarik completed his litany, commending the souls of the fallen to the eternal care of their ancestors, a revelation born of his meditation came over him. Where previously he would have raged impotently at the loss of so many brothers, brooding alone for days on end at the injustice of the galaxy, a new clarity and wisdom now settled upon him. It was as if the script inscribed on the stone tablet before him by his primarch had been written just for him, for they spoke words the meaning of which Sarik had never truly understood though he had read them countless times. In the crucible of the battles fought these last few days, Sarik had been re-forged, like a dulled blade returned gleaming from the hand of the master artificer.

Sarik felt renewed purpose and resolve deep in his heart. Though the tyranids represented a dire threat to the very survival of mankind, they were also the agency by which the champions of the Imperium would come together and find honour and glory beyond measure. Even now, garbled reports were coming in of the terrible enormity of the tyranid invasion. Sarik's battle-brothers in his own and many other Chapters were dying, giving their lives to hold at bay the most devastating incursion the Eastern Fringe had ever witnessed.

Sarik swore, to his primarch and to his Chapter, that he would stand at their side come what may. By his savage pride and the honour scars carved into his weather-beaten face, Sarik vowed that the tyranids would know the wrath of the White Scars, and of all of humanity.

ABOUT THE AUTHOR

Andy Hoare worked for eight years in Games Workshop's design studio, producing and developing new game rules and background material. Now working freelance writing novels, roleplaying game material and gaming-related magazine articles, Andy lives in Nottingham with his partner Sarah.

HUNT FOR VOLDORIUS

ANDY HOARE

An extract from

HUNT FOR VOLDORIUS

by Andy Hoare

'RELEASE IN TEN,' the pilot announced calmly over the vox-net. 'Drop bay portal opening.'

Kor'sarro Khan, Captain of the 3rd Company of the White Scars Chapter of Space Marines, and holder of the honoured rank of Master of the Hunt, turned his gaze from the command terminal to the scene outside the Thunderhawk's canopy. Flashing red lumens made the inside of the strike cruiser's drop bay appear as a scene from the underworld, putting Kor'sarro in mind of the tales the Chapter's Storm Seers told at the great feasts. The sound of wailing sirens added to the hellish impression, sounding like the lamentations of the damned. With a grinding rumble transmitted through the hull of the gunship directly to Kor'sarro's bones, the great doors below the Thunderhawk ground open. In seconds, a deep, metallic boom passed through the strike cruiser and the doors were fully open, the Thunderhawk suspended by its drop cradle above the yawning opening.

'Portal bay open,' the pilot reported. 'Release in five.'

With the drop-portal open, Kor'sarro saw for the first time the surface of Cernis IV. From this height, the land appeared white and serene, glistening with scintillating reflections of the violet lights that danced in the upper atmosphere. As captivating as the lights were, the Master of the Hunt knew that what created them represented a terrible danger to the drop mission his force was about to undertake.

'Release!'

An instant after the pilot's announcement, the huge metal claws holding the Thunderhawk above the portal sprang apart. The gunship dropped through the opening with gut-wrenching force, the surface of Cernis IV leaping upwards to meet it. Kor'sarro fought against the staggering G-force to raise his head and look upwards at the rapidly receding form of the strike cruiser, *Lord of Heavens*. He noted with satisfaction the release of the other four gunships, each holding its place in the formation.

The Thunderhawks levelled out. Rather than dropping straight downwards, each now arrowed prow first towards the surface. Already, bright flames began to lick the leading edges of the gunships' blunt forms.

'Gravimetrics picking up turbulence, as predicted,' the pilot said, addressing Kor'sarro directly. The Techmarines had warned of the disturbance the gunships would meet as they undertook the drop, an effect caused by the complex interactions of Cernis IV's many natural satellites.

'Compensate as you see fit,' Kor'sarro replied. 'But keep us on target.'

The cockpit began to shudder, wisps of flame dancing

across the outside of the armoured canopy. The Thunderhawks were effecting their drop on a heading that no ordinary human troops could undertake, for the gravitational forces would overcome them long before the drop vessels touched down. The White Scars were no mere humans, however; they were superhumans, genetically enhanced Space Marines whose augmented physiologies could withstand such forces and more.

'They'll never see us coming,' Kor'sarro growled, his words drowned out by the roaring of the upper atmosphere as it burned against the gunship's hull. Kor'sarro longed to feel the earth beneath his feet, to breathe the air of the world below, to engage his enemy and complete the hunt. Though masters of the lightning strike, the White Scars preferred to fight across the wide spaces of a planet's surface. Kor'sarro always felt a notion he imagined was akin to helplessness during a planetary drop. As the buffeting increased still further and the cockpit shook with mounting violence, the captain gripped the arms of the grav-couch fiercely.

'Approaching overlap point alpha,' the pilot reported. Kor'sarro caught the note of concentration in the warrior's voice, the only hint of the tension the Space Marine must have been experiencing.

As the gunship dived on and the surface of Cernis IV swelled to fill the view from the cockpit, the shuddering reached a new pitch. Kor'sarro saw that six of the planet's small moons were rising, and it was this that was inflicting the violent disturbance as the Thunderhawks raced onwards. Although the Techmarines had predicted the effect, there was still a risk that the titanic forces might prove too strong for even the mighty Thunderhawks. At a single word, Kor'sarro could order the gunships to change course, coming about to a new heading that would avoid the worst of the gravitational pressures. Yet to do so would be to abandon the best chance of taking the target by surprise, for none could expect an attack to come from the vector the White Scars were taking. The target was far too valuable to lose, and Kor'sarro would take any risk to achieve victory. His honour, and that of the entire 3rd Company, depended on it.

'Entering point alpha!' the pilot called out, his voice barely audible over the roaring against the hull and the violent shaking of the cockpit. The turbulence increased by an order of magnitude as the gunship entered the point where the gravitational influences of the moons converged. Kor'sarro imagined his body was being pulled in several different directions at once, and knew that it was only his genetic enhancements that kept him conscious. He knew too that his survival relied not only on the Thunderhawk resisting the immense pressures that strained its armoured hull to breaking point, but also upon the pilot's own efforts not only to remain conscious, but to keep the vessel on its heading.

'Terminal point alpha reached,' the pilot announced through gritted teeth. There was no turning back now, even if Kor'sarro had been willing to order a change in heading. He mouthed a silent prayer to the Emperor of Mankind and to Jaghatai Khan, revered Primarch of the White Scars.

The view through the canopy was now entirely obscured by rippling white flame as the atmosphere of Cernis IV burned against the armoured panels. Kor'sarro's enhanced vision protected his eyes from damage. Warning klaxons wailed as the forces outside took their toll on the gunship's hull, which groaned audibly as it was wrenched in multiple directions. The temperature inside the cockpit rose to that of a furnace as the vessel's cooling systems laboured to maintain survivable conditions. Sweat ran from Kor'sarro's brow, obscuring his vision as he looked to the pilot.

'Brother Koban,' Kor'sarro addressed the pilot. The Space Marine's face was a mask of determination as he battled with the gunship's controls. Kor'sarro knew that the pilot was nearing the bounds of his endurance. 'Draw your strength from your ancestors,' Kor'sarro shouted over the roaring winds and the wailing alerts. 'Have faith in the primarch!'

'Honoured be his name!' the pilot replied by rote, visibly emboldened by his captain's words. The Space Marine redoubled his efforts, mastering the bucking control column, and the gunship responded instantly. The buffeting calmed, and in moments the white flames licking the outside of the canopy faded and danced away.

'My thanks, brother-captain,' the pilot said, nodding his head towards Kor'sarro.

'You have but yourself to thank,' Kor'sarro replied. 'And the Great Khan, honoured be his name.'

As the last of the flames engulfing the Thunderhawk's blunt, armoured prow flickered and died, the surface of Cernis IV became visible again. The entire view from the cockpit was now filled with the pure, glittering whiteness of the planet's northern polar region. Where before the surface had appeared to shimmer with reflected light, Kor'sarro could discern individual points of jagged, violet-hued brightness. Each of these was a towering crystalline formation, some as tall as a man, others rearing hundreds of metres in the cold air. Each crystal tower reflected the violet auroras that pulsated in the skies above, casting the entire region in an unearthly light.

The Techmarines had been unable to identify the material from which the crystals were formed, but warned that they were clustered so densely across the northern pole that they presented a significant threat to a successful planetfall operation. The remote likeliness of any force attempting such a mission in the perilous region had simply added to its desirability, as far as Kor'sarro was concerned, and the order had been given.

'Landing zone identified,' the co-pilot announced.

'Altering course,' the pilot replied, bringing the gunship around to the coordinates scrolling across his command slate. 'Brother-captain?'

Kor'sarro confirmed that the other four Thunderhawks of the strike force were in formation. One was trailing a line of thick black smoke from its starboard engine. None of the Thunderhawks had come through the drop untouched and there was little that could be done now. He could not even risk a vox-transmission to determine the extent of the gunship's wound. Only faith in the Great Khan would see them through.

'Final approach,' Kor'sarro ordered.

On his word, the gunship banked before diving for the frozen surface. The landscape rushed upwards dramatically as the Thunderhawk's air brakes shed the vessel's momentum. In minutes, the largest of the crystal towers were discernable, their multi-faceted, mirror-smooth flanks reflecting light in all directions.

'Beginning approach run,' the pilot said, his attentions focussed on the closing towers. As the Thunderhawk levelled out the pilot fed power to the engines. Crystals the size of cathedrals flashed by on all sides, and for an instant Kor'sarro was assailed by the sight of a thousand gunships flying in an insane formation all about. There was no way of telling which were the real vessels and which were reflections on the mirrored surfaces of the crystal towers.

'Adjust three-nine in eight point five,' the co-pilot said, not taking his eyes from the augur screen before him.

The pilot merely nodded, before yanking hard on the control column. Kor'sarro's seat restraints tensed as his weight was thrown suddenly to port, but to his relief they held. The largest crystal tower Kor'sarro had yet seen flashed by the gunship's starboard. Due to its multiple, reflective faces, the crystal had not been visible by eyesight. Only the co-pilot's augur warning had saved the vessel from being smashed to atoms against its sheer side.

'That was too close,' breathed the pilot. 'My apologies, brother-captain.'

'None needed,' Kor'sarro replied. 'Attend to your duty.'

The pilot returned his attentions to the fore, bringing the gunship into a wide turn that brought it around a huge crystal tower that Kor'sarro had not even seen amongst the riot of reflections. Leaving the tower behind, the pilot corrected the heading, Kor'sarro craning his neck to ensure that the other vessels were doing likewise.

'Delta twelve!' the co-pilot called out suddenly.

The pilot heeded his battle-brother's warning with instinctive speed. The Thunderhawk was thrown violently to starboard as the pilot avoided a needle-like tower that reared out of nowhere as if seeking to skewer the vessel. For the briefest moment, Kor'sarro caught sight of his own reflection in the needle's mirrored flank as the formation flashed by mere metres away.

Kor'sarro had no need to turn his head to look

through the rear of the canopy in order to follow the progress of the other four gunships, for their reflections were all about, mirrored in a thousand glassy crystal flanks. One Thunderhawk pitched to starboard, while two went to port, the needle flashing by between. The last gunship, still trailing smoke from the engine damaged during the planetfall, was not so fast to react. To his great honour, the vessel's pilot almost managed to avoid the crystal spire, but his starboard wing grazed it nonetheless. In an instant, the end of the stubby wing was shorn away, and the entire needle exploded into a million shards. The devastation was reflected from a thousand surfaces at once. Kor'sarro's senses were all but overwhelmed as innumerable shards, both real and reflected, cascaded in all directions, impacting on the hull of his own gunship like anti-aircraft fire.

'Hunter Three's going down!' the co-pilot called out. 'I can't get a reading, there's too much interference from the shards.'

Kor'sarro processed the terrible decision in an instant. Just as quickly, his mind was made up. 'Maintain vox-silence,' he ordered. 'But keep the channels open.'

The mission was all.